PRAISE FOR GREGG OLSEN

THE LAST THING SHE EVER DID

"Gregg Olsen pens brilliant, creepy, page-turning, heart-pounding novels of suspense that always keep me up at night. In *The Last Thing She Ever Did*, he topped himself."
—Allison Brennan, *New York Times* bestselling author

"Beguiling, wicked, and taut with suspense and paranoia, *The Last Thing She Ever Did* delivers scenes as devastating as any I've ever read with a startling, pitch-perfect finale. A reminder that evil may reside in one's actions, but tragedy often spawns from one's inaction."
—Eric Rickstad, *New York Times* bestselling author of *The Silent Girls*

"Olsen's latest examines how a terrible, split-second decision has lingering effects, and the past echoes the present. Full of unexpected twists, *The Last Thing She Ever Did* will keep you guessing to the last line."
—J. T. Ellison, *New York Times* bestselling author of *Lie to Me*

"Master storyteller Gregg Olsen continues to take readers hostage with another spellbinding tale of relentless, pulse-pounding suspense."
—Rick Mofina, international bestselling author of *Last Seen*

"Tense. Well-crafted. Gripping."
—Mary Burton, *New York Times* bestselling author

"With *The Last Thing She Ever Did*, Gregg Olsen delivers an edgy, tension-filled roller-coaster ride of a novel that will thrill and devastate in equal measure."
—Linda Castillo, *New York Times* bestselling author

Nonfiction

A Killing in Amish Country: Sex, Betrayal, and a Cold-Blooded Murder

A Twisted Faith: A Minister's Obsession and the Murder That Destroyed a Church

The Deep Dark: Disaster and Redemption in America's Richest Silver Mine

Starvation Heights: A True Story of Murder and Malice in the Woods of the Pacific Northwest

Cruel Deception: A Mother's Deadly Game, a Prosecutor's Crusade for Justice

If Loving You Is Wrong: The Shocking True Story of Mary Kay Letourneau

Abandoned Prayers: The Incredible True Story of Murder, Obsession, and Amish Secrets

Bitter Almonds: The True Story of Mothers, Daughters, and the Seattle Cyanide Murders

Bitch on Wheels: The True Story of Black Widow Killer Sharon Nelson

If I Can't Have You: Susan Powell, Her Mysterious Disappearance, and the Murder of Her Children

LYING
NEXT
TO ME

GREGG
OLSEN

PINNACLE BOOKS
KENSINGTON PUBLISHING CORP.
www.kensingtonbooks.com

PINNACLE BOOKS are published by

Kensington Publishing Corp.
119 West 40th Street
New York, NY 10018

All Kensington titles, imprints, and distributed lines are available at special quantity discounts for bulk purchases for sales promotion, premiums, fund-raising, and educational or institutional use.

Special book excerpts or customized printings can also be created to fit specific needs. For details, write or phone the office of the Kensington Sales Manager: Kensington Publishing Corp., 119 West 40th Street, New York, NY 10018. Attn. Sales Department. Phone: 1-800-221-2647.

PINNACLE BOOKS and the P logo Reg. U.S. Pat. & TM Off.

First Pinnacle mass market paperback printing: May 2023
ISBN-13: 978-0-7860-5015-4

10 9 8 7 6 5 4 3 2 1

Printed in the United States of America

For Chris Renfro,
who is brilliant,
patient, and kind.

The female giant Pacific octopus, *Enteroctopus dofleini*, is a cunning creature. Larger than her male counterpart, she hunts only in the blackness of night. With more than two hundred suckers on each of eight undulating arms, she moves through the water with slow, graceful movements to stalk her prey. She is cunning too. She has the ability to change her appearance, color, and texture to suit her environment as she lies in wait. If brought aboard a boat alive, even full-grown, she can free herself through a space the size of a half dollar. One of the largest ever found, an incredible monster more than twenty feet across, was caught by divers on the western shore of Hood Canal near Lilliwaup, Washington, in a deep-water site of the Salish Sea locals call Octopus Hole.

CHAPTER ONE

ADAM

I hold my daughter tightly to keep her from the jagged shards of my wife's broken wineglass. It's the only tangible indication that something terrible has happened. I gulp for air. The salmonberry thorns that clawed me as I ran up from the beach to the highway have shredded my bare arms. The striations of oozing blood leak slowly and don't require a bandage, though one's offered to me. Someone puts a blanket over my shoulders as I sit on the five-foot-high bulkhead that separates the crescent beach from the three cabins behind me. It's a kind gesture, and I don't resist it—even though I know it won't help calm my trembling. I don't look up. Instead, I sit there, wondering if I've done everything I can.

Everything I should have done.

Aubrey shifts in my arms, her brown eyes taking it all in.

The woman in the cabin next to ours came out for Memorial Day weekend with her grandchildren. She's doing her best to remain calm. She's told me her name, but my brain is so addled, I can barely grasp anything new.

She taps my shoulder.

"Adam, how about I take Aubrey to my cabin?" She glances upward to the sloping driveway that leads to the cabins. A black SUV with gold accents inches its way to the parking area. The Mason County sheriff has arrived.

My eyes, vision blurry without my glasses, somehow meet hers, and I give her a slow nod. "I'm sorry. I've forgotten your name."

"Teresa," she says.

"Right." I put my hands on Aubrey's shoulders. "Honey, I want you to go with Teresa. You can play with her grandchildren."

Aubrey's confused, scared. She's been part of the trauma. "I want Mommy."

"I know," I tell her. "We're going to find her. I'll be right here. Okay? Just for a minute."

"We made popsicles this morning," Teresa says.

Aubrey swings her attention to the nice older woman but stays mute.

"Cherry punch," Teresa adds, selling a distraction to a three-year-old with grandparental skill.

"Go on, now," I tell her. "Daddy will be right here."

My little girl turns to go with Teresa, and I head in the direction of the SUV, my pace quickening to a run over the broad lawn along the bulkhead.

"Thank God you're here!" I call out to the officers. My voice cracks a little, and I reel in some emotion. *Need to be clear. Need to tell them what happened.*

It's a man and a woman. He's the older of the pair, with silver hair, wire-framed glasses.

The woman is familiar to me. Her hair is long and pulled back. Her face is a smear of freckles.

"Lee?" I ask.

"Adam. It's been a while."

Her partner, who identifies himself as Zach Montrose, gives her an interested look. "You know each other?"

She keeps her eyes on me. I see a faint smile of reminiscence, but this is not a happy reunion. How could it be?

"We grew up together," she says. "He was Kip's best friend."

Kip was her older brother. We went all the way from kindergarten through high school together. He enlisted in the army and never came back from Afghanistan. The last time I saw Lee was at the memorial service the Husemanns held to remember their son. I remember standing in front of the congregation at the Shelton Bible Church and recalling the kind of person Kip was ("shirt off his back . . . never knew a stranger . . . always ready to help someone"), my eyes refusing to look in the direction of his parents and sister because I didn't want to break down. I like to be in control. I like to make sure that everything I do is done with purpose.

"Small world." Montrose surveys the scene.

"I heard you were a police officer," I say. Lee has green eyes. That's what was familiar about her.

"I'm a detective," she says, the flash of any warmth in our quasi reunion suddenly gone. "Let's go over everything that happened."

"We've got to find her," I plead.

"That's what we do," Montrose says. "Let's talk over there." He indicates the sun-bleached cedar deck of the Wisteria, the cabin Sophie and I had rented for the long weekend.

I provide the basics. The weekend at Hood Canal was a surprise. Sophie said I never plan anything special for the family, and I knew she was right. I saw an article in the *Seattle Times* that reminded me about a trio of 1920s cabins near Lilliwaup that had been lovingly restored. Each was named for a flower by the previous horticulturalist owners. Sophie loves old homes; that's the reason we've been living in sawdust and commotion for the past five years as we restore an espresso-brown 1922 Seattle Craftsman.

I look at Lee across a weathered picnic table. She's scribbling notes.

"I thought it would be fun. I thought we'd have a chance to relax, unplug. Focus on our family."

"Have there been problems?" Montrose asks.

I shake my head. "Just too much work. Too little time to just enjoy life. Nothing more than that."

There *is* more than that, of course. There is in every marriage. And yet, as I sit there with the detectives, I know that none of that needs to find its way into anyone's notebook.

"Adam," Lee says, "I'm sure this will be difficult. I need you to tell us everything that happened. Don't skip the slightest detail. What might seem inconsequential to you might be the key to finding out who took your wife."

"And where she is now," I say.

"Right," she says. "Where she is. That's why we're here."

I couldn't get off work from SkyAero early Friday because my director was up to her neck in some kind of leadership training that's supposed to make her more effective with our team. She insisted that I stay to run some reports so she could focus on learning more ways to help her team members create work-life balance. The irony of this wasn't lost on me.

Sophie and Aubrey took the Seattle–Bremerton ferry and arrived at the Wisteria cabin first, at about five thirty. I drove down from the Renton plant where I work and crossed over the Tacoma Narrows Bridge, coming up through Belfair to Lilliwaup, getting to the cabin a little before eight.

I explain all of this to the detectives while Montrose writes and Lee listens.

"Did anyone see you arrive?" she asks.

"I don't know," I say. "I think so. Teresa—that's the woman

watching Aubrey now—had her windows open and lights on when I got here. She probably saw me arrive. Or her grand-kids did."

"What about the other cabin?" Lee asks.

I want to skip to what happened, but I'm following their directions to ensure that I provide every detail.

"A couple driving a blue Lexus arrived late last night," I say. "But I didn't talk to them."

Montrose makes a note of that. "Was there anyone else?" he asks.

This isn't Grand Central, I think. But I don't say it.

"The old guy walking his dog," I say. "Some kids from one of the houses up the beach were out this morning. No one else. Not that I could see. I mean, I wasn't looking for people. I was here, you know, to be with Sophie and Aubrey."

Sophie's name causes another crack in my voice. I reel the emotion in.

I tell them that I made a fire when I got in. Sophie had stopped at a store and bought sandwiches and a couple of steaks. We had a glass of wine and watched one of the DVDs that the owners had provided, a collection that was mostly kid-friendly comedies. Aubrey fell asleep around nine, and Sophie put her down. Not long after that, an hour or so, we went to bed.

The next morning, I tell them, I made waffles.

"Aubrey's favorite. Really about the only thing I'm good at making."

I hear my daughter's laugh, and I see Teresa's oldest grandson doing his best imitation of Tarzan on a heavy rope swing that juts out over the beach from the limb of a massive western red cedar.

Montrose prods me. "Then what happened?"

"Aubrey and I took a skiff out to drop crab pots," I say. Aubrey, ensconced in a bright orange life jacket, couldn't wait to be out on the water, which was literally as smooth as glass. Not just *like* glass—like a flawless sheet of window-pane. We went back and forth all morning, I tell them. "There was nothing special or out of the ordinary about it."

"Take your time," Lee says. "We need to know everything."

I tell them that while Aubrey and I rowed around and worked the pots, Sophie was reading a novel with a cup of coffee that later morphed into a glass or two of chardonnay.

I'd baited the pots with tins of cat food, and we checked them about every half hour. It wasn't about catching crabs. It was about spending time with Aubrey and seeing it all through her eyes. Everything was a first for her. Her first time on the water. Her first encounter with a gull. A seal. I remembered times on the water with my own father. Not only connected with nature, but with each other. *Shipwreck. Pirate. Captain Ahab.*

Lee's partner pushes. "And then it happened?"

He annoys me. I feel as if he's trying to catch me in a lie or something. I know he's doing his job, but my wife is missing. He could show some compassion.

"Yes," Lee says. "What was the first thing you saw or heard that suggested something was wrong with Sophie?"

I'm surprised by the need to steady myself a little. I'm stronger than this. I pull myself together and tell them what happened.

We're out about a hundred yards from the shoreline. Sophie has moved from the deck of the Wisteria to the massive concrete bulkhead. Her book has been abandoned but not her wine. She sits there and waves to us. Aubrey heard a dog bark just north of the crescent beach, and I'm rowing in that direction. She wants a dog, but Sophie and I stay firm that we can't bring any pets into the house until construction is complete. It's mostly a delay tactic on Sophie's part. I love dogs. I grew up with golden retrievers. Sophie isn't as much of a fan. It's one of the few things we really disagree about. Sophie is the kind of woman who never deviates from whatever she believes to be true. Her undying confidence is at once an asset and a detriment. When we are on the same page, we are unstoppable. When her plans or ideas conflict with what I think is best, we edge toward a knock-down, drag-out fight that I will never win. Five years into our marriage I've learned that, as tough as I can be at work, I acquiesce to Sophie's ambitions, plans, and ideas at home. I do that to keep the peace. I do it because she's everything to me.

As I row back toward the cabin after failing to find the dog for Aubrey, I hear a scream. It's not piercing, but it's jarring enough that I swivel my attention to the shore. I see my wife and a man struggling. The wineglass has fallen and shattered. Sophie is yelling at the man, but I can't hear what they are saying. I turn my back to them and row as fast as I can.

Aubrey, who is facing me, thinks it is a game. I work out twice a week, but I can't get the boat to move fast enough, though the surface is so smooth. Aubrey sees the terror in my eyes, but she misreads it. "Fast!" she calls out. "Fast!"

Sophie is not a large woman. She's 110 pounds dripping wet. But she's strong. She can beat me in a marathon, and she has. The next time I check over my shoulder, I see the stranger do the unthinkable. He balls up a fist and punches her. She drops to the ground.

"What the fuck!" I yell. "Leave her alone!"

I can't get there. I am rowing. My glasses fly into the water when I wrench my head around to check on Sophie. What was so clear now becomes a smear of color and shapes. I see the man scoop up my wife and carry her off behind the Wisteria.

My heart jumps from my chest.

"Holy fuck! Stop! Leave her alone."

Aubrey knows now it's not a game we're playing. She starts to cry. I want to jump out of the skiff and run through the shallows to get to my wife, but I can't leave my daughter adrift in a boat. I'm hyperventilating now. I tell myself to get it together. Twenty more yards. That's all.

"Help!" I yell in the direction of the Chrysanthemum, the middle cabin, the smallest of the three that face the beach. I'd seen lights on the night I arrived, but nothing after that.

"Someone help me!" I call out as loudly as I can. Loud enough to be heard in a storm, I think, let alone on a quiet morning. "Someone's got my wife!"

I jump out of the skiff, grab Aubrey, who is still crying, and run up the concrete steps from the beach to the lawn. I set her down.

"Everything will be okay," I tell her. "Stay right here. Don't move. Okay?"

"I want Mommy," she cries out.

"I know," I say, trying to calm her. "I do too."

I hear voices in the cabin, and I wonder if I've hallucinated everything. The sunlight on the water had scrambled the images of what I'd seen. I run up the steps of the deck and inside through the kitchen to the living room facing out over Hood Canal and the conifer-crusted hillsides beyond.

"Sophie?"

It's the TV, of course. Sophie's gone. An infomercial for a pressure cooker is playing.

I'm in a pressure cooker.

I breathe in for a second. My heart is about to burst from my chest. I'm going to have a heart attack. I'm going to fall on the old fir floor that Sophie coveted that morning as we ate waffles. *What is happening?*

I return outside just as a woman and two children come back from wherever they've spent the first part of the day.

"Someone took my wife! Call 911! Help me!"

The woman sees the look in my eyes that indicates unequivocally this is no joke. She tells the boy and the girl to go inside the Chrysanthemum, and she reaches for her cell phone.

As I run, I yell for the old man with the dog to call 911 too. Cell service is terrible. My own phone only works a quarter of the time here—and never when you need it most.

Like right this minute.

Up the steps past the hot tub I trace where I saw the shadowy figure of the man carrying off my wife. I'm moving as fast as I can. I'm tall, and the salmonberry thicket that arches over the trail to the road above the cabins cuts into my arms and hands.

"Sophie! Sophie!"

Nothing.

At the top I see nothing. No sign of her. Nothing at all. A silver Honda Accord whizzes toward me, and I practically throw myself in front of it, but instead of stopping, the driver veers past and flips me off.

"Fuck you! My wife! Someone took my wife!"

The car disappears, and I can't read the plates without my glasses. I suck air into my lungs and run back down the trail to the cabin.

The woman in the middle cabin identifies herself as Teresa Dibley. She tells me that she's called the sheriff. "What happened?" she asks.

"I don't know," I say. "My daughter and I were out checking pots, and I saw someone arguing with my wife, then he hit her. He grabbed her. Carried her. My glasses fell. I couldn't see everything clearly. She was right here." I point to the glass, now in shards, from which Sophie had been drinking while she sat on the bulkhead.

"Have you been drinking too?" she asks.

"No," I insist. Why would she say something like that? I'm shaking. I'm out of breath. I'm in shock. I'm not drunk. I know what I saw. Or what I partially saw. No doubt.

Someone took my wife.

Her eyes show a mix of concern and alarm. "Sheriff is on the way," she finally says.

I work her like a witness. "Did you see anything when you pulled in? I think he took her up to the road."

"No," she tells me. "I mean, nothing that stands out."

I think then of abduction cases I've seen on TV. I wonder if the woman is thinking of them too. I know how many, maybe most, turn out. The ones in which some freak takes a girl or woman, holds her captive, does whatever a dark mind can imagine.

"We have to find her," I say.

"Police will be here soon."

"Right. When? Where are they?"

"Dispatcher said nearest officer is twenty minutes away."

I look at my phone. I can't hide my frustration and fear. Sweat is pouring from under my arms and down my temples. I try to slow my breathing.

"Twenty minutes might as well be an hour," I tell her. "He could take her anywhere. There's nothing but gravel roads and forest for miles around."

She doesn't respond. My guess is she's thinking the same thing. She reaches for me but thinks better of it. I try to comfort her.

"It'll be okay," I tell her. "She'll be found. She'll be all right. She's strong. Really strong. Mentally. Physically."

The woman brightens a little, and Aubrey is out of her life jacket and back in my arms again, holding me C-clamp tight. I hold her and ignore that my bleeding arms are coloring her pale blue *Paw Patrol* T-shirt with a pink-and-red swoosh that I wish had been left by the strawberries I put on her waffles that morning. The dog walker and his black Lab approach while we stand there trying to make sense of what's transpired. He's older, maybe in his seventies, and speaks with a very slight accent I can't quite make out. Dutch, maybe?

"Everything all right?" he asks. "I heard you calling out. I called 911."

"I called too. The sheriff is on the way," Teresa Dibley tells him. She nods at me. "He says he saw someone take his wife," she says, her eyes on her grandchildren as they perch on the deck of their tiny cabin and take in everything. "Right here," she goes on, trying to contain her own anxiety. She fails. "Right off the beach!"

"Did you see anything?" I ask him.

He nods and murmurs something about the shock of what's happened, but I don't really hear his response—it's clear he saw less than I did. People gravitate toward danger and drama to show concern, yes. But also to silently count their blessings that nothing like this has happened to them. That being close to the unthinkable takes them off some list that God or fate keeps track of.

I'm safe.

Not going to happen twice in the same place.

Nothing will hurt me.

Please, God.

I finish telling the detectives everything I know, and I breathe in. They don't stop. They continue peppering the air with questions, seeking details that I must admit, in the turmoil of the moment, have turned into a messy blur. Lee implores me to remain calm as she and her partner continue scribbling notes and exchanging glances. I know that what happened just now is probably like nothing they've ever handled before.

"We need to find her," I repeat, my voice breaking.

Lee puts down her notepad.

"We're on it, Adam."

CHAPTER TWO
LEE

While Montrose collects the broken wineglass in case there are prints from Sophie Warner's attacker and a tech takes a sample of Adam's blood to compare with some small spatters on the glass, I methodically walk the perimeter of the first cabin, looking for evidence. Sophie, thirty-three, is my age. She's a mother, which I'm not. She works at Starbucks headquarters in Seattle, where she is a graphic designer responsible for many of the coffee giant's in-store promotions. From what Adam said, there have been no problems at home and there was no reason to believe that his wife knew the man who took her or, for that matter, why anyone would take her.

The sun bears down on me. The trail dividing the brambles up to the road above is dry, hard, compacted soil. Sword ferns and trilliums, undisturbed, edge the path. I cannot make out any footprints. I can see, however, evidence that matches Adam's account of being cut by the brambles as he ran after his wife. When I reach the top, I look down at the way I came. The cabin blocks most of the view, but a sliver of the shore and the bulkhead where Sophie was sitting is

visible. I spin around. At my feet is an indication that someone might have stood there observing the cabins below. I
collect a single cigarette butt and take a photograph of loose
gravel next to the trail leading to the Wisteria. Slight inden-
tations in the gravel indicate that a car or small truck might
have been parked there. No telling when, of course. Or if it
had anything to do with what happened down by the beach.

I meet Montrose inside the shingled single-story cabin,
which is flanked on one side with a mammoth, anaconda-
like vine of its purple-hued namesake.

"How's he holding up?" I ask.

He gives me a little shrug. "Seems okay, considering.
Find anything?"

"Not really. A cigarette butt. Looks like it's probably
been there awhile," I tell him as we move through the cabin.
The kitchen sink is stacked with a bowl used to mix waffle
batter and a couple of plates. The green tops of a handful of
strawberries lay on a paper towel on the counter. I can see
Adam on the deck through the kitchen window. He's sitting
now, his daughter in his lap, his phone pressed to his ear.

Montrose looks over in their direction. "Calling his
wife's folks."

"Wouldn't want to make that call," I say.

"Nothing could be worse."

No argument there. From what Adam told us, Sophie is
gutsy and strong. She's got a fighting chance if some weirdo
grabbed her. At least I hope so. Before getting my shield, I
taught a self-defense class.

"Who does something like this in broad daylight?" I ask.

"Some crazy person," Montrose says. "Someone who either stalked her or saw an opportunity and took her."

Off the dining room is a bedroom with bunk beds. The
bottom bed is unmade, its sailboat-themed coverlet is pushed
to the floor. A child's stuffed animal, which I now know is a
character from *Paw Patrol*, from the same graphic that's on
Aubrey's shirt, is tucked next to the pillows.

"We need to talk to the girl," I say.

"She's pretty little," he says.

We head through the dining room on our way to the master bedroom. I notice a pair of women's sunglasses adjacent to what I assume is Sophie's purse. Just sitting there like a tableau of a life now on pause.

"Right," I say, processing the space. "But she still might be able to tell us something."

Montrose is the first to notice it when we enter the bedroom. The bed's right side is smooth, and the pillows are stacked neatly against the headboard.

"Looks like only one side of the bed was slept in," he says. "Kind of interesting."

"You don't believe his story." My words come out a little defensively, and it surprises me. I know Adam Warner, but not that well.

Montrose has been a detective a lot longer than I. He's back on his second chance, though, having left the department for two years following a substance-abuse problem that could have ruined his life. He's got great instincts, but I don't always agree with him. I like to be right too.

"A few holes in his story," he says.

"Like what?"

"Like that he couldn't get to shore in time to save her. A hundred yards out? Biceps like his? Guy spends a lot of time to look that strong. Seems like he could have gotten to her."

"He couldn't even see."

"Right. The glasses."

"Yes, they fell off."

Montrose makes a face. "Pretty convenient."

"You're mad because you missed lunch."

"Only a little mad."

I sigh. "Fine. Food later. Let's remember. The evidence is our guide here. Not your gut."

Montrose pats his belly, which hangs over his belt like a canopy.

"I like my gut."

I give him a smile. His gut is empty.

"Besides, abductions like this just don't happen. Not in front of someone's house."

"This isn't someone's house," I say. "It's a vacation rental. Transient. People come and go."

A carved wooden-bear coatrack and a slipcovered sofa decorated with faded denim pillows dominate the living room. I notice a throw on the sofa.

I circle the room. "Maybe one of them slept out here."

"You mean like they weren't getting along and he's a liar?"

Now I give Montrose a look. "I mean just what I said. I don't know the why. You don't, either."

The sole bathroom in the cabin is surprisingly spacious for something built in the 1920s. A claw-foot tub commands the space against the interior wall; a toilet and shower take up the rest of the space. Sophie's cosmetics bag is open next to the sink. A pair of pristine white towels, damp to the touch, hang on brass hooks next to the door.

On our way out, Montrose pokes his head through a doorway that I assumed was a closet.

"Nice," he says. "A sauna."

"Not a fan," I say.

"Hot tub too," he points out. "Might just want to stay here myself."

I give him a nod. "We might be here a lot, but we won't be in the hot tub or the sauna."

Montrose looks in my direction. I can see the twinkle in his eyes behind his wire frames. I wait for it, but it doesn't come. I am certain that my partner will make some crack about Adam Warner being in hot water or the fact that we're going to need to apply some heat here.

But he doesn't. And I'm grateful for that.

CHAPTER THREE
LEE

Teresa Dibley offers coffee or soda, but I decline. She's grandmotherly, because that's what she is, but immediately I learn she's more than that. At sixty-two, she's raising her son's children—Clark, twelve, and Destiny, seven—because her son and daughter-in-law would rather use drugs than parent. We stand on the deck of the Chrysanthemum and watch as the kids play with Aubrey by the rope swing. Destiny is blond and very shy.

"Destiny doesn't really know her mom, and frankly, I hope to keep it that way. Not that my son is any better. But I can tolerate him, I guess, because I have no choice."

"I'm sorry," I say.

"I picked up Destiny from the hospital when she was four days old. The only trace of her mother on the girl is the ridiculous name she gave her. Hope to change that someday. I'm just biding my time until the state of Washington gives me the final stamp of approval. It's stupid; it's cruel, but that's the way it is."

Teresa is slender and fit in shorts and walking shoes. Her

sleeveless T-shirt is emblazoned with the logo of the Hama Hama Oyster Saloon, just past Lilliwaup. Her hair is pewter with streaks of black, and she wears it pulled back from her face.

"You weren't here when Sophie vanished?" Montrose redirects the conversation, removing his glasses and wiping the lenses with a handkerchief pulled from his pants pocket.

"No. Kids and I spent the morning going up Staircase."

I nod, thinking of the times I'd scaled it. "Nice hike."

"Yes," she says. "Destiny got tired, but she's a pretty good sport. Didn't cry or anything. Even so, we came home early. Clark insisted. Wanted to gather oysters at low tide this afternoon anyway."

"What did you see when you got here?" I ask.

"I saw Mr. Warner. Adam. I didn't know his name. They came in last night. We left early this morning before anyone got up. It'd been a long night. Destiny and I slept on the Murphy bed and Clark on the sofa. I'm doubtful about renting a studio again. The Chrysanthemum is just too little for three people."

"When you got back from Staircase," I go on, "you saw Mr. Warner?"

She nods. "Right. He was on the lawn in front of the cabin screaming for me to call 911. He was in pretty bad shape. There was no doubt that something very traumatic had just happened."

"What exactly did he say?" Montrose asks.

"His wife was gone," she says. "That someone had taken her."

She stops and wheels on Clark, who is back on the rope swing over the water. "Careful!" Teresa yells. "You almost knocked Destiny over!"

The blond-headed boy glances over at us. "Sorry, Grandma!"

I notice Adam is still on the phone. He's pacing and looking over at us. He's like a dog tethered to a chain, working his way over the lawn, back and forth. At one point he throws his hands up in the air and looks over at me.

"Find her!" he says to me. "Do something!"

We're trying to, I think. I motion to him that I'll be with him in a minute.

"Did you interact with Sophie?" I ask.

She shakes her head no.

"Was there anything happening last night at their cabin? Anything remarkable at all?"

Again she shakes her head. "I wear earplugs at night. You would too, if you had to sleep on a Murphy bed with a wiggle worm like Destiny. Girl's a talker, even in her sleep."

Clark comes over from the swing. His lips are stained red from a cherry ice pop.

"*I* heard something," he says.

I forget how keen a child's hearing is.

"What did you hear, Clark?" Teresa asks.

"Destiny got me up to get some water. It was late. I gave her the water and went back to bed, and while I was lying there, I heard a loud noise. A door slamming. Then a car started. I looked outside but didn't see anything. No lights or nothing."

"What kind of noise, Clark?"

The boy looks blank eyed. "I don't know. Just a loud noise."

Clark wasn't making this easy.

"A noise a person makes?" Montrose asks. "Or something else?"

He looks upward. "No. More like something falling," he says. "Or maybe like the sound our door makes when it slams shut. I don't know. A noise."

Clark's a kid doing the best that he can. Describing a noise in the middle of the night—outside of gunfire—isn't easy.

"Do you know when you heard it?" I ask.

"You mean what time?"

"Right," I say. "About what time?"

"Late," he says. "Dark. Probably after two. That's about the time Destiny gets me up at home for a drink."

"She's still doing that?" Teresa asks, changing the subject to one that touches on her responsibilities.

"Yeah," he answers, now with an older-than-his-years exasperation. "Every night. Can I have another popsicle?"

Teresa doesn't put up a fight. "Take one to your sister and Aubrey too."

"Have you met the folks next door?" I ask, indicating the southernmost of the trio of cabins.

"No," she says, "but they were here late. The lights were on, shades drawn. Their car was here. Must be late risers."

Before we leave, Teresa gives us the name and contact number of the property owner for all three cabins. Montrose heads back to the car to call the man for whatever information he can provide about this weekend's renters. When he's done, he'll check in with the uniformed deputy who's been gathering information from the neighbors who've arrived to watch and the remaining renter we haven't spoken with yet.

I make my way down the beach to the home of Axel Bakker, the elderly dog walker. When I told him we'd want to talk with him, he'd pointed his house out to me and invited me to drop by as soon as I had the time. He and his dog weren't going anywhere.

Axel Bakker's house on Canal View Road is a Hood Canal classic, built in the 1920s when the area along Washington State's saltwater fjord was talked up in LA as the Next Big Thing. It's a silvery weathered-shingle bungalow with cream-colored shutters and a red door. When I walk up from the beach, Mr. Bakker gives me a wave from a raised vegetable garden.

"How did the peas do?" I ask, joining him.

He shrugs. "About as lousy as ever."

Mr. Bakker is pushing eighty, but he's in remarkable shape. His face is as tan and wrinkled as an old paper bag, but his light blue eyes spark with intelligence. Winston, his dog, is at his feet.

"What's your name again?" he asks, squinting at me.

I tell him.

"I told your partner what I saw already." He gives me a once-over and then returns his gaze to what he was doing. "Not that Mason County worries about wasting money, God knows."

"You might feel differently if Sophie were your daughter," I say.

"Probably so." He finishes staking a tomato plant with some jute twine and invites me inside.

No, I think as I go in. Not a house. A *museum*.

The furniture is burled wood mostly. Some upholstered pieces are covered with coastal weavings from the Salish tribes. The folks at *Antiques Roadshow* would be aghast at such mutilation for sofa pillows. The walls feature Hood Canal memorabilia: "Oysters for Sale" placards, a carved sign from the long-gone Tahuya dance hall, and an array of black-and-white photographs that tell the area's history of shellfish and timber.

"Dad built this place during Prohibition," he says, catching my interest in his collection. "Made some money here too. Bunch of locals did. Good place to make and run booze into Seattle."

"Doesn't seem so remote now," I tell him as he gestures for me to join him on one of the big burled-wood chairs.

"Nope," Mr. Bakker says, sliding off his shoes, a shabby pair of blue Crocs. "Goddamn Californians have ruined the place. Taxes going up every year. Forced my neighbors to the north to move. They'd been here nearly as long as I have. Now they live in a damn subdivision in Mesa, Arizona, and wish to God every day that they died here instead of moving. I hope I have a heart attack on the beach one day . . ." He looks down at Winston. "Not for a while, though. Winston has to go first, and this dog has a few more years left in him."

"He's beautiful," I say, petting Winston's head.

"You didn't come for a history lesson or to pet my dog."

"No," I say. "I didn't. I'm here to go over what you saw on the beach when Mrs. Warner was abducted."

"I didn't see much," he says.

"I understand," I tell him. "I'm here because sometimes after a traumatic event, people are able to pull more from their memories. You agree it was traumatic, right?"

Winston works on a flea, and Mr. Bakker scrunches his papery face. "For the woman and her husband? Yes, 'traumatic' is a good word. For me? I don't know. I served in the army, and I've seen a lot of things. Nothing like that on my daily beach walk, that's for sure. Though one time I thought I saw a rape being committed, but it was some kids messing around on an air mattress."

I nod and ask him to tell me what he saw that morning. "One more time, please," I say.

He launches into a repeat of what he'd told Montrose in their first, perfunctory interview. He'd been out walking Winston as he always did at that time of the day. He saw Adam and Aubrey out in the rowboat about a hundred yards from shore. The next thing he recalled was that he heard someone yell. He looked first to Adam, who was frantically rowing to shore, then over to the bulkhead.

"And you saw Mrs. Warner?" I ask. "And her attacker?"

Mr. Bakker fishes for his glasses in the front pocket of his shirt.

"I know I'm as old as dirt," he goes on, "but I can see just fine with these on. It was fast, and there was a lot going on, but yes, I saw it happen." His tone is slightly defensive, and his Dutch accent moves a bit more to the forefront.

"I'm not here because I don't believe you, Mr. Bakker. I'm here because a crime has been committed and we need to find out what happened. And who did it."

Winston is not a lapdog, but Mr. Bakker lets him crawl up on his lap anyway.

"Right," he says. "Okay, fine."

"Tell me what you saw on the shore."

He takes a breath and then slowly lets it out. "I was a distance away, but like I said, I can see just fine with my glasses. I saw Mrs. Warner struggling with a man. It was fast. I saw her and looked down to step over some rocks to get there, and when I looked up again, both of them were gone."

"His height? What was he wearing?"

The old man thinks carefully, his eyes closed for a moment. "Average," he finally says. "Might have had a baseball cap on. Orange jacket. *That* I'm sure about. Although it might have been a red. Orange, I'd say."

"I don't believe you mentioned that jacket to my partner," I tell him.

He gestures with open hands. "Didn't ask me."

"Okay," I go on. "This is good. This is helping. What about Mrs. Warner? Can you recall any details about her? What *she* was wearing?"

He thinks a minute. "A straw hat—*that* I remember very clearly. And a white dress," he says, though with a little less certainty. "Maybe light blue? She was definitely wearing a dress. You know the kind of light, filmy thing those gals wear now over their bathing suits. I've even seen them at the IGA dressed like that. Practically see-through. Not that I'm really complaining."

I smile. It's a creepy remark, but this isn't a creepy old man.

"A cover-up," I say.

"If that's what you call it."

"Anything else?"

"No," he says. "She vanished. Poof. I looked back up, and she and whoever was attacking her were gone. I called 911. The husband was almost to shore when I got done."

"What was his demeanor like?"

"Like I said, the man was frantic. Didn't know which end was up. His little girl was crying, and he told me to call 911. Said his phone didn't have service or something. Probably T-Mobile. Pretty bad out here."

He goes on to say Adam left Aubrey with the vacation renter in the cabin next door while he ran up the trail behind the cabin looking for his wife. They waited for the police to come.

"And while you were waiting, what happened?" I ask. "How was Mr. Warner?"

"Why are you asking about him so much?"

"It's routine."

"He was out on the boat when it happened. I can verify that. That's the God's truth."

"I know," I say. "But we need to ask. So tell me: What was his behavior like?"

Winston moves back to the floor to work on his flea.

"He was a mess," he says. "His wife just got snatched. How do you think a man is going to behave?"

Fair enough, I think.

We talk a little more about what he saw, how his vision was decent—though he was overdue for a new prescription for his glasses.

"Damn Medicare," he says. "So much red tape."

While the state of his vision is of some concern, he's so sure about what he saw that I relax a little. He shows me around his place. I see a silver-framed photo of him and his wife, a wedding portrait.

"Beautiful couple," I say.

He looks at the photograph. It's a black-and-white that

was hand-tinted by someone who knew what they were doing. Not clownish but subtle, with only enough color to bring the nuances of life to an already lovely image.

"You want to know what traumatic is?"

I don't say anything. Behind his thick lenses, I can see dampness in his eyes.

"Losing her," he says. "That guy must be in a world of hurt. There's not much more painful than losing your wife. Real lonely too."

"I'm sorry," I tell him as I make my way to the front door. "Winston is good company, I hope."

"Winston?" he asks.

Mr. Bakker looks confused, so I bend down and rub the top of the dog's head. "This guy, of course."

His already knotted brow constricts a bit more. "That's not Winston," he says. "That pup's been gone for years and years. This is Reggie."

When I make my way back to the crime scene, I find Montrose and fill him in on the interview with Mr. Bakker. A little reluctantly, because older people get trashed all the time for being out of touch and confused when they don't deserve it, I mention that the old man had told the dispatcher the wrong name of his dog.

"Kind of a small thing," I say.

Montrose squints into the sun and takes off his glasses to remove a smudge. "Could be a big thing."

He's right. Other than Adam, Mr. Bakker's the only witness to the crime.

CHAPTER FOUR
CONNOR

"Was that a cop?" I ask Kristen as she returns to the bedroom of the Lily, where I've been resting like pancaked roadkill since we arrived the night before. I thought I saw a uniform in the doorway when I fought my way to my knees on the bed to see who'd knocked but couldn't stay there long enough to be sure. Every muscle in my body aches, and my head feels like it's packed with a dozen loose ball bearings, all rolling around like the vintage pinball machine my dad bought us when my sister and I were kids.

"Yes," Kristen says. "A woman went missing, and they're looking for her."

I try to right myself on a pair of down-filled pillows, but they are too squishy. I look at my phone. It's after two in the afternoon. I plunge back into the cloud of linens and comforters, but manage to lift my head a little. "Missing from where?" I ask, now feeling a wave of nausea that I refuse to give in to. "Don't follow you."

"Staying in the first cabin," she says. "Someone took her, I guess."

It's hard to process those words and repeat them. "Took her?"

"I don't know much more than that. I told them you've been under the weather. We'll need to make a statement later. No big deal. Our civic responsibility and all."

I give her a slight nod. Kristen's the most beautiful woman I've ever seen. She's blond and blue eyed and probably could have been a model if she'd wanted to be one. In fact, I'm sure of it. She could have been anything. She's that smart. She's thirty-nine and in line for a partnership at a Seattle law firm.

"Drink this," she tells me, handing me a glass of tepid milky liquid. "Found some baking soda in the pantry. This'll make you feel better."

I balance myself on floppy feather pillows and drink the now-foaming concoction in a few big gulps.

"Thanks, babe," I say. "Sorry about last night."

The kindness melts from her face, replaced by her practiced, Oscar-worthy look of disappointment. I've seen her use it in the courtroom, turning to a jury when a witness states the wrong thing.

But, honestly, I *am* sorry.

She pretends to struggle for words. I know it's a pretense, because my wife never has a shortage of opinions about every subject you can imagine.

Especially when it comes to me.

"You were drinking all day, Connor," she says, letting out a leaking tire of a sigh. "All day. I should have left you at home. And I sure as hell shouldn't have let you get your hands on that bottle of tequila."

I wince at the word *tequila*.

"I don't know," I say.

Kristen sits on the edge of the bed. "You *do* know."

She's right. I *do.*

I want to remind her that she could help matters. Pouring me drinks and then later complaining about my alcohol consumption isn't fair. I can't tell her that. I know that she loves me, and really, this is my battle.

"Yeah," I finally say. "I've got to stop."

She could offer up a kind of "I've heard that before" retort, but thankfully, she holds back.

"That's correct," Kristen says, taking my glass. She's full-on kind right now, a pendulum of emotions. All for me. Her smile is sad but genuine. She looks at me with those blue eyes that see through me. She loves me more than anything, but I know that my time with her could end at any moment for the mistakes that I have made. And the one I keep making. I need help. Treatment. I hate that word because it makes me feel like a weakling, but after last night, I think there will be no more second chances with her. And when she makes up her mind, there's no changing it. I've often wished that I could be so sure of things too. But I'm not. I'm too easy. Too malleable. I'm a ball of unbaked dough. My wife is a rolling pin. Despite some major ups and downs, I admit that the dynamic has somehow worked for us. I didn't always think that it would, but what do I know? She's a lawyer. I'm a waiter. A really good one. But, yeah, a waiter.

"I couldn't do it for my dad," she reminds me, underscoring the fact that she is the adult child of an alcoholic, which has framed much of her personal story. "I can't do it for you, Connor. You're going to need to take each and every step toward recovery on your own. I'll be there, right behind you, but I cannot lead you through this."

The truth is I've tried before and failed.

"I feel like a loser," I say. "I'll make an appointment for next week. I'll see my doctor first, see what he recommends for treatment and what it will involve."

"Honey," she says. "I have faith in you. I really do. Connor Moss is absolutely not a loser."

"I feel like one sometimes," I say.

She takes me in with those beautiful blues. "You're going to have to fix that on your own too."

Kristen starts to leave and then suddenly turns around and gives me a sweet but knowing look. She's an angel. She really is. No other woman would have put up with me.

"You need a shower," she says. "You smell like a distillery."

I manage a smile in return. "Never again, Kristen." I don't add the word *promise* into the conversation. That's a concept that I've overplayed in the past. More than a few times.

I hoist myself up from the bed and make my way to the bathroom. It's a small space tiled from floor to ceiling in a mosaic of beach glass. The window is open, and I can hear the sounds of the highway above the beach. A siren passes by. I assume it's additional police, driving down the hill to the little row of cabins.

Missing. Abducted. Taken. The words play in my head as I turn on the shower and wait for the water to warm. It seems unreal. TV-like. Investigation Discovery. I catch my reflection in the mirror. I'm tall, in good shape. My hair's holding up better than my dad's ever did, and I'm grateful for that. I look a little green around the eyes at the moment, but I'll drink lots of water and get past this hangover. My right shoulder is a web of scars from a car accident years ago. For a waiter, I'm not too bad. For a man married to a high-powered woman, I'm not the catch that I could have been.

Or once was.

The sight of my scars and the noise of the running water and the sirens trigger a memory. It's one that I keep buried. Not because I truly want to forget it—forgetting it would be a mistake—but because that moment changed my life forever. And not in a good way. Hot water cascades over me, and I lather up, running my soapy hands over my sore body and feeling the slightly raised skin of my shoulder. I pick at a knife cut on my hand, and red swirls down into the chrome-plated drain.

That reminds me too.

It was long before Kristen. I was twenty-four and visiting cousins in Huntington Beach. The *rich* cousins. I'd completed my degree in sociology at USC and was doing what I'd been doing far too much for far too long. My cousin Rob and I'd spent the day at the beach drinking beer from a red plastic Coleman cooler. We were wasted. Really wasted. I remember we ran out of beer, and Rob actually went around the beach with a wad of cash, buying more from whoever had any. Rob was persuasive. He was the kind of guy who had a big white smile and a sleepy casualness that made him approachable and fun to be around.

It was too much. But we drank more. At one point I passed out while Rob was playing volleyball with some cute girls down the beach. The sun felt so good. I felt so great. Sloppy, but sloppy at the beach isn't terrible. In fact, at the time I was convinced things couldn't get any better.

Big wrong.

I had started my job search a few weeks before and was already getting some pretty good bites. An interview with Los Angeles County to work on a youth-offender program was scheduled for the following week. It wasn't a dream job, but it was a start.

When the sun sizzled into the distant edge of the Pacific, Rob returned and suggested that we hit a few bars. He'd motioned to a couple of girls a few yards away. They were like everyone in LA. Perfect. In every single way.

"They want to meet up," Rob said, indicating the girls and fixing his secret weapon on them: that big white LA ortho-engineered smile flashing down the beach at them like a searchlight.

A tall blonde looped her beach bag over her shoulder and gave me a little wave.

"Sounds awesome," I said.

The last thing I really remember about that night was getting Rob into his bright red BMW convertible. He was in no condition to drive. I wasn't, either, but I was confident that if I stayed off the freeway and was extra careful, I'd be able to get us home. I was heading south on Pacific to Beach Boulevard when Rob started making the kinds of sounds that indicated he was about to hurl. No one likes that noise—or what was about to happen. Indeed, I'm one of those people who actually sympathy-pukes when I hear it.

"Hold on, Rob," I said. "Let me pull over."

"Man," he said, "going to blow chunks."

"Stick your head out the window!"

I opened the window and gave him a little nudge so he could get his head in position before I found a place to stop. Cars lined the side of the road. There was nowhere to pull over, so I sped up to find one.

I didn't see the van in time. I didn't see the stoplight change to red, either. I was going forty-five miles an hour, and I somehow managed to swerve. I believe in God because of that. The van was packed. A family of seven from Phoenix had driven to Disneyland and had been working their way around the sun-drenched sights of SoCal.

Next thing I knew, I woke up in Huntington Beach Hospital, tubes everywhere. It was hard to process, while it shouldn't have been. Blood had been drawn, and a cop was outside my door.

"What happened?" I asked a doctor.

Her expression was grim. "You ran a red light."

That's right. I'd been the one driving.

"Jesus," I said, trying to sit up. I hurt like hell. My shoulder was bandaged like a cast. I couldn't move. None of that mattered. My mind went to my cousin.

"Rob? My cousin?"

"You're both lucky," she said. "You're luckier than he is. But you are both alive."

Later I found out that Rob had suffered a brain injury from which he was never likely to fully recover. That kind of truth is a heavy thing on someone. It was my fault. I knew it. I should not have driven. I thought I was in better shape than he was. I was so stupid.

I was also a criminal. Because I'd injured another party, I was charged with a felony DUI, and not a misdemeanor. I was so low that I wouldn't have fought it if I could. Rob was never mean about it, but I assumed that his kindness was the result of his head injury. That he really didn't understand the lasting consequences of our day on the beach. I served only one night in jail and was put on probation. The light sentence wasn't because I wasn't at fault but rather the result of an overcrowded justice system.

Lucky. Unlucky me.

If God had given me any gifts that day, it was that I hadn't killed anyone, that those five kids with Mickey Mouse T-shirts and bags of souvenirs returned to Phoenix with a good story to tell and nothing more.

Felonies, however, don't ever go away. They follow you like the blackest of shadows. With a criminal record, it was no surprise that I didn't get that job with LA County. In fact, I couldn't get any job that I wanted. Waiting tables, it turned out, was the best I could do in the short term. In time, the short term became the long term. It wasn't all bad. I met Kristen at my work, a bistro in the University District. She was just out of University of Washington Law School, and I'd moved up to Seattle for a fresh start. She was four years older, a lot smarter, and had the kindest eyes I'd ever seen.

I really was the luckiest guy in the world when she said yes when I asked her out. I'm still the luckiest guy. Every time I look at my wife, I see goodness. That's why what's happened between us over the last few years feels so painful.

CHAPTER FIVE
ADAM

I don't understand. I told them what happened. And yet the Mason County detectives who answered the call are barely moving. Talking to that grandma and even her grandson when they should be sending out some kind of AMBER Alert or an APB to find Sophie. *Something.* Maybe they have? Sophie has been missing more than four hours now. Aubrey's hopped up on sugar from those damn ice pops, and I'm sitting here wondering what I should be doing to find her mom.

Find Sophie.

Bring her home.

Get my wife back.

Save her.

I think of all the things that I should tell them, but when the detectives come at me, it's their agenda that trumps everything that's running through my mind.

"We noticed that either you or your wife slept on the sofa last night," Detective Montrose says.

His tone feels accusatory. Or maybe I'm imagining it. I don't know. I've never been the husband of a missing wife. I push back because I know they are blaming me for what happened. I've seen crime shows on TV. Cops always blame the husband.

"Really?" I strain to keep my cool but fail. "That's what you're saying to me? What the fuck? So what! I slept there because Sophie's been battling a cold. We almost canceled this trip because of it. What are you trying to put out there? That we had a fight or something?"

"We're just asking," Lee says. "We have to ask."

"Fine," I answer, my lips taut over my teeth. It's a physiological reaction. I cannot control it. "What are you actually doing to find her?" I ask, fighting hard for composure. "She's not here. You can see that. Some sick fuck took her. Why aren't you going door-to-door or searching every goddamn ditch between here and Potlatch?"

"We've already sent out a statewide BOLO for your wife," Montrose says. "But we don't have much other than her driver's license picture from the DOL database. We don't know if the man took her on foot or in a car. Or a truck. There's not a lot for anyone to go on."

"Adam," Lee says, "honestly, my partner is right. We don't have much to go on. Your description from a hundred yards out without glasses gives us only an idea about who we're looking for. Red jacket. Hat of some kind, according to another witness. Average height and weight."

"That's the best I can do," I say.

"Right," she says. "I know."

I'm counting on the police to believe me, but I know from watching TV and reading the paper that you become a target as soon as you report that your wife has died or is missing. Sympathy erodes in five minutes and turns to suspicion, and then accusations fly. First they are quiet. Murmurs of those who have no real standing. Then a trickle that turns into a tidal wave. I didn't consider that any of that could ever happen to me. I never considered until that very moment that my wife would be missing.

"Did you hear anything unusual last night?" Detective Montrose raises his pen to pad, waits for my answer.

"I would have told you if I had."

"Around two? Very late." This time it's Lee who is speaking.

"No. Nothing. Lee, why are you treating me like this?" I hold her gaze, unblinking. "You know me. You're asking me questions like you don't believe anything I've said."

Lee swallows. Her pale white skin blushes a little. She used to turn red when I teased her when we were kids. The color is pink, not red. But there's color there. Good. I feel like shit. In fact, there are plenty of bad feelings to go around at the moment. They aren't focusing on what's happened to Sophie.

They are focusing on me.

I shouldn't be surprised. But I guess I am.

"The noise was loud," Lee says. "The boy heard it. Said it sounded like his door at home slamming shut."

"I didn't hear anything," I tell her. "Are either of you even listening to me?"

Suddenly I feel like I'm in quicksand, sinking out of view. Going down while the two Mason County cops look at me from above. I'm going lower and lower. They are hunched over me now. As I sink under the weight of their questions, I realize that there is no way that I can truly control what's happening around me. I'm not at work, where I can lie to my director and do what I want. I can't tell my team to ignore what the higher-ups are dictating and do what I think is best. Not that I ever tell anyone to do anything unethical. Not really. Cutting corners to get things done faster isn't wrong. Here, I'm at the bottom.

"We're just doing our jobs, Adam," Lee says.

"Sure doesn't feel that way to me. I saw someone hit my wife, grab her, and carry her off, and you're ignoring all of that."

"No one is ignoring anything," Detective Montrose says. "We just want to know how things were going with you and your wife. Maybe Sophie got mad and took off. My wife did that to me. Went to her sister's for a weekend and let me stew at home with a bottle of gin."

Lee keeps me in her gaze, but I can see her body stiffen a little. She didn't know what her partner was talking about. I imagine that if they tire of Sophie's case on their drive back to Shelton, the stability of his marriage will wind its way into their conversation.

"My wife and I are solid," I say. "Even if you want to fully discount what I told you I saw, then fine. Do so. Have whatever's happening to her right now on your hands. I told you what I saw. There's no drama, and there's no way she would have run off. We were happy."

A car pulls into the parking area adjacent to the Wisteria.

"Your in-laws?" Lee asks.

I shake my head. "No. They won't be here for another hour."

I stand there for a beat. Silent. Me in my quicksand. Aubrey is suddenly back in my arms. I can tell that she doesn't know what's really going on. I'm unsure too.

"I saw what I saw," I finally say. My words hang awkwardly in the air.

"Of course," Lee says.

"What's next?" I ask.

Detective Montrose glances past me over the darkening shore of Hood Canal as an enormous cumulus cloud shutters the sun. He doesn't say anything. Neither does Lee. I wonder if their silence is a police tactic of some kind or if they simply don't have an answer.

"Are you staying here tonight?" Lee asks.

"Where else would I go?"

"I'm not sure this is a good environment for your little girl."

"Thanks for your interest, Lee. My wife is gone, and I'm not leaving. Her parents are on their way. I expect that they'll take Aubrey with them."

I turn to my little girl. She looks scared, confused. And I don't know how to make it better.

"You want to see Grandma Helen and Grandpa Frank?" I ask.

She gives me a little nod.

Lee speaks up. "That's a good idea, Adam. But before that, we'll need to interview Aubrey."

"I don't know about that. She doesn't know anything. She's just a little kid."

"She's also a witness," Montrose says.

"It has to be done, Adam," Lee says. "Procedure. You understand."

Part of me does, of course. But even so, I think that pressing a three-year-old for details about the worst thing she's ever seen can only make the ordeal worse in the long run. An interview would be traumatic.

"I don't know," I finally say.

"I've done this before," Lee says. "You can be present, but you need to let me talk to her." She looks over at Montrose.

That goes for him too.

CHAPTER SIX
LEE

While her father and my partner look on, Aubrey Warner and I sit on the concrete steps that lead to the beach. We face the water, and all the commotion behind us fades away. The strangers. The police vehicles that fill the parking area shared by the three cabins. Lights on one still flashing. Especially the worried look on her father's face.

"Aubrey," I tell her, "I know you are a big girl."

She smiles a little. "I am big."

"I know," I say. "I need you to help me."

She finds a mussel shell on the step and offers it to me. "Mommy likes shells too."

It's my easy opening.

"Tell me about your mommy," I say, taking the blue shell. "Did you see your mommy on the beach before she went away?"

"A bad man took her."

"What did he look like?"

She turns to Adam and Montrose and points.

"Like him."

"Like your dad?"

"No. Like *him*."

She means Montrose, who's older than Adam.

I ask her if she can describe the man further, but she's at a loss. He was a man.

"He took her. He took Mommy."

"Yes," I say. "I know."

"Find Mommy."

I want to hug that little girl. I want to promise that we will, but I know better. I know that promises like that can come back to haunt you.

CHAPTER SEVEN
ADAM

Watching your child being questioned is among the hardest things imaginable. Intellectually, you know that the investigator is doing his or her job, but you cannot fathom the point of it. A little kid can't remember what they had for breakfast unless they refused to eat it. They can't tell you if something occurred ten minutes or two hours ago. It takes everything I have to let Lee pry out nonexistent details from Aubrey.

But I do. I do it because it has to be done.

Just as the interview concludes, I look up to see my in-laws' maroon Buick making its way down the driveway.

I told them what happened on the phone, a conversation that would have been best in person.

"What do you mean someone took her?" Frank said to me. "*Who* took her?"

"Someone," I said. "I couldn't really see."

"What the hell are you . . . what kind of man would let something like that happen?"

Dumb shit. Mr. Big. Blowhard. Those are the words that

come to mind when I think of Frank Flynn. I don't say them to his face. I don't say them to Sophie's, either. I just grin and bear his complete obnoxiousness. At night, when I grind my teeth, I'm almost certain that Frank is the cause of it all. I'll be damned if I'll put a night guard in my mouth every goddamn night just to find a way to live with him in my life.

Frank spills out of his car and puffs his way over, with Helen trundling along behind him like one of those suitcases on wheels. He's wearing his weekend gardening getup. She's dressed like she was yanked out of a tea party. She probably was. She never misses an opportunity to plan something away from Frank. I don't blame her. She's mousey, yes. She's also clever enough to get away from her husband. Even with the tiniest opening.

Aubrey bolts to her grandma, bouncing past her grandfather like a ball in a pinball machine. She doesn't like him, either. That makes me smile most of the time. Though not right now. This is not a day for any smiles.

"Goddamn!" Frank bellows at the detectives. "What happened to my daughter? Where is she? She's my only daughter, for crying out loud!"

Lee identifies herself and her partner as detectives from the Mason County Sheriff's Office.

"Jesus!" Frank says, letting out an exasperated sigh. "Can't we get some cops in here that know how to work a case? Some from Seattle?"

Helen tugs at her husband. She's weak, but Sophie is her daughter too. "Frank, that's not how it works."

I flash to what I imagine their long drive from Seattle was like. I'm all but sure that she sat there in stony silence while he railed about how stupid Sophie was to pick me.

I hear Frank's voice in my head.

"A SkyAero manager! Goddamn, she could have picked anyone!"

I know Helen wouldn't defend me. It isn't that she doesn't care for me. She just doesn't have a spine.

Frank shoots his wife a bone-chilling look just then. *His wife.* His possession. His pet. His thing. I've often wondered if he hits her when no one is around. I imagine he beats her in places that those long sleeves cover no matter the season.

Then he faces me.

"They are going to find her, Frank," I say, though the words come out more like a hopeful whisper than an emphatic statement. The blowhard does that to me. Sucks all the air out of the room. Leaves no one with an opportunity to come back at him. For a little tyrant, he's a goddamn master.

"If anything happens to my Sophie," Frank says, nearly vibrating with anger and kicking the dirt with the toe of his shoe, "it's on you!"

CHAPTER EIGHT
LEE

While Adam Warner and Helen Flynn gather Aubrey's things for the trip back to Seattle, Montrose and I talk with Sophie's father. It's after four, and the sun is baking us where we stand, so we move under one of the cedars between the first two cabins.

"Some tension there between you and your son-in-law," Montrose says.

Frank Flynn nods. "He's a prick, so yes. Always acting like he's Mr. Hotshot. Always in line for some big promotion that, to be honest, never seems to come." He stops a second and looks in the direction of the Wisteria. "He's a good father, I guess. Probably the best thing about him."

"How about as a husband?" I ask.

Frank doesn't skimp on adjectives. "Disappointing. Egomaniac. Full of himself."

Pot, meet kettle, I think.

"You two don't get along," I say.

"We do," he says without hesitation. "For the most part.

He knows his place, and that's half the battle when someone joins the family, isn't it?"

"I guess so," I say, wondering why joining anyone's family should be couched in terms that include the word *battle*. I remember how tight Adam's family had been when we were growing up in Shelton. My parents had divorced by the time I was sixteen, and Adam's parents were not only together but happy. They took Kip to Disneyland one time. God, how I wanted to go too. Adam knew this, and he made sure that Kip brought me back some mouse ears with my name stitched in lavender thread on the back. I still have them somewhere. Mr. Warner worked at the mill, and Mrs. Warner was an elementary school librarian. Good people.

"Everything okay between them?" Montrose asks. "Marriage okay?"

"A few bumps in the road," Frank says, his tone suddenly colored with reluctance. "But not since Aubrey was born."

"What kind of bumps?" I ask.

"Sophie wanted to move to New York," he says. "She's a graphic designer. A great one. Not some flake freelancer who thinks that graphic design is the gateway to a fine arts career. Sophie's smarter than that. More talented too. She had a chance to work for one of the biggest agencies in the world, but Adam wouldn't leave his job at SkyAero. Like that was some prize. Jesus."

Coming from a town like Shelton, SkyAero doesn't seem like a disappointment to me at all. When I heard from someone in town that Adam had made his way up the ladder at the Seattle aerospace company, I thought it was great. I'd only been on a plane three times in my life. Adam's success was a big deal. Impressive. Better than the ups and downs of the mill in town or a job at the shipyard in Bremerton, like a lot of local guys. And girls too.

"But they worked things out?" I ask.

"Stalemate," Frank Flynn goes on. "She still wanted to

go. He still insisted that he was on the way up to the top of whatever it is he does. I told her to leave him, and I think she almost did. Not long after that, she got pregnant. Her last chance at greatness was done. Kaput. I blame him for that."

I hold my tongue. I don't see how having a child stymies any opportunity. My parents raised us on a shoestring, and we felt loved and encouraged. Dad worked his ass off. Mom too. And they did it all with a high school diploma and an unfailingly optimistic attitude.

"But they worked things out, right?" I ask.

Frank fiddles with the keys to the Buick. "Yeah. I guess so. I wasn't happy about it. I really thought that the pregnancy might give her good reason to assess where she was going, but, well . . . you can't live your kids' lives, you know."

I don't think that he believes that at all. Ten minutes with this guy makes me all but certain he'd like to treat his daughter like a ventriloquist's dummy. His words. Her voice. His plan.

We watch a couple paddle by slowly in bright green kayaks. They can hear what we're saying, as the water carries our conversation toward them like a speakerphone. When they pass, Montrose speaks up.

"Has Sophie indicated that there was anyone bothering her?" he asks. "Maybe at work?"

Frank shakes his head. "No, an old boyfriend from high school that couldn't let go, but that was a long time ago." He takes his wallet from his pocket and produces a couple of photographs of his daughter. He holds one out.

"She's beautiful," I say.

"Always looked like a movie star to me," he says. "So, yeah, lots of interest from coworkers and clients, but she just brushes it off. I told you she was tough, right? She's able to deflect any unwanted attention. That's what's so maddening about her being with Adam."

"What are you getting at?" Montrose asks.

"Crap," he says. "She wasn't all that interested in Adam. Not really. You can see why. A girl like her. A guy like that. I'm sure it sounds like I hate my son-in-law. It's not that. I just hate average. I deplore it. Adam pursued her. He was relentless. Didn't want to lose her. I figured she'd shake him off like a turd on her shoe, but nope. He got her. He reeled her in."

I ask him if I can keep the photo. "I'll return it later."

"No," he says. "That's all right. I have others. Keep it, Detective. Just find my daughter."

I can hear Helen, Aubrey, and Adam as they emerge from the cabin. Helen is carrying a tiny pink suitcase. I recognize it from the bedroom with the bunk beds. Aubrey is carrying a well-loved stuffed dog by one arm, nearly dragging it over the surface of the deck. Adam is right behind them as they come down the steps and approach the shade of the cedar. His face is expressionless. Hard to read. Maybe heartbroken. Probably in shock.

CHAPTER NINE
ADAM

Helen is mostly silent as I inventory Aubrey's things in the cabin. She's always been mostly silent. I can't think of the last time she really said something of any real consequence. I know that she has been beaten down by her husband and that the world he's created barely leaves any room for her. I know that Sophie stayed in their house after college because she wanted to be there for her mom. Helen is weak, yes. It isn't because she suffers from depression (though she does) or that she is an alcoholic (I wouldn't blame her for that extra glass of wine early in the afternoon). She seems to inhabit the fringes of her own world. As if Frank rules their world and allows her to coexist with him as long as she keeps the house clean and does his laundry.

I try to be friendly to her. There is no chance that Frank will change his mind about me. He doesn't change his mind about anything. Hard-line. Always right. Early on, I saw Helen as my way into some kind of a normal in-law relationship. While there were flashes of a possibility that she could soften the blow of having a father-in-law like Frank, it just didn't go my way.

"I'm scared," she says to me as we stand outside the cabin.

Helen's eyes are blue, and for the first time since she and Frank arrived, I notice how red they are too. I expect she'd cried all the way from their home in Federal Way while Frank went on and imagined every terrible scenario that could have happened to Sophie. As if an abduction by a stranger wasn't traumatic enough on its own.

I imagine his nonstop harangue:

"Serial killer got her.

"She's probably being raped by some madman right this minute.

"She's been sliced and diced."

And then, while she would lean her head against the passenger window, flattening her hair on one side as I noticed she had, she'd cry and move her lips with words that float like dust into the air-conditioning unit of the Buick.

"She's going to be found, Frank."

"What? Did you say something?"

She'd keep her focus on the road because to make eye contact with Frank meant that he'd have cause to shut her down with some kind of verbal punch in the face.

"We can't lose her," she'd say.

"Frank's going to blame you," she says to me now. Maybe it's a warning. Maybe it's meant to hurt me the way her husband hurts her. "He's going to use this to prove to Sophie that you are a poor excuse for a husband."

She never gazes at me once as she says this. She drops the bomb and runs for cover by going into the bathroom to assist Aubrey with the faucet.

"When's Mommy coming back?" Aubrey asks. She looks concerned, but it's clear she doesn't know anything other than that her mom has gone somewhere. Not the how of it. Or the why.

"Soon," I tell her.

She looks up at me. "I want to wait for her to come back," she says.

"Right," I say. "I know. But you can't. You have to go home with Grandma and Grandpa. Daddy will help find Mommy, and then we'll come home to get you. All right?"

It's a stupid plan, but Aubrey seems to take it as a good idea.

"Honey," Helen says to Aubrey, "everything is going to be all right. Promise."

I don't know how she can make that promise, but I'm grateful for it just then. I can almost forgive her for what she said outside the bathroom door. She was just echoing Frank's words. The kinder thing to do would be to not pass on such poison. As I watch Helen take my daughter's hand, I wonder if sometimes I mistake quietness for kindness. Silence for caring. When it gets right down to it, no one ever really knows what other people are thinking. I want to like Helen Flynn, but there might not be anything there to actually like.

"Car seat's in Sophie's car," I say.

I watch Frank wave his arms as he undoubtedly makes a point to the detectives that I'm a piece of garbage and that Sophie would have been better off with someone else.

"*Anyone* else," he'd say.

The two detectives and my father-in-law are silent as we approach. There's nothing quite like being tossed under the bus on the worst day of your life. Leave it to Frank Flynn.

My father-in-law makes a show of exiting the parking area by our cabin by revving the Buick as if it were some hot rod. The detectives head back to the station after promising to keep me posted on developments, and I am alone. Aubrey's gone. Sophie's gone. I am unsure of what to do. So I sit on the bulkhead above the beach, and I play the events of the afternoon over and over in my head. I think of the crab pots, Sophie, the call for help, the police, the strangers around me. Each mental image of what happened hangs like a noose around my neck. Heavy. Sad.

The crunching sound of oyster shells under Teresa Dibley's feet knocks me out of my thoughts. Her face is etched by years of heartache and summer sunshine.

"Grandson found them in the bottom of the boat when you were gone," she says, holding out my glasses.

"Thank God," I say, putting them on and suddenly seeing everything more clearly. The faces. The heavy scene coalescing around me. All of it.

"Clark's a good kid," she adds, indicating the boy, back on the rope swing. He's gangly, all lanky limbs and a head of hair that'll go nearly white as the Pacific Northwest summer begins its annual sprint.

"Is there anything we can do for you?" she asks.

Her eyes are kind. The first real kindness anyone has exhibited since Sophie went missing.

I shake my head. "No. I just don't know what I should be doing. Looking for her? Staying here in case she comes back?"

My last question is a stupid one. She's not just going to come back.

"Have you eaten anything?" she asks.

I shake my head. "Not really hungry."

"Right. But you need to eat. We're grilling burgers tonight. Maybe a few oysters too."

I thank her. "I think I'll just go inside and lie down."

She gives me a sad smile. "Hang in there, Adam. Let me know if you change your mind now, all right?"

"Promise," I tell her.

CHAPTER TEN
KRISTEN

The pristine white of the bedsheets is blemished with reddish smears. At first, it passes through my mind that I inadvertently left a lipstick on the bed the night before. Damn. But when I look closer, its shade and consistency bother me. I touch the red and call for my husband.

Connor enters from the hallway, a white towel around his trim waist even though he finished his shower a while ago. He's been sprawled on the couch in the front room all this time, making quiet moaning sounds.

"Are you all right?" I ask.

He puts a palm to his forehead. "Brain's pounding like a jackhammer," he says, dropping the towel and fishing for some clothes on top of a white lacquered dresser. "But yeah. I'm fine."

I study him, and then he follows my gaze to the red on the sheets.

"Are you bleeding?"

He shakes his head. "Not really. Maybe a little. Cut from work reopened."

I cross the room to his place by the dresser and study the slice along his forefinger.

"Lot of blood for that small a slice," I tell him.

"What can I say?" Connor asks, stepping into some boxer briefs. "I'm a drunk and a bleeder."

I worry that he's going to break out in song and bastardize the oldie "I'm a Believer." He's like that. Ordinarily I don't mind. I'm just worn down at the moment. Work. Our marriage. Our prospects for parenthood. All of those things stack up at times, and levity doesn't do much to alleviate the situation. In fact, in those instances in which Connor tries to bring a little lightheartedness to a problem, there is often an endearing miss. It's me. Not him. I just can't get the list of things I need to do out of my head. It's how I'm wired. I'm on time. I'm always prepared. If someone tries to switch gears on me, look out. I just don't operate that way.

Last night I slept on the cabin's gray velvet sectional, which faces the water and a river-rock fireplace. Connor was too drunk and agitated to share the bed with anyone. Naturally, it wasn't how I hoped our first night of the long Memorial Day weekend would be. We've been trying to get pregnant off and on for more than four years. Seriously. Clomid. Folic acid. OvaBoost. We've done basal temp. We've collected my eggs and frozen them. We routinely collect Connor's sperm to go into cryopreservation so that I can get a syringe during my lunch hour and double up on the efforts while at work. Yes, at *work*. I'll disappear into the executive lounge and lock the door and do my thing. It's fine. Really. I've never been one to shy away from doing what I have to do to get things done. Meeting at nine. Court at one. Insemination at three. Commute home at six thirty with my legs somehow clamped tightly the entire way.

I know Connor has a headache, but I also know that he won't let me down. He's good that way. That's part of what's made our increasingly unbalanced marriage last as long as it has. Sure, I thought he'd be something more than a waiter. I didn't marry him for his money, but I had hoped that he'd find a path to a better job. I tried to help. I even petitioned the court to see if there was anything we could do about that felony conviction in California. He was young and stupid at the time. But not *that* young. And I knew the law well enough: a felony isn't expunged because someone's wife wants it to be.

I'm a little groggy. The drive with a drunken husband got into my head, and I took an Ambien—maybe two—before I put Connor to bed and made up the sectional for the night. Even so, I need to get things done. I'm thirty-nine, and I'm running out of time. I did what so many women in my generation did: I waited. I wanted to get everything settled in my life, my career, before embarking on motherhood. That men never deal with this is beyond unfair. Biology isn't fair. Fertility isn't fair. There's a man in my office pushing sixty with a young wife and a two-year-old. I want to be happy for him. He's a nice guy. It's hard to be genuinely enthusiastic if you can never have what's in front of you—when it comes so easily to others.

The bulge beneath my husband's boxers grows. I look at it approvingly. More than that: like I can't believe my eyes. Connor likes that. All men do. Like it's some miracle. I don't see it that way. I see it as a soldier standing to attention, ready to plant his flag for his country.

The sad truth is, our lovemaking has become a process, purposeful. An activity that doesn't revolve around intimacy but instead calculation. We have sex because I want a baby. There is a need inside of me that cannot be denied or set on the back burner for a moment longer.

Damn biology.

I'm naked in the bed, and Connor comes for me. He's fully erect. That's one of his best qualities. My husband's penis is as quick to attention as an eighteen-year-old's. I spread my legs and apply Pre-Seed, a sperm-friendly lubricant. There's no foreplay to get me wet, and really, I'm a little beyond that right at the moment. Connor lubes his dick too. He's smiling at me, excited. He *is* eighteen at times. I put my legs up high. I want him inside me as far as he can go. I want those swimmers to get where they need to go. I want to feel that hot spurt against my cervix. And then it's on. Connor thrusts, and I moan. It feels good. I like sex. Really I do. I want to be totally into it, yet I can't quite get there. I keep thinking over and over between his thrusts: *Will this be the time? Will something finally happen? Will we make a baby?*

It doesn't last long. We're both wired now with accomplishing our goal. Off my list. Off his back, I think.

Thankfully, he doesn't say much when we have sex. No "baby" this, "I'm giving it, take it, I'm coming" that.

When it's over, Connor slides off me and puts a pillow under my thighs to keep the dream alive.

I'm quiet.

"You all right?"

I don't answer right away, and when I finally do, I ramble. "I'm not sure. I think so. I *hope* so. My mind's just elsewhere."

We've stopped making predictions on whether or not this level of effort will result in a baby. One time I felt a peculiar tingling in my pelvis, and I was sure that conception was happening at that very moment. But no. Nothing. I loathe the idea of coming up empty handed, that the trying has become tiresome. We've both been checked by a fertility doctor. I'm not perfect, but there is no reason why I can't get pregnant.

Connor's sperm could make it across the English Channel.

He's younger. He's got a felony. He's a waiter. And he's as fertile as a rabbit. I'm everything my husband isn't. I love him, but I also feel a biting envy. In the balance of power, he wins when he shouldn't.

"I'll get cleaned up and dressed while you gestate awhile,"

he says with a grin, getting out of bed, fetching some clothes, and disappearing down the hall.

I lay there, legs held slightly upward, scrolling through the cracked screen of my iPhone. I check messages but don't answer any. I'm here on vacation. I want to live distraction-free and keep my singular focus. I've made a list, and I need to get everything done.

I hear my husband turn on the TV. He's settling in while I, as he says, gestate. I turn to examine the blood smears on the pillow next to me. It appears more than just the residual of a reopened kitchen injury.

In fact, I know damn well it is.

A little later, the detectives and the missing woman come to mind. How could it not? It's all over the news—traditional and social media.

"We need to go make a statement," I say.

CHAPTER ELEVEN
LEE

"Abduction in broad daylight." Montrose drives us back to the sheriff's office in Shelton, the late afternoon sun turning the highway into hard edges of shadow and light. My partner can take a common statement and turn it into the bull's-eye on a dartboard.

"Happens," I say.

Montrose always makes a point of being in the driver's seat. I let him—not because he's a man but because holding the steering wheel steadies the tremors in his hands. Parkinson's, I think, but I'm not a doctor. Our eyes met one time when he was trying to pull money from his wallet and struggled a little. We never said a word about it, though I could see the mix of desperation and humiliation in his eyes. And the plea: *Don't say anything. Don't tell anyone.*

"Yeah, it happens," he allows. "To kids." He swerves slightly to dodge a dead opossum. "Not to a grown woman. Mom says her daughter was strong. Did yoga or something like that twice a week."

"Maybe her attacker subdued her with something," I say. "Like that guy in Portland that kept the bottle of chloroform in his glove box."

"Always ready to collect some young woman," Montrose says. "Maybe. But look at where this happened. It wasn't some parking lot at a mall where a guy would hang around like he's fishing or hunting."

"Right," I say. "The beach where she was taken isn't exactly remote, but it does take some effort to get to it."

"*If* she was taken."

"He said she was," I say.

"Yeah, he did," he says as we drive past billionaire Bill Gates's compound near Alderbrook Resort. Montrose points that out every time we do. But not this time. He's holding on to the wheel tightly. His knuckles are white. He's concentrating on two things: his tremors and Adam Warner's story.

"What are you thinking?" I ask.

"Maybe she left him," he offers. His tone is less than emphatic. "Maybe he's lying. Maybe he's responsible."

I knew that Montrose was going there. I could see the way he looked at Adam when we were taking his statement. I don't want to defend him. I want the evidence to dictate the outcome of the investigation. But I know Adam. I have known him a very long time. I remember when he used to come over and hang out with my brother and how much I wanted to be a part of their little club. But that was a nonstarter. I was a girl. Even worse, I was a kid sister. Out of all my brother's friends, I liked him the most. He had the best smile, and he used it on me all the time, making me feel special. So there. I liked him.

Not that I would tell him all that.

"You could knock me over with a feather if Adam Warner's lying to us" is what I say. "We grew up together. I'd put my money on almost any other kid in Shelton that I knew back in the day over Adam."

"Maybe you shouldn't work the case," he says flatly.
I ignore his tone. "I'm fine. It was a long time ago."
He takes his eyes off the road and glances at me.
"If you say so," he says.

My office at the Mason County Sheriff's Office has a
window that overlooks a withered old plum tree, its bark a
silvery patina that reflects sunlight back into my face. Every
year an arborist comes out to inject fertilizer, test the soil,
and clip off more dead limbs. It's a historic tree, planted by
one of the town's founders, but anyone can see that it's
about done. There was a time when I felt that way about
Shelton. The town's primary employer, a sawmill, expanded
and contracted for decades, leaving everyone in town wondering where it would end up, robust or shuttered. It's survived
so far. Barely. Everything about our town—our festivals, our
sports teams, our commerce—had been about timber. Sure,
we had a gorgeous Pacific Northwest setting, set against the
verdant foothills on the pristine waters of the southern end
of Puget Sound. That alone, we all know, would never have
been enough to make us a tourist destination. Too far from
Seattle or Tacoma to be a bedroom community. We survived
because we're stubborn. We're the children of loggers.

And we have a prison just up the hill. Business is always
good there.

The plum tree will be firewood someday. Maybe a log
cut from its trunk will be saved and put into the archives of
our little museum. But more than likely, firewood will be its
final disposition.

While Montrose is in his office down the hall running reports on those we interviewed, I make note of Dispatch
recordings. It's always my first step. I need the basic frame-
work to be clear and as tight as possible. The calls are more
than drama. They are the first marker in what happened, a

marker that cannot be denied in court—and often kicks off most prosecutors' cases. There are no suspects, despite what Montrose was suggesting. All we really know at the moment is when things were reported to us and what our witnesses said.

At 11:42, Teresa Dibley calls to make the first report.

Dibley: "The wife of the man staying in the cabin next to us was abducted."

Dispatcher: "Your name and location."

Dibley: "Teresa Dibley. I'm renting a cabin with my grandkids for the weekend on Hood Canal in Lilliwaup, near Octopus Hole. Live in Port Orchard."

Dispatcher: "Where are you calling from?"

Dibley: "The address? I don't know. Just off the highway on Canal View Road. I don't know the exact address. But there are only three cabins here. You can't miss it. Wait a minute . . ."

A long pause.

Dispatcher: "Teresa? Are you still with me?"

Dibley: "Hang on. Yes. I was looking for the address here in the cabin. Can't find it."

Dispatcher: "That's all right. We've got the location. Can you see the man?"

Dibley: "[Unintelligible.] No. No. My grandson says he ran up the hill."

Dispatcher: "All right. I'm going to hang up. Help is on the way. Twenty minutes out."

At 11:44, Axel Bakker phones Dispatch that a woman had been abducted from the beach between Hoodsport and Lilliwaup.

Bakker: "Police?"

Dispatcher: "Yes, what is your emergency?"

Bakker: "We need the sheriff out here right now. Man says that his wife was kidnapped from the beach. I saw it. Out walking my dog."

Dispatcher: "What's your name, sir?"

Bakker: "Axel Bakker. Dog's name is Winston."

Dispatcher: "Where are you calling from?"

Bakker: "I don't know the exact address here. I live a few doors up the beach at four-two-two-three Canal View Road."

Dispatcher: "Are you at home now?"

Bakker: "No. I'm on the beach. I'm walking over to the man and his little girl."

Dispatcher: "All right. You saw an abduction."

Bakker: "Yes, partly. I saw her. The man in the boat with the little girl called over for me to get help."

Dispatcher: "Is the man all right? Is the little girl all right?"

Bakker: "How should I know? I never talked to him. I saw what I saw, and he yelled at me to call you. Are you sending someone?"

Dispatcher: "Yes, sir. Stay calm. Stay where you are. We have a unit not too far away heading there now."

Bakker: "Hope you get here soon. Never seen anything like this before, and I've been around awhile. Seems like a TV show or something."

Even before meeting him, I could make some assumptions about Axel Bakker based on his call. He was older: his voice was fractured by age and shaky with emotion. He'd been thrust into the unthinkable. Despite his age, his only frame of reference for something like what he'd witnessed was TV. And he was a decent, caring soul. He felt it was necessary to provide the dispatcher with his dog's name.

Montrose and I were working a burglary case near Alderbrook when we stopped what we were doing and responded to the scene. Even so, it took us twenty minutes.

We arrived at 12:04.

It is interesting that the first caller, Teresa, didn't see anything transpire and was just relaying what Adam had told her. Axel had seen the crime occur but called in a couple of minutes after Teresa.

I wonder why that was.

Montrose pokes his head into my office.

"Connor and Kristen Moss are here," he says.

I grab my notepad, hoping to fill it with an explanation for the unthinkable. "Right there."

CHAPTER TWELVE
LEE

Connor and Kristen Moss are an undeniably good-looking couple. He's dark, with almost-black wavy hair that is cut shorter on the sides, although not in a Third Reich style. His handsome features are angular, and his arms, bare in a UW T-shirt, are more sinewy than muscular. His wife is the opposite. She's a stunner. Of the pair, she's by far the more intense. Around her neck dangles a platinum-and-sapphire art deco pendant. It amplifies the blue of her eyes. As Montrose and I take seats across from them in our too-bright interview room in the Mason County Sheriff's Office, I thank them for coming. It's near the dinner hour. Montrose likes to eat at the same time every day. That's not going to happen.

"You could have just called," I tell them.

Kristen answers right away. "Of course. But as an officer of the court, it's my duty to ensure that you have everything you need. Not that I"—she stops a beat and self-corrects—"not that *we* know anything."

"Of course not," I say, though I get to decide that. Not them.

"The lady in the little cabin next door filled us in on more of the details. Stuff that's not on the news," Connor says. His voice is quieter than his wife's. "A total shocker."

"Yeah," Montrose finally pipes up. "I hate the old shop-worn expression 'Things like that don't happen around here,' but it's right on the nose. They don't."

"Yeah," Connor says. "That's what Kris and I were talking about all the way here. Sure, back in Seattle, but not here. We've been coming out here for years. Kind of our place, and now this."

"Makes me rethink where we spend our long weekends. Maybe we should scratch the cabin off our list and start going to Hawaii for our vacations like everyone else," Kristen adds.

We talk a little more and learn that she's a lawyer for a downtown firm, and he's a waiter at a tony restaurant that I'm sure is a far cry from the Mill Wood, our best Shelton eatery.

"Headwaiter," Kristen says.

I nod. I see the distinction, and even more so, I see Kristen's need to shore up her husband's career. I know that my partner will make some snide comment when they leave.

"You arrived early this morning," I say. "About what time?"

"That's right," Kristen says. "We couldn't make it earlier on Friday. Too many things going on, so we left at ten p.m. Arrived at the cabin well after midnight. Honestly, I'm not sure of the exact time."

"I was beat," Connor interjects. "I can't say for sure what time we got there. I crashed immediately. Zonked out."

Kristen gives her husband an annoyed look. "We both have demanding jobs, and yeah, you crashed hard."

"Did you notice anything unusual at the cabins?" Montrose asks. "You go there all the time, right?"

Connor answers. "Been there, yes. All about the same. Same octopus art on the walls. Same beach."

"Did you see or talk to the occupants of either cabin?" Montrose goes on.

Kristen takes this one. "I did. Connor slept most of the morning. I chatted with the lady next door a little. She seemed sweet. Had her hands full with those kids."

"So, Connor," I say, "you were there all morning? I thought you were both out on a hike or something."

Connor rubs the back of his head.

"I get migraines," he says. "I took some meds and was literally out like a light. Kris went out alone."

She gives her husband a look. "It's been happening more and more. I tell him to go see another specialist, but what do I know? I only practice law. Not medicine."

And there you have it. Kristen Moss is one of those lawyers who find a way to work their job into every conversation.

"Where did you go?" I ask Kristen.

"Where didn't I go?" she answers with a question. "I drove over to Cushman and hiked around part of the lake. Probably got too much sun. Nothing major, though. I use copious amounts of sunscreen."

"What about you, Connor?"

"Put on my noise-canceling headphones and slept. I was sick. Too much to drink the night before. Migraine today. That's about it."

"Did you hear anything?" Montrose asks.

"No," he says. "Headphones are top of the line."

Of course they are, I think.

Kristen pushes back from the table and gives her husband a look so that he'll follow suit. He does. She slides her business card in my direction.

"Connor's cell number is on the back side if you need to reach him. I've also included my private line at the firm."

Did she mention she was a lawyer?

* * *

"Well," Montrose says, "that was a big nothing burger."

"Yeah," I add, "but at least we know a good attorney."

He gives me a smile. "She was interesting, I'll give her that. Poor SOB she's married to—he's probably forever stuck with her telling people he's not just any waiter but the *head*waiter."

"We don't know anything about them," I remind him.

"And they don't know anything about the case. Miss Independence and Mr. Migraine. Jesus! What a pair! I almost feel sorry for the people of Hawaii. Those two are going to be the most annoying thing that happened there since that moron sounded the false missile-attack alarm."

We talk a little more as we head back down the hall to our offices.

"All we got is the husband and the dog walker. The husband didn't have his glasses on, and the dog walker is in his eighties."

"He's seventy-seven," I say.

"Whatever. My point is our eyewitnesses are not exactly 'top of the line,'" Montrose says, echoing Connor Moss's remark.

"They saw someone take Sophie," I say.

"Adam Warner says that. The old guy walking the beach saw Sophie and a struggle. He couldn't say for sure who was dragging her off."

"Then what do you think happened? She's gone, you know."

"Yeah. Right. She's gone. And I don't know what happened. The 'some weirdo abducted my wife' story seems far-fetched."

"It happens every day," I remind him. "Just not in places like here."

Montrose gives a little shrug. "No doubt," he says. "But in broad daylight? At eleven in the morning?"

"The time is unusual," I allow. "I wouldn't expect such a bold move from someone who wasn't after her specifically."

"And she drops a wineglass," he says. "Was she an alcoholic or what?"

"I didn't get that from talking to her folks," I say. Immediately I feel foolish, because I didn't even ask them. Eleven a.m. *is* early for a drink. Even on vacation. While I didn't think to ask about the wine, something inside makes me doubt her folks would tell me if their daughter had a drinking problem—certainly not in the first hours of an investigation.

"The truth is," Montrose says, now sitting in his ancient office chair, held together by duct tape, a MacGyver fix that he considers a badge of honor, "we don't know a goddamn thing about Adam and Sophie Warner." He pauses a bit. "I mean, *I* don't. But you do, don't you, Lee?"

CHAPTER THIRTEEN
ADAM

The cabin creaks with every step as I pace the burnished old fir floors. It's after eight thirty, and the sun still illuminates the water out the window. An ancient Seth Thomas in the kitchen ticks like a metronome, reminding me that I'm alone, while I need no reminder. I've never been one to pace before. On this evening, however, I have a lot to process. I pass by the room with the bunk beds where Aubrey slept the night before. I wonder how she's coping with her grandparents. She's three, but she's smart. She knows that her grandpa hates her father. And I know, without a bit of doubt, that in the battle for her affection, I will always beat him. It might be the only thing even he'd concede. Helen is probably running a bath now, filling the tub with bubbles and making sure that the water isn't too hot. She's decent. Sometimes I see traces of Helen in Sophie, the parts of her personality that I have always detested. Sometimes, when something she disdains or disagrees with gets pointed in her direction, she pretends to not hear. She always says *fine* when she's anything but. Sophie disappears into the bedroom and drops the blinds to create a dark fortress so she doesn't have to face what disturbs her. I didn't know that when I married her. I saw her as she showed herself to the world: fun, smart, sexy. Funny how those things are often a smoke screen from one's true self. It's easy to act all those things. Up for adventure. Head nods at complex scenarios when she's not really listening. Ready for bedroom play even when there is no bedroom. In the beginning, Sophie was all those things. I didn't know they were a construct. I thought they were key parts of who she was.

Service is lousy, but my phone blows up anyway. I slump onto the big blue sofa in the living room and scroll through the texts that started coming in around six and haven't let up.

Dude, heard about Sophie.

Need me to come up?

What the hell!

She's going to be found.

You coming back tonight?

Aubrey's OK. Right?

Holy fuck.

What happened?

Are you OK?

The texts are from friends and family who caught the drama from the news and social media. I respond the best that I can, but I don't know how to really answer. Obviously, I'm not fine. Yes, she's going to be found. No, I don't need anyone right now. What could they do anyway? Words and heartfelt concern won't do me any good at the moment. I could pretend that they would. I could lie. The truth is far more complicated than that. I love my wife. I hate her too. I loved the idea of us. But—and this is hard to admit to myself—that was a while ago. Before Aubrey. After she was born, our life pivoted away from us to become something else. I'd become a father. Sophie, a mother. I learned that mother is more than father. Mother trumps everything. Father is a role. Father is biology. Mother is sacred. Motherhood consumes every bit of a marriage. Every last crumb.

I set down my phone and go for the whiskey that I brought from Seattle. Though I expected we'd be together this weekend, I knew there would be plenty of time for me to sit and sulk and drink. I pitched the weekend as a chance for us to get back on track, and Sophie accepted the pretext. I mean *accepted* in the way someone agrees to come to your kid's baseball game. They don't want to be there. They don't get anything out of it. But they come because you asked and they were too slow to drop an excuse that you couldn't easily torpedo with a feigned look of disappointment.

I don't talk about the state of our marriage to anyone. I never have. I've always had the feeling that Sophie is the same way. She's like her mother. She retreats and keeps things inside. She learned that from watching Helen as she built an invisible wall to keep Frank at bay. I am not Frank. I am not a thing like him. But learned personality traits aren't often based on present reality but on a past from which there is no escape. Our marriage is quietly rocky. Silently in shambles. I love her without a scintilla of doubt. But Sophie? I don't know how she really feels about me. If she loved me at all, she'd have never done what she did.

I take a slug of whiskey from the bottle, and the sweet burn fills my throat with familiarity. Thinking of Sophie has always been my drinking game. It's funny to love someone so much that it hurts.

I call Helen.

"How's Aubrey?" I ask.

"Anything new there?" she asks, her voice breaking with worry.

"No. Nothing. Haven't heard a peep. How's Aubrey?"

"She doesn't understand what's going on, so she's fine."

I can hear Helen's voice fracture a bit more. It's easy to forget that inside her cool and placid exterior is a human being. Not nice to think, I know. But that's how I've always seen her.

"Frank's foaming at the mouth," she says, pulling herself away from the emotion that is making her shatter.

"What's he doing now?"

"He's in his office. He's been on the phone with everyone from the FBI to the news media."

"The FBI?"

"Kidnapping," she says. "Frank's convinced that someone's got Sophie and will ask for ransom. Of course he'll pay. I know you would too."

"Of course," I tell her, "but there's no ransom. This isn't a kidnapping."

She doesn't say anything for a second. She's thinking about what her husband has told her to say to me.

"We don't know that," she says.

I hear Frank in the background. He's coming toward the phone.

"Who's that?" he asks.

"Adam."

Frank takes the phone. "What are you hearing on your end?"

"Nothing," I say. "Sheriff's working it."

"Didn't you see those detectives? A couple of backwater idiots if you ask me."

I don't say anything.

"FBI can't get involved unless they're convinced it's a kidnapping. Ransom request and all that. Can you believe that bullshit? Not a federal crime. Bet they'd feel differently if it had been their little girl."

He always calls her that. *His little girl.* Like she's stunted at six and not a grown woman of thirty-three.

"I think we would have heard from a kidnapper by now," I say, though I'm not sure of the logic of what I'm saying. While Frank rants on, I mull it over. I think of what I could say to him. Her phone is at the cabin. My phone is in my hand. Unless the kidnapper has my number because this was a planned abduction and not the act of some random freak, it's doubtful he'd be able to contact me. Sure, he could call the police, I guess. Or the news media. A direct conduit isn't a likely option.

But I don't say anything. Frank only likes the sound of his own voice.

"I called KOMO TV," Frank finally says. *Make that, announces.* "Linda London is going to see what she can find out."

Linda London is the last of the old guard at a Seattle TV station that has tried, with reasonable success, to make itself over into a news source for the hipper, younger Seattle crowd that has taken over the city since Amazon began its winning quest for world domination. Linda is pushing fifty, but despite a face-lift and Botox injections that have left her nearly expressionless—even at a fire scene in which two were killed—she's determined to fight for airtime to the bitter end.

I can't stand her. I've mentioned this before. Frank knows this. I'm sure that's why he handpicked her.

"Great," I say. "Any help is appreciated. Got to find Sophie."

I hear a car pull in, and I look out the window in the direction of the parking area. It's the blue Lexus. The couple from the third cabin, the Lily, has returned. She's got her arms hooked around him, leading him across the lawn. I keep my ear to the phone to hear what Frank says next, but he's done. He doesn't even say good-bye. He just hands the phone back to Helen, who in typical form offers up a non sequitur.

"We had cherry pie for dessert tonight."

"Bye, Helen," I say. "Give Aubrey a good-night kiss from me."

I call my family next. First my mom in Chandler, Arizona. Then my dad away on his annual hunting trip in Spokane. Finally, my brother, Keegan, in Los Angeles. I tell them all the same thing, and they reveal themselves in their responses.

Me: "I wanted you to hear from me before the news picks it up."

Mom: "Oh, dear God."

Dad: "Sure she didn't run off with anyone?"

Keegan: "Need me to fly up?"

I know Keegan would drop everything at the Orange County hotel he's managing. He'd be here by morning.

"I'm okay, Bro," I say. "Let's see what the police find out. They're on it. One of them is Lee Husemann."

"Kip's little sis?"

"Yeah," I say. "Small world."

We talk a bit more, and I hang up and go back to my whiskey.

I make my way to the sauna and turn on the thermostat. I think of my dad and how he disparaged Sophie as though it was something that I'd wanted him to do. How my mom invoked God and then started to pray while my phone cut in and out. It didn't matter. Saying her prayer was more important than God or anyone else hearing it.

The sauna is off the kitchen. It's heated by a Swedish electric firebox and lined in knot-free cedar planking. Opening the door after turning it on is to invite a blast of hot air in the face. It's a slap! It's about right for how I feel at the moment. I've stripped off my clothes and grabbed a towel, which I wrap loosely around my waist. I sit on the wooden bench and let the heat make the sweat from my forehead roll down and catch up with my tears.

Despite what people think about me at the office or in my private life, I'm not heartless. I feel things. I truly do. I just don't see the need to make a big deal out of my feelings. I'm allowed this. I am alone. My wife is gone. I know that whatever happens next will take a course all its own.

Can't control the world. Can't really regulate the people around you. Never could.

A half hour later, I pass out on the sofa, bottle in hand.

Next thing I know, my phone buzzes like a swarm of killer bees. It's nine a.m. Shit. I overslept. How could I?

A text from my brother reads: Check your Facebook.

CHAPTER FOURTEEN
LEE

It's nearly eleven, Saturday evening, when I leave the office, and I'm wired from seeing Adam and the trauma of what he's going through. I catch the scent of the fireworks display that had just echoed over Oakland Bay Junior High's field—one of the highlights of Shelton's annual Forest Festival. I breathe it in. To the outsider, such a celebration is corny, I'm sure. I don't care. This is who we are. Logging competitions and a Paul Bunyan parade compete for our town's attention with one of those rickety traveling carnivals every Memorial Day weekend. The logging competition with springboard, hot-saw, and standing-blade categories is the biggest crowd pleaser in a place that was built on sawdust-strewn ground. I ran for Queen of the Forest when I was seventeen but didn't make it. Most every girl in town tries out.

Even today.

I still have my grandmother's pretty emerald-green and silver-embroidered sash from her reign in 1948. After she died, my mom was going to throw it out, but I saved it from the trash bin. I loved my grandma more than anything. She never let me forget that after everything that happened to me, I was going to be all right.

"No one is going to steal your future, Lee."

As I turn the knob to open my front door, I can't help but feel a renewed hope that she's right.

My little blue house is hushed as I rummage through the freezer. I find a frost-coated Lean Cuisine and put it in the microwave and watch the carousel turn under the dim light. I look around as my sad, and very late, dinner spins in the window.

Everything around me is a reminder of where I come from and who I am. My grandmother's blue-and-white Delft plates hang on the wall above my flea-market-find dining table. She hung them on her wall in her big old house in Tacoma. My mother's mother was the kind of woman who made everything untouchable, saving cherished items solely for a special occasion. The silver in the top drawer of the hutch was never used but never tarnished, either. Those blue plates were to be seen, admired, talked about. Never used on a dining table. My mom was the opposite. She said that nice things were meant to be enjoyed and that her mom was more of a hoarder than a giver. I wonder where I fall in that spectrum.

I live by myself. I own a cat, for God's sake. I know that I've built a wall around myself. A good one too. I know that I've hoarded my life. Sometimes I think I have good reason to, but most of the time I realize that what I do today is part of the chain reaction, the legacy, of what happened to me when I was twelve.

When Adam Warner found me.

I saw the car the day before. It was a sedan, blue in color. Even though I know cars because my brother knew them, I cannot make out what the make and model were in my memory. Charlene and I passed the car on Tamarack Lane on the way to school. Charlene and her family lived two doors down, and while we weren't best friends, we were good walking-to-school partners. She talked a mile a minute, which was fine. I was pretty much a listener back then. I could easily pick out the bits of truth from her exaggerated tales—something that would serve me well in the job that would become my life. The morning before it happened, Charlene was talking about some uncle of hers who lived in Latvia or someplace like that and how she'd been invited to stay in his castle the next time she made it over there.

"I didn't know you've been to Europe," I said.

"Haven't you?" she asked, avoiding my question in the way that she always did.

"No," I said. "We saw the redwoods in California last summer. That's about as far as we've gone."

"That's pretty cool," she said, adjusting her dark brown braids and hiking up her backpack. "Did I tell you that my dad's brother sailed from San Francisco to Hawaii in a boat he made of redwood?"

She hadn't. But I knew she would.

The next day Charlene had an early morning dental appointment. She'd told me on the way home the night before that she'd discovered that one of her back teeth was coming in at some weird angle. "Dentist said he'd never seen anything like it," Charlene had bragged. "Not ever."

The blue car was there again.

And then I was gone.

I get up to answer the ding of the microwave. Millicent follows me. It's funny how the most traumatic events that happen to you are always there behind a sometimes-impenetrable memory. I pour the steaming water over the Earl Grey tea bag. I try to distract myself with my cat and the tea, but I know that the trigger has been pulled. I'm going to replay the "incident," as I've come to call it—my mother's term that I gladly adopted—one more time.

With feeling.

Without Charlene-like exaggeration.

With the knowledge that it shaped the person I am today.

Albert Davis Hodge was his full name, though I didn't know it at the time. I didn't know people like him inhabit the planet.

He was standing next to his car when I walked toward him. He had a kind face. Glasses. Hair that was neatly combed. Even though the words out of his mouth were completely at odds with the fact that I'd seen his car the day before, I didn't think of it until later.

"I'm lost," he said, pointing to a copy of the newspaper he was holding.

I leaned in close to read the address on the classified ad he'd circled. I'd seen my father give directions to a stranger before. It was just a nice thing to do.

"Yeah," I said, "you're on the wrong side of town. You need to turn around and go the other way."

"Crap!" he said. "Excuse my French."

"No problem," I told him.

"I'm Al."

I did think, for just a second, that him saying his name was strange. Why would he introduce himself? I'm on my way to school. I don't need to know his name. I don't need to tell him mine.

But I do.

"I'm Lee," I said.

He went back to the ad and made a perplexed face. "Clear across town? Now I'm really turned around. I'll never get there."

He took off his glasses and wiped the lenses on his blue-and-red flannel shirt. Al was older than my brother, Kip, but not much. Maybe twenty. Definitely out of school. He seemed young to have a car like that big blue boat, but I dismissed that too.

"I'm a cat breeder," he said. "I have a cat they're going to buy."

"I like cats," I said.

"Want to see her?" he asked. "She's a Persian, with blue eyes."

Stupid. Stupid. Stupid. I know. I should never have leaned in to look. I knew better. I was raised not to get into a stranger's car. Not to engage with someone you didn't know. Be polite. Smile. Be respectful. Look them in the eyes. But never let anyone touch you. Or get close enough to hurt you.

"Bad things happen everywhere to little girls," my father said when we were splitting logs in the backyard one Sunday afternoon not long before it happened. The impetus for the conversation was a story that had been blared all over the news. A ten-year-old from Chehalis had been snatched in front of her house. The news media was all over the story, of course. Reporting every *nothing new* as if it were something. In the end, the news was as many expected. Her mangled body was found in a tangle of blackberry vines that had overtaken a vacant lot one street over. She'd been savagely attacked, though at the time I didn't see the brutality behind a physical beating. I didn't know what grown men might do to a little girl. My father did. "Even here in Shelton," he told me, dropping the ax into the buff grain of an alder log. "High alert for strangers, Lee. At all times? Got it?"

I said that I did.

But that day I didn't. That day the incident happened.

When I peered inside, I could see right away that there were no kittens in his car. Al's hand went over my mouth and nose.

Lights out.

Duct tape, it turns out, is useful for many things beyond household repair. When I woke up, my wrists and legs had been bound. My lips had been sealed shut. I remember running my tongue over my front teeth, feeling the sticky residue of the adhesive. It's a nothing moment, I know. But it's one of those things that lift the curtain every now and then. I hate going to the dentist, because after a cleaning by the hygienist, my tongue wanders over the slickness of my teeth. Even when I tell myself not to, I do it. I feel the smoothness and think of the glue from the duct tape. Every single time.

I knew he did something to me "down there," as I would later call it. I was sore and bloody. I think that I cried, but I really don't remember. I know that my brain called out for my parents and my brother. I knew for a fact, as I lay there naked and terrified, that if they didn't find me, I'd die like that girl from Chehalis.

I wish I'd known her name back then. I wish that I had paid more attention to her story. I should never have looked in that car. I wonder if she'd done the same thing. If he'd wrapped her in duct tape before he did what he did.

I eat a few bites of my dinner, but my stomach is in knots, and I don't even know why I tried to eat something. A minute later, I'm lying on my bed there with my cat, fully clothed, bedside light on.

The light is always on.

CHAPTER FIFTEEN
ADAM

I drive the half mile to Octopus Hole and push to the front of the crowd of onlookers. It's what I know will be the worst Sunday after the worst Saturday of my life. My heart strikes like steel against steel. I'm there for a reason. The others are there to watch a show. It's been twenty-four hours since Sophie went missing, and what her father insisted had happened has. She's gone. I can see by the way the police hold back the people gathered there that just beyond the dock at Octopus Hole is the floating body of a woman. She's face-down, nude. I don't need to see her face to know it's her. I can tell by her hair, her legs, and her delicate wrists. I can even see the small hummingbird tattoo that she'd had done when she was seventeen—something she always insisted that her parents hadn't known.

I expect her little rebellion will be known now.

"I think that's my wife," I say.

A deputy who looks all of fourteen acknowledges me, as does another officer.

"This isn't really happening," I say, though I know it is.

"Sir, please come over here," the fourteen-year-old says.

My gaze remains glued to the water and the bobbing figure of my beautiful wife.

"What?" I ask, confused.

"Here," he repeats. "Come here."

Briefly all eyes are on me. Briefly, because it is almost impossible to take your gaze away from what you likely have never seen in your life. Or ever wanted to see.

Crying is foreign to me. Really. And yet in that moment when I see the anguished face of a teenage girl, tears streaming down her cheeks, I find my own eyes start to leak.

Another officer puts his hand on my shoulder.

"I know this is rough," he says. He's older and might actually know how hard it is to see your wife, the mother of your only child, floating like a discarded mannequin on the inky saltwater surface of Hood Canal. She looks so white. She's chalk. She's a doll made of chalk. A crime-scene tech arrives to document everything she can before the body is removed from the scene.

"Do you need me to call someone for you, sir?"

I look up. "My in-laws. Sophie's parents."

"Are you sure it's her?"

"Even from here I can see her tattoo. It's her." My fingers find their way to my eyes, and I quickly wipe my tears. "I saw they'd found a body on Facebook. My in-laws don't have a Facebook account, but they might know someone who has. Need to tell them. She's their only child."

The deputy nods and leads me to an ambulance that arrived before I did. He goes to confer with another officer while I sit on the back of the vehicle. There was no need for an ambulance. Sophie wasn't going to be saved. She was utterly and completely dead.

"Sheriff's detectives are on their way from Shelton," he says. "Unless you feel strongly about calling your wife's parents, we'll have local law enforcement make a notification. But despite the tattoo, we're going to need you to make a positive ID."

"I did," I tell him. "It's her."

"Right," he says, his voice even, "but we need you to see more of her."

"She's my wife," I say. "I know her body like my own."

"I'm sure you do. In this instance, sir, we need you to look at her face. All right? They are bringing her out of the water now. Before we prepare her for travel to the morgue, we'll have you come up and look at her. Okay?"

I don't want to look at her. I don't want to see her face. I'd like to remember her as she was before spending a night in the water.

"Fine," I say. "I guess I can do that."

"Good," he says. "Stay right here."

I watch him as he pushes back the crowd, parting it enough so I can see that she's out of the water now and on a gurney, coming my way. A deputy is holding up a blanket to give her some privacy or to spare the onlookers from a real-life horror show. I'm not sure which it is. From where I sit on the back of that ambulance, I can see it all: a chalky-white body rolling toward me. My hand goes to my mouth. I might be sick.

Sophie's eyes are open. They stare up into the nothing-ness of death. I think of a fish in the market just then, look-ing up from the crushed ice that surrounds it. Seeing nothing. I only glance over her eyes. Seeing her looking at me is a jolt that makes me turn away. I can't speak. I know they want me to say that it's her. And it is. There's no doubt about it. But it seems my lips won't move. The deputies look at me like I'm an alien, but I can't help it. I can't explain my muteness. I just sit there leaning over her and trying not to vomit.

"Is this your wife?" asks the older of the two that were apparently assigned to me.

My eyes meet his. He's full of sympathy, but just beyond

that he's giving me that look that indicates he's very glad that it's me and not him. I see that look at work when I make an unpopular assignment. *Better you than me.* I blink and remove my glasses. My voice croaks out a response.

"Yes," I say. "That's Sophie. That's her."

I don't move. I sit there. The crowd parts again. This time, it's for Lee Husemann and Zach Montrose. The detectives from Mason County are back.

CHAPTER SIXTEEN
LEE

Adam watches his wife's body from a few yards away. On his face, he wears the saddest look I've ever seen. And I've seen plenty in my ten years in law enforcement. I've seen a mother holding her lifeless baby outside a burning house. A father throw himself in front of a car when he found out that his wife had killed herself. The endless tears that come from the kind of grief everyone can recognize as inconsolable but are unable to really feel until it becomes their turn. Adam looks pale. His eyes are red. I think he's shaking as he looks over in my direction. This is what a broken heart looks like.

Montrose checks in with the techs and the responding officers. Our county is too small for a coroner. Kitsap County, just to the east, handles suspicious deaths for us. This quite obviously is one of those.

"Where are you going to take her?" Adam asks me.

"They'll take her to Bremerton, where she'll be autopsied and examined by Kitsap's forensic pathologist. We'll find out what happened to her."

"I saw what happened," he says, some anger working its way to the forefront.

Anger is good, I think. It can be healing.

"Yes, I know. She was abducted."

"Right. Some guy—some guy who's still out there—took her."

"I know," I say.

His focus narrows. "Why aren't you out there looking for him? He's got to be around here. He didn't take her far, did he?"

"It seems not," I say, letting him unspool a little. He needs it. He'd never admit it, but Adam Warner is in shock right now. Within twenty-four hours, his life—and his little girl's—has been turned upside down. I tell him I need to check in with my partner and provide instructions for the pathologist. Since it is a holiday the next day, I'm thinking that they'll keep her body in the chiller until Tuesday.

I go look at the body and then find Montrose by the dock.

"A couple from Canada were kayaking, and they found what they thought was a blow-up doll," he says, indicating a man and woman standing on the grass up from the shore. "Here on vacation."

"Been a lousy vacation for a lot of people around here."

Montrose ignores my remark. "Deputy took pictures of all the lookie-loos," he says. "Smart kid. Says he read somewhere that the perpetrator often returns to the scene of the crime."

"You think?" I say with sarcasm.

"I know," he says. "I thanked him for the good police work. How'd he get here before us?" He indicates Adam, who's now sitting on the grass with his face in his hands. "Nobody who responded notified him. I asked."

"Deputy says it was on Facebook. Pretty much how everyone finds out everything these days, Montrose."

"I hate the Internet," he says, rattling a Tic Tac container. "No good's come of it."

"You can order things online."

"I don't need anything that I can't get at the IGA or the mall in Olympia."

I offer up a half smile. He plays up his disdain, but I know better. I've seen the Amazon boxes in the back of his car.

"Looks like bruising on her wrists and on her thighs," I say.

"Sexual assault," Montrose says. "Kind of fits with this kind of crazed abduction, I guess."

"Well," I say, "we know she didn't run off with some other guy."

"Yeah," Montrose says. "She was dragged off."

"I pulled all the sex offenders from the registry," I say. "Local parolees too. After the scene is secure and cleared, let's knock on a few doors. My money's on someone who's done something like this before."

"Or someone who has worked themselves up to something like this."

I go over to Adam.

"Deputy Cronin can take you back to the cabin," I say.

"I can drive myself," Adam says.

"Are you sure?"

"I'm fine to drive. I've got to get my things and go tell Sophie's parents. I've got to find a way to tell Aubrey."

"We can send a chaplain," I say.

He gets up. "No. Sophie wasn't religious. I'm not, either. I just need to wrap my brain around what's happened here." He stops and studies the group of spectators, the police cars, the ambulances. "What happened?" he asks.

"Someone murdered your wife," I say. "We have reason to believe she was assaulted too."

"Assaulted," he says, blinking back tears. "Yeah, I saw that, remember? She was forcibly abducted right in front of our vacation rental."

I have to tell him. Better from me than from someone on Facebook.

"We'll have to do a thorough exam, Adam, but I'm sorry to say that it appears that Sophie may have been sexually assaulted too."

"Raped?"

"That's what it looks like."

"If she was raped," he says, "then there'll be some evidence as to the identity of her killer, right?"

Just like the kid cop who took photos, Adam watches crime TV. Seems as if everyone does. If I had a drink for every time I sat in a bar with a TV on and there was some crime report and someone piped up that there was a problem with the chain of evidence or fruit of the poisoned tree or some such, I'd . . . well, be drunk.

"It's not guaranteed," I say. "She's been in the canal a few hours, at least. The water might have washed away some of what her killer might have left behind."

"There are a lot of *mights* there," Adam tells me.

"I'm afraid so," I say.

Montrose joins us just then. "I'm very sorry about your wife," he says to Adam.

Adam gives him a nod. "Just go catch who did this to her, Detective," he says. "Just find him."

CHAPTER SEVENTEEN
LEE

Carmine and Delia Winters sit at a picnic table. They are in their early forties. He's trim and wears a mustache that's meant to be noticed—a handlebar that looks so waxed that I'm all but certain a wet towel could be hung from its tips. His wife, Delia, is a striking woman with dark hair and penciled brows. He's got on a UBC T-shirt, and she's wearing a tank top, blue in color. A pair of hoodies, also UBC, are folded neatly on the picnic table. The two of them are watching everything around them with the kind of peculiar expression that comes with seeing the horrific and the fascinating in a single glance. A car crash comes to mind.

I approach and introduce myself as one of the detectives investigating the case.

"Do you know who it is?" Carmine asks.

"Yes, but we're not releasing that now," I say.

"Well, we've already told the police everything," Delia says.

Her husband puts his hand on her shoulder. I can tell she

doesn't want to go over it again because it's painful to talk about, not because she doesn't want to be bothered.

"It's fine," he says. "This is a bit of a shock. Never in our lives did we think we'd find a dead body."

No one ever does. And those who do probably never forget it.

"I'm sure it was a terrible shock," I say. "I just want to hear a bit more about how it was that you found her."

Delia answers. "We're here on holiday from Vancouver," she says, starting slowly, staring me in the eye. "Stupidly," she says, "not realizing how busy things would be here with Memorial Day weekend. I guess you have a lot of war dead to remember in America."

She stops herself before going on. "We got the last cottage at Mar Vista Beach just down the road."

"A cancellation," Carmine says. "Lucky for us."

"The only thing lucky about this trip," Delia says.

"We brought our kayaks and put in at Mar Vista. It was early. About seven? Right, Dee?"

She nods. "Right. The current was in our favor," she goes on. "Took us barely three-quarters of an hour to make it here. I brought some breakfast snacks and some coffee, and we thought Octopus Hole would be a good spot to eat."

"Right," he says. "I was paddling behind Dee, so she saw it first."

"I thought it was a blow-up doll," she says. "I'm embarrassed to admit that. Not because either one of us have ever seen one in person, but it just seemed like that's what it was. Naked. Bobbing up and down a little."

"When we got up close," Carmine says, "it, or rather *she*, was in the reeds, and I poked her with my paddle. I thought it was a big joke at first."

"We both did," Delia adds. "We don't think there's anything funny about it now, of course."

They tell me how they went to shore as fast as they could and phoned 911.

"Was there anyone else here?" I ask. "Did you see anything?"

"No," Delia says. "It was just Carmine and me. And her, of course." She looks in the direction of the body.

"Did you notice any cars?" I ask. "Trucks? Other vehicles?"

Again an emphatic no.

I watch Montrose talk to some new arrivals at the crime scene. I know he's wondering if the killer has shown up. He's a big believer in that. Me? I've never seen it happen.

"This place is probably packed with people in the day," Carmine says. "But it was morning. The air still had a chill in it. Besides—and I mean no offense by this—Americans aren't early risers, right?"

I offer a faint smile from across the table. "Many aren't," I say. "You're definitely onto something."

I take down the rest of the Winters' information. She's an administrator at the University of British Columbia. He works for Muji, a large Japanese retailer, building out new stores in the city. I know for a fact that they will tell this story over and over when they get back home. In time, they'll forget about all of the things that made their holiday special up until the moment they found Sophie Warner's lifeless body floating in the pristine, blue waters of what many consider America's only fjord.

They will only talk about the dead lady in the water.

CHAPTER EIGHTEEN
ADAM

I return to the Wisteria to pack my things. Sophie's things. What else am I supposed to do? I could stay here parked outside the cabin and cry. I almost want to do that, but I can't find the tears. I'm in that place where it all seems like something happening to someone else. Not me. There is no reason to stay another minute, I know. Sophie is dead. She's been found. I know everything that has happened is extremely real. I grasp that everything that happened is decisive, final.

Inside, I find her sunglasses, vintage Fendi. The pair stares at me from the dining tabletop. As I put them away, I remember when she got them on our trip to Martha's Vineyard.

That was a happy time. And seeing those sunglasses somehow propels me to think of all the reasons I loved Sophie and how long it has been since I'd seen evidence of those things. How we drifted apart before Aubrey. I know I had a part in it. I was busy. I was wrapped up in the idea that the more I gave to my job, the more I'd get in return. Fuck me.

It just meant less time with her. It meant an opportunity to fail in a marriage that I didn't want to fail. I can see how she fought for us to survive. I really can. She greeted me with a kiss that lingered. She texted me ideas of places we could go. A trip. Restaurants we could try. She made excuses to her folks so that we didn't have to spend time with them—or rather, so I didn't have to.

I was an idiot. I was blind to everything. And still she didn't give up. Sophie was a fighter. She was the kind of person who stood up for others, then herself. Certainly she had mood swings. I wonder now how much of her depression was chemical and how much was caused by me.

We were a sinking ship headed for the bottom of the ocean. I was sleeping on the sofa half the time. We never used the word *divorce*, but that's where it was going. I'd stay late at work. Go out with the gang. She'd do the same. I remember I used to come home to an empty house that felt so devoid of any kind of warmth it felt like one of those extended-stay hotels.

And then everything changed.

I came home from work to find the house filled with the smell of Sophie's famous lasagna. Famous, because I bragged about it constantly to anyone whenever the subject of favorite food came up.

Now that she's gone, I find myself going back to that night of our new beginning. We laughed about our situation.

"I don't want a roommate," she said.

"Me neither," I said.

"I'm tired of feeling alone even when I'm in the same room with you, Adam."

She was crying then, and I put my arms around her and held her.

"How did this happen to us?" I asked.

"Me," she said. "My fault. I just let the distractions pile up, and when they got so all-encompassing, I just shut down."

"I've got some skin in the game too," I admitted. "I let

things get out of hand at work and here. I forgot what's important. Yeah, I did."

After dinner we made love, and I held Sophie all night. We'd found each other again. Our second chance, I thought, would never need a second chance of its own.

A month later Sophie woke me one morning with a nudge. She stood over me next to the bed holding a pregnancy test wand. She looked happier than I'd seen her in a very long time.

"We're going to have a baby."

"Huh?" I sat up and put on my glasses.

"You're going to be a father, Adam."

As I sit there in the cabin, I want to pound my fists against the table. But I don't. The most important days of my life are bookends now: Aubrey's birth and Sophie's death. Between the two were hope, love, and the promise that whatever mistakes I'd made were gone forever.

Just like Sophie.

I set down the sunglasses and look out the rippled glass windowpane. Teresa Dibley is on the lawn in front of the cabin. I realize now that she's been waiting for me. When I go out, I find myself going to her like she's a friend. Maybe it's the way she wears her hair, but she reminds me of my mother. Grief propels me in her direction.

"She's dead," I call out. "Sophie's dead."

She puts her hands out, and I take them. "I'm so sorry. I saw it on the news. Clark showed me on his phone. I'm so sorry."

The words *thank you* come out of my mouth, but I don't actually hear them.

Her eyes are wet. "Is there anything I can do?"

I don't even know this woman, but she's offering to help. I wonder if other people are like this too. Is this stranger an anomaly? Would I look the other way or offer assistance?

"No," I say. "I'm going home now. Just need to go see my daughter."

She nods. "Are you sure you can drive? You've been handed the biggest hurt ever, and after a night like last night, I don't see how you can consider driving anywhere."

I'm not sure what she means.

"You were up so late," she says. "Saw the light on."

I give her a quick nod. "Yeah, I couldn't sleep. Sat in the sauna. Drank too much and tried to keep positive. Even though, after what I saw, I doubted there'd be any other outcome than what happened today."

Her damp eyes stay on me.

"Can I help you pack?" she asks.

I don't want help. I just want to find a way to understand what happened yesterday and how in the world I'm going to get through everything that is to follow.

"No," I tell her. "I can manage. Just a couple of overnight bags. You want the food in the fridge?"

"How about I put the cabin in order—you know, wash the dishes and work the owner's checklist?"

I accept the offer. I need to get out of here.

CHAPTER NINETEEN
ADAM

For the first time ever, I welcome the traffic clusterfuck I encounter on the way back into the ever-swelling Seattle-Tacoma metroplex. Even on a Sunday. Even on a Sunday before a paid holiday. It's always beyond comprehension. The Tacoma Narrows Bridge might as well be suspended in amber. Archaeologists will need to chip us out ages from now, after all the twisted metal and carnage piled at the eastern landing has at last been sorted out.

And I couldn't be happier. Anything to postpone my arrival at my in-laws'.

A fantasy unspools in my mind as I drum my fingers on the motionless steering wheel. Both Aubrey and Sophie are part of it. We're at the Wisteria, and we're roasting marshmallows in the fire pit on the oyster shell–strewn beach. Sophie fixes on Aubrey as I let our little girl attempt to roast her own.

"Keep the stick away from the flame," I tell her. "We're going for golden brown, not black the way Mommy likes them."

"Sorry," Sophie says, "but burned marshmallows are very yummy."

"Yummy if you like eating ashes," I say.

We all laugh as we sit there on bright blue Adirondacks, taking in the evening air and enjoying the spitting sparks of the cedar-and-alder fire. The waves draw closer, and the lapping sound adds a kind of relaxing tranquility to the scene.

"Maybe we can catch some crabs tomorrow," I say. "Gather some oysters."

"Crab is good," Sophie says, sipping from her wine. "No oysters for me, please."

"Aubrey looks exhausted," I say. "Let me take her inside, put her to bed. I'll be back."

Sophie gives me a smile. "Good," she says. "I love it here. I won't move an inch."

The other cabins are dark when I carry Aubrey back up the steps to the Wisteria. She's asleep. I feel her warm breath on my face.

In my fantasy I know that something bad is going to happen. I feel a heaviness cover me like a black tarp.

"Night-night," I say, putting her under the covers.

Aubrey looks up and smiles before shuttering her eyes. I turn out the seashell lamp next to her bed and return to Sophie and the fire on the beach.

"How did we get here?" Sophie asks.

"We drove our cars," I say, teasing.

She makes a face and signals for more wine. "Funny," she says. "I mean to this place in our lives when everything seems so perfect but isn't?"

"I don't know," I say as I fill her glass, the firelight flickering off the bottle. "It just happened."

I look into the fire pit, and for a second I imagine her face in the embers. She's the most beautiful woman I've ever seen. I felt that way when I first saw her. I feel that way now. I think I always will. I feel a smile come to my face.

Then I'm back to being alone in my Adirondack facing the placid waters of Hood Canal. No Sophie. No Aubrey.

I don't want to go inside the Wisteria.

And when I go home, I realize, I won't want to go inside my house.

Going inside will make it all so final. So empty. So good-bye.

It would be the best time for a cigarette. If I smoked. At work, I admit I find myself a little envious of all of the solitude and thinking time smokers in my group steal from the workday as they trudge multiple times a day to space outside SkyAero's gates. To a hater, it appears as if they've managed to create some kind of homeless camp on the shore of the Duwamish, that sluggish green river that flows into Puget Sound. They think on the way to and from their smoking encampment. They stand on the muddy shore and think.

My wife is gone now, and I go back in my memory, in that weathered chair looking out at the blackness of Hood Canal, and think. A few lights flicker across the water. I hear a seal dive in from the swim float out in front of me.

She's gone now.

Sophie is gone.

I replay the moments of our life together. First, as a kind of greatest-hits montage. When we met. When I couldn't get her out of my mind and knew that she was the one. When we took that trip to Paris before we got married. Her beautiful smile. Her laugh. How she begged me to make an offer on that house in Mount Baker because her artist's sensibility saw an amazing home, while I saw a money pit.

And then the flip side, the B-side.

How I noticed that I was no longer the only one of the two of us who worked late into the night. I was trying to show my boss, Carrie, how serious I was about my career. And really, nothing more. She absolutely flirted with me, but she did that with anyone who made eye contact with her and didn't have a sandbag stomach. And Sophie, she started texting me just before the time I'd head for my car for the soul-crushing commute up I-5 and home.

No rush tonight. Big project here.

Made a boneheaded mistake on a display for China. Thank God we caught it in time.

Janna and I are grabbing a drink.

New concept taking more time than I'd like. Might need to camp out here.

SAM has a reception tonight. Going after work.

I knew in my bones what was going on with Sophie, but I couldn't bring myself to confront her about it. At work I'm direct, because that's the role I've chosen to play to move my career forward. With Sophie, for some strange reason, I just couldn't be that way. I was so lucky to have her as my wife. So proud of her. By being with her, I was somehow a better person. Smarter. More successful. Even better looking. Make no mistake: having Sophie on my arm was never about showing her off as some kind of wifely accessory. *I* was the accessory. I was the lucky SOB that had the woman any man would have wanted.

The truth is, I didn't actually want to know for sure what she was doing and, getting to the point, with *whom* she was doing it. To know there was another man between us was something I just couldn't quite process. I never really cheated on her. I could have. I had my offers. My boss, but she doesn't count. The cute girl sitting next to me at the oyster bar in Heathrow. The girl who watered the plants in our building before cost-cutting measures pushed the duty onto the employees.

Sophie cheating on me was like a cancer diagnosis that

never really came—because knowing meant dealing with it. I could feel the tumor growing inside, getting bigger and bigger. First a walnut, then a peach, now a cantaloupe pressing against my rib cage and reminding me that I needed to see a doctor. Sophie's affair was my tumor, the one I was prepared to ignore until I quietly dropped dead in my sleep. None the wiser. Going peacefully.

In my fantasy-Adirondack, I see and hear another seal plunge into the water off the platform floating in the canal. Aubrey loves the seals. She wanted to pet or even kiss one when we were out on the boat and a pup sidled up next to our rowboat. I smile at that memory and pull a bottle of Maker's Mark up to my lips. I'm not a fancy drunk. Like all managers in my office, I do only what's necessary to get the job done. I take steps one at a time and never backtrack.

As I drink, I notice the lights go on in the Chrysanthemum, the little middle cabin Teresa Dibley is staying in with her grandkids. Off, then on. Off again. Those kids must be a nightmare for their grandmother. But a nightmare insufficient to keep my thoughts from bouncing back to Sophie's affair. *Affair.* God, I hate that word. It legitimizes a deep betrayal by casting it as if it were either wonderful or nothing at all. A love affair. An extramarital affair. A business affair. A gala affair. Put one's affairs in order.

A sorry state of affairs.

I imagine putting a note in my Maker's Mark bottle and tossing it into the waters of Puget Sound to let the world know how I feel about my wife.

Goddamn you, Sophie. You really fucked up our lives. Big-time.

I don't, of course. Instead, I drink. I'm not feeling angry at all. Just empty inside.

A car horn. Another, then quickly a third. Terrible harmony.

Oh shit. The bridge deck opens before me as traffic slides away up the span.

I throw the car in gear and accelerate, waving frantically over my shoulder before realizing I don't give a fuck if the honkers are angry with me.

Did I fall asleep, or into some kind of fugue state? The Maker's Mark is still packed away in its box with a bag of trash on the seat behind me, so at least I didn't actually drink.

I'm left with a hangover, though—that yawning emptiness my dream or fantasy left inside me.

I pull myself together and stop at the Mobil off the exit to Sophie's folks' place. I slide my credit card and top off the tank. It takes all of two minutes. A girl with a bad sunburn gives me a nod while she waits for her Camry to fill up and puts her empty water bottle and fast-food wrappers into the receptacle by the pumps. Before I drive off, I follow suit, pushing down hard on my own garbage.

"I practically live in my car," she says.

Sophie used to say the same thing before she got the job at Starbucks, when she commuted to Microsoft in Redmond.

"Yeah," I say. "Me too."

CHAPTER TWENTY
ADAM

Frank and Helen live in the same house on the course of the Twin Lakes Golf and Country Club in Federal Way that they did when they brought Sophie home from the hospital. It's impressive in its own way, a sprawling rambler with a cobblestone driveway and landscaping that proves a control freak lives there. Most of the shrubbery is sphere perfect. The lawn is as flawless as a pool table. I feel each cobblestone bump in my stomach when I drive up to park. I make my way to the front door and try the knob, but it's locked. It's about Aubrey's bedtime, so I half hope that she is sleeping and I won't have to face her. Seeing Frank will be enough. I expect that he'll find a new batch of blame for me. He's resourceful that way.

Helen answers. She looks nearly as pale as the cream sweater she's wearing over her rack-of-bones shoulders. I reach for her without saying a word, and we hug each other in the doorway.

"I'm so sorry," I say. "So sorry."

I feel Helen's frail body crumple as she lets go. I know immediately she already knows what happened to Sophie, but I get the feeling that every time someone mentions how sorry they are or how much they loved Sophie, it will wound her with another bolt of pain. Concern will only underscore the hurt that's taken over every grain of Sophie's mother's tortured being.

"Come in, Adam," she says. "We've put Aubrey down, but she's still awake."

"She doesn't know about her mom?" I ask.

Helen steps back and glances to the gleaming slate floor under our feet. "Frank told her," she says. "He felt like she had a right to know." She looks at me with an expression that mixes her own sorrow for her loss with a bitterness aimed at her husband. It's classic. Frank Flynn is a grandstander. He needs to be the first and the loudest. The most memorable too. Many times he has been, but not for the reasons he's assumed. He just had to beat me to my daughter. Had to get there first to tell her that her mother was dead.

"He was very gentle about it," Helen goes on.

I don't want to cause a scene. I refuse to turn the worst moments of my life into the beginning of a war. I almost laugh at that: the war began long before Sophie and I were married. I've tried with little success to ignore it. Frank wanted his girls all to himself: first Helen, then Sophie, and later Aubrey. I was the asteroid that hovered just outside his orbit. Out there, but not really there. If there at all, only once in a great while.

Frank's in the living room sitting next to an air purifier, at which he aims his omnipresent cigar smoke. It's pointless. Like the Buick, the house reeks of his cigars. I wonder how Helen can tolerate it.

Or if she even notices anymore.

"We lost our Sophie," he says as I approach.

"Lost her," I say, holding the phrase in the thick air and

wondering why he's treating her death as if she's on some random carousel at baggage claim. She's been raped. Murdered. She's in a refrigerator in a county morgue.

"My little girl," Frank goes on. "What in the world are we going to do now?" He looks at me but directs his words at his wife. I am nothing. Just like always.

"We have plans to make, Frank," she says.

An inch-long ash threatens to fall, and he finally stubs out his cigar. "We will never make plans again. What's the point? Why bother? What am I going to do now with this life? Make plans to do things with you?"

"I didn't mean that," Helen says. "I meant funeral plans."

I know the futility of changing the subject—their fight will resume later a hundred times anyway.

Regardless, I speak up. "I think I should talk to Aubrey."

"She's asleep. I told her. She's fine." Frank's words are birdshot in my face.

I doubt she's sleeping, and I know that no three-year-old is going to be fine hearing that her mommy has gone to heaven.

"Helen says she's awake," I say, looking over at Sophie's mother, trying to reel in some support.

"She's not, Adam," Frank says. He struggles for a beat to get out of his leather lounge chair but gives up. He's stuck. *Good,* I think.

"She needs her father," I say.

I know I've just flipped the switch: Frank's going to lift his leg to pee on me.

"She needs a stable home," he says.

He fails at getting up again. Good.

"What are you getting at?" I ask.

"Don't play stupid just because you're in front of my wife. I know that you were a lousy, unfaithful husband. My daughter forgave you. But I never did."

I feel my face grow hot. I never had an affair. Ever. Not one time.

Sophie did. She cheated on me. I feel like screaming that at the big, fat, balding boob. But I don't. I never even told Sophie that I knew about her affair. Confrontation would have made it worse. And honestly, I just didn't know where I stood. I thought if I pushed her to make a choice that the love of my life wouldn't have picked me at all.

"I never cheated on her," I finally say. "Not one time."

Helen speaks up. "See, Frank. I told you. Adam says he didn't."

"His word is dog shit."

Just then Aubrey appears. She's wearing a pale pink nightgown, a garment I don't immediately recognize.

"Hi, baby," I say.

"Daddy!"

She runs into my arms, and I lift her up to the popcorn-and-glitter ceiling.

"Mommy's in heaven," she says.

"She is, Aubrey," I tell her as I feel my in-laws' gazes drill into me.

"I want to be an angel," she says.

"You are an angel right here on earth," I say. Holding her takes away some of the anger I feel toward Frank, and I reluctantly set her down. I shift to my mother-in-law. "We need to go home, Helen."

"Why don't you spend the night?" she asks.

"I have to go to work tomorrow."

"Like hell you do," says Frank. "Tomorrow's Memorial Day."

He's got me there. "Oh," I say. "Right."

"And even if it wasn't, your stupid job can wait. Your wife's been murdered. What's the matter with you?"

I don't want to stay there. I hate being there.

"Please," Helen says.

I finally give in.

"All right. I'll stay over."

"Do you like my nightie?" Aubrey asks. "It's Mommy's. It's from when she was a little girl."

Helen smiles a sad smile. "I found it the other day when I was reorganizing the garage. I was going to give it to Sophie so she could pass it on." She bends down to her granddaughter and strokes her hair. She plants a kiss on the top of Aubrey's head. "She'd think you were the prettiest girl in the world right now. Right, Frank?"

Frank doesn't say anything and I know why.

To Sophie's father the prettiest girl in the world will always be the one in the refrigerator at the county morgue.

The guest room in the Flynn house says everything about my in-laws—and how they feel about actually having guests. In one corner is Frank's antique humidor, a mahogany-and-glass piece that he bought in an auction in Tacoma. Paid a lot for it. Bragged about it. Then, like the moron he is, he refinished it from top to bottom. Stripping off the patina of the old wood, polishing the brass hinges, and making it look like it was something off the shelf at a Drexel furniture store. He ruined it. Sophie and I laughed about it. Neither of us said a word to him, however. Someone else must have had the pleasure. It was moved to the guest room from a place of prominence in his home office.

The bed, and no joke, is a rollaway. Not kidding. A torture device with a metal bar that never fails to dig into one's back around two a.m.

The Flynns were never big on having visitors. I'm all but sure that's because Frank doesn't like to share his space with anyone. Frank doesn't like to share anything. His wife. His daughter. His stupid antique humidor.

Helen had made up the rack anticipating I'd stay over. She even turned on the rummage-sale-reject light on the nightstand. I don't get it. Everything else in Sophie's parents' house is of the best quality. Everything but this room. I sit on the edge of the bed waiting for it to spring shut like a mousetrap. I *feel* trapped. I want to take my daughter and go home. I want to pull in some air and breathe. I want to mourn my wife's death before everyone I know tells me how *they* feel.

Too late for that, I know.

"Adam?"

It's Helen in the hall outside my door.

"It's unlocked," I say.

She cracks open the door. "Linda London is about to give a report on Sophie."

I get up and follow her to the enormous TV that Frank bought for himself last Christmas. A commercial is on advertising a Memorial Day appliance sale.

"Sit down," Frank says, or rather commands. "Sophie is top story and she deserves it."

Like being top story when you are dead matters.

When KOMO News comes back on, a pretty blond anchor introduces "veteran reporter" Linda London from "a tiny town on Hood Canal rocked by tragedy and shrouded in mystery."

The news writer pulled out all the stops.

Linda stands next to the water's edge. It's a live shot, so she's illuminated by floodlights that do her no favors. Every line on her face highlighted and edged in shadow. She recounts the "gruesome discovery" and how the family is devastated.

Frank shoots me a look. "I talked with her before you got here. Not on camera. Just over the phone."

Of course you did.

Linda interviews one of the onlookers, and the girl reiterates how shocked they are about what happened. "Like, we are a safe place here," she says while a young man in a Patrón tank top next to her bobbles his head up and down in agreement.

Patrón leans toward the camera, looking for part of his

girlfriend's fifteen minutes. "Things like this don't happen around here," he says. "A drowning now and then, okay. Not a murder. We aren't a murdering kind of place. You can put that on the news."

London takes the close of her segment to drop a bomb.

"Sources close to the investigation," she says, "indicate that a person of interest has been identified. They won't tell us who it is, but we expect more details to come."

Frank, who is sitting in his chair like the world's ugliest Buddha, looks over at me. "I wonder who it is."

"We all do, Frank," Helen says, cutting the awkwardness of my silence.

"I'm going back to bed," I say.

"How can you even sleep?" Frank asks. "Considering everything."

I know that's shorthand for *everything you've done*.

I ignore him and start back for the guest room. I'm not completely sure, because the TV competes with Frank's voice, but I think I hear him say, "Don't worry, Helen, that SOB is going down."

As I try to drift off, I realize that sleep will elude me once more. There's no way to compartmentalize what happened and what will happen next. I'm trapped in that mousetrap bed and held captive by my wife's murder.

CHAPTER TWENTY-ONE
LEE

It's ten a.m. Monday, Memorial Day, and Frank Flynn is on the phone. His call doesn't surprise me in the least; in fact, I'm a little surprised he waited this long. Even our short time together at the site of Sophie's abduction in front of the Wisteria was enough for me to know that he'd be as hands-on with the case as we'd allow. He peppers me with questions about what I know, and I am as candid as I can be. Most of what I would hold back isn't known—and won't be until after the autopsy tomorrow.

"You need me to come in for a statement?" he asks.

"I already have your statement," I say. "Unless you've omitted something you think I should know."

"I'm pretty sure my son-in-law killed my daughter," he says.

That's about as direct—and as expected—as can be. Doesn't matter that we have a witness who backs up Adam's story of a struggle on the beach while he was one hundred yards offshore with his daughter. Frank Flynn's dead certain his son-in-law killed his daughter.

"Why is that, sir?" I ask.

Sophie's father doesn't mince words. He reminds me of my own father. My dad isn't a hothead like Frank Flynn. But then, my dad never had to talk to a police detective investigating his only daughter's murder.

"He was having an affair on her," Frank says. "Probably someone at work."

"How do you know that?"

Again he charges at me with full force. "My daughter told me. That's how."

"All right," I say, wondering why he didn't mention it at the cabin when Montrose and I were first there. Mr. Flynn doesn't seem to be the type to hold back. "When did she tell you this? What else did she say?"

I want to point out that if Adam had an affair, it doesn't mean that he is a killer. If all men who had affairs were killers, our prisons would need to be run like timeshares.

Frank Flynn does a little backpedaling, a move that I'm sure is almost foreign to him. "Sophie never came out directly and said it to me," he says. "She was too proud for that. My girl was never one to give me or her mother any cause for worry. There was something going on with her and her husband." He stops for a beat. "You should talk to Janna Fong, her best friend at Starbucks. I bet she knows a whole lot. I've got her number right here."

I take down Janna Fong's information and tell him I'll look into it, but it's more out of courtesy to a man who's just lost his daughter than because it's a real lead. I know better than to remind Frank of the witness to the struggle on the beach. He'd just say the old man was blind, or had just seen Adam's accomplice doing the dirty work. There's not much more I can do until I get the autopsy results anyway.

"I'll call Janna," I finally say.

"She lives in Tacoma now," he says. "Got married last summer. Nice guy, I'm told. Not like my son-in-law. That's for sure."

* * *

Montrose is off with his kids on the peninsula for the holiday, and it's quiet in the office. I reach Janna Fong after a couple of tries. She's already heard the devastating news about Sophie and is eager to help in the investigation.

"In any way that I can," she says, her words coming into my ear so quietly that it's almost like a whisper.

I tell her that I'll come to Tacoma.

"If you're home," I say.

"Yes," she says, giving me the address. "I'm here all day. I'm not doing anything. Husband has to work, which is fine. We need the extra money. Please come. Sophie was my friend. I can't believe this has happened."

Janna Fong greets me at the door of her beautifully remodeled Victorian in tree-lined North Tacoma. She wears her black hair in a loose bun, and her neck is adorned with a thin strand of coral beads. I notice her very obvious baby bump, and I give her a smile.

"Two more months," she says. "Feels like two more years. Do you have any kids?"

I shake my head. "No. Someday, I hope." I do.

Janna offers tea, and I follow her to her kitchen. It's painted a light peony pink. Its open shelves hold a collection of jade-colored glassware. It feels like we've stepped into springtime. I love it.

"I've cried my eyes out," she says, pouring the tea from a pink vintage teapot. The scent of jasmine fills the air. "All of this seems like a bad dream."

She's shaking, and I pat her hand.

"I'm sorry," I tell her.

"Thank you," she says. "I haven't seen Sophie for a few months, but we talk all the time. She's my girl. *Was* my girl." She takes a quick, deep breath. "My best friend. I went through some tough times with a guy before I met Richard—

that's my husband—and Sophie got me through all of it. I can't believe she's really gone."

"I know," I say. "I'm here because of something her father told me. It may or may not have some relevance to what happened on Saturday."

I leave out the words *rape* and *murder*. I've changed it into *what happened* because this nice girl across the table from me in this fantasyland kitchen doesn't need all the ugly that would come with having those truths specified just now.

"Mr. Flynn?" she asks. "I've never met him."

I'm a little surprised by that, but he never said he knew her personally. "He says that Sophie and Adam went through some hard times in their marriage and that you might know something."

She stirs stevia into her tea. "Any time with Adam would be a hard time," she says. "But that's me. Adam and I were oil and water. Just not the right mix. Sophie loved him, for the most part."

"What do you mean, 'for the most part'?"

"She could put up with his constant scheming to get ahead. He viewed life like it was like that old board game. Risk? My brothers and I used to play it. High stakes. Conquer the world. You know, war."

I know the game. Risk was Kip's favorite. I remember a time when Kip and Adam and the other boys played a game of Risk that lasted an entire weekend. The basement smelled like pizza and a locker room. Mom had a fit when the game was over. Dad thought it was funny and was a little proud that Kip played so hard to win. I wonder if Kip thought about Risk when he was off in Afghanistan.

"What about problems in their marriage?" I ask.

"None that I could really see," Janna says.

"Her father thinks that Adam was having an affair."

She sips her tea. "He probably was. He's the type to do it.

Not because he didn't love Sophie. I mean, she was everything. Beautiful. Cute figure. So talented. He might have strayed a little, but it wasn't major."

"'Strayed a little'?"

"Some weird stuff too," she says with a shrug. "Sophie used to tell me that she wondered where he was after work. Thought he was off with some waitress from a restaurant near the factory or maybe with some recent finance graduate on a rotation at SkyAero."

Staring into her teacup, she suddenly stops.

"What is it?"

"I remember her saying something about an affair before Aubrey was born, but she wasn't specific. When I really put my mind to it, I can't come up with anything that would point to anyone. Just a feeling."

"A feeling?"

"Yeah, I remember her asking me what I would think if he ran off with a waitress."

"A waitress," I repeat.

"Yeah," she says. "We kind of laughed about it. I told her that he'd never run off with someone beneath him. I don't mean to be a snob, and I'm sure there are plenty of nice waitresses out there, but really, for Adam, it would be too big of a step down."

"I know you said it was a feeling," I say, "but do you think that Adam was cheating on her recently?"

Janna shrugs a little. "Honestly, I don't know for sure. We talked about all kinds of things—my boyfriend of the moment, our jobs, her baby when Aubrey was born—but Adam wasn't our focus. He was there, of course, like a shadow she could never shake."

I take her words and rearrange them. "Did she want to shake off the shadow?"

She offers a faint smile. "I think so. She told me that he

was a bigger control freak than her father at times, and if you've heard anything about Mr. Flynn—who I never met—you know that's saying quite a lot."

I don't want to dwell on Mr. Flynn. Instead, I say, "A moment ago you said 'some weird stuff' in reference to Adam. What did you mean by that?"

She hesitates. "I don't know. Kinky stuff, I guess. One time when Sophie and I went shopping in Bellevue, we took Adam's car. When we put our stuff in the trunk, there was one of those sex dolls inside."

I have no idea what she's talking about.

"What kind of doll?"

She makes a disgusted face. "Those blow-up dolls that guys mess around with, I guess. Anyway, she was angry that it was still there. Said Adam told her it was from a friend at work. Bachelor party joke or something along those lines."

I process that and set it aside before moving on.

"Lately, Janna," I say, digging in, "how was Sophie? Happy? Troubled? Any feelings on that?"

"Better. That's for sure. Things settled down after Aubrey was born. I think having a baby was good for her—good for them. They argued still, but they always had that little girl to come back to. Sophie was private, but not so much that I wouldn't know."

"So they were happy?" I ask.

"As happy as they could be."

"I'm not sure what you mean."

Janna offers me a second cup of tea, but I decline.

"Being happy takes a lot of work. With a demanding job and a child, at the end of the day, how much time is there to be happy? Me? I'm exhausted now. I can't imagine how beat-up I'll feel when Sophie is born."

Her baby's name catches in her throat.

"I decided when I found out what happened."

"It's a lovely tribute."

"Sophie was amazing." Tears roll down Janna's cheeks. "I don't know that I'll ever get used to referring to her in the past tense. It's so wrong. You have to catch the guy who killed her."

"We're working on it."

She hesitates a little. "I don't know who it is, but I just can't imagine it's Adam. I just can't get there."

"Why's that?"

Janna takes a deep breath. "He's a jerk. He's insufferable. He's stuck on himself too. He's all of that. But he also knew that he was lucky to have a girl like Sophie. She was the best thing that ever happened to him. And Aubrey? She was icing on the cake. No marriage is perfect, and they had their problems. I hope you know how much I loved her, because what I want to tell you can come out wrong."

She stares at me. I can see that she's about to let her tears fall.

"Say it," I tell her.

"Sophie and Adam deserved each other. They really did. She was private. Quiet. She also had a depressive, dark side, and he was oblivious half the time. A shitty match for survival if you ask me."

Before the drive back to Shelton, I check my messages. There is one from Adam.

His voice is soft. He's not whispering, but I get the impression that he's talking in a low voice so as not to disturb anyone. Maybe his little girl?

"I hear you have identified a person of interest," he says. "I'm still processing everything and wondering what I'm going to do now. Just wanted to call and thank you for everything. You were always special to me. Your entire family was."

He's thinking of Kip. Not me. I know it. He's remembering how our father took him and Kip fishing on Neah Bay every year from junior high school to the summer Kip enlisted in the military. I went a couple of times when I was older. But it really was *The Adam and Kip Show* all the way. I was merely an add-on, the awkward girl with a crush on my big brother's best friend.

For no reason I can name, I listen to the message two times more before deleting it.

CHAPTER TWENTY-TWO
LEE

The Kitsap County Coroner's Office sits on a hill above a landscape quilted by rows and rows of shiny new cars, just off Auto Center Way in Bremerton. I drive up to the parking area alone. Montrose is ferrying his kids in three different directions before he comes in, since as he put it "Tuesday is Monday this week" and his family's all upside down.

I'm thankful for the simplicity of my life.

To the left as I pull in I see some navy recruits working out on a field adjacent to the complex. I think of my brother whenever I see the young faces of the men or women who serve our country. They join for many reasons. Some to fight. Some to get out of a bad situation here at home. Others do it because struggling for something is the fuel for their very existence. Like Kip. He was that way. A fighter.

My heart stops as I recognize a maroon Buick parked in a visitor's spot.

Frank and Helen Flynn are here.

I have no idea why they'd come. Adam has already identified Sophie, and there is no need for them to put themselves through an experience like that.

The coroner's assistant, Celia Greene, meets me after Security lets me inside the building. She's in her twenties, with cropped blond hair and what looks like a dozen earrings on each ear. Just below her neckline peeks the top half of a calligraphic tattoo. I can't make out what it says, and I know I'll try later when I go to sleep. I'm like that. A puzzle solver who never misses an episode of *Wheel of Fortune*, something I'd never admit to anyone out loud.

"Good God," she tells me without as much as a hello, "the victim's father is a real ass."

I keep my facial expressions to a minimum. "What's up?"

She rolls her eyes upward. "He insisted that he wanted to see her. I told him that the body was prepped for an exam and that an ID had already been made. He could see her post-exam, when the body's released to the funeral home."

"That didn't satisfy him," I say, knowing already that probably nothing satisfies Frank Flynn. He's left at least seven messages for me since Saturday. Each message offered a pointed—and unsolicited—suggestion to "help" with the investigation.

"No," she says. "He and his wife are in the viewing room waiting for someone to lift the blinds."

"Can the pathologist make that happen?" I ask.

"Sure," Celia says.

In Loving Memory. I think that's the tattoo. The tops of the letters indicate *I*, *L*, and *M*. The spacing is about right. I wonder who's being remembered on her chest, but I don't ask.

"The little girl is with Deb in Records," she adds.

I'm stunned. "They brought her?"

"I know. Right? Who brings a three-year-old to the morgue?"

"Frank Flynn does," I say. "That's who."

"I could tell that Mrs. Flynn was none too happy about it. She barely said a word."

I want to tell Celia that's Helen's normal MO, but I don't. I head into the viewing room, where I find Sophie's mother clutching a box of tissues and Frank positioned in front of the viewing window as though he doesn't want to miss a football play on TV.

He glares at me. "Jesus," he says. "I thought you'd never get here."

I'm actually ten minutes early, but I don't bring that up.

"I'm here now," I say.

I hear the sound of tissues being pulled from the box. Helen is already sobbing.

I place my hand on her shoulder. "You don't need to be here, Mrs. Flynn."

She nods at me and then looks at her husband.

"She wants to be here," he says. "This is our only child. We want justice for Sophie, and we're going to be involved in everything that we can."

"I'm sorry," she says, more mouthing the words than actually speaking.

Frank hurls a look so powerful that Helen immediately looks away as if she'd been struck in the face.

"We all want justice," I say. "That's why I'm here. That's why I'll be fighting for Sophie until I catch who's responsible for her murder. Do we really need to be at odds over something we obviously agree on?"

Frank keeps his attention locked on his wife for several seconds before turning back to face me.

"You say the right things," he says, "but I did some checking on you. You don't have the best record, you know."

"Frank!" Helen says. "Please."

He's referring to the case of a young woman who was found strangled and murdered in Mason Lake. We think her boyfriend is behind her death, but we've been unable to build a case strong enough to charge him.

Frank shakes his head in exaggerated disgust. "I wonder how Cathy Rinehart's family feels about now."

I know what he's doing, but I refuse to take the bait. I wonder what kind of man uses someone else's hurt to make another feel terrible.

"Heartbroken," I say.

He doesn't flinch. Frank's not a flincher. He faces everything head-on like a runaway truck without functioning brakes.

"Angry too," he shoots back, before dropping a little bomb. "I called Cathy Rinehart's father, and he gave me an earful."

I get it. I do. Grief is a powerful motivator. I do my best not to push back at this man in front of me. He has every right to be angry at the world. However, he has no right to try to grow a club membership of the parents of murder victims whose murderers have eluded justice. I intend to nail Cathy's killer. I intend to find Sophie's.

"Mrs. Flynn, are you sure you want to see Sophie now?" I ask, knowing that I need to tread lightly here. "You don't have to."

As I'm sure he always does, Frank answers for his wife. "She wants to," he says.

But I don't care. Whatever they have going on between them—and I have a good idea what that is—I don't need to be a part of it. Helen is a person. She's not a thing.

"I'm asking *her*," I say.

Frank fumes. His head is a big red stoplight now.

Helen looks flustered, which I have already figured out is one of her most recurrent states. Apparently, she's not used to seeing anyone go around her husband. "No," she says a little weakly, before catching his stare. "I mean no, I'm sure that I want to see her."

"All right, now," I say, "after you see her, we'll shut the

blinds again. After you two are gone, I'll observe while the forensic pathologist conducts a thorough exam to determine what caused her death and to collect any evidence that might be present on her body."

Frank motions Helen to join him as he faces the window.

I press a button, and the blinds on the other side of the glass rise.

"Goddamn it," Frank says almost at once as he sees Sophie on a steel gurney, lightly covered by a sheet. "Goddamn *him*. He really killed my little girl. That son of a bitch!"

Helen doesn't say anything. She stands there statuelike while her husband rants. Her hands have turned into crab claws, and the tissue she's been holding is now wadded into a near-perfect sphere.

I ask the question for which I know the answer—a question that was already answered by Adam at the crime scene.

"Is this Sophie?"

Frank swings around. "Goddamn it," he says. "You idiot! Of course it is!"

"Frank, please," Helen finally mutters. Her words are sucked right into his gaping mouth along with all the air in the saddest room ever built. It passes through my mind that the interior decorator and the contractor had worked together to try to make the space as calming as possible. A soothing palette of blues and light grays playing over a base of soft white. An abstract painting of clouds hangs over a sofa that I imagine is stained with a zillion tears.

Frank ignores his wife and jabs a finger at me. "You goddamn have to arrest Adam Warner for this! He's the killer! We know it. *You* know it. Now get on with it, or I swear I'll make you wish that you had."

I breathe in his threat. I could make something of it if I was unsure of my skills as an investigator and if I was bereft of compassion for the father of the dead woman on the gurney.

Instead, I press the button, and the blinds fall downward. I open the door and indicate to the Flynns that they should exit.

"Aubrey's this way," I say.

Helen doesn't look at me. She walks by, her head down. I can feel the heat of Frank's stoplight head as he passes.

"You better keep us informed," he spits out.

"I'll tell you everything that I can," I say. "But just to be as clear as I can—just to be as clear as you've been just now—there will be things that I cannot comment about, because I want the killer who did this to be convicted and put away for a very long time."

"You mean you'll keep us in the dark?" Frank asks. "That's just dandy."

"I want the same thing you want," I say.

He puffs up his considerably puffed-up body. "Then arrest my son-in-law and be done with all of this."

"We don't know what happened, Mr. Flynn," I say. "But we will."

I don't tell him that I know for sure that Adam Warner couldn't have done it. It isn't because the evidence—what the eyewitness says he saw—doesn't point to him at all. It's because I know him. I know his character. He isn't the type of guy to hurt anyone. He is good. After all, he saved *me*.

I watch as they collect Aubrey. The little girl reluctantly puts down a teddy bear that Celia gave her—a tool that the coroner's office employees use to calm and distract children at the scene. Frank says the plush toy is dirty, and she should leave it. Aubrey looks more like her mother than her father, and I wonder how that will play with the Flynns and Adam as they try to carry on. I wonder if they'll see Sophie's face when they look at Aubrey as she grows up. I wonder if they will hear Aubrey's laugh and instantly think of the woman who was recovered from the reeds at Octopus Hole. I wonder if Aubrey will exist on her own, or if they'll turn her into a constant reminder of what has been lost forever.

* * *

Dr. Tamara Collier has been the pathologist for Kitsap County for six months, having replaced a longtime and much-admired pathologist who'd left to work for the Makah Nation on the Olympic Peninsula. Our county has only sent Dr. Collier a handful of cases—two were deaths associated with car accidents, one a house fire, and the case that Frank Flynn shoved in my face like a rancid cream pie: Cathy Rinehart.

We exchange hellos, and as she ushers me inside the exam room, she lets me know she's already determined the cause of death.

"Blunt force trauma to the back of the head," she says, looking at me over her drugstore readers. "Someone hit her hard. Swung for the fences."

I don't like the analogy. I've never been much for sports.

"I see," I say as she rotates a beam of light onto Sophie's head. Her hair had concealed it at the crime scene, but it was there, the bruising and gash in the back of her scalp.

Dr. Collier is so short that she steps on a booster to do the exam. She's wearing green scrubs hemmed with masking tape. I think of two things just then. She's resourceful, and Kitsap County is too cheap to get her a custom size.

"Is that bruising around her neck too?" I ask.

"Good eye. It's faint, but yes. Looks like the SOB that did this choked her too. I don't think it's what killed her. I'll have to get in there to figure that out." She glances at her saw. I'm not sticking around for that.

"What about sexual assault?" I ask. "At the scene, we thought we saw some indicators."

She looks at me. "Did you now?" she asks, in a tone that shifts the dynamics in the room. She's very short, but she's big on what she's been called to do.

"I'm not a pathologist," I'm quick to say. I've had enough conflict for one day. "Wondering what you were thinking."

She peers over the tops of her drugstore readers. "I'd say

so. I'll do the swabs of everything, every which way, and see what the lab tells us. But, yes, I think you and your field team were right." She stops and looks back at the body in front of her, the light shimmering over Sophie's lifeless skin.

"I don't suppose you'll have much luck with any trace," I say.

"It might have helped if you'd bagged her hands."

"She'd been pulled from Hood Canal," I say. "I didn't think that there was any need."

The pathologist looks up. "Meg Fleiss was pulled nude from the Mississippi, a floater no less. Lab in Biloxi found clothing fibers on her nipple rings that matched a suspect. She'd been in the water for seven days."

I don't completely see the relevance. Sophie didn't have any piercings that could hook a fiber.

"DNA?" I ask. "Under her nails?"

Dr. Collier returns her gaze to Sophie's body. "No. Nothing. But next time, bag the hands. Always bag 'em."

I stand there as she takes long cotton swabs and runs them along the inside of Sophie's mouth, her vagina, her anus. She swabs twice for each area and puts the swabs into separate tubes, sealing them and then noting the contents with the case number.

As I watch the pathologist work, I know that this might have been my fate if Adam hadn't found me. I don't know when my assailant would have come back or why he ditched me there. Why I was so compliant. I hate thinking about where it might have ended. I'd have been on a table, bloody water running into a drain, my brain removed and weighed, my organs cataloged and then returned willy-nilly to the cavity of my body. I'd have been just like Sophie Warner.

"Lab is running behind," she says, revving up her saw: my cue to leave.

"Okay," I say, pulling myself back into the moment. "Thanks, Doctor."

I have an urge just then to scream out and curse Albert Hodge and what he did to me. I never, ever think about him. I did my best to banish that day into the background of my life, like some flub in a school play that I just didn't want to think about ever again. Sophie on that table brought it all back. Seeing Adam Warner brought it all back too.

"You okay?" the pathologist asks, turning off her saw.

"I just feel a little sick," I fib.

She gives me an empathetic smile. I know she's trying to be kind. "I get it. Have to have a strong stomach for this. My dad said mine was made out of cast iron. Grew up on a farm in Ellensburg. Slaughtered Angus . . ."

She's still talking as I bolt from the autopsy suite to the restroom down the hall. Inside, I run cold water in the sink and spoon it up to my face. It helps a little, but only a little. Celia, the coroner's assistant, emerges from a stall.

"God," she says, "that man was such a jerk. Don't let it get to you."

"Yeah," I say, not letting her know that as bad as Frank Flynn was, he wasn't the source of my little moment.

I don't want her to know what I'm really thinking or how I feel. When you have something that you carry inside and never talk about, you don't ever unleash it on a stranger. And since you've never talked about it, you don't know even how to really frame your thoughts. You fear that your words will tumble out in a way that will only make things worse.

If that's even possible.

"I got a text from my partner," I lie. "Need to get back to Shelton. Do me a favor and let Dr. Collier know that I want to be the first to know the lab results, okay?"

"Sure, Detective," Celia says. "Don't worry. You'll catch this guy. I have faith in that, faith in you."

I know she means well just then, but her kindness only makes me feel more pathetic.

*   *   *

When I check my messages back in the car, I find two.

The first is from Linda London, the reporter from KOMO. She's nothing if not direct.

"You need to go on air and talk about Sophie Warner's murder. I'm getting lots of pieces of the story, but our viewers are demanding something official. I have a crew headed your way."

I don't call her back.

The second message is from Teresa Dibley, the woman staying with her grandkids in the tiny cabin next door to the Wisteria.

"Probably nothing," she says, "but I'd like to talk if you can find the time. The kids and I are staying through about four o'clock today. Squeezing one more day out of what's been a traumatic holiday, to say the least."

Teresa I call back.

"I thought of going home," Teresa Dibley tells me, "but I prepaid, and there are no refunds." We're back on the deck of the Chrysanthemum, watching Clark and Destiny row around the glassy waters of the protected beachfront. "What happened here," she adds, her voice soft, "is almost too much to take."

"I understand," I say.

"Those two haven't had it easy," she goes on, looking at her grandchildren. "Lots of drama. They're good kids, but I don't know that I got them in time. Sure wish I were twenty years younger."

"You're doing great," I tell her. "Your grandchildren look happy."

She smiles in their direction and offers me some ice tea. It's hot out on the cedar-plank deck despite the cooling breeze gliding off the water, so I gladly accept.

"Something's been bothering me," Teresa says, handing me a glass. "I read the news story about the case. And well, I don't want to be the person who meddles in what you are doing. It isn't my style at all."

"No," I say. "This is good. I need to hear what you're thinking."

Teresa sets down her glass. "When Mr. Warner returned from, you know, finding Mrs. Warner?"

She's upset. I see it in her eyes.

"Yes," I say. "I know this is hard."

She looks a little embarrassed, which was not my intent at all.

"Sorry," she says, reeling in her own sadness over what happened. "Anyway, he was a complete wreck. Just barely able to make it from his car to the cabin. I've never seen anyone wrapped up in that kind of grief. And I've seen a lot. With my son. My daughter-in-law too."

Just then Clark waves at his grandma from the rowboat.

Teresa immediately jumps to her feet. "Destiny! You keep that life jacket on, or you'll never set foot on a boat again."

Teresa looks at me and shakes her head. "That one will be the one that puts me into an early grave."

I smile. "The ones that test the limits sometimes do the most amazing things in life. That's what I've always thought."

"You'll feel differently when you have a child of your own," she says.

"I hope to someday."

We drink our ice tea, and Teresa gets to what she wanted to talk about when she called me.

"Sunday afternoon, I offered to get the cabin in order so that Mr. Warner could leave right away. You know, no one wants to lose a cleaning deposit if they can avoid it, right? It was the least I could do, considering what he'd been through."

I feel my heart rate pick up. I'd been through that cabin too. "You found something," I say.

"Oh, no," she says. "Not really. But I did notice something that seemed at odds with what the news said. They said that Friday, the night before she died, the Warners had dinner at the cabin. Sandwiches or steaks. I'm not sure which they had."

"And Saturday morning they had waffles for breakfast," I say.

"Yes," Teresa says. "I saw that too. There were two plates in the sink and a bowl that had been used for batter. The dishwasher was empty. There were no other plates or glasses or anything."

"Maybe they ran the dishwasher that night," I suggest.

"Right. I thought about that. When I went to clean out the refrigerator, I found three store-bought sandwiches. Two were roast beef, and the other was a half-eaten peanut butter and jelly."

I process her words. "And two steaks?" I ask.

She gives me a nod. "Yeah. Both of them were still in there. It made me wonder when I read the news story. It didn't seem to add up."

She is right. It doesn't.

"The sandwiches were from IGA in Hoodsport," she continues. "I think that's probably where the steaks came from too."

I ask if there was anything else that seemed unusual.

"I know Mrs. Warner was drinking wine when she was taken. The bottle was in the refrigerator. It was a sauvignon blanc, a screw-top. I used it last night to make some steamers the kids and I dug down the beach."

"Is the trash still in the cabin?" I ask, hoping to fix what I know now is a lapse in the investigation. The idea of a mistake makes me sick to my stomach. Teresa Dibley sees the switch in my demeanor from interested to concerned, but

she doesn't remark on it, and I'm grateful for that. I'm starting to sweat too.

She shakes her head and sets down her now-empty glass
and motions that Clark is taking his sister too far from shore.

"One more thing," she says, getting up. "The wastebaskets
and the trash can under the kitchen sink were all empty. Lin-
ers gone too. I thought that was strange. Why take the trash
with you if you're going to leave the food behind?"

Chapter Twenty-Three
Lee

Montrose and I are eating our lunch and playing bingo with the sex offender registry, parole records, and notes on recent LE contact with locals as we try to find who might have taken and assaulted Sophie Warner. There are four nearby whose crimes include rape. Two of those used a weapon. Only one of those held a woman captive.

According to the reports, Jim Coyle, forty-nine, lives barely two miles from the cabins in Lilliwaup. He is a truck driver for a small freight line based out of Port Townsend in nearby Jefferson County. He was arrested for kidnapping when he was twenty and sentenced to seven years. The incident involved a longtime girlfriend who had just broken up with him. He wanted one more chance, but she refused. He held her at gunpoint for more than four hours before releasing her. He claimed their sexual relations the day before had been consensual, but the young woman insisted otherwise.

At least at first.

Coyle pleaded guilty and served his time. Two years after his release, however, his victim appeared on national TV and told the world that she was sorry. She'd found God and wanted to make amends.

"He didn't hurt me," she told a chubby, bald TV psychologist. "It was partly my sin too."

Semiexonerated or not, we decide to pay him a visit.

An hour later, we drive past the road to the cabins and find ourselves at Coyle's address. Montrose has sharper eyes than I do. He sees the entrance to the Coyle property right away. It's narrow—too narrow, I think, for a semi—and it's shrouded under a canopy of big-leaf maples and hemlock trees.

"Creep lives here," he announces, pulling in.

"And you do all this without GPS," I say.

He shrugs. "GPS is for wusses."

A man wearing paint-splattered blue jeans and a tank top emerges from a single-wide trailer at the top of the long, rutted driveway. A tuft of white chest hair protrudes over the top of his shirt. It's so long I think that it might possibly be braidable.

By the time we park, Jim Coyle is right next to the driver's side, looking us over with an unfriendly glare. "See the 'No Trespassing' sign?" His face is ruddy from the sun. His eyes are so brown that it is hard to distinguish the iris from the pupil. He doesn't smile. In fact, it looks as if he hasn't ever. He has no laugh lines on his face.

Montrose opens his door so Coyle has to step back, and I join him outside the car. As Montrose makes the introductions, it's immediately apparent that Coyle is used to people like us stopping by uninvited.

"I know why you are here," he says.

"Really?" Montrose asks.

Coyle folds his arms across his chest, pushing his tuft nearly to his chin. "I made a mistake a long time ago," he says. "I met the wrong girl, and she set me up."

"You held her at gunpoint," I say.

"I pled guilty to that. Yeah, I sure did. But that bitch is a liar, and she proved it later when she decided to ask for forgiveness. Called me. Harassed me. Said she was sorry. What am I supposed to do with that? Judge says nothing. Case stands. I am a goddamn rapist, and that's why you're here. Such bullshit."

A yapping Pomeranian, one of my least favorite dogs, sweeps down from the trailer, and Jim scoops it up.

"Where were you the other day?" I ask.

"I was running a load down to Longview. Got back here this morning."

Montrose looks around. "Where's your rig?"

Coyle shifts his dog up to his left shoulder. "At the lot in Chehalis. Brakes are a little sticky."

"No one likes sticky brakes," Montrose says.

I give my partner a bit of a side-eye. He always promises to rein in his immediate disgust for a person of interest with a criminal record, but he never seems to get there. When I look past Coyle, I see his pickup truck. It's red. On the back bumper, I can make out the green fringe of some reeds.

If I can get a decent sample, I can find out if it is the same kind of plant material as on the shore at Octopus Hole where Sophie's body was found.

"I don't have to say anything more to you. I don't have a lawyer, but I guess I could get one. Now we're done here."

"Let's go," I say to Montrose.

The man without the smile turns and heads back to the mobile home, and Montrose and I get back into the car.

"What got into you?" he asks.

"We need to come back," I tell him. "But we need a warrant."

"You were looking at something behind him. Did you at least see something useful?"

"The Ford," I say. "It matches something I saw on Facebook."

Montrose looks over and shakes his head. I know the

look. God, I know it better than anything. I wait. Three. Two. One. Here it comes.

"'Facebook'?" he asks. "Seriously? Now we're using that piece of self-absorbed crap as an investigative tool? What's wrong with your generation?"

"Nothing that we can't fix once your generation is gone." I snap this back at him with heat.

He stays silent until we're back on the highway.

"Okay, now that our little tiff is over, tell me about the truck you read about on Facebook."

I manage an embarrassed smile. "It's more than what I read. Last night I was scrolling down the Mason County Crime Watch page, and someone posted that just before Sophie's disappearance, they saw a red pickup truck parked on the road next to Canal View. There was no one in the truck. Poster shared it because he'd read on another thread that Adam Warner had told police that he ran after the man who was carrying his wife and he thought someone might have been waiting just off the road above the cabin."

"I know all this, Lee."

"But here's something you didn't know: I think that there were some reeds consistent with what I saw at the body recovery site on the back bumper of his truck."

This time *he* gives *me* the side-eye.

"You a forensic botanist now?" he asks.

"We need to do two things, and we need to do them fast," I say.

"All right. What's on your list?"

"Find out if Coyle was really on the road and when. Find out more about that truck from the Facebook user who posted about it. Then get a warrant to return. If Sophie was in that truck, we're going to need to prove it."

We pull over to a spot along the highway that opens up to a magnificent view of Hood Canal. The water is so dark that it almost reads indigo—with or without sunglasses on. The tide is high, and a slight breeze is magnified by the channel, sending frothy white waves over the rocks that bolster the edge of the road along the shoreline. My phone service is spotty, but I'm able to retrieve the name of the Facebook poster. I ask Dispatch to get me an address. Montrose is on a call to the trucking company. It seems like he's on hold a very long time.

"Okay," he says. "You sure?"

He disconnects the call.

"Not at work Saturday," he says. "Called in sick."

I don't want to jump to conclusions, because it's not how things are done, but I do. "He's going to be our guy," I say. "Isn't he?"

"I got a strong feeling about him." Montrose runs on coffee and instincts. Many cops do.

I look down at the screen on my phone. "Let's go pay Sheila Simmons a visit."

"Who's that?"

"The Facebook poster. Dispatch just came back with her contact info. She saw a pickup truck on the highway above the cabins about the time of Sophie's abduction."

He rolls his eyes, but gives in. "Which way?"

"South," I answer, looking at her address on my phone. "She's in Hoodsport."

Sheila Simmons's address leads us to a small yellow house adjacent to the public library. It's as tidy as it is small. Not quite a tiny house, but I'd be surprised if she had more than seven hundred square feet to work with. I knock—after all, this is my big Facebook lead and Montrose is at once befuddled and irritated by the way people are circumventing the norm in favor of social media.

"First music," he once lamented. "Then TV. Then news implodes. Is everything going to self-service? What happened to the days when everyone was on the same page because what we saw and read was handed to us?"

I ring the bell, but no answer.

"She's probably out somewhere streaming some music," he says without a trace of irony.

I tuck a business card with *Call me* scrawled on the back, and we head back to Shelton. On the way, we run the case over and over.

"Why would Coyle lie to us if he wasn't knee deep into this?" Montrose asks.

"Why would he abduct a stranger and dump her body practically in his own backyard?" I ask.

"Freaks," he says, "especially those who have been freaks for a long time, don't think like other people, Lee. Their wires are all messed up. Someone who rapes and kills some woman, a stranger, doesn't even see people as anything but a conquest. A prize. A chance to feel like they're a big winner."

"Winner over what?"

"Us," Montrose says as we pass by the mix of expensive megahomes and those more modest structures of the original weekenders that line the highway. Many are named with a play on the owner's surname: Boyd's Nest and Potts of Gold. Others play on puns: Shore Thing, Going Coastal, and my personal favorite, Latitude Adjustment. Seriously.

"It's us versus them," he says. "And news flash for Facebook or Twitter or whatever you post on: we're going to win this one."

CHAPTER TWENTY-FOUR
LEE

Montrose is off at a doctor's appointment late in the day when Facebooker Sheila phones, falling all over herself apologizing for not getting back to me sooner. She's more than just eager to talk to me. Frantic actually. She says she can come by the station whenever I like. All I have to do is tell her a time.

I say now is fine, and twenty minutes later she's in the reception area. She's in her late twenties. She's wearing jeans and a scoop-neck tee with "Hama Hama" embroidered on the front.

"I work at the oyster saloon," she says when I take her into the interview room and pull out a notepad to capture whatever it is she's going to share—that she hasn't already posted on Facebook. "I was there when that lady's husband came in asking for leads on his missing wife. Now dead wife, I guess."

"So you talked to Adam Warner and his father-in-law?" I ask.

She shakes her head. Her hair is curly, and it literally bounces like a Slinky when she moves her head.

"No. Not really. I just heard them talking. The older guy did the talking mostly. Said that someone had abducted someone—his daughter, I guess—and asked if we'd seen anything. He said it happened in front of those cool old-timey rentals with the flower names. Believe it or not, I knew the place."

"You did?" I ask.

"Yes. Stayed there a few times with a guy I dated. Lived with his parents, and we needed a place. Okay, at the time I lived with mine too. Anyway, I pass by there every day."

"But something caught your eye that day?"

"Right. I was on my way to work. It was around ten thirty, and I was late. I'm supposed to be there at ten thirty. Anyway, I saw a truck parked there on the side of the road."

"Where exactly?"

"Right before the turnoff to the cabins."

"What kind of truck?"

"I'm not a truck person. More of a Jeep girl. I think that it was a Ford. Maybe a Chevy. Big. I really don't know what make, but I can tell you the color."

"That'll help," I say, though I already know from her Facebook post.

"Red," she says. "Red."

"Okay. Fine," I say. "Did you see the driver?"

Her curls bounce again. "No. No one was in the cab that I could tell. I was going pretty fast, so I can't swear that no one was inside; but as I whizzed by in my Jeep, I did think to myself that it was a dumb place to park. Shoulder there's not great. Ten yards past there is a wider spot on the shoulder. Even has a picnic table there."

"If you saw the truck again, do you think you could ID it?"

"Like for real or a photo?"

"Either," I say.

She looks at me. She's putting the puzzle pieces together. I can see it.

"That means you know who the truck belongs to, don't you?"

"I can't tell you anything about the investigation," I tell her.

She pushes back from the table. "That's not really fair," she says, her demeanor moving swiftly from concerned citizen to irritated twentysomething. "I'm telling you a whole lot, and my followers probably deserve an update."

Her last words get to me. I wonder if she's made up the truck now. I wonder if she posted her story just so she could add something to a popular news feed and get a lot of so-called likes. I hate that Montrose might be right about social media. I see it as potentially powerful in crime solving. Montrose sees it as a chance for every weirdo on the planet to insert him- or herself into a criminal investigation.

For *likes.*

I thank Sheila for her time and tell her that I'll be in touch. She might have seen the red truck. It might have been Jim Coyle's. And while it was true that he'd lied to us about driving his truck to Longview, it was pretty thin evidence. No judge was going to let us push around someone who was previously, though only partly, the victim of a false police report.

"That news reporter from Seattle wants to talk to me now that I'm part of the investigation," Sheila says. "Can I?"

"We don't tell citizens whether they can go on TV or not. It's up to you."

"What should I tell her?" she asks. "About the person of interest."

I'm exasperated now. "You can tell her anything you want. I haven't told you anything here, so leave me out of it."

Sheila pretends to look hurt. I know she's not.

"I'm just trying to be helpful," she says as I lead her back to Reception and the door to the outside.

"I appreciate that," I lie. "Thank you for coming in, Sheila."

I'm the biggest idiot in the world. Montrose's going to tell me so. I'm going to deserve whatever snide remark he makes about it. I'm going to sit there and take it. The only way out will be the truth.

And I have no idea what that is.

CHAPTER TWENTY-FIVE
ADAM

Our house in the Mount Baker neighborhood of Seattle is—*was*—an apt indicator of the state of our situation. The remodeling project that had cost us more than we could afford has been on hold for a few weeks. The contractor doing the floors screwed up and installed some bullshit engineered crap when we were very, very specific about what we wanted. Sophie even more than me. I went ballistic on the guy, who barely spoke English—or at least pretended not to be as fluent as he had been when we hired him. I probably scared the crap out of him. I hope I did. At the time of my tirade, scaring him into making good on the contract was the point.

"You want me to call Homeland Security on you?" I actually asked.

Sophie gave me a look. I'd gone too far.

When Carlos left, she turned to me and let me have it.

"You know," she said, her eyes popping a little, "I get that the flooring situation isn't what we wanted, but you don't need to threaten a man's family, Adam. Sometimes I feel like I don't even know the man I married."

I didn't say so, but I considered it at the time: *Sometimes I don't even know the woman I sleep with every night.*

And now she's gone. The arguments are over. Permanently. I never had the chance to tell her that I didn't really intend to send Carlos packing for the border, that I really wasn't the hard-ass she thought I was.

I look at my watch's showy dial, bigger than a manhole cover. Helen and Frank were due at seven to return Aubrey. They are never, ever late. I drink some Maker's and wander around our unfinished house. I'm not exactly sure why I started boxing up some of her things, but that's what I find myself doing. Maybe Helen finding Sophie's old nightgown in the garage and giving it to Aubrey was the trigger. Or maybe I drank too much whiskey.

Yeah, that could be it.

I started with all of the things in the house that were gifts from my in-laws. The truth is that Frank is cheap, and Helen's taste is all in her mouth. On the coffee table was a cheap ceramic bowl that Frank insisted was some kind of treasure from their trip to Mexico. He was too stupid to remove the tag from the bottom. It was four dollars US. There were also framed photos, silver-plated, I'm sure, that Helen has given us over the years. All hold images of Sophie and Aubrey, but mostly of Sophie. Sophie as a child, on a pony at the Woodland Park Zoo. Sophie standing next to one of her paintings in high school. Her father raved that Sophie could have been the next Picasso if she hadn't become a SkyAero manager's wife and a graphic designer for Starbucks.

"They don't even make a decent cup of joe," he said.

I've kept the photos with Aubrey.

I drink a second whiskey. This time, to pace myself, I drop a ridiculously large ice cube into the glass.

When the bell rings, I see the three of them standing on the front step in view of our peephole. Helen looks like she's been browbeaten all the way from Twin Lakes. Aubrey looks excited to be home. Frank is sulking, which is his usual attitude when he thinks no one is looking. He saves his over-the-top puffer fish routine for when it counts.

I swing open the door and drop to my knees for Aubrey as she rushes to me. I lift her up, swinging her in the air the way I always do. This time I don't do it for her. Or for me, either. I do it to show Frank Flynn that no matter what he thinks or hopes, the little girl that looks like his daughter loves me best.

Wallpaper Helen speaks first, which in itself is nearly a first.

"We were thinking on the way up . . ." she says, looking around the living room, and taking in my boxing activity.

I set down Aubrey. She immediately rushes to her room to reconnect with her toys. "Yes?"

". . . that maybe," she says tentatively, "Aubrey should stay with us—you know, until things get settled."

I'm unsure what she's getting at. I want to say that things *are* settled. Sophie is dead. My life. Aubrey's life. They're changed forever. Nothing could be more settled than that.

God, I shouldn't have let them guilt me into leaving Aubrey with them Monday night.

"We have Katrina," I say. "Aubrey will be fine here. I'm here."

Frank stays uncharacteristically mute.

"Yes, but I'm home all day," Helen goes on. "Aubrey shouldn't be watched by a stranger."

I'm pretty sure Frank is using Helen as a human shield, and she's too weak—or too exhausted by him—to do anything about it. "Katrina's not a stranger," I say. "She's been with us since we brought Aubrey home from the hospital. You didn't say anything about her being a stranger when Sophie was alive. Why now?"

I know the answer, but I'm glad I asked it anyway.

"Don't talk to my wife like that!" Frank says, finally unleashing his inner prick.

"I'm sorry," Helen says, her features melting. She's embarrassed. A feeling she knows so well.

"You don't need to be sorry," Frank insists as Helen blinks hard. I expect she's about to cry again. I wonder if her tears could fill a bathtub or maybe even a swimming pool. Next he faces me. "Look, Adam, we have never really gotten along."

No shit, I think.

"And you know the reason for that, right?" he asks.

Except that he's a prick, I honestly don't. No man would be good enough for his only child.

He doesn't wait for an answer, and I take a gulp of my drink. The ice in my glass crashes against my front teeth, and I wince a little.

"Frank, please," Helen says in her more-than-ever mousey voice.

He flicks her away like lint. "Aubrey should be with an intact family," he says. "She's been through so much."

I want to laugh. So I do.

"'Intact family'? You've got to be kidding. Captive, yes. Sophie used to tell me that she thought her mom was a victim of Stockholm syndrome—that she had lost any sense of who she was because you dominated her like she was a science project."

My eyes scrape over Helen. I feel somewhat sorry for her. At the same time, watching her wriggle under Frank's thumb all these years has been revolting. Sophie wanted to liberate her mother. She loved her. Right now, I just want to jolt her like an online electroshock therapy kit.

"She called you," I say, "'my Stepford mom.' Just so you know."

Helen puts her fingers to her lips for a second, trembles a little, and then walks toward Aubrey's room down the hallway, which gleams like polished brass with that goddamn over-finished oak flooring.

"You little piece of crap," Frank says to me, keeping his voice low as if he wants to spare the others. "I won't have you insult my wife." His head is getting red. It's a barometer of anger. "You didn't need to say that. We're all on edge. We've all been dealt the hardest blow we could have ever imagined. Helen's teetering on the edge."

From what I've seen, she's lived her whole life that way.

I take a seat on one of our Stickleys—genuine, not reproductions, as Sophie insisted. I don't want to get into it with my father-in-law. If there could be a best thing about Sophie's death, it would be that I'll almost never have to see this dickhead again. If he wants to see Aubrey, he's going to have to change the way he acts. I'm sick of it.

I'm sick of *him*.

"Pour yourself a shot and sit down," I tell him. "You're going to need it."

He looks at me with a quizzical stare. He's sizing me up. He thinks I'm going to engage with him in a way that he can win. But he can't.

"Go on, Frank," I say as he looks at the bottle.

He senses something. I can feel it. I like it. He turns the red wax cap on the Maker's and pours a healthy shot. He slugs it back.

"You love Aubrey," I say.

"She's my blood," he says.

"Right. She's the last thing you have of your daughter."

He stares at me. His eyes bulging again. "What are you getting at?"

"You want to see her, right?"

"It's my right," Frank says, setting down his glass. "Grandparents have rights."

I like where this is going. Fun, I think.

"Only if they're fit," I say.

"What are you getting at, Adam? Can you just come out with it? I'm not one of your flunkies at the plant."

"I don't work in the plant, Frank," I say.

Frank doesn't even blink. "Just spit it out, man," he says.

I look at my dead wife's father with what I hope are laser beam eyes burning into his own cold, cruel ones. The ones that never looked at me with anything but disappointment, distrust. Even hate.

"If you want to see Aubrey," I say, letting each word soak in like rancid syrup on a short stack, "you'll need to be less of an asshole. To me. To Helen. Understand?"

Frank's lips tighten, and his nostrils flare.

Heart attack, maybe? This is the best moment in a day of utter misery.

"Are you threatening me?" he finally asks. "Seriously? Is that what you're doing, Adam? You don't want to do that."

I sip my drink, the cube crashing into my teeth.

"What I don't want to do is put up with any of your bullshit anymore," I say. "My wife is dead. *Your daughter* is dead. I don't need to hang out with you and Helen just to make her feel good. I loved Sophie enough to put up with you, but I don't have to anymore, Frank. I don't have to put up with you for one more second. I could tell you right now that you'll never see Aubrey again, and you know what? She's three. She'd forget about you just like she'll forget about Sophie."

I let those words hang in the air before finishing. He lets me.

"Maybe not seeing you anymore would be the best thing for her," I say.

"You're out of your mind," he says, which is a short retort from the likes of Frank Flynn.

"No," I spit back. "You're out of time, Frank. When you marry a girl, you're stuck with her family. Now that she's gone, I'm goddamn free of you. Now, get your wife and go."

Frank stands there facing me and finally gives me his best—what he came to say, I suspect.

"You killed Sophie," he says.

He thinks it will hurt me, but it doesn't. I stand my ground with a man who seemed to have only one quest in life: to diminish everyone around him. Not me. Not Sophie. Not Aubrey. Not anymore.

He can do whatever he wants with Helen. She may be brainwashed, but she can get the hell out if she wants to.

"Just keep saying that," I tell him. "Every time you piss me off, I'll erase another visit for you and Aubrey."

Helen emerges from the hall. I'm unsure how much she's actually heard. Enough, I hope.

I don't get up. I'm done pretending that I ever liked these people. That they ever gave me any reason to show any kind of respect. He is a bully. She is the soggiest of milquetoasts.

"Adam, please don't keep Aubrey away from us," Helen says.

I ignore her.

"I put some of Sophie's things in a carton by the front door," I say to neither one of them in particular. "Do me a favor and take it with you."

The house feels lighter when the door closes. I can hear Frank cursing at Helen as they go down the steps to their car, but it doesn't bother me in the least. I head down the hall to Aubrey's bedroom. She's already in bed waiting. She's like a little angel, and while I have no idea how things will turn out for her, I think that less time with the monsters that raised her mother is a very good thing.

CHAPTER TWENTY-SIX
LEE

A summer's night in Shelton is all I need to remember why this place is where I'll end my days.

My town.

My *home*.

I doubt I could ever think of Shelton as anything but that, no matter what happened here when I was a girl.

I stop for cat food at the minimart down the road from the sheriff's office.

Shannon Carson is behind the counter. She and I were high school classmates, though not close. She's been working nights as a cashier to pay for an online degree in accounting for almost two years. I congratulate her when she tells me she just finished her classes.

"This is a town of late bloomers," she says, putting Millicent's food into a plastic bag.

I can't argue that one.

"Heard about the case you're working on," she says.

I'm sure everyone has, I think.

"Yeah," I say. "Sad one."

She waits for me to elaborate, but I don't.

"Yeah," she says to fill up the dead air between us. "Nothing like that happens around here."

I can't argue that one, either. While the rest of the world changes with the times, we stay mostly the same. Mostly. The Skyline Drive-In Theater, a fixture and location for more rites of passage than could ever be counted, is still in operation, just as it was when the first cars lined up for outdoor movies in 1964. We are the Christmas Tree Capital of the World, and that's no phony creation of a too-eager chamber of commerce. Simpson owned our lumber mill when my dad worked those brutal shifts, but didn't mind. Hard work was fine with most everyone back then. When I became a deputy on patrol and then later a detective, I seldom worked a case in which I didn't know someone by name or reputation. Shelton was and always will be that kind of place. Everyone knows everyone. We hike in the Olympic foothills in T-shirts and shorts at the first hint of warm weather, clam and crab on our rocky and sometimes stinky beaches like the Skokomish people have done for centuries. We grab hold of every minute of our dappled summers, because we know that by the end of September our feet will grow webs until spring.

Newcomers with buckets of cash from Seattle jobs or real estate they've unloaded think we're quaint, if not a complete throwback to another era.

We smile at that, if only to ourselves. It's good to be all of that when the alternative is big-city life and all the problems and discontent it seems to bring with it.

We'll take small-town any day.

Back home with Millicent circling my ankles, my phone buzzes. I see it's Frank Flynn, and I cannot stomach another one of his calls. Honestly, I've never felt this way about a victim's family member. But Sophie Warner's father is the kind of man who makes the worst possible moment in his life even grimmer. It's after nine, and the late hour gives me a weak excuse not to answer. I could be asleep. Obviously I'm not. I look at my phone and wait for the tone to indicate a message has been left. It takes a while. This, I'm sure, is going to be classic Frank Flynn—not a good thing at all.

"Detective," he says, "I hope you are out somewhere building a case against my goddamn son-in-law. Helen and I were over at his house tonight. He had the nerve to threaten me. Said he'd keep Aubrey from me if I kept pushing for the truth. Well, it doesn't work that way. No one pushes Frank Flynn around with a threat. Adam's up to something. You need to get in there and question him. Put him under a hot lamp or something. Wish you could waterboard him. I wish I could beat it out of him. Don't make me do that. Do your goddamn job and shake the truth from him."

As he goes on, I can hear Helen in the background sobbing about Aubrey, repeating her name over and over.

Frank stops addressing me and speaks to his wife.

"This is bigger than Aubrey, Helen! This is about our Sophie. Pull yourself together!"

Then back to the message he's intent on leaving.

"He was behaving very strangely tonight. He didn't confess, but he said and did some things that point in the direction of his obvious guilt. He said he was glad Sophie was gone. He was. He said so. And get this, Detective: he'd put all sorts of her things in a big box and gave them to us. It was like he couldn't wait to erase her from his life. Who does that but a goddamn guilty man? I expect you to get off your ass and put a bow on this case. You know who did it. *He* did it. Call me back."

I get a beer from the fridge and drink it standing up by the kitchen sink. I'm just like my father then. He always did his best thinking in the kitchen, beer in hand, looking out the window.

It's dark outside. The neighbor's floodlights cast a bright

white glow against the picket fence that separates our yards, sending bars of light across my lawn. I hear the cat door swing open as Millicent comes back inside.

It has been a long day. The longest, really. The morgue. The encounter with the Flynns. The confrontation with Jim Coyle. The nonsense with Facebooker Sheila. The call just now. I'm feeling the pressure—my own, and others'. I can't let this be another Cathy Rinehart case. I know that when I go to sleep, I'll be thinking of her and how we've let her down by letting her killer escape justice. It happens. Maybe more often than I know.

I run the shower to make sure that the chemical smell of the morgue no longer clings to my hair and skin. I step inside and let the water pour over me. As I turn my wrist, I see the tiny hairpin-shaped scar that is the sole physical reminder of my own victimhood. It makes an appearance about this time every year as the sun slightly tans my freckled skin to reveal the thin, white tracing.

Whenever I see it, I turn away.

CHAPTER TWENTY-SEVEN
LEE

"You know you shouldn't work this case, Lee."

Zach Montrose is standing in the doorway to my office. I know what he knows the second those words come from his nicotine-stained lips, but I don't admit it. I think that I can work this case. I am indebted to Adam, of course. But it's more than that. I owe Sophie and every other girl or woman who is abducted a shot at justice. It never leaves my mind that I am the lucky one.

Personal connections are strong and powerful motivators, not distractions. That's what this is about. I see that by the look on his face.

I think of doing an end run and bringing up his medical appointment for early stages of Parkinson's, but I don't. He hasn't told me directly. A new girl in HR did. I don't want to burn her.

More than anything, I don't want to hurt him.

"Why didn't you tell me that Adam Warner was the one who found you?" he asks in a tone that's decidedly more disappointed than angry.

I probably *should* have told him. It came to me the second I knew that it was Adam's wife who had vanished. It's just that it's something I don't like to revisit in any way, shape, or form.

Montrose slides into a chair next to my desk. He's wearing a chambray shirt and faded Wranglers. Ordinarily I'd tease him about his sartorial selection. How he looks like a blueberry popsicle. It's our little game. Not today, however. Not in the moment where he's come to me with something that I should have already confided.

"How did you find out?" I ask, directly peering into his eyes.

"Ran into Belinda Stephens at Safeway," he tells me. "She should have been a cop instead of a librarian."

Or the town crier, I think.

"Belinda was always good at putting two and two together," I say.

Montrose folds his arms over his burly chest. "Am I the only one in town who didn't know? I feel kind of like an idiot here, Lee. I don't like to be made the fool."

"Not my intent," I say. "I really am sorry."

"Don't you see how this could compromise an investigation?"

"Ordinarily, yes," I say. "Sure. But it was a long time ago. He only found me. He didn't do anything. Just found me."

"Right," he says. "And that couldn't possibly give him a pass with you, right?"

"There's no pass here, Montrose. Yes, I am grateful for what he did then. Very grateful. Seriously, it is something that I don't think about. But I wouldn't give the pope a pass when it comes to a case. You, of all people, should know that. I do things by the book."

Montrose fidgets some. I know this man. He's thinking. He's a great partner, and he has my back, but he's also totally by the book. He has to be. He can't afford any more slipups, because he hit rock bottom once, and he's damn sure he's never going back there.

"Lee, like it or not, he's someone we need to consider. We don't know yet where this is going to lead."

I don't defend Adam, though part of me truly wants to. I could remind him of Axel Bakker, and he could counter that he's old and his eyesight is poor and he didn't really see anything. I could say something about Aubrey being there too, and he could say that she's only a child and didn't know what she saw.

But I don't.

"We always follow the evidence, Montrose. There's never been a time when we didn't have a bias about something or someone, but it didn't get in the way of finding the truth."

"This is a pretty big bias to overcome, Lee."

"If my father had molested a neighbor kid, do you think I wouldn't report it?"

He shakes his head. "Not the same."

"It is too," I say. "You know me. You know that I would never protect anyone who'd harmed someone. Not one inch of latitude. Seriously. You know that, right?"

Montrose thinks a moment. I know he knows I'm right. I know that he knows me. It crushes me a little that he'd bring up the past in a way that suggests I could be weak enough to hide the truth about a heinous crime.

"Yeah," he says. "I know it. It's just that I'm not the only one around here that will wonder if you're doing your best work."

"Sheriff knows me better than that too."

He gives me a shrug. "Others like to gossip. Gossip sometimes becomes a reality for some."

"I'll deal with that if it comes up, Montrose," I tell him. "Okay?"

"Okay," he says. "Something else we need to deal with."

"What's that?"

"Getting Adam Warner in here for a real talk. Like today, ideally. You want to call him, or you want me to?"

"I'll do it," I say. "No problem. Anything else?"

Before he answers, I pull out the Warner file.

"Let's get down to business," I say.

"Lab's got a backlog," I tell him. "Dr. Collier thinks it will take a while. A Mason County murder doesn't appear to be a priority."

"Should be," he says.

As I go through my list with Montrose, I feel the air lighten in the room. The tension of what transpired between us fades. We're focusing on what will move us forward.

"Let's see here," I say, running my index finger down my hastily scribbled list. "Oh yes, I have a call I'm supposed to return. Multiple calls, actually. All from Linda London."

Montrose makes a face. "Don't you do it," he says.

"Don't you worry. I'll toss her over to PIO and let them deal. Obviously," I add, "we're not giving any interviews yet."

The *yet* was important, a major lesson learned. I gave an interview to the *Olympian* early in the Cathy Rinehart case. It was a huge mistake. In the interview, I said I'd told the family that I was certain we'd solve their daughter's murder. I knew better. Never make a prediction about what you cannot truly control. That case file sits atop the otherwise perfectly ordered credenza behind me. It will never leave there until justice is served. It both mocks and haunts me every morning when I hang up my jacket or stow my purse.

We are a small staff at the Mason County Sheriff's Office. Our county is vast, with a sparse population tucked here and there among some of the most stunning Northwest scenery one could imagine. Truly postcard stuff. Whenever we can, Montrose and I work together on a major case. We separate for our own tasks, though. Like right now, he's off following up on Jim Coyle, our best bet for the case—and I'm making my "no problem" call to Adam, and returning the call of Frank Flynn, the bane of my existence. It's a measure of how much I'm dreading calling Adam that I choose to lock horns with his father-in-law first.

"I'd like a call back right away when I call," Frank barks, right out of the gate. "There's something really wrong with law enforcement that forgets the families of the victim."

"Hello, Mr. Flynn."

He's baiting me, but I ignore it.

"Your message said you had something important to tell me," I say, my pen poised to make a note of whatever it is that the victim's father feels is so urgent to add to the investigation file.

"He's wiping Sophie out of his life," he says. "He's unloading everything she held important in her life."

I don't understand. "I need to know more. Slow down."

"I will not slow down," he says. "If I slow down, then you and your lousy detective partner are going to botch the case like you did the Rinehart girl."

"What do you mean 'wiping her out of his life'?"

"Stuff," he says, almost like ejecting a wad of spit from his mouth. "Anything that mattered to her, he's removed it from the house. We were there when he was doing it. Gave back photos and other mementos. Really hurt Helen when he did that. Seriously. He couldn't wait to get rid of her things. Just like he got rid of Sophie."

"Maybe the reminders are too painful for him."

Wrong thing to say.

"*I* have a reminder," he says, his voice pulsating with bitterness. "Seeing my daughter through the window at the morgue."

That was bad. A terrible situation. One that Sophie's dad managed to make even worse by arranging to be there in the first place.

"I'm sorry," I say. "I know all of this is very painful."

I can hear Frank take in a big breath. He's locked and loaded. There is nothing I can say to this man.

"You want to know what's painful?" he says, now yelling into the phone. "Painful is knowing that some son of a bitch piece of crap that sat at your Christmas table killed your little girl. *That's* painful. I think what he did to Sophie will kill Helen. Then you'll have *another* victim on your hands."

"We have a witness, sir," I remind him. "He was on the water with your granddaughter."

Frank's not having any of it. "Witness is an old codger," he spits out. "I saw him on the news. Glasses as thick as Coke bottles."

I let him rant. Axel Bakker had his problems, but his eyesight seemed fine. Glasses or not.

"Why aren't you listening to me?" Frank asks.

Half my job is listening.

"I am," I tell him. "I promise."

"He's a piece of crap. Thinks he's God's gift. Might have hired someone. Adam's always bragging about his flunkies at the office and how he gets them to do all his work."

"I'm on this," I say, trying to close out a conversation I had no intention of having.

"You better be," Frank finally says as he comes up for one more gulp of air. "You better fucking be."

On the surface, what he's saying is troubling. Really troubling. Yet I know from experience in my own life that people handle stress and grief with different, sometimes seemingly nonsensical actions. My mother cut my hair supershort after I came home that day because she was sure that my hair was what had attracted Albert Hodge to take me in the first place. I looked like a boy for two years. Even though I went on, Mom stayed stuck in "what could have happened" mode. It took the life out of a woman who had up to that point lived in full color. Joy. Love. It was like a slow-growing cancer.

*   *   *

It's not yet noon when a text from Dr. Collier confirms most of what I already know—and something I didn't. Sophie was beaten to death with some kind of blunt instrument. She died sometime Saturday. The time spent in cold water makes it difficult, if not impossible, to say anything more precise. The killer left his DNA in her vagina. As far as the pathologist knows, the sample hasn't been run through the system yet.

Backlog at the state crime lab, she reminds me in her text. Still hoping we get a hit in a few days, though.

The tox screens, however, have come back, and while Sophie was clean of any controlled substances, reports indicate a large dose of diphenhydramine, what most people think of as Benadryl, was present in her body.

I make a note of the dosage.

Adam said that his wife had been fighting a cold, so the Benadryl doesn't come as a surprise. The tox fits Adam's narrative to a T.

But something else doesn't.

I reach for my desk phone and dial Dr. Collier.

"Hello, Detective," she says, picking up.

"Doctor, thanks for the preliminary. Still waiting on the DNA, right?"

Music plays in the background. It's cheerful. Katy Perry's early stuff, I think. "Still waiting," she says.

"I noticed that your exam reports her stomach was basically empty."

She lowers the volume on Ms. Perry. "Pretty much," she tells me. "Let me look. Hold a second."

In a moment, Dr. Collier gets back on. "That's right. Empty. Some sesame seeds in there, but nothing else. Clean as a whistle."

"When was the last time she ate something?" I ask her. "Can you tell?"

"Hard to say," she says. "These Seattle gals are always on some kind of diet or cleanse. Taking Seattle out of the picture, I'd say she hadn't eaten anything for at least twelve hours. No food. No water, either. She was a little dehydrated."

"No sandwich?" I ask, thinking of what Teresa found in the refrigerator. "No food the night before she was abducted?"

"That's what I said," she goes on. "No nothing."

I thank her, and we end the call—and I have to fight the temptation to lay my head on my desk.

Sophie didn't eat dinner the night before her murder, even though she purchased groceries in Hoodsport.

Adam said they had wine and dinner and watched a movie.

The next morning, only Adam and Aubrey ate strawberry waffles.

I rack my brain to think of a plausible explanation— maybe Sophie was ill and too sick to eat that night and that morning?—and I don't know why I'm doing it.

I'm a detective. A detective would pose these questions to the only person who could answer them. And she'd do it as quickly as she could.

CHAPTER TWENTY-EIGHT
ADAM

The funeral director at Western Hills Memorial Park seems confused. Befuddled even. He's a short, pudgy little man, and I imagine that baffled is his go-to expression. His coffee breath comes at me like the puff of a geyser.

"Your wife's parents called and wanted to come in to see about caskets," he says. "You know, to assist with the sudden expense."

"You don't need a casket for a cremation," I tell him. "Do you?"

I know the answer. I know exactly what that piece-of-shit ex-father-in-law of mine is up to. I also recognize that James Deacon of Western Hills is trying to get me to cough up as much money as possible for Sophie's funeral.

I'm not opposed to caskets for burials. I'm not a pro-cremation hard-liner, either. Lots of people in my office have preached the benefit of cremation over burying their folks. They say it's because it's better for the environment, which seriously is so Seattle. Really, it's because it's cheaper. That's Seattle too, though none of my friends out of state would believe it. They think we swim in money and live in million-dollar homes. And we do. The homes, that is. They *are* pricey. If they were anywhere else in the country, they'd go for a sliver of their grotesquely inflated value.

"Look," I tell the man, "my wife had strict opinions about her last wishes. I'm honoring those."

"Did she leave it written down somewhere?"

Coffee Breath fiddles with a brochure. This guy is annoying. His palms are sweaty, and his shirt is a size too big. I bet he has just the one blazer, because I can see two different stains on it. Egg and tomato. I'd say breakfast and lunch.

"No," I say, holding my ground and actually enjoying a little jousting with this dweeb. "She's my wife," I explain with exaggerated emphasis. "She told *me*. She didn't tell her parents because she thought they were busybody idiots, okay? Do you really want to get into the ugly of my wife's family? Because if you do, I'll tell you right now, you don't have enough time in the day to listen to me and plant all the stiffs in back."

James Deacon blinks and mutters something about being sorry or being misunderstood. I think he's just angry that he's being cut out of a fat commission on a high-priced, throwaway box.

"What about a mausoleum?" he asks, rallying. "It would be nice if there was a place you and your little girl could come every now and then to remember her. We have several—"

I cut him off. "We'll remember her just fine on our own. I'm spreading her ashes in Hood Canal, where she died. It's a place that she loved. She didn't care much for marble. In fact, when we redid our kitchen, she specifically told our contractor that marble was out of the question."

"Oh, I see," he says. "I guess you aren't going to need any upgrades for the memorial service."

There isn't going to be one, I think, so no, I guess not.

"I'm still thinking about that," I say. "It happened so fast. Not really sure what I'm going to do."

I don't want to look like a complete ass. Yet I'm pissed off at Sophie right now. I'm angry with her for a thousand and one things. Some I don't want to think about. Some I can't get out of my head. I don't feel up to celebrating her life. I know people expect me to, but grief is funny. It gets mixed up with residual feelings that don't just go away because someone is dead.

"Most people have services within a week," he says, a little hopefully.

"I'll think about it," I say, turning to leave.

"Do you want to look at some packages before you go?" he asks, opening up the brochure and smoothing it flat. "Give you an idea, sir?"

I give him a look. It's a hard glare, actually. "No, thanks. But I would like to know when the cremains will be ready."

He looks surprised. A new look for him, I think.

"We've had her on hold because of Mr. Flynn's insistence," he says, "but now that you've cleared all that up— how you want to align her interment with her expressed wishes—we'll have everything ready for pickup tomorrow."

"That's great," I say. "I'll text you my home address. You can deliver, right?"

"Most people want to send someone," he says, again doing that baffled expression he offers up a hundred times a day.

"Most people haven't lost their wives to a murderer who dumped the body in the water. Jesus, man, you are making this harder than it needs to be. You really are."

"I'm sorry," he says. "Yes, we can have Mrs. Warner's cremains delivered."

I give him a perfunctory nod.

He gives me a look of utter disgust. I don't care at all. I want him to report all of it back to Frank Flynn. I can see the big red ball of Sophie's dad's bald head going scarlet right now. Boom. Like a train crossing.

That's the only thing that's made me truly smile in a very long, very sad four days.

A young woman at the front desk catches my eye as I leave. She certainly wasn't there when I arrived. She's extremely pretty. Probably no more than twenty-three, maybe even younger. I wonder why she's working in such a morbid industry. She looks normal, like Marilyn in the old *Munsters* TV show, stuck in a funeral home with the likes of creepy James Deacon. I give her a good look. Big brown eyes. Long, curly dark hair. In another time and place I'd have asked her out without a thought about it. I'd be able to brag to my friends that I picked up a hot chick at a funeral home. It wouldn't matter how truly hot she was or what the sex was like, I'd get lots of points for the audacity of it all.

By the time I return to my car, I get the call. Just as I knew I would.

"Hi, Frank," I say, as if the call is unexpected. "What's up?"

"What's up?" he says, all puffed up, I'm sure. "I just got off the phone with Western Hills. Jesus Christ, what kind of a man are you? Denying your wife a proper burial!"

"She didn't believe in that, Frank."

"Yes," he says, "she did. In fact, we had a plot for her. It's not like you had to pay for anything, you goddamn cheap son of a bitch."

I half hope that Frank has a heart attack just now. It's a fleeting hope. Despite smoking, drinking, overeating, and having a heart the size of a peanut, Frank Flynn will probably outlive us all. A nuke could drop, and Frank could be the king of the roaches. He'd like that. Roaches wouldn't talk back. Lord of the Roaches. I like that. That face of his is still red, I'm sure. Frank doesn't like to be challenged, questioned, or contradicted. He's a control freak of the highest order. I want to tell him that Sophie was embarrassed by him more times than I could count. And I'm in finance. But I don't. I crank up the AC.

"It's not about the money, Frank," I say. "Sophie had life insurance. If I wanted to, I could build her a goddamn mausoleum on my own."

Frank is flat-out seething. I love it.

"You make me sick, Adam," he says. "You are a piece of garbage."

I hold the phone away from my ear, letting Frank rant into the open air. His words going out into space. That makes me smile, big-time. Teeny-tiny Frank's voice ricocheting around various planets, with no one to hear any of it.

After nearly a minute, I press my phone back to my ear. He's still going strong. In fact, *very* strong.

"You fucking asshole," he spits into the phone. "You don't even know what kind of a war you've started, do you?"

I move the phone away from my ear again. I see a man waiting for an Uber and I feel like offering a ride so he and I can have a good laugh when and if Frank ever shuts the hell up.

"Frank," I cut in, "you are really irritating me right now. This call is about done."

"*I* called *you*," he says. "*I* decide when it's over."

That's a good one, I think. Like Sophie's dad has some magical power that can force someone—other than poor old doormat Helen—to listen to his unremitting rants.

"I need to go, Frank," I say, without waiting for a response. I'm just plowing on. "Thanks for the call. Give Helen my love. How she puts up with you, I'll never know."

With that, I turn off my ex-father-in-law. Click, and he's gone.

I consider blocking him from my contacts list, but he'll find a way to wriggle into my life and blame me. Annoy me. He has no idea how much I loved his daughter and how much she despised him. How much I hate him too. People believe what they want to believe. My mom always said that. My mom was one very smart woman.

I'm about to set the phone down when I see I have a voice mail. Turns out it's from Lee. I can't say why, but seeing this snuffs out the little high I'd been riding after hanging up on Frank.

CHAPTER TWENTY-NINE
CONNOR

"You had quite an ordeal," Micah tells me when I let myself in the back door of the restaurant early Wednesday afternoon. He's in the big walk-in pantry going over inventory before dinner service.

"It was all right," I say, taking off my jacket and looking over the night's fresh sheet. "The scallops always go fast," I say.

Micah doesn't care about shellfish at the moment.

"An abduction and murder," he goes on, pulling me into the nightmare of my three-day vacation. "That's got to make for a memorable Memorial weekend."

My chest constricts, but I stay silent. How the hell would he know anything about it?

"The woman from Mount Baker," he carries on. "Happened up in Lilliwaup, where you said you were going. KING had a copter out. And there was your car!"

I don't want to think about the weekend, but the news coverage makes it all but certain that I'll have no choice in the matter.

"We missed most of the excitement," I lie. "If you can call that kind of thing exciting."

"Sarah's all over it," Micah says, looking up from his tablet. "She's a big crime buff. She says she's sure the husband must have done it."

Sarah is Chef's wife. And he's right. She's a huge crime buff. She's never without her nose in a thriller of some sort when she's waiting around the Blue Door for her husband to turn things over to the staff so she can go home.

"The husband probably *did*. I wouldn't know. We didn't see anything."

"Really? Nothing?" he asks, setting down his iPad and sending a shopping list to the printer. I hear the sound of the printer running in the office, and I go over to pull the paper for him.

"Here," I say, handing it over.

"Thanks, Connor," he says. "Sarah will be very disappointed. She was hoping that you'd have some inside scoop on this Warner dude. Poor wife of his. Beaten and tossed like trash into the water. What a piece of garbage he is."

"Anyone who would do that is shit," I say.

"Yeah," he goes on. "Sarah's going to pick your brain, I bet."

"Nothing to pick," I say. "We weren't even there when it happened."

I finish prepping the tables. It's a small restaurant with a fussy, well-heeled Seattle clientele, mostly in the tech sector. Micah has aspirations for a lot more than the Blue Door, and his food really warrants it. I never want to be the one who lets him down. I'm the oldest waiter here and the one with the most experience. I serve the best tables. I make the most in tips. *By far.* It's a great partnership. Suddenly as I fold a white napkin, the wound on my finger opens and oozes blood. It's like a red warning sign. A Rorschach splatter.

Flashing at me. The events of the weekend rush at me, and I feel uneasy. I don't know exactly why. I felt fine when I arrived at the restaurant, but now I am shaky and upset. It's like my brain is trying to reboot, and it just can't get there.

I run my wound under the tap, sending pink down the drain.

Down the drain.

The truth is I don't know where that cut came from. Was it from work? Was it somewhere else?

I've never left a service in my life. I fight it. I try really hard to pull myself together. Yet I can't imagine how I'm going to get through an evening with nothing but smiles and charm when inside I feel like I don't know myself anymore. I don't know what I've done. Not at all. Deep down, I feel I must have done something.

What happened at the cabins? If I did something so terrible, was it terrible enough that I could really have no memory of it?

Like most of the car accident in Huntington Beach?
Was it something like that?

I find Micah. He's talking with Lynnette, our front-of-the-house. She's my age. Stunning. Long black hair that she wears swept back and a black dress slit up to there to show off her perfectly shaped thighs. I've seen Micah and Lynnette together—*closely* together—many times. I've wondered who was using who. That isn't on my mind at the moment.

"Chef," I say, "man, I hate to do this to you. I feel sick. Like food poisoning or something. Maybe oysters from the canal. I don't know. Just came on like a Mack truck. I can't be here."

"That's strange, Connor," Lynnette says, somewhat suspiciously. "Food poisoning happens pretty fast. When did you eat the oysters?"

"Yesterday," I say.

Sweat pours down my temples. My armpits stain my white shirt too. I look bad. Really bad. To Lynnette's point, it doesn't goddamn matter when I ate the oysters at all. I'm sick. *Look at me.* I'm about to hurl. I need to get out of there. Micah sees my very real symptoms. He reaches over to pat me on the shoulder but thinks better of it. I wonder if he thinks I have the flu. He's smarter than Lynnette, for sure.

"Dude," he says, "get out of here. Go home. Let me know how you're doing."

"I'm really sorry, Chef," I say, backing away to get my jacket from the peg by the back door.

"No problem," Micah says. "We'll get by."

As I get ready to leave, I hear him tell Lynnette something about what happened up at the cabins in Lilliwaup. I'm sure she's all over it. She loves a little drama, and she manages to *make* a little drama out of very little things.

"Wow, maybe he's having a flashback or something," she tells Micah as she leans in close enough to smell his neck. What, she thinks I can't hear her? Or just doesn't care. When she bends a little closer, the slit of her dress opens like a flower, exposing more leg. She might like a little drama, but I know our boss likes a little leg. A perfect match, those two.

"No," Micah tells her. I give a quick nod good-bye. "Connor and Kristen weren't even there when it happened. They were out hiking or something. If I know those two at all, they missed everything."

I wait for my bus as the sounds of early evening dim the space around me. The air is cool and I shake a little. I need to get home. I stand among a dozen other people thinking the same thing, though for reasons I'm sure are absolutely different from mine. Be with the family. Feed the cat. Do something. I'm surely alone in what I need to figure out. I text Kristen that I got sick and left work for home. She doesn't answer. That's fine. I don't know what more I can say except that I'm feeling sorry for something I don't think I did. But I'm not certain.

God, please help me.

I promise never to ask again.

Never for myself anyway.

CHAPTER THIRTY
LEE

Adam is in Reception, and I feel sick. Nerves, I think. If I told Montrose how I felt, he'd go to the sheriff and get me bounced off the case. I doubt I could argue my way back in, either. I glance at the plum tree outside my window. It reminds me of the branches that covered me when Adam found me.

"Ready?" Montrose says as he swings by, notepad and coffee cup in hand.

"Yep," I say, although I'm not really sure I am.

"You sure you can do this, Lee?"

"Don't ask again," I say. "I would tell you if I had any doubts, Montrose. You have to know that by now."

"I'm not a fan of your old buddy, you know," he says. "And I like Coyle for this. But this will be fun anyway. And something we need to do."

He offers a smile and quick nod. Montrose goes to the interview room, and I make my way to Reception.

Adam brightens and gets up when he sees me. He's wear-

ing two-hundred-dollar jeans and a crisp button-down shirt.
I can't tell if it is white or the palest shade of blue.

"Hey, Lee," he says, putting down a copy of the *Shelton-Mason County Journal*.

"Old home week," I say, studying the front page.

"Yeah," he says. "Just seeing if I recognize any names."
He follows me.

"Did you?" I ask, glancing back.

He shakes his head. "Not really. Maybe a couple. Shelton's not the same as it was."

"Actually, you'd be surprised how little it's really changed," I say.

Our chitchat relaxes me. It appears to relax Adam too.
That's good. His face falls a little when he sees Montrose.

"Hey, Adam," Montrose says.

"Detective." He looks over at me. "I thought I was just going to be talking to you."

"It's not a talk," Montrose says. "This is an interview.
About your wife's murder."

Adam's face goes a little pink. "I know that, Detective. I just didn't know that there was going to be two of you." He looks at me once more. "Kind of feel ambushed here, Lee."

"Not the intent," I tell him. "Just procedure. We're a small team here, but when we can, we prefer two detectives in the room. This will be fine. Take a seat, okay?"

Adam sits down across from us. I notice the beginnings of a little underarm sweat staining his formerly pristine shirt.
He's nervous. That's fine. I'd be nervous too if I were hauled into the sheriff's office to talk about the murder of someone close to me. Not because I'd be guilty, but because being so close to evil is pretty daunting stuff.

"We're going to record this, Adam," Montrose says.
"Again, procedure."

Adam keeps his eyes fixed in my direction.

"Should I have a lawyer here, Lee?"

Montrose responds right away. "Do you think you need one?"

"You are not a suspect," I say, which is how I feel. Unlike Montrose. He hasn't written Adam off his list yet. I'm hoping that this interview ties up the loose ends we collected while interviewing others associated with the case.

Adam appears to relax in his chair. Montrose presses the "On" button on the recorder.

"Okay," I begin, "we're going to cover a few things that need clarification, Adam. Some of these things might seem inconsequential to you or even hard to remember, but do your best. Okay?"

I realize that I just gave Adam an out by saying he might not remember. Montrose's going to ream me on that later. If he caught it.

"We've been going over some witness statements," I say.

"Right," Montrose jumps in. "You know we've been out interviewing people, and we have some statements that are in conflict with your account of what happened."

"Really?" Adam says, blinking. "That surprises me. I was kind of a mess when we talked, but I thought I'd covered everything as accurately as possible."

"Let's start with the 911 call made by Mr. Bakker," I say.

"Okay, what about it?"

"He says you told him that your cell phone didn't get reception there."

"Yeah. That's right."

Montrose leans forward a little. "Then how come you were able to phone Sophie's parents to get them there?"

"Cell service wasn't great," Adam says, "but sometimes it worked. I guess it worked then."

"All right," I say. "Can you tell us what Sophie was wearing when you last saw her?"

He looks down at the table, then back at me. "Yeah," he

says. "She was wearing a white beach cover-up over her bathing suit. I think she was planning on laying out in the sun or maybe swimming. Water gets warm in that little cove."

"Did she have on anything else?" I ask.

"Sun hat," he says. "Got it in Santa Barbara the summer before."

"Let's revisit your description of your wife's attacker," Montrose says.

Adam thinks a beat. "I never saw the bastard's face. So if you want me to ID a photo or something, that's not going to work. It happened so fast, it was a blur."

"We understand," I say, though I know Montrose doesn't. "Can you remember anything more about him? Hair color? What he was wearing?"

"He came at Sophie from behind. She screamed, and I started rowing. I saw that it was a man. Bigger than her."

"Okay. Fine. What about his clothing? A hat?" I ask.

Adam looks upward. "I don't remember a hat. He was wearing a red jacket and khakis, I think. I can't swear to that, but that's what comes to mind. You try remembering something when you're in the middle of something like that. It's not easy."

No, I think, it isn't. But *I* did. I remembered every detail of what Albert Hodge was wearing when I was abducted. Every single thing. How he smelled. The scar on his abdomen from an appendix surgery. The watch that he wore was a Casio digital; the face was white, the band, black leather. He wore a flannel shirt and Levi's 501s. His jeans smelled of motor oil.

We move on to the food that Teresa Dibley found in the refrigerator. It was at odds with his story that they'd eaten a late supper.

"You said Sophie bought sandwiches for dinner that night," I say.

"Yeah," he says, "at the local store just before you get to the cabin."

"And you ate them?"

"Sophie wasn't that hungry," Adam says. "She was fighting a cold. But, yes, we ate. Not much."

I don't tell him that Sophie's stomach was empty.

And in that moment it seems like he's reading my mind. I wonder if I'm telegraphing excuses to him because I know he didn't hurt his wife, despite my partner's assessment.

"You know," he says, "I don't think she ate after all. She bought sandwiches, and Aubrey and I ate some of one."

That makes sense, I think. There were two untouched and one that was half eaten in the refrigerator.

"The next morning you made waffles," Montrose jumps in. "But Sophie didn't have any? Is that right?"

Adam shifts in his chair. The sweat blooms under his arms have dried. He's calm. Cool. "Yeah. She wasn't a morning eater. More a cup-of-coffee kind of girl."

"But she was drinking wine," Montrose says. "Before eleven?"

"We were on vacation," Adam answers. "She called it wine o'clock, and sometimes it was pretty much all day."

"Did you buy the sandwiches or did Sophie?" Montrose asks.

"She did," Adam says, looking a little puzzled now. "What's the big deal about the sandwiches?"

"Nothing," I say. "Just pinning down the time line."

"Do you think someone stalked her at the IGA?" Adam asks out of the blue.

Montrose looks at me, then over to Adam. "No, do you?"

"Not really," Adam answers. "She mentioned that the guy behind the meat counter checked her out, but that was Sophie. She not only got a lot of looks, she never missed a chance to tell me about them. I know that sounds bad, talking about her that way. But she was proud of the attention. I was too. It just was the way things were."

"Did the man at the meat counter intimidate her or make her feel uncomfortable?" I ask.

"No, not really," he says. "Like I said, she liked the attention. Don't you?"

I ignore his remark. It's odd. It feels combative and unkind. Not like Adam at all. Suddenly the room goes quiet, and Adam asks for a bathroom break. Montrose directs him to the men's room down the hall.

CHAPTER THIRTY-ONE
ADAM

The urinal at the sheriff's office has a deodorant cake the size of a Frisbee. I stand there doing my thing and wonder where the interview is really going. I can't be sure, but I sense that Detective Montrose is pushing me as a suspect, and Lee is doing her best to hold him at bay. She knows me. He doesn't. And as far as who ate what the night before—who gives a crap? I couldn't even remember my phone number when the cops on the scene asked for it. Traumatized. Big-time.

I zip my fly and flush.

At the mirror as I wash my hands, I see myself the way others likely do. At least I think so. I'm not *GQ*, but I'm not *Farm Quarterly*, either. I'm going to hit forty soon, and I'm told that's when a man is at his peak in terms of power and sex appeal. I could lose the glasses, I guess. Though that might make me look older. Older is not what I'll need if I'm going to duke it out for another run up the ladder.

I replay what I told the detectives that day and what I'm saying now. I have no reason to change my story—things happened as they happened—but somehow the pleaser in me emerges, and I find myself trying to fill any tiny gaps just to make things smoother. I've done that at SkyAero. Carrie asked me to run a report and then soften the figures so that she'd look like she was achieving her target. It wasn't a big deal to lie for her. In fact, I didn't even think of it as a lie. I felt I was only making what was supposed to happen occur at a more accelerated rate. I'm all about moving quickly to get the job done.

I can tell by the way Lee looks at me that she's attracted to me. It might be because of what happened at the end of Tamarack Lane. Or maybe it was before that. She had a crush on me, though she was a kid, and I didn't really see it at the time. She's pretty enough. Nice body. I like her red hair. Not fire-engine anymore. Just nice. She's come into her own. I like what I see, but I want to reel it back inside. Sophie's dead. She was murdered. I don't know why I'm thinking of other women.

Montrose pokes his head into the bathroom.

"You done?"

"Yeah," I say. "Just washing up."

I wonder if he'd knock on a stall door to roust me.

"Great," he says. "We're ready to start back up."

The detective with the smoker's breath reminds me of my first boss. He was such a controlling prick. Always checking up on his team members to make sure we were doing what he asked. That pretty much amounted to doing *his* work along with our own. Detective Montrose is probably pissed off that he's teamed up with a younger, less experienced partner. A woman too. I bet that really frosts him. When he looks in the mirror in his run-down Shelton house, I bet he knows what every man his age knows.

He's maxed out on where he's going.

I go for the door. I'm looking good. I can do this. Despite some huge setbacks, and a reset button that has been inexplicably pushed on my life, I'm the opposite of Montrose and his ilk. I'm only starting over.

CHAPTER THIRTY-TWO
LEE

With Adam back in the interview room, Montrose and I have silently agreed to a cease-fire. He's sure about Adam, whom he now considers a class-A liar. I don't see that at all. I do know, however, that what we are about to discuss will almost certainly change one of our opinions.

We're about to get very personal. A man confronted with accusations of adultery will often lie. Frank Flynn is pretty much insane in his hatred of Adam, so strike him and his tale. Janna Fong told me what she believed, but she didn't have an ax to grind. Not that I could tell. She was on Team Sophie, but her now-dead best friend hadn't given her any assault weapons for the assassination of her husband.

"Adam," I say, without preamble, "were you having an affair?"

He shakes his head. "Seriously?"

This is hard, but it needs to be done. "It might be important," I tell him.

He lets out a disgusted sigh. "It's none of your goddamn business," he says, digging in.

"It has obvious relevance," Montrose says, a little gleefully. "What's the story?"

Adam looks at the wall, his demeanor suddenly changing from defiant to embarrassed. He folds his arms over his chest. That quickly, there is a sheen to his forehead.

"Look," he says, "I'm not proud of it. But yeah. All right. I had a thing with a coworker. It was meaningless. Work-related."

That stops me. I wonder what kind of place SkyAero is if having an affair is considered work-related.

"Who was it?" I ask.

"My boss. Carrie LaCroix."

"When was it?" Montrose asks.

"A few years ago," Adams says.

"A few years ago," Montrose repeats.

"That's what I said."

"Did Sophie know about your affair?"

"It wasn't an affair. So no, Sophie didn't. She didn't know because it was nothing to me. Just something to do. Maybe advance my career. I don't know why in the hell I slept with that woman, but she offered, and I said yes."

"She offered," Montrose says, his tone on the edge of sarcasm.

Adam narrows his gaze at Montrose. "Yeah," he says. "Probably hard for you to understand that concept, but, yes, she was into me, and I took it."

"And Sophie didn't know?" I repeat.

"We never talked about it. I cheated on my wife. I'll admit to that. I did. So put a big fat checkmark after my name. Lots of guys do. And if you're trying to say that I had something to do with Sophie's disappearance because of that, you would be barking up one more wrong tree."

Adam gets up. His eyes stay pointed at me.

"I really expected more of you, Lee," he says, shaking his head. "I never thought for one second out of all the people in the world that you'd shit on me. Jesus. Sometimes you can't even trust your own instincts about people."

"I'm just doing my job, Adam," I say, a little afraid my voice will crack. Thankfully it doesn't.

He gives me one more look. "If your job is to piss on people whose lives are ruined by a random act of violence, they should give you an award."

"We have more questions," Montrose says, now pulling himself back into the show.

"Take your questions and shove 'em up your ass, Detective," he says. "I'm done."

A few minutes later, Montrose joins me in my office. My eyes land on his hands. His tremors are almost always more pronounced later in the day. He catches my gaze and shoves them immediately into his pockets. I pretend not to notice.

"Are you all right?" he asks.

"Yes," I say. "I mean, no, not really."

"He's a jerk. I know you think he's great for something he did for you years ago. But I also understand that guy could benefit from a personality transplant. He's an egomaniacal loser. That's the worst combination."

"I'll give you that," I say. "But he's also right about something. He didn't kill his wife."

"We don't know that."

I point to my computer screen. It's a preliminary report from the lab. It came in while we were prying into Adam's personal affairs.

Montrose leans in to get a good look, but the type is too small.

I look up at him. "The semen found in Sophie's body wasn't Adam's."

He is clearly stunned.

"How do you know that?"

"Blood work from the sample we took. He's not a secretor. Sophie's assailant, however, was."

Montrose tries to read the screen, but he gives up. He really needs new glasses, but he's too thrifty to pay the co-pay.

"That doesn't make any sense," he says. "Then whose is it?"

"Don't know yet," I say. "Running that now."

"So he's only guilty of being a jerk," Montrose says.

"I guess so."

The jerk that pulled me out from under a web of plum tree branches will probably never talk to me again. It has been a day for the ages. I'm ready to get a bottle of wine and go home to my cat.

God, I have such a full life. Ridiculously full.

And I follow through: I get a good bottle of chardonnay from the top shelf at the Safeway on Franklin. It's not a celebration. I just think a better bottle will help more than my usual bottom-shelf twist-top. When I arrive home, Millicent is there to greet me at the door.

Yes, ridiculously full.

I sit there in my kitchen drinking—from a glass, at least—and staring at my phone. Finally I do what I know I should never do.

I text Adam.

I'm sorry about today.

I keep my eye on my phone while stroking my cat and wish that I could do the day over. I *am* sorry. I was doing the right thing. But that doesn't make it feel right.

No reply comes from him.

CHAPTER THIRTY-THREE
ADAM

Seeing Lee at her office with that doofus partner did what seeing her always does to me.

It made me think about the day she went missing.

Kip and I were in homeroom when the principal's secretary came to the slit of a window in our classroom door and motioned for Mr. Saperstein. It was Twentieth-Century History, and I was glad for the break from the teacher's monotone recitation of the New Deal. I called it the Big Deal just to get under his skin a little when he called on me.

Mr. Saperstein, with his wholly ridiculous goatee and horn-rimmed specs, shut the door and went over to Kip. His eyes bugged out from behind his glasses, and he leaned in very close to Kip's ear.

"You're needed at home," he said, his voice charged with emotion.

Kip looked confused. "What's up?"

"We can't talk about it here," he said.

"Is it my mom?"

"We can't talk," the teacher repeated. "Please gather your things and go."

Then Mr. Saperstein looked at me. "Adam, I'm excusing you too."

Ordinarily, I would have been elated, but I knew that this was not a chance to hang out and have a good time with my best bud. Mr. Saperstein thought that Kip would need some moral support.

It had to be bad.

I thought that maybe one of his folks had dropped dead. Or maybe the house burned down.

That something had happened to his sister, Lee, was the furthest thing from my mind.

Mason County Sheriff Jack Masters was at the Huse-manns' house when Kip and I got there. In fact, there were four cop cars in total. Right then we both knew two things: There had been no fire. And since there were no ambulances in the queue, it was likely that no one had had a heart attack.

It was something else.

Sheriff Masters was older—though I was a teen and thought that anyone over fifty was ancient—and well known to everyone in Shelton. He'd been around forever. He'd come to our classrooms to talk about the perils of drug use when we were in second grade. He came in fifth grade to share insights about "stranger danger" and then in seventh to remind us again about the perils of drug use. He had gray hair even then and a belly that indicated that Mrs. Masters knew how to cook—or that he couldn't pass by a drive-through window without braking. He was decent, though. When we were in high school and did the kinds of things everyone does, Sheriff Masters lectured us but also gave us rides home.

"Drink like this again," he told me one time, "and we'll need to take it up with your folks."

When we were caught speeding, Sheriff Masters gave us a warning. "Look," he said, "you're smarter than this. Cars can careen out of control. You don't want to be the teen missing from graduation because you're dead or in jail. No more, okay?"

Mr. and Mrs. Husemann were in the living room when we came in. It was apparent right away that only Lee was missing from the family. Mrs. Husemann bolted for Kip and held him. I remember feeling so sad and awkward, and I lingered behind him while his mom cried harder than any woman I'd ever heard in my life.

"Lee's missing. She didn't get to school. She's vanished."

"Missing?" Kip asked.

Missing, I thought. *Wow.*

Mrs. Husemann was a pretty lady with auburn hair that was obviously her pride. She wore it long—longer than most moms did. It was a mess that morning. Her eyes were red. My mom always said that Mrs. Husemann was "put together," but this morning I could see that she was completely undone.

Mr. Husemann was the strong, silent type, like my own dad. Maybe like all men back then. I could see that while he hadn't been crying, he was on the edge of falling apart. His mighty, stacked-brick shoulders heaved a little when he spoke to the sheriff.

"She'd never run away, Jack," he said.

"I just have to consider everything," Sheriff Masters said. "I know your girl. She's a good kid." He acknowledged us with a quick nod. "Kip, do you know of anything that might have happened?"

Kip kept his attention on his folks. "Like what?" he asked. "Dad's right. Lee's not a runaway."

"Right," he said. "Okay. Has she said anything to you that might help us find her? Someone bothering her? A place she might hide out if she was upset about something? Maybe upset about school or a boy or something?"

Kip shook his head. "Lee's not like that. She's good. She's happy."

Sheriff Masters looked in my direction. "You have any ideas?"

"No," I said. "But maybe we should look for her?"

"We got that handled, son," he said.

"We need to do something," Kip shot back.

That afternoon the word was out that we were searching for Lee. She'd been missing for a few hours. In a small town like Shelton, I'm pretty sure that everyone knew by noon. No Internet. Few mobile phones. Just the old-fashioned way of getting the word out: Moms called other moms, dads spread the word from barstools or at the mill. Kids congregated in the hallways of the high school. Everyone speculated about what might have happened.

The Shelton High School basketball team—Kip and I were teammates—joined in the effort to find Lee, with one of the deputies providing us some basic instructions of how to conduct a search. He didn't really give us a protocol, and I doubt any of us would have followed it anyway. An inch-by-inch grid was the way they might look for evidence, and that's fine. We were looking for our buddy's kid sister.

Kip and I were paired up.

"She's dead," he said to me as we scoured the neighborhood.

"You don't know that."

We went from house to house along Tamarack Lane. It was almost like a parade, in that there were people sitting outside watching us, urging us, offering to join in.

"I know my sister," Kip said. "She's not a flake."

"No. She's not."

"So someone took her and killed her."

"Maybe he only raped her," I said.

As if rape were ever an "only" anything.

Kip was stoic about everything that was happening; oddly matter-of-fact about it. It was pretty much how he was about everything. I knew it then and I knew it later when he went to Afghanistan.

"My parents will never get over it," he said.

"Sure they will," I said. "We'll find her and bring her home."

"No they won't. Not if she's raped."

His words hung in the cooling air. It was a strange response, but I understood because I knew his family. They were very conservative. I'm sure that having a daughter who was raped would be more than difficult for them. I didn't let it pass through my mind that they would rather have her dead than living with the lasting impact of a sexual assault.

Or living with the label of victim.

"She was raped, you know."

"Must have asked for it."

"Some of these girls these days . . ."

That she was a sixth grader would be lost to time. Some drunk somewhere would twist it into her fault—the way people do when they try to keep random evil at bay by affixing blame. It is always easier to sleep at night if the monsters outside your house only knock when you give them cause.

Tamarack Lane is a dead end. Literally. And while there is a "No Dumping" sign posted there, people continue to leave yard debris, grass clippings, and the occasional discarded household item. That evening Kip and I poked through the discards there in search of his sister. Well, Kip poked. I had my mental grid set up and was working systematically through it. It was beginning to get dark, and Kip said that we should knock off, go get a couple of flashlights and try the park.

The park had already been searched by another pair by now, I knew, and I was only about halfway through my grid here. Kip was antsy, however. He couldn't focus. Which made sense, when I thought about it. If he focused and succeeded in finding his sister in this tangle of blackberry vines, yard waste, and trash, he might never recover from what he found.

I probably wouldn't, either, but I was going to finish my grid.

"You go," I said. "Get the flashlights, and I'll finish here and meet you by the swing sets at the park."

"Thanks, man," he said, his voice rough. I wondered what he was thanking me for until I caught a shimmer of a tear on his face as he turned away. I knew then that Kip was relieved to be getting the flashlights on his own because he was beginning to fall apart and didn't want me to see.

I pretended I hadn't.

"All right, bud," I said. "See you in a few."

CHAPTER THIRTY-FOUR
LEE

I could hear twigs snap, but I couldn't scream. Someone was near. Was it my attacker, back to fulfill a promise interrupted by someone who'd seen his car? His words played over and over like Kip's favorite CD.

"Don't say a word and don't move a muscle. I'll know if you do. I'll be back when it's dark, and then I'll take you home."

The movement of someone coming. Was it someone sent to find me? Lying there in the dark, under a shield of tree branches that the man in the blue-and-red flannel shirt had used to conceal me, I could hear someone call my name.

"Lee!" the voice came.

My attacker had told me to stay quiet. To wait for his return. To say a word, to call for help, would mean he'd find me again. Kill me. Kill my family.

I believed him.

So stupid, I know now.

Though I was frozen there, I wanted to live.

I heard my name a second time. I tried calling out, but nothing could move past the tape that sealed my lips.

"Lee!" came the voice once more.

It was familiar.

It was Adam Warner.

When I think about the moment when he leaned into the dark of the branches covering me, I cannot help but find tears in my eyes. It's like the moment in a movie when the lovers meet on the top of the Empire State Building or when they find out it was the other who had been emailing them the whole time. Adam and I weren't lovers, of course. But it was that kind of emotion that burbles to the surface in a way that I could never fully comprehend.

I was shivering and rocking back and forth to move the branches that were meticulously placed over me.

"Oh, God!" Adam said, dropping to his knees and uncovering me.

It was Adam, of course. But to me it was an angel as he gently pulled off the tape from my mouth. He was crying. We both were. I didn't care that he was seeing me naked. I only cared that he'd found me.

"I was so stupid," I said.

His gaze never traveled down my body.

"You're going to be okay," he told me.

Promised me.

He undid the silver tape from my bruised and bloodied wrists and then my ankles. His hands were shaking as he did that and repeated over and over, "You are going to be okay, Lee. You're going to be fine."

My lips hurt from the tape.

"Promise?" I asked, though really it wasn't a request, but a plea.

He looked right into my eyes. "Would I lie to you?"

I shook my head.

"No," he told me. "Never."

Adam put his jacket on me and when he held me, I felt the warmth of his sweaty chest. He was breathing hard. Sharp puffs of breath brushed against the rawness of my face. For a flash it made me think of the man who took me. Only for a second. I didn't ever want to think about him again. Or what he did to me, first in the car, and then in the vacant lot where people discard things they don't want anymore.

I was alive. Adam found me.

I drink the rest of my glass of wine. I feel as if I'd been transported back to a moment that sometimes feels as foreign as a new experience can feel. It's as if I'd been remembering a story that someone else told me—something they heard from a third party. Like the old game of telephone. I'm not sure if what I remember is really how it happened or if I was made to remember only the good parts: Adam finding me. Then my brother coming with a flashlight and dropping it on the ground as he took me from his best friend's outstretched arms and carried me home.

Millicent purrs.

"He told me that everything would be okay," I tell my cat.

She looks up in the way that felines do. It's barely an acknowledgment that I've spoken to her. I put meaning into it, of course.

"I'm okay," I say.

Millicent shifts in my lap and drops to the floor.

"Thanks," I say as she pads toward the cat door and disappears.

Albert Hodge was never tried for his assault against me. He was never tried for the murder of the ten-year-old from Chehalis he attacked before me. Instead, he did what I came to wish more purveyors of evil would do. Hodge took his own life as the police pounded on the door of his Terry Travel Trailer. Inside, they found underwear belonging to me and his only other known victim. I was happy when I heard the news. Again, as though it had been something that happened to someone else and not me. I was spared reliving it all by sitting in the witness box in the Mason County courthouse. While the truth was different, of course, both my parents insisted that our story be that I'd been physically assaulted. Not *sexually*. I had lied about the kittens because I'd felt so full of shame to have been stupid enough to volunteer to get into his vehicle. It's easy to compound a lie with another. Each lie, a brick in the wall of my own protection.

"She's very lucky," Sheriff Masters said in an interview with the paper. "We got to her in time to save her from the worst kind of abuse."

Everything returned to normal after that. I almost forgot about it. Really I did. I tried to anyway. Only one time did Adam and I even broach the subject, and that was at my brother's funeral. We were standing in the back of the church where my folks had put together a display of Kip's life. There was a picture of Adam, of course. He and Kip stood together, arms slung over each other's shoulders. It looked to be at about the same time as the incident.

"I remember that shirt," I said while we stood there.

It was the same one he was wearing when he found me.

"Yeah," he said. "I thought it was so cool. My first concert: Metallica."

"You were wearing it the day you found me," I said, still looking at the photos.

He didn't say anything for a while as he sifted through the images.

"Right," he finally said. "I remember."

We had never talked about it. I knew that it wasn't the right time or place, but I still wanted to say something.

"Thank you," I told him. "For finding me."

He pointed to Kip's photo. "You were everything to him, Lee. He loved you so much."

That was like Adam. He always knew the right thing to say. He understood how to shift a conversation to a place that moved the content from the maudlin to true compassion.

CHAPTER THIRTY-FIVE
ADAM

Lee and I had a bond that was invisible but titanium strong. Finding Kip's kid sister after she went missing was the greatest thing I'd ever done, yet I didn't feel the need to make an issue out of it. I worked the search like I do everything. I made a mental grid of where we'd gone, then kept working the grid and did what I could to keep Kip from cracking into a million pieces. It's what I do in the office today. Seriously. The team I lead is full of people who don't know how to dot the i's or cross the t's. The sheriff's office gave me an award, but I never put it up anywhere. Felt a little silly to be rewarded for doing what anyone else would have done.

Anyone just lucky or born smart enough to be a hero.

Lee and I never really talked about what happened after I transferred her to Kip's arms. I think there were plenty of times when she wanted to say something, but I didn't see the need or the reason to dredge it up. She'd catch me alone and start to say something, but I'd find a way to deflect it. Just before Kip's funeral she mentioned something about how

I'd saved her life and whatnot, but as always, I didn't feel right about making a big deal of it.

"No thanks needed," I told her firmly.

I should have been more gracious.

She was a wreck all day as she shepherded her parents through what I'm sure was in the top two of the most difficult days of their lives. I could see her breaking apart in front of me, and it made me feel weird, awkward.

"You saved my life," she repeated. "I owe you."

I deflected it, as always. "You don't owe me anything."

She tugged at me a little. "You don't get to decide."

I looked at her with empathy but held firm. "I'm afraid I do."

"You are a hero," she said.

We stood there in front of a bunch of photos: a display of Kip's life from babyhood to fighting for his country on the scorching sands of Afghanistan.

"That's a real hero," I said.

Lee nodded.

"I thought of going into the army like Kip," she said.

"That's cool," I told her. "He'd like that."

"Right," she said, regaining her ebbing composure. "I decided against it. So much work needs to be done here at home too."

"No argument there," I said.

"I'm going to be a cop," she said. "A detective. Someday I'm going to stop men like Albert Hodge."

I put my hand on her shoulder. She was trembling a little, but she was fighting hard to maintain.

"I think that's a great idea."

Before she could speak, I put a lid on the conversation.

"Let's go check in on your folks."

I could count the times I returned to Shelton after Kip's funeral on a single hand. I didn't go to any class reunions or anything like that. I wanted to shake the sawdust off my clothes for good. I wanted a better, bigger life than my father had. And yet, it was still a part of who I was. Who I used to be anyway. Every now and then I'd check the *Shelton-Mason County Journal*'s web page to see what was happening in the place I'd called home until college gave me the excuse and means to escape. I read about DUIs, funerals, levies that failed.

It both surprised me and made me very happy to see that Lee Husemann had been hired on as a Mason County sheriff's deputy, then later that she made detective. Her picture was online, and I looked at it on my SkyAero laptop, taking it in for the longest time. I could still see traces of the girl I knew, but Lee was all grown up now. She looked pretty, which I guess she always was, but she'd been a kid when I last really paid attention to her. She stood there with a couple of other new hires, looking confident. She wore her red hair a little like her mother did, which brought a smile to my face. I thought of reaching out to her through Facebook. I even found her profile. But I didn't message her. Just as she was a reminder of the place I left, I was sure I was a very real reminder of the worst thing that had ever happened to her.

CHAPTER THIRTY-SIX
ADAM

Carrie looks at me with smoky, sad eyes—rainy campfire eyes. Without saying a word, she ushers me into her office and shuts the door. For a second it feels like old times, but it isn't. Carrie is seven years older than I am, a sturdy brunette with nice teeth and a habit of touching my knee whenever she's speaking. For a time, Carrie was fun. Serviceable for what I was looking for at the time. I assume she felt the same. What we had was never more than "an office fling without strings."

Her words. Not mine.

"Are you okay, Adam?" she asks.

"Sophie's dead," I say. Though my answer is obvious, it is meant as a gut punch. I consider Carrie the reason my career has stalled at SkyAero. She throttled my way up the ladder by telling the Ethics Department that she was "uncomfortable with my behavior." Word had gotten out that we were fucking like mad, and that was her corrective move: tossing me under the bus. Her meeting with Ethics was a black mark that has followed me like a dark shadow. The Ethics team is a one-way funnel of accusations and reprisals.

This was long before Aubrey.

We still fucked after that, God knows why. Well, I guess I do. Carrie was such an eager participant. We fucked all over the SkyAero plant. Mostly in areas where no one could see or hear us, though one time we did it midshift when a massive auger was running and rumbling. She writhed with great enthusiasm. I mean, *really* enthusiastically. It wasn't against the rules per se. Nowhere in the company's massive canon of employee behavior literature is there any mention of the plant being a sex-free zone.

"I know she's dead," she says, oblivious to my jab. Carrie is oblivious to everything. That's what I think made her a decent boss. Sandbagging me aside. "I can't imagine what you're going through. Are you okay?"

She gives me her practiced look of phony empathy. And immediately the hand is on me like a hermit crab that's found its shell.

"I don't know," I say. "Still trying to wrap my brain around it. It doesn't seem real."

"How could it? It's a shock. I couldn't believe it, either. None of us could. Are you sure you want to be here already? We wanted to reach out and let you know that you should take some time off. You need to talk to HR about EAP."

I've always felt the employee assistance plan is for losers. I've referred many of my team members over the years and never seen anything tangible come from it. They told one guy who was having a hard time with his wife's cancer diagnosis to take it one day at a time. She had less than thirty.

"I think work is the best thing for me," I say for a couple of reasons. One, it is easy work. Two, I don't know what I'd do sitting around the house with Aubrey and the nanny all day.

"I don't know," she says, moving her hand up my leg about an inch.

I can't tell if it is opportunistic or predatory behavior. Or if she's just trying to demonstrate some sympathy. I decide to test her.

"Maybe we could grab a drink after work?" I ask.

"Oh, Adam, of course," she says. "I'm here for you. We're all here for you."

I thank her for her support and return to my desk, a cubicle in the middle of a sea of other cubicles. The only thing that distinguishes mine from my subordinates' is that I have a little round table and two visitors' chairs. Carrie looks at me from across the room through the enormous glass panels that surround her office. I give her a nod and wait a beat or two for the rest of my team to begin coming, one by one, offering condolences, telling me that, like Carrie, they are there for me.

They don't even know me, though they pretend to. They laugh at my jokes as though I were the funniest man on the planet. They listen to my suggestions as if I just redefined how we were going to beat the competition to Mars—and do it cheaper than anyone could have ever dreamed. They always smile at me. Bring me coffee. Cookies too.

I'm sure they don't even like me. Not much anyway. They do it for the same reason I bang Carrie LaCroix.

Ben Walker pokes his head into my cubicle.

"Sorry about Sophie, dude," he says.

"Thanks, Ben," I say.

"Can I have next Tuesday off?" he asks. "Have a chance to catch some waves in Maui."

I give him a quick nod. "Sure, man," I say, in a way that mocks his surfer speak. He's too clueless to get it, though.

My wife is dead. My life is turned upside down. And my boss wants to fuck me. And my right-hand man wants to go to Maui, man.

Just what I expected.

* * *

Nothing I do after Sophie's death should matter to anyone, I think, as I watch the top of Carrie LaCroix's head and her eyes looking up at me with a gaze of admiration. We skipped the after-work drinks. We're in her bedroom in the subdivision she calls home in Renton. I haven't been there in a while, but a drawer full of condoms indicates that others have. My hand touches my belly, and I think that I need to lose a few as her head bobs and I ejaculate. She's a spitter, not a swallower, which is fine.

"I've missed you," Carrie says, sliding up my naked body and propping herself up with a ridiculously frilly pillow from some outlet store. That was one good quality about Sophie. She didn't do the girly-girl bit. I never had to shove a teddy bear off the bed when we had sex.

"Missed you too," I say, though I haven't even thought of her like that since she figuratively screwed me over with her Ethics Department complaint. But then again, I'm a wreck, and I feel like I'm spinning out of control. Sophie is dead, and I'm pissed off at her. Carrie is there. Ready. Just like always.

"I want you to ride me like a forklift," she says.

Carrie likes aerospace and factory sex talk, for some goddamn reason.

"Spread your wings," I tell her without the slightest embarrassment. "I'm coming in for a landing."

She murmurs some expression of utter delight, but my mind is elsewhere. Carrie LaCroix is a lousy lay. A crummy distraction. It comes to me just then that making like a plane going into a hangar is only a little better than nothing. I feel like telling Carrie that, but she seems so happy right now.

When I get home, Katrina is packed up and ready to go. She's twenty-three and from Romania. Her English is perfect, and she's great with Aubrey. She's attractive, no doubt.

But as stupid as I am for sleeping with Carrie, I'm not about to put any moves on Katrina. I need her as a nanny.

"Sorry," I say, "had to work late."

"Business is important," she says. "But so is family."

I give her a disarming smile. "Thank you for everything," I say. "I'm a little lost right now. Not sure how I'm going to get through all of this."

"You are a smart man," she tells me. "You'll find a way. Aubrey is asleep. She thinks her mother is an angel, you know."

"She doesn't understand the finality of death," I say, pulling off my jacket and laying it over the back of a chair.

"She will learn," Katrina says. "Good night, Mr. Warner."

I almost tell her to call me Adam, but I don't.

"Good night, Katrina. See you in the morning."

I pour some Maker's into a glass and head down the hall to check on Aubrey. She's curled up like a kitten in her bed. I adjust the covers a little and sit on the rocker that Sophie bought to nurse her in. I want to cry, but I can't. I just can't make the tears come.

I get up and fix another drink. And then another.

During the night, I'm convinced I feel Sophie breathing. She's on her side facing me. Her breath comes at me in soft puffs. I can't sleep. I lay there looking at the ceiling. I don't know what to do. I want to tell her that I know everything and that she's hurt me to the core, but that opens up a host of problems. I wonder as she's lying next to me if I ever really knew her. Or if she knew me. As I peel back the years before this moment, I don't know if I was in love with the idea of her or something as shallow as that. I thought it was her. I thought it would always be her. I remember how Frank accosted me just outside the church sanctuary just before our wedding. He was in full-on jerk mode. That was before I knew that was his normal personality.

He patted my shoulder like we were buddies. I thought he was going to wish me well.

"If you ever hurt her," he said, "I'll kill you."

Whoa.

Hurt *her*?

What about *me*?

CHAPTER THIRTY-SEVEN
LEE

Friday morning, Montrose is suspiciously chipper, considering his normal morning gloom and his disappointment over Adam being ruled out as Sophie's killer.

"Are you going to let me in on it?" I say, finally.

"Whatever do you mean?"

"God, you're a horrible actor. Something's happened. You're going to make me guess?"

"You could try."

I sigh and study him. "It's good news?"

"Actually, great news."

"We don't get *great* news. Wrong department." I eye him. Force myself to think. "All right. You were waiting for Jim Coyle's employer to call you back."

He winces just perceptibly. Pay dirt.

"So they called back. How'd it go?"

He gives up the game. "It went fucking fantastic, Lee. He's been messing with them for years, and they're going to cut him loose. He's never where he's supposed to be. And get this: they have no record of excessive absences related to any medical condition. Yeah, he's missed work, but they think it's because he's a drunk." He pauses and pretends to look at his watch, a Rolex he flashes whenever he can. I suspect it's fake, but never call him on it. "I expect he's getting his pink slip right now."

"Let's bring Coyle in," he says.

Our phones ping at the same time.

"Nice. Search warrant for Coyle's place," Montrose says. "Gonna be a great day."

"You drive," I tell him.

All it took was one lie for Jim Coyle to transition from person of interest to murder suspect. It was more than that, of course. Coyle had a criminal record that included violence against a woman. He lied to his employer about his whereabouts. He lived within minutes of where Sophie had been taken. There was more. All circumstantial, obviously. Coyle had a truck that matched what Sheila Simmons—the crime-scene Facebook poster—had said she'd seen on the highway directly above the Wisteria, Chrysanthemum, and Lily cabins around the time of Sophie's disappearance.

What's more, I noted in my report after our first contact with Coyle at his property that the back bumper of his truck had reeds stuck to it that appeared to me—not that I'm a botanist—like what I'd seen where the kayakers had found Sophie's body.

Armed with a search warrant, Montrose and I arrive at Coyle's mobile home. His truck is missing, and the minute we get out of the car we hear his dog yapping. I love all animals. I love my cat. But the truth is, I don't care much for the incessant yapping of any dog, which, I am sure, is owing to the fact that my neighbors have a Chihuahua with the lung capacity of a Saint Bernard.

"He's not here," I say.

"The damn Pomeranian is."

I smile. Montrose and I are a match on something besides espresso and beer.

I knock on the door; its thin aluminum sheeting reverberates like a snare drum.

"James Coyle," I call out with some volume, to ensure that my words are heard over the barking Pomeranian, which by now has gone completely berserk. "Mason County detectives Husemann and Montrose here. We're here to execute a warrant on these premises."

Montrose and I look at each other while we wait a moment.

I check the door and, surprisingly, find it unlocked.

We look at each other again.

"Maybe he'll shut up if we let him out," Montrose says.

"God, I hope so."

The puffball with teeth is yapping, and we need to find Jim Coyle. So we go inside. The dog makes a break for it, and we let it scoot itself out into the yard.

"Oops," Montrose says.

Coyle's house is small and reasonably tidy for a single guy. Even the throw pillows on the sofa are squared up against the armrest. It's clean but not very homey. The walls are barren except for a canvas print of a big blue Pacific octopus. Its arms reach out over the edge of the frame. I look closer, and I notice the figure of a woman bound by one of the animal's eight legs. It's creepy, and I motion to Montrose to take a shot of it with his phone.

The front room is set up for TV and beer drinking. On the wall opposite the octopus print are three neon beer signs, Rainier, Hamm's, and Rhinelander. The TV is an old-school pecan console that straightaway reminds me of my grandparents'.

"Hasn't he heard of a flat-screen?" Montrose says as we

move through the cramped space looking for any sign Sophie Warner might have been there.

"Not everyone cares about seeing the facial pores of his favorite celebrity."

Montrose takes photos of the room.

"Says the Hulu streamer."

I ignore his remark. I'm drawn to a piece of yellow paper on the small kitchen table.

"He left a note," I say, picking it up and reading.

> *I've been this route before. I know that no matter what I say or do you'll find a way to blame me. I should have killed that bitch when I had a chance. She was a liar. All of them are. And even when she admitted she lied, I was left to rot in prison. Please find a home for AJ.*

"He's got some major issues there," Montrose says, reading over my shoulder.

We bag the note and work the rest of the scene inch by inch.

"I wouldn't make a guy like that for a suicide," Montrose says.

"You never know what's inside anyone's heart, Montrose."

He shrugs. "Yeah. Kind of defiant there. Doesn't ask for forgiveness. Just a home for his dog."

The bedroom is too small for a double bed. A single bed, all made up, fills half the room. It's spotless and organized. His clothes hang on wooden hangers, and an examination of his chest of drawers reveals everything from socks to underwear to T-shirts and jeans, folded neatly.

"Prison will do that to you," Montrose says.

I know I shouldn't feel sorry for Coyle, but I do. A little.

It's possible that he was overcharged for his crime, a kind of undoing of his life that could never be righted. Maybe he fixated on Sophie. Saw her at the IGA and followed her to the cabins just beyond Octopus Hole, then came and took her the next day. His health was failing. His job was in jeopardy.

When we showed up, he could envision his future. And it was ugly.

"Some self-pity in that note of his," Montrose says. "When we find him and bring him in, he'll have some real reason to feel sorry for himself."

"It was a suicide note," I say. "We're not going to find him alive."

"Guys like that are all talk," Montrose says. "Trust me. I've been in this line of work longer than you have. Just saying. Not trying to make it seem that I don't appreciate your insight, but this time I'm right."

We've had this conversation before. In the past I've pushed back. This time I let it slide.

"We'll need to get out a BOLO," I say. "Statewide, I think. He could be anywhere."

"I agree," Montrose says. "Let's get the tech up to process the scene here. No sign of Sophie, but you never know what they'll vacuum up."

"What about the dog?" I say as we shut the thin door to the mobile home and seal it with crime-scene tape.

"What dog?" he says.

I make a face. "I get it. But we need to call Animal Control."

"Fine, cat lady."

Within the hour Mason County has issued a Be On the Lookout for James Edward Coyle, forty-nine, and his truck, a red Ford F-250 with Washington plates. He is wanted in conjunction with the abduction and murder of Sophie Warner and should be approached with extreme caution.

* * *

These days things only move fast or faster. Within thirty minutes of the BOLO our PIO had already fielded four media calls—including Linda London, who is always on the hunt for clickbait stories.

Stories start on Twitter and then jump to Facebook and finally onto the electronic pages of legacy media sites. Everyone with a pair of thumbs and a smartphone pounces to express shock and outrage and joy, as if their take on a case matters to those investigating it. The truth is, sometimes it does. Sometimes the right individual will see a story, and we'll get the call that will end in justice. That's always the hope.

I've thought of calling him many times since the interview. But I didn't. Now I have to. He picks up on the first ring.

And he blasts me straightaway.

"I saw the news on my feed just now. You should have called me, Lee. It's not right. Sophie was my wife. I should be the first to know."

He seems anxious, and I don't blame him, but that's not how it works.

"I couldn't," I say. "But I'm calling now."

I hear him take a breath. "You really think he's the guy?"

I can only imagine how he's feeling. "Not sure," I say. "But we're going to bring him in."

When we find him, I think.

"Crap," Adam says abruptly. "I'm at work, and I have another call. I have to take it. Call me with any updates, Lee. Okay?"

I promise that I will.

CHAPTER THIRTY-EIGHT
ADAM

She circles like a buzzard outside my front door. Linda London is one cosmetic procedure away from snapping and taking out someone's eye, and I almost feel sorry for her. She was on TV when I was a teenager, and I thought she was old back then. Over the years, the veteran talent has been replaced on Seattle airwaves. Some kicked out without a mention, to be replaced by someone solely driven by living in a city famous for the things they love the most: Amazon and Starbucks. I admit she looks decently preserved, especially through the small lens of my front-door peephole, but as she lifts her hand to knock, I can see how old she really is.

Hands can never pass for younger unless covered by expensive gloves.

She knocks again.

Dogged reporter, I think. *Works even on a Saturday.*

She knows I'm home because my car is parked on the street.

She rings the bell for the third time.

I give in and open the door.

"Adam," she says, as if she knows me, "I'm glad you're home."

"Hi, Linda," I say, playing her game of familiarity.

"Can I come in?" she asks. "Just me. No camera. Just want to tell you about the disturbing call I got early this morning."

"This isn't a good time," I tell her. "Our nanny just put Aubrey down for a nap."

It feels strange when I say the word *our*. There is no *our* anymore.

"It will just take a minute," she says, her blue eyes working overtime to transmit trust and sincerity.

"Fine," I say, again giving in. I shut the door behind her.

She smells like my grandmother's perfume. Or it might be the scent of her hairspray. I was never good with things like that. Sophie said I had a nose for business but not much else. I pretended to think it was funny, but it really wasn't. It was a dig.

"You want coffee or something?" I ask, not sure if she's there to help me or find me a spot under a Metro bus tire somewhere.

"That would be wonderful," she says. "Coffee's actually good for you. I did a spotlight report on its health benefits last week."

I imagine that most conversations with Linda London are like that: peppered with the updates she makes to her Linked-In page in preparation for the day they fire her in favor of some much younger blonde with big white teeth and bright, communicative eyes.

She follows me into the kitchen, and I pour her a cup and one for myself.

"I'm really sorry about your wife," she says, settling in as if we were about to have a cozy chat.

"Me too," I say.

"You must still be in shock. I'm really sorry for intruding during a very personal time."

I know her game. Anyone with a double-digit IQ would. "But you felt compelled to," I say.

She looks at me strangely, unsure if I have just mocked her or lauded her. She chooses lauded.

"That's right, Adam. It's all right that I call you Adam?"

"It's my name," I say. "So, yeah, it's fine." I force a little smile, a grim one, but a smile nevertheless. She responds with her practiced look of concern, and we're off.

"Frank Flynn called me and said some really horrific things," she starts out. "Really horrific. I'm just dumbfounded. Really I am. What he said was so damning yet so utterly not true that I had to come over and see you. I didn't bring the camera guy. I would have. But we can do something later. This is more personal. More private. Just you and me."

"Go on," I say, setting down my coffee cup so I can feel the full force of what Frank Flynn had to say.

She sets down her cup like it's a piece in a chess game.

"He said that you and your wife were having marital problems."

I don't even flinch. I let her words end in a long beat of silence. I want her to shovel out everything that she thinks she knows about Sophie and me.

"An affair," she finally says.

I drink coffee. It's my move. I answer truthfully. "I didn't have an affair." Carrie didn't rise anywhere near that level. She barely rose above whacking off into a sock.

"He was pretty adamant that you did," she goes on. "Said that you and Sophie hadn't gotten along for years and that you were seeing someone from work."

"If you knew who I worked with," I say, "you wouldn't even think that."

She clearly doesn't know how to deal with my retort. Again I let the air stay stagnant, silent, between us. In the bright light of the kitchen, without the benefit of makeup and filters, her face is a shrinking balloon. I see a plastic surgery scar behind one of her ears when she leans down to check out something interesting in the bottom of her coffee cup.

The pause is so effective.

"He said that you were there when Sophie's body was found," she says.

"I was," I say. "Within a few minutes anyway. So were a lot of people. It was on Facebook, which, by the way, is close to putting the likes of you out of business."

Linda flutters her lashes and shakes her head. She's pretending that my remark has hurt her feelings. I know it hasn't. I know that every day she gets on Facebook and massages her page like it's her last chance for relevancy.

She pushes. "Don't you think it's even a little strange that you were there?"

"What's so strange? Sad. Painful, I get. But I was still at the cabin, less than a mile away," I tell her. "I got an alert on my phone, so I went. I'd never been to Octopus Hole before, if that's what you're getting at, Linda."

She blinks. "I'm not getting at anything. Your father-in-law put forth some pretty strong accusations, and it's my job to find out what's true and what isn't."

It's your job to stir the pot, I think. I also wonder, with Sophie being dead, if Frank Flynn is still my father-in-law. I hope not. I hope that I can just lop off his branch from my family tree. Helen's too.

"I understand," I tell her, though of course I know she's a liar.

She looks around with her obvious and practiced sympathy. "He said that you purged the house of all things that belonged to Sophie."

I knew that would piss him off. Good. I'm glad. I bet he's railed about that to everyone from the kid taking the money at a drive-through to his buddies at the golf course.

"That's not exactly true," I say.

"'Exactly,'" Linda repeats. "What does that mean?"

I keep on her. "I boxed up a few of her things. Not everything. I boxed up what I thought Frank and Helen might want to have and what I no longer wanted to live with. Mostly things that had to do with them, not me. I wasn't purging my wife's memory from this house. Not at all."

"Your in-laws are concerned," she says.

Suspicious, you mean, I think.

"Look," I say, "my in-laws are grieving. *I'm* grieving. I have a little girl to think about. Maybe I got a little drunk. Maybe I was a little stupid. Maybe it was too soon. Giving back some family photos that meant nothing to me and some bullshit gifts that I could just have easily tossed out with the trash isn't a sign of anything. I loved Sophie. I never cheated on her. I don't want to forget her."

The reporter with the shrinking balloon face looks away. I think I got her. I think I shut her down.

And then she rises from the dead.

"I think there was a love affair," she says. "I've been asking a lot of questions. People you know. When people talk, things happen."

Now she's irritating me with a threat.

"I think you should leave now," I say.

"I'm not done with my coffee," she lamely says, as if that would be a reason that I'd keep her at my table for one more second.

"I'll get you a to-go cup," I say.

I'll throw it on your stretched-like-a-drum face, I think.

"Linda, time is running out for you," I say as I lead her from the kitchen to the front door. She's scanning the room, looking for anything that will bolster Frank's claims, but there isn't more to see. I have purged the living room of all things Sophie.

"Linda," I say, "don't come back."

"I'm just doing my job, Adam."

"And don't use my first name as though we are friends."

"You use mine," she says in a weird tit for tat.

"Good-bye, Linda," I tell her. "Thanks for making the worst thing that has ever happened to me and my daughter even more painful by regurgitating lies in the guise of phony concern for the truth. I can't wait until you're shitcanned right out of the newsroom."

There had been a love affair.

But I wasn't the one who had it.

I look at my watch, a gift from Sophie that I've decided to keep. Aubrey and Katrina are at the park and won't be back for an hour or so. I head down the hall to our bedroom. *My* bedroom now. I swing open the closet and start putting all of Sophie's clothes on the unmade bed. I smell her. I remember the last time she wore *that* dress. *That* jacket. I feel her all around me. When I'm finished, I go to the kitchen and get the box of garbage bags that I'd set on the counter before Linda London arrived. I don't want to live with any reminders. I'm so angry with my dead wife. Everything that belonged to her, in fact, is headed for Goodwill. I had considered pitching it all in the dumpster behind a gas station on the way to work. But I couldn't do that to her. That would be too cold. And as mad as I am, I'm not a bad guy.

CHAPTER THIRTY-NINE
KRISTEN

Connor is a total, certifiable wreck. My heart goes out to him. It really does. No matter our ups and downs, there has always been something about my husband that—and I'm loath to use this particular phrase—has brought out the mother in me. *Ugh,* I think now. Connor is not weak, but it's a fact he's more fragile than I am. It's the way things worked out. I get to be the strong one. The breadwinner. The one who does the finances. Not because he's not man enough to do those things; it's just that, well, that's who I am.

I pour him a drink, because it's the only thing that I think will calm him. I do this knowing that it's completely wrong.

"You're shaking," I say.

He stuffs himself into the folds of our white couch. His black denim stains the Italian leather, but I don't say anything about that. Not now.

"I feel like shit," he says.

I find a place next to him. "What happened?" I ask.

"I don't know," he says, drinking. It's a big gulp, and I

know he's on his way to getting drunk. Stress is a big trigger for Connor. It has been that way since the day we met. I don't pretend to know everything that goes through Connor Moss's head, but I've been with him long enough to dissect his personality with a modicum of astuteness and accuracy.

He's thinking. His mind is knitting together what happened in SoCal more than a decade ago and the tragedy at Hood Canal over Memorial Day weekend. One involved a car. The other a stranger abduction. The events are not similar at all.

However, one thing *is*, and I know just what he's going to say.

"I lost time," he says.

"You were drunk," I remind him. "You were almost killed."

He takes his eyes from mine.

"Right," he says—ironically, as he drinks more.

I give him more tequila. I have a glass too, but I mostly shift my ice cubes around. I've never cared much for drinking. I'd seen how it ruined my parents' marriage. Of course I'd pick a man with a similar issue. Even with my bachelor's from Seattle U and a JD from the University of Washington.

Intelligent me.

"But, Kristen, the blood," he says, "I don't know how the blood got there."

He glances at me, then back at his drink. He looks like he might cry.

"Honey, you cut your finger at work," I say, though unconvincingly. "You thrashed around in the bed. I could hear you from the other room. You were pretty drunk. You bled. No big deal, babe."

"But you were gone that morning. I was in the cabin."

"That's right," I say. "You were dead to the world, and I went on a hike. That's it. That's the story."

He studies his empty glass.

"Is it a story?"

I shake my head. "No. I don't know what you mean."

His eyes are pools of anguish. "The blood," he says. "My shoes."

He's never mentioned it before. I didn't bring it up. But, yes, his shoes were peculiar. When we went to get dressed to go to the sheriff's office in Shelton, I watched my husband study his shoes for a long time. He seemed perplexed. They had sand from the beach stuck to them, and when he picked them up, particles sifted to the hardwood floor.

"Weird," I'd heard him say. "I don't remember going outside."

"From when we got here, Connor," I'd said at the time. "You probably walked on the beach. I don't know. I was busy unpacking our things."

"I didn't walk on the beach drunk as a skunk," he now says, shaking like a leaf. The white couch is devouring him.

"You are screwing with yourself," I say. "Stop it. Stop it right now."

My shattered husband sets down his glass. "I don't know what happened. I don't know at all."

"You didn't do anything," I say. "You couldn't have. You aren't that kind of a person, and I wasn't gone that long. And really, when you get down to it, babe, if you did something to that woman—and there's no way you could—what did you do with her?"

Connor exhales for the first time since we began the mental trip back to the cabin.

"That's right," he says. His tone becomes something close to hopeful. "I couldn't have done anything with her. I wouldn't have done anything *to* her."

I nod and change the subject.

"How about you take a shower and we go to bed early?" I give him a smile that's merely an invitation, one in which there is never a need for an RSVP. Not when I am ovulating. Which I am.

"What about the sushi?" he asks.

"You hungry?"

"Not really. Maybe later. Maybe after."

He catches my smile, and I know he's with the program. His anxiety is his problem. I'm keeping my focus. Maybe tonight will be the night. Every night that it isn't is one day closer to it never happening at all. I watch him pad past the dining table to the master bedroom. He's a drunk, but he's still attractive to me. I want him inside of me.

I make my way to the kitchen and make some tea from the herbs that I've stashed in the cupboard and drink it down, looking over the house: four bedrooms and only two people. I wonder if it is a curse. That my idea of filling the house up with children was ruined by virtue of thinking so far ahead. Planning is for dreamers and fools.

After we have sex and Connor goes off to the kitchen to eat some sushi, I lay there in the bed like I'm an airplane-seat tray, my legs once more in the upright and locked position. I'm trying. I *really* am. It flashes over me that it will probably work now. Now that we're not seeing Dr. Y.

That high-priced quack.

Simple and direct is better in any course of action. I was so foolish to think that I had to bring science into the equation. Natural is best. Let nature take its course. I feel that way about my marriage too.

It feels great.

Really it does.

I promise.

CHAPTER FORTY
KRISTEN

I peer through the nursery window at Virginia Mason Hospital and look at my sister's latest arrival. It's a boy. Her fourth. He's beautiful, of course. All babies are. He's got a mop of dark hair that is actually brushable. She hasn't decided the name. She's like that. So busy popping them out she can't even take a breath to come up with something until the last minute. I'd call him Bradley, after our father. But she won't; she'll pick something stupid like the last one, Preston. Ugh. I scan the space. There are four Isolettes filled with babies. So many in one place. Each little person will be heading out the door for a lifetime with their parents. There'll be birthdays. Christmases. There'll be graduations. There'll be every special occasion that anyone could imagine. I want to reach through the glass and hold one. Any one. All of them.

A nurse gives me a concerned expression from the other side of the nursery. She points in my direction. I snap out of my thoughts and follow the trajectory of her scrutiny. I turn my hand upward.

Blood.

I'd dug my fingernails into my palms. It didn't hurt. I didn't even notice that I'd done it.

It was only a little blood anyway. Barely a speck.

It's early last fall, and I see my doctor's smug face on my phone. I ask a young law student, there for an informational interview, to excuse me while I take a call. When he shuts the door behind himself, I swivel my chair to take in the view from the Seattle high-rise of my law firm. I'm on the forty-first floor and face northeast. A ferry cuts through the dark blue waters of Puget Sound to Bainbridge Island, and the Olympics are out in full force: only a dash of snow softens the jagged peaks.

"Hi, Doctor," I say. "It's good news, right?"

Dr. Yamada lets out a long, irritating sigh. He hates it when I preempt every conversation with the hope that whatever he's about to tell me is going to be good. Admittedly, I've been overly hopeful during this ordeal. Stupid. Hopeful. Me. I took a regimen of Clomid the previous year, and nothing. Still I hoped. I was good at hoping, which is peculiar, considering hope doesn't get anyone very far in a law practice. Facts move the needle here. Facts trump hope and wishes and dreams.

In this case, I think, I loathe facts.

For the six months just ending, I've been injecting myself with gonadotropins to stimulate my ovaries. It was as awkward as it sounds. It was all about getting good healthy eggs to drop at the right time. I've been working it like an Olympic athlete. For his part, Connor's been milked like a 4-H Holstein. I, on the other hand, was turkey basted like a . . . well, a turkey.

We seriously should move out of the city and get a farm.

"You need to come in," Dr. Y says.

"You need to tell me why," I tell him.

Another sigh. He's annoyed with me, but he's a patient doctor. I was lucky to pick him.

Or was I? Maybe he's the one who failed here.

"You know why, Kristen," he says. "We aren't getting anywhere."

The ferry glides out of view. It's a calming image. But calm I'm not.

"That's because you're not doing enough, Dr. Yamada. This is your goddamn fault. I should have listened to my friends. I need to try some alternate methods. You've wasted all my time with chemicals, pills, and shots. God! What an idiot!"

I stop. Not because I have nothing more to say, but because I want him to feel my pain.

He feels nothing.

He has four kids.

"You know that's not true," Dr. Y says as calmly as he can. I can picture the shock on his face at my tirade. Everything about this man is gentle, kind, and caring. But at the moment I don't care. He doesn't want to be a mother. He can say all the time that he understands, but he hasn't a clue. Not really. His practice is thriving. Apparently there are a lot of empty wombs in Seattle.

I'm crying now, and I'm not going to continue talking to him.

"Fuck off, Doctor," I say, before cutting him off and throwing my phone across the room. It bounces off the wall, just missing my JD diploma. I can hear the sound of the screen shattering. *Perfect.* I deserve that. I can't even make a baby. I'm in tears now. Ashamed for what I said. How I acted. But most of all because I don't know if that other part of me, the part that I want now more than anything, will ever materialize. I look at the time. I have a deposition in ten minutes.

The time. It's always moving forward. It's my enemy.

On the way home I stop at a holistic remedy center on Stewart. While the city is growing younger and younger, and more and more places like this are springing up, I find that it's a bunch of women my age or older in the pregnancy section. We're all there on that last quest. We don't speak to each other, and we don't actually connect. I fill my shopping basket with a list I pulled from the Internet: red clover blossoms and leaves, nettles, milk thistle, and my favorite, the appropriately named motherwort.

A young girl at the counter gives me a slight smile, and I don't know if it's meant to make me feel bad or encouraged. She's about twenty-five and pretty. Her hair is tipped in a pretty shade of dark blue. Cobalt, I think.

The color of my sister's children's eyes.

"I've heard good things about milk thistle," she says. "One of our customers made a tea of it every day and got pregnant in a month. No shit. A month."

This girl knows her herbs.

"Thanks," I tell her. "It's for a friend. I'll let her know."

She gives me a nod.

I'm lying. She's probably lying too. Nothing seems to work when you've waited too long.

I get back into my Lexus, the black leather seat sucking me in behind the wheel. I don't know how much more I can take. I really don't.

Connor calls and I pick up.

"Hey, babe," he says. "Working late?"

"Heading home," I tell him.

"Restaurant was slow, so Micah gave me the night off. I'm at home. Want me to scare up some dinner?"

I don't say anything.

"Kristen? Did I lose you?"

His words seem prophetic just then, or maybe even accurate to the moment we're in right now.

"I'm here," I say as I pull off the freeway and head up the

hill toward our place in Ravenna. "How about sushi? I can pick up."

"I love sushi," he says. "I'll chill some wine."

"Sounds good," I say.

"I love you, babe," he says.

Another pause. I turn the car onto a side street.

"You too," I finally say.

But, honestly, I don't know if that's true anymore. I don't know if I can keep this marriage going when all that I want feels like a goddamn perpetual failure. Connor is a good man. But we could divorce, and I could tell people that it was because he just couldn't keep up with me. He was a waiter, for God's sake. I could say that I outgrew him. I could. That's a pretty easy sell. It wouldn't matter that the reason is that I failed him and seeing his face every day is a reminder that two people really don't make a family. I don't care what couples with dogs say. Dogs are great. However, fur babies are not children.

I'd be happy to take that to a jury anytime.

CHAPTER FORTY-ONE
CONNOR

I watch Kristen take her multicolored cocktail of hormone and fertility pills with her morning coffee. Her blond hair is damp from the shower, and despite her wearing not an ounce of makeup, I doubt that there is a more beautiful woman on the planet. Sometimes, in moments like this, I wonder how I could have even looked at another. She lifted me up from nowhere and set me down carefully in this life.

She gives me a smile.

"Never give up, Connor. Everything will be all right."

I don't know if she's thinking of getting pregnant or if she's telling me that I'll be all right.

In any case, I am grateful.

When Kristen's gone to work, *Iron Chef America* comes on, and I watch it with the volume low. Chef Micah Reynolds at the Blue Door has tried three times to get on the show but has never made the cut. He's a nice guy and very talented. But part of me wonders if he has what it takes to get to the next level and become a competitor against the likes of Bobby Flay and Masaharu Morimoto. Just because you want something, doesn't mean it's yours. I never believed in "Name it, Claim it."

Micah and his wife, Sarah, were having similar fertility issues too. I didn't know it for the longest time—not until I heard him say something to her about basal temperatures. I'd been around restaurants all my adult life and knew that wasn't a cooking term. Kristen and I were in the muck and mire of the same thing.

One night after work, when the staff was gone, Micah and I were drinking a little as we shut down the place.

"I feel your pain," I told him.

He looked at me with his famously hooded eyes. "How's that?"

I probably shouldn't have brought it up. It was personal. But I did anyway.

"I heard your end of the conversation the other day," I said, weighing his reaction to every word. "Kristen and I are going through the fertility nightmare too."

Micah is a big guy with two gold earrings and a thinning ponytail. He's got a barrel chest and forearms that don't look like any other cook's I've seen. He could punch me out. Instead, he nodded his head slightly.

"Yeah," he said. "You too?"

"On and off again," I said. "With the wife I have, I doubt she'll ever give up."

"I have one of those too," he said while lifting a bottle of good tequila from the back bar. Next he proceeded to pour a healthy shot in a coffee mug for me; the glassware was already in the washer, and he likes to leave nothing in the sink for the next day. I waited for him to get his own in the cup he was drinking from.

We knocked them back together.

"It's rough," Micah told me, before revealing that it was tougher on his wife. By far. "I have two kids with Darla," he said, "so I know it's not me."

I motioned for another shot—because it was Patrón. And it was free. Only one of which is a good reason to drink. The free part has always been my downfall. I live on the bottom shelf at the liquor store. The truth was, I've been working on being an alcoholic since my DUI. Maybe I already was one back then? Who knows?

Micah poured the booze.

"Yeah," I said. "Me too."

He gave me a wary look. "I didn't know you had a kid before Kristen."

No one at the restaurant did. It's not something I would ever discuss. Not even a mention.

"Not before," I admitted. "It's something I don't talk about with Kristen or anyone. I just know—like you do—that it isn't me who can't get the job done."

He pulled back and didn't press the point.

"Puts us in a real bind," Micah said, offering another shot.

I covered my empty glass. I'm smart enough to know that I can't get drunk with Chef here. He's the owner too.

"Yeah," I told him. "Every month we go through the same thing over and over. It kills me, and it's killing her. She doesn't want to give up and adopt or do IVF with someone else's more viable eggs. She wants her own."

"Sarah is the same," he said. "I've told her that we could adopt, and of course, she already has a couple of stepkids. Not good enough. Wants her own baby. Like it's some kind of fucking badge of honor to be a mother."

I gave in and took his offer of a third shot. After that, I insisted to myself, I was done. Really I was.

"Let's be honest, Chef," I said.

"Go on," he said. "Hope that we always are, Connor."

"This baby thing is driving a wedge between us."

Micah took our mugs and started to wash them by hand. "How?" he asked.

I leaned against the bar while he ran the tap.

"The constant failure," I said. "I can never say, 'It's sad, it's terrible, and it's unfair, but you can't get pregnant, Kristen. We have to move on.' Instead, every month feels like a referendum on our life."

Micah gave me a quick nod. "I hear you loud and clear. I'm right there with you."

"Yeah," I went on, feeling the tequila pretty good. "It's a blame game, and yet I'm not playing along with her. I can't. I know that this is on her. I love her. I don't want her to think anything bad about herself, but the constant bitching about our failure is tearing me up."

He rolled down the sleeves of his white shirt. "Sarah's not so bad," he said, "but I must admit that every now and then she gives me a little zinger. The other day she said men over forty have less than fifty percent of the potency of men in their twenties. *Potency?* Like we're a bud from the pot store!"

I let out a laugh, and it felt good.

"So that's why we're hungry after sex," I said.

Micah gave me a courtesy grin, but I immediately switched the tone back to what had been eating at me. "I am tired of feeling like a goddamn failure," I said. "I'm tired of jacking off into a tube so that she can do the deed when it's best for her."

"Like a piece of meat?" he asked.

I got where he was going. "Okay. Every man's dream, I guess. And it wouldn't be so shitty if I could see a way out of it that would keep her happy."

"People with fertility problems work their way through this," he said, quickly adding that he and Sarah had been to a counselor. "It takes a while. It's harder for the woman, of course. They see a baby in someone's arms and are immediately reminded of what they don't have. On TV. On the streets. Sarah gets a load of it every Christmas when her sisters show up. One had twins. The other, four kids. She looks at them, and despite all that she is, all that she's accomplished, she feels less than."

I'd seen that look in Kristen's eyes too. "Yeah," I said. "Nothing to do but let acceptance set in."

"That's right," Micah said. "Sarah wouldn't be happy that I shared all this with you."

"Yeah," I said. "Kristen wouldn't, either."

We set the security alarm, turned off the lights, and made our way for the door. The street in front of the restaurant was dark, and a homeless guy in purple sweats was sprawled out in the doorway. We stepped over him knowing that, as hard as we think we have it, there's someone out there in far worse shape.

Not having a baby isn't the worst thing in the world.

Unless, of course, you want one.

CHAPTER FORTY-TWO
KRISTEN

Marcy Teaberry has been my assistant at the firm for three years. She's ten years younger and in some ways reminds me of who I was a long time ago. She's ambitious, but not overly so. She treats the staff beneath her with the same kind and thoughtful regard she offers to those who could advance her career. She's so nice, I think, I could actually be happy for her if she got a promotion. Her rise in the ranks wouldn't be built on trashing someone. As mine was. I'm not proud of that. Marcy is trustworthy and predictable. In a law firm like ours, those attributes are in short supply and seldom linked.

She comes into my office with a stack of binders. The binders are black like her daily uniform. She sets them on the table softly.

"Traffic was the worst," she says. "Sorry I'm late."

"I didn't even realize," I say, though, of course, I did.

"Jaxon was up all night," she says, as though a second excuse were needed.

This is where she doesn't remind me of me. First, she has a son. Second, she's named him Jaxon. If God or a fertility doctor were to give me a child, I would never call him something as low-class as Jaxon. Nicholas or Alexander top my dream list for a son. For a daughter, Katherine, after my grandmother, has always seemed perfect.

I bet if Marcy has a daughter, she'll call her Amber. The name will be both a nod to her lower-class roots but also to the coloring that I'm sure the girl will inherit from her mother. Marcy's hair is flame red. She wears it in a pixie cut that's somehow modern and less childish than it sounds. Her skin is milk white and blemish-free. Looking at her, no one would guess she recently had a baby. Her baby belly is gone from hard work, good genes, or Spanx. Maybe all three.

I sit there quietly while she says my name a couple of times.

And a third: "Kristen?"

"Oh. What?" I ask. My head is lowered to look at my laptop.

"Are you all right?"

"I'm fine."

"Okay," she says, fanning open the top binder, which is the thickest. "Let's cover the Bradford depos. Sound like a plan?"

"I'm sorry," I say, barely looking up from my work. "I'm not okay, Marcy."

I can feel myself starting to crumble. I'm grateful that the door is shut and that Marcy is the one who is going to catch me when I fall instead of someone who would see opportunity in what I am about to say.

She leans closer over the desk. I can smell her perfume. Heavy on the gardenia. A touch of spice.

"What is it, Kristen?" Her eyes are full of concern.

Genuine concern, I think. Though I admit that I use that same look in a courtroom, and it is almost always far from a genuine representation of what I am really thinking about my client and what he's done.

My eyes puddle.

"I don't want to talk about it," I say.

"Something's going on," she says, now coming to my side of the desk. She puts her hand on my shoulder. "Is it about starting your family?"

She goes there right away. Fecund women do this. If you've struggled to conceive and stupidly mentioned what you have been going through, then no matter what is going on, that drags you down. The source of your pain is always about the baby.

The one you don't have.

The one you will never have.

The one they already have.

"No," I finally say. "I'm just scared, Marcy."

"Scared about what?"

"I can't talk about it."

"You can," Marcy says. "You clearly need to. Whatever it is, it's tearing you apart."

I gently push her away and turn to the floor-to-ceiling windows overlooking Puget Sound. I know she'll see what's on my screen and ask me about it.

"That case isn't solved yet?" she says, seeing the *Seattle Times* story on the murder of the young mother on Hood Canal. "Must have been traumatic. Being there when something so terrible occurred."

Marcy's predictable all right.

I watch the rolling white clouds as they bump into each other over the blue-gray waters of the Sound.

"Marcy," I say. "I'm worried . . . and I'm scared."

"Jesus, Kristen, now you're scaring me. What is it?"

I turn slowly to face her. "I'm not even sure how to say this but . . ."

"But what? Say what?"

In the courtroom, according to the old-timers' joke, this is a Perry Mason moment, the scene in which the bombshell is dropped to a cacophony of gasps from the jury box.

"I'm scared that Connor was involved in what happened."

There *is* a gasp. Only one. From Marcy.

Her eyes widen. "What do you mean?"

I tell her about the blood on the sheets. The sand on the soles of Connor's shoes. How he couldn't really account for his time from the moment that we arrived until the police came. How I never saw him after we got to the cabin.

"I put his drunk ass to bed and shut the door," I tell Marcy, exposing a little more on my life with Connor.

She knows he's a drinker, but she probably doesn't know how bad things have been in the past. Or what they've really been like lately.

"Those things don't mean much," she says, trying to calm me.

"I know," I tell her. "I know Connor better than anyone too, but even he's not sure what happened after we got to the cabin. He's making me think that he might have done something. It's really messing with my head."

"I can see that," she says. "But it's a . . . forgive me . . . a stupid thing to have messing with you."

I attempt to pull myself together and give her a slight smile.

"Thanks," I say. "I know that he'd never hurt anyone. He's not that type. Not really."

The last two words get her attention. As I thought they would.

"'Not really'?" she asks. "What do you mean by that?"

I turn away again. "Sorry. I just don't want to go there. There are some things that should be kept in the marriage. I've forgiven him. That's all that matters."

My words come at her with a concrete decisiveness. She doesn't ask anything more.

"I'm going to the kitchen," she says. "I'm getting you some tea."

"I have a special tea," I say, not telling her it's supposed to improve my odds of getting pregnant. I'm not a quitter on that quest. The tea's a belt-and-suspenders move, as my dad, also a lawyer, would have called it. The theory being, it's impossible to try too hard. "Just bring the hot water."

"Will do," she says. "Now, Kristen, please. Please stop thinking whatever you've been thinking. Connor is a good guy. He had no reason to hurt a complete stranger."

I don't mention Sophie Warner isn't a stranger at all.

She'll hear that soon enough.

CHAPTER FORTY-THREE
ADAM

Carrie LaCroix bursts into my cubicle. She's wearing a skirt that would raise eyebrows in a shithole bar and, even more noticeable, an anxious look on her face. Sophie has been gone for more than two weeks, and Carrie has been stomping around on six-inch heels in search of ways to insert herself into my life.

Insert. That's a favorite Carrie command for sure.

"I need to talk to you, Adam," she says, nearly out of breath.

I look up from the mind-numbing financials on my computer screen. "What's up?"

"Conference room," she says.

"Got to finish up this report for your meeting," I tell her.

She thumps my shoulder. "Forget the fucking meeting. This is more important."

It has to be big, I think. Carrie is concerned about only one thing: her career. I wonder if the company is for sale or if there has been another reorg that has left her with an additional rung to climb. She's running out of time to get where she thinks she needs to go.

Just like me.

I lock my computer and follow Carrie down a corridor plastered with images of airplanes and smiling men and women of every color and ethnicity. It's not wallpaper, but it feels that way. And seriously, none of the images resemble the reality of our workplace in the slightest.

She shuts the door behind me and spins around to face me.

"Linda London just door knocked me," she says.

I hold her words for a second before answering.

"That bitch," I say.

"Right," Carrie says. "She's that all right. She's also hell-bent on sending you to the gallows for Sophie's murder."

I don't correct her by informing her that Washington doesn't have that option for the death penalty. Carrie is only up to speed on subjects that help her. She campaigned for Hillary because she thought a woman in the White House would help her rise in the ranks at SkyAero.

"Linda is trying to stay relevant, Carrie," I say. "Ignore her."

Carrie takes a seat next to me. I can smell the fear coming out of every powdered pore of her body.

"Kind of hard to when she brings up our affair," she says.

I want to remind her that there hasn't been an affair. I only slept with her to get something out of it. It wasn't about romance or even sex. It was about two people using each other to get what they wanted. Carrie's too stupid to understand that, of course.

"Look," I say, "you need to take a chill pill."

"Chill?" she asks, her eyes widening and then just as quickly growing hard. "If it gets out that you and I had an affair, then I'm done here. You know that. I'll be recast by senior management as someone who doesn't follow the rules."

You'll be viewed as the predator you are, I think.

"No one will ever think bad about you, Carrie," I say. "You're a two-time Manager of the Year finalist. You're golden around here."

"Gold tarnishes," she says.

Again I don't correct her. It actually doesn't. This time I put my hand on *her* knee. It feels awkward and weird, but she does it to me all the time when she wants to make a point.

"It's going to be fine," I say.

Carrie puts her arms in the air, like she's directing traffic. "What are you *talking* about? One more whiff of impropriety and I'm done here. They don't tolerate things like this at Corporate. You know that."

I want to remind Carrie that all of our so-called ethics training is the result of our higher-ups being caught with their pants down around their ankles and their dicks out. But I don't. I kind of like seeing her frazzled. It's actually a whole lot better than having sex with her.

"And then there's the other matter," she says, dangling what I know is really a threat.

"And what's that?"

"Your personal problems. You know, the investigation."

If she were a guy, I'd punch her.

Instead, I reassure her.

"Don't worry," I tell her. "But since you've never asked, I'll tell you right now: I didn't kill my wife."

She waves her arms again. "I know that, Adam," she says, though I doubt she thought it until just now. She's a very literal kind of person. She takes things at face value. I should have told her I didn't kill Sophie while she was blowing me the other night. Maybe then she might've slammed the door in Linda London's face, and all of this drama between us would have ended right there.

"So are you all right?" I ask.

She shakes her head. I think she's about to cry. Last time

I saw her cry was the second time she was passed over for Manager of the Year. She's an unfortunate crier, all smears and mascara stains.

"She taped me saying something," she says. "I'm really sorry, Adam. She just tricked me."

I'm more than curious about what Carrie said, but I underplay it.

"She's like that," I say. "What did you say?"

She takes a deep breath. "I'm sorry. I told her that there had been talk around the office of an affair."

"Between you and me?"

"Oh, no," she says, her eyes now cast downward. "I made it seem like it was some other girl. Maybe in Accounting or something."

She's a moron.

"Why would you say that?" I ask, stone cold.

"It just kind of came out," she goes on. "I thought that if I shifted her to some other storyline, it would get me out of this mess."

"There is no one in Accounting, Carrie," I say.

Carrie's tugging on her creeping hemline. She makes a show of it. Like always.

"Right," she says. "And if she digs, that's just what she'll find. No one. She'll figure out that it was all office gossip, and at the same time she'll be glad for my lead."

Your bogus lead is a trip to nowhere, I think. *It won't placate a reporter on her last legs.*

"Don't get so caught up in this," I say before swinging the symbolic knife in her direction. "You have as much to do with Sophie's murder as I did."

I watch the expression on her face change. She's cogitating on what I said, something she never does in a meeting. Not even once that I could recall. She knows that if I go down for something I didn't do, she's going right down with me. I'll make sure there's more than a whiff of impropriety associated with her.

She gives me a long, penetrating gaze. "I don't like your tone," she finally says.

I give her a faux-concerned look—one that mirrors hers in every budget-crisis meeting.

"There is no tone here," I tell her. "We're innocent, Carrie. Some freak killed my wife. It's random and gross, but that's what happened. People always think the husband did it, you know, to get with his floozy mistress. That's not what happened here. You aren't a floozy. And you aren't my mistress. We're free and clear here. Just sit tight."

She doesn't say another word.

For once.

I know that Carrie will be more careful now. I know that she'll stay clear of Linda London and the likes of her. We had no real love affair—by Clintonian standards anyway—but whatever story Carrie tells will make her look like a liar, a businesswoman clinging to the remnants of a once-promising career. There is no way the media can paint what happened between Carrie and me as anything but sexual harassment. I am her subordinate. After all, she took advantage of *me* by holding the keys to my promotions, the raises that I'd earn in the future.

Hashtag Me Too.

CHAPTER FORTY-FOUR
LEE

Adam's boss looks like something out of a magazine. We don't see many like Carrie LaCroix in Shelton. At least not out and about. It's Friday morning, and she's come before going to the office to meet me at a Seattle coffee shop with something big to tell me.

"Can't talk about it over the phone," she'd said. "It's a delicate matter."

There's obviously no casual Friday at SkyAero. She's dressed to the nines. Her suit looks very expensive. Her nails are done in a tasteful bing cherry hue, and her makeup's applied better than a YouTube expert would have done. She's a few years older than me, but she proves the point that people with money have access to better cosmetics.

Immediately I capture an energy from her that hides under her flawless skin.

She's nervous.

"I took the liberty," she tells me, indicating a pair of coffee cups. "Hope you don't mind. I'm kind of like that."

I thank her and wonder what she means by the remark. Kind of what? Presumptuous? Kind of busy? Kind of thoughtful?

I choose thoughtful.

"Carrie," I say, calling her by her first name, which she insisted on when she called me to meet her. "You were very upset on the phone."

She sets down her cup. "I was. I *am*. I'm sorry about that. I don't do upset very often. Most of the people who work with me—my team of superstars—think that I'm a rock and don't have any feelings whatsoever, but I do. I really do."

"That's all right," I tell her. "We all hide our feelings to get things done. I imagine that our jobs are somewhat alike. I need to be strong for people who have been victimized, and tough with those who do harm to others."

Carrie smiles. "I guess we are. The corporate world asks a lot of women, just like I'm sure law enforcement does."

I really don't think the two are that related, but I give her a slight nod. She's called me with something to say about Adam Warner, and I need to hear it. Though I would never admit it to anyone, especially Montrose, I'm there for myself as much as I am for Sophie. It feels terrible and selfish to think that, but I can't help it. I know Adam never could hurt anyone, yet between Frank Flynn and now the woman across from me, I'm beginning to wonder how well I know him.

Or if I knew him at all. It has been a long time since I was twelve.

"I'm not sure if I need a lawyer here," she says.

"Why would you need a lawyer?" I ask. "Have you committed a crime? Or been party to one?"

Carrie shifts her body in her chair to let a young man slip by.

"No," she says. "Of course not. Never."

"Then why would you think you need someone's counsel to tell the truth?"

Her eyes flutter. "I don't know. It's a little complicated. I haven't got a thing to do with what happened to Sophie, and really, I don't think that Adam did, either."

I feel a little relief come to me with that last remark.

I urge her to continue. "Something's bothering you, Carrie. You need to tell me just what it is so that the investigation can cover all of its bases. All right?"

"Right," she says. "I understand. That's why we're here."

"Yes," I say. "That's the reason."

"He won't be happy with me."

Her words are leading me to a place I don't want to go. What she has is very personal, and it might rewrite what I think of Adam.

"His being happy with you isn't crucial in the long run," I finally say. "What's important is that I get all the information I can for Mrs. Warner's case."

Carrie fidgets with the clasp on her Kate Spade purse.

"Well," she says, "it's not that I think he's a killer. If that's what you think. God, no. He's not that tough. I've seen him back down in the boardroom countless times. Between you and me and the fence post, he'll never make director level. Especially now."

That's the world she lives in. Adam too, I think. Everything is about the corporate climb.

I put her back on track. "Carrie, what's troubling you about Adam?"

"Okay," she says, now playing with the plastic lid from her coffee cup. "I saw a news report about Adam having an affair with someone."

"Linda London's story?" I ask.

"Right. That's the one."

She grows suddenly silent.

And I let her.

I want her to think very carefully about what she's about to say. I don't want to prompt her. It's awkward for a few beats. Awkward, however, is fine in an interview. I'm troubled far more by the person who rattles off his or her story as though it's a speech they've memorized and expects some kind of a prize.

"Okay," she continues, "I can't say that Adam and I were having an affair, but we did have an intimate encounter or two."

Intimate encounter sounds like corporation speak to my ears.

I remain expressionless and urge her to continue.

"I don't want to say it was a fling," she says, "but I guess that's what it was. *Booty call* is what the kids call it, I guess. That sounds so tasteless to me. I guess *fling* is better."

Fling really isn't much better, I think. He was married, after all.

"It was a few years ago. Maybe three or four. I can check my calendar. I keep records for everything."

"So the affair wasn't recent?"

"I'm going with *fling*," she says, correcting me. "*Affair* seems too personal for what it was. It was just sex. Really, that's all it was. He was going through some stuff with his marriage, I think. I was divorced. It wasn't ideal, but I think being with Adam was what I needed at the time."

She's treating Adam like he was some kind of counselor.

"Right. No strings. Just something you needed," I say. "And he and Sophie were having problems?"

Carrie rakes her nails through her hair.

"He never really said. I just know that he was always working late and she was always working late and their marriage seemed to be teetering. I've seen it before. Of course, it's happened to me too."

"Did the fling continue for a period of time and then end amicably? As I understand it, you still work together, right?"

Carrie snaps the lid back on her cup, a smear of red lipstick in a half moon on its outer edge.

"It wasn't completely amicable," she says. "It wasn't a problem between us, but one of our team members saw Adam and me one afternoon and, well, reported that she thought we were too cozy. It was just how we were sitting. I went to our Ethics Department. I'm not proud of it. But I didn't see I had a choice."

I'm confused. "To turn in the complainer for what?"

"No," she says. "I had to make a preemptive strike against Adam. I couldn't let our inconsequential liaison ruin my career. I told Ethics that he was being a little too familiar with me and it made me uncomfortable."

She sees the look on my face. It's hard to explain what I'm feeling just now. Adam betrayed his wife. His lover betrayed him. Not so nice in the big city.

"I didn't sandbag him," she says. "I know people might think that. But those that do don't understand that being a woman in a position of power makes you a target twenty-four seven. The guys above me want nothing more than to keep me under them on the org chart. Don't let anyone tell you that things are fair. They aren't."

Carrie climbs off her soapbox.

"Things aren't fair anywhere," I say, not because I believe it completely. At least, I hope things are fair elsewhere. I got the detective's position over three men, and I think it was because I was the best candidate and not because someone at the hiring office was trying to make things fair.

"What was the outcome of your report?" I ask.

"It wasn't that bad," she says. "I indicated to Ethics that I was only marginally uncomfortable and that I didn't think Adam was doing anything that should result in any kind of corrective action. They gave him some online sensitivity training."

"I'll bet that wasn't well received by Adam."

"He was a little mad at me," she says. "You can't stay angry very long, or it makes things worse. He got over it."

"And that's the sum of the affair? I mean fling."

Carrie's phone buzzes, but she ignores it.

"Yes, that part of our relationship. It stopped. Sophie got

pregnant with Aubrey, and the ship was righted. All good. For me, it was a time that I didn't think about."

"And it was over," I say.

She thinks a second. "Not really. We did get together one more time. Recently."

"Just how recently?"

"After he got back from Hood Canal."

"I see," I say, while managing to keep my coffee in my mouth. I keep my expression flat. At least I try to.

"I honestly don't think it was about anything other than forgetting for just a moment how his life had been turned upside down. We didn't talk about what happened over Memorial Day weekend. It was just sex."

This isn't the Adam that I know.

Or knew.

And honestly, I don't understand the concept of "just sex." Just sex? Why not find another activity to pass the time? Maybe Skee-Ball or something like that.

"I'm going to be dragged into this, right?" she asks.

"Why would you be?"

"If you arrest Adam like that reporter says."

"Do you know what happened to Sophie?" I ask.

She winces at the question. "Of course not," she says, her voice rising a little. "And I don't think Adam could have hurt her anyway. He's weak, like I said.

"I wouldn't give Linda London an interview if she asks you," she goes on. "But if you do, I trust you won't bring me up. I wanted to do the right thing, that's all. In case, you know, he did it. Do you think he did?"

I offer no expression, but I give her something to think about.

"Well, there was an eyewitness that saw the abduction, Carrie."

She gives me a little shrug and snaps her purse shut. "I heard that," she says, "but I also heard that the guy's about a hundred years old and isn't sure what he saw."

Linda and Frank are the A-Team of misinformation, I think.

"He's sure," I tell her. "He's not that old, by the way. Don't pay attention to what Linda London says, all right? She's selling a story."

"I guess so," Carrie says. "I just thought I'd come forward first—you know, a preemptive strike."

"Understood," I say.

"I told my director this morning," she says, getting up from the table and glancing at a text. "I think they are going to make Adam take some time off from SkyAero."

I get up to leave. I notice that I'm shaking a little. I don't like to shake. I push back on my own thoughts about Adam Warner and his affair with Carrie LaCroix. One bad act doesn't always lead to another.

Not always.

CHAPTER FORTY-FIVE
ADAM

Earlier this morning I was notified by Tricia, our Human Resources representative, to come to her office at the end of the day. I asked her what it was about, and she indicated it was "process and procedure" that needed to be addressed. I thought it had something to do with changing my dependents now that Sophie was gone. I poked my head into Carrie's office to ask what she knew, but she was on a call and waved me away.

I don't want to think that anything worse can happen to me. I've lost my wife, and people in the office have come one at a time to check in with me. The guy who routes our mail made a point of asking if he could help me with anything. It's been nice. I know that there are decent people everywhere, but mostly on the levels far below my name on the org chart.

I admit that it's hard to focus on work with distractions of the magnitude of a murdered wife, a police investigation, a father-in-law from hell, and a TV reporter who won't go away. I read the comments on a story posted in the *Seattle Times*, and mostly they were about the mystery of who had taken my wife and if there had been other, comparable attacks. A poster from British Columbia wrote that they'd had a similar case up there: a student from the University of British Columbia was abducted in the middle of the day. Her body was found in the Fraser River. She'd been beaten, strangled, and raped.

Just like Sophie.

I think of the Canadian couple that found my wife's body. They were connected to UBC somehow. I wonder if anyone else will think of that. I contemplate if I should call Lee or if inserting myself into the investigation in any way will only make things worse.

Carrie stops by. It's almost noon.

"I'm off-site for the rest of the day, Adam."

She lingers a bit, looking at me and then turning away.

"See you tomorrow," I tell her.

"Okay," she says, her voice trailing away from me. "Sounds good."

The HR office is one building over from mine. I pack up my laptop and wave good-bye to the rest of my team and make my way through a warren of cubicles to the stairwell. It's a little after four p.m. by the time I find myself in Tricia's office. But we're not alone. A man who identifies himself as Tricia's coworker is there too. On the desk in front of her is a single sheet of paper, facedown.

This is not good. It's not about beneficiaries.

"What the hell is going on here?" I ask, feeling my pulse starting to race.

"Can you calm down?" the jerk next to her says.

"Can you fucking tell me what's going on here?"

"I'm sorry to tell you this," Tricia says, "but we're terminating your employment today."

"Holy shit," I say. "What for?"

"Can you tone down the language?" Jerk says.

I give him a hard look and then return my attention to Tricia and that paper. She slides it across her *Titanic*-size gray laminate desk.

"It's all right here," she says.

I scan the document, picking out the words that have brought me to this moment: "Inappropriate behavior reported by two colleagues . . . a failure to embrace the company's code of conduct despite diversity and sensitivity training . . ."

"This is a load of bullshit," I say.

"I'm sorry, Adam," Tricia says, "but I'm going to need your laptop and your badge."

"If this is about Colin's bachelor party," I say, "I had nothing to do with that blow-up doll he left in my office as a supposed thank-you. I deflated it and got it out of there pronto."

Colin was a douche.

I can see by the look on Tricia's face that she has no idea what I am talking about. This wasn't about a blow-up doll, inflated or not.

Just then I notice uniformed security outside her door.

"This is fucking unfair," I say. "Insanity!"

Tricia ignores what I'm saying. "The company wants you to acknowledge that you've read this," she goes on. "Failure to do so will forfeit the six months' severance we're offering."

"I won't sign anything," I tell her, ripping off my badge and dropping my laptop bag to the floor with a thud. "I didn't do anything!"

Jerk speaks up. "Sign it or not. Up to you."

I am so irate I feel like punching out that guy's lights. I'm not very fond of Tricia at the moment, either. God, I thought we were friends. I told her that her kid was cute when he looked like a mutant Wookiee when he was born. Carrie turned me in. She'll pay for this. Big-time.

Goddamn her. Goddamn all of them. Sophie's death brought all of this on. Damn her too.

The security officer follows me out to the parking lot. I don't say a word as we walk across the sticky asphalt. All I can think about is that the thing that I loved more than anything in the world is gone.

That night, while Aubrey sleeps, I drink Maker's and dig through the computer that Sophie and I shared before we abandoned it in favor of our phones for everything. I find the photo I'm seeking. I have to admit that I kept it not because Carrie was particularly hot, though she kind of was, but because I knew someday that I could use it. At the time there wasn't a term for it. Now, I know, I'm about to engage in a little revenge porn.

I go to Facebook and type:

Damn it! I've been hacked! If you see some posts, they aren't from me. Seriously pissed off!

Next, I upload Carrie's ready-to-take-flight photo and start tagging all of our mutual SkyAero friends. There's a pretty good list of them, because the boss with the biggest office gathered his leadership team together and told them they needed to engage with our team more. He said Facebook would be a good idea. Up until now I had to scroll through my news feed to endure photo after photo of food, braggarts, and their trips to Morocco, kids that are cute only to their parents. I gave out likes like confetti in a parade because my boss's boss said social media makes people more connected.

Now I'm giving them something they'll never forget.

The last person I tag is Carrie. She's about to go viral, which is a pretty good trick for someone I now consider toxic like a disease.

With almost a flourish, I post it. It feels good. Better than sex with her, that's for sure. I sit back and drink some more and watch the fireworks.

Payback is a bitch, bitch, I think.

I hear Aubrey calling for me. I set down my drink. I bet my phone will start ringing any minute.

Holy shit, I'll say. *I knew I'd been hacked. I'm going to contact Facebook now. Carrie LaCroix? Naked? Wow, that's embarrassing. Thanks so much. Jesus, seems like everyone is a victim of something these days.*

Aubrey asks for some water, and I bring it to her. I can hear the buzzing of my phone all the way in her room. I have been through the wringer since Sophie died. Hell, I've been to hell and back. This bit of revenge isn't really like me. And yet for some reason, I did *save* the photo. So I guess that leaves me to wonder: Is it like me after all?

CHAPTER FORTY-SIX
ADAM

The next day, Aubrey and Katrina are at Woodland Park looking at the baby goats and lambs in the children's zoo while I sift through more of Sophie's things in her dresser drawers and ponder what life will be like without her. Even though I knew about her affair and, yes, hated her for it, I still had a love for her. Sometimes hurt so deep gets buried by hope. I thought, *Sure, we can do this. We can make this work. I don't want to know who he is or why you thought he was your soul mate. We all do crazy. I did Carrie LaCroix.*

I find the gold-and-sapphire bracelet that I gave her for our first anniversary. She used to wear it all the time on that slender, beautiful wrist of hers. She acted like we couldn't afford such extravagance when I gave it to her, but I dismissed that out of hand.

"I'm on the way up," I told her. "In line for a big promotion."

God, I was stupid then. I guess Sophie was too. She believed me.

I put the bracelet in a box for Aubrey but think better of

it. I'm out of a job now. I might need the money down the road. I put it in the box with other jewelry that I intend to sell. One is a diamond pendant that belonged to Frank's mother. Can't wait to unload that one and then tell him that some stranger cut the diamond into a nipple ring or something.

He'll go berserk.

Helen will cry.

It will make me feel just a little bit better.

The bell rings, but I ignore it. Then a fist hammers the front door, so begrudgingly I follow the noise down the hall to answer. Through the peephole, I see Carrie. I expected her to call, but instead, like an insistent and rushed pizza delivery boy, she is making her presence known in person.

I weigh the possible drama, but I open the door anyway.

Her face, absent of makeup, is puffy from crying. Her hair is a mess. I doubt Carrie has ever looked worse.

"What are you doing here?" I ask her. "It's the weekend. Shouldn't you be off sucking up to someone?"

She shoves her way inside and lunges at me. I push back, and she retreats a little.

"You fucker!" she screams.

She can be direct. That is one of her decent qualities.

"Seriously?" I say. "*You* fucked *me*. You turned me in to HR. I got canned because of you. What kind of a crazy bitch are you?"

Her hands are fists now, and she intends to pummel me. I almost want her to, but I step away from her.

"You never should have posted that photo," she yells. "I can take you to court over that! It's against the law."

I put on my best version of innocence. I knit my brow and widen my eyes at the same time. I'm uncertain if the look works, but it is all I have at the moment to placate this pissed-off woman standing in my living room.

"I was hacked, Carrie! Get a grip!"

Her lips stretch to a thin rubber band. "You are a goddamn liar, Adam."

I'll give her that. In this circumstance, I *am*. It's easy to lie to the face of someone who's betrayed you.

"How could you do that to me?" she asks. "I thought we were friends."

This is unbelievable.

"You cost me my job, Carrie. You ended my career." Before she can say another word, I play the sympathy card. "Right after my wife died! You took me down when I'd lost everything. Thanks, Carrie. That's how you treat your friends?"

"I'm going to press charges," she says.

I shrug. "Fine. Go ahead. I don't care what you do."

I do, of course, but only a little.

"You'll be hearing from my lawyer."

I lead her to the door. "Looking forward to it. I suppose I'll need to make the other photos and that video of you available to the prosecutor."

She stops in her tracks. "What video?"

I push her out the door.

"The video in which you're sucking my cock behind the flight line at work. The company logo is right above your head."

Her mouth hangs open, which in this instance only reminds me of the video.

Nothing comes out. Carrie is stunned. I push one more button.

"You'll have some major explaining to do on that one," I tell her. "You were my boss. Not cool, Carrie. You'll probably get fired for not wearing safety glasses on the factory floor. I'm done, Carrie. So the video will be payback. You fuck with me again, and you're done too."

Then I slam the door. That felt great. Better than being with her on the factory floor, that's for sure.

I go back to the bedroom and continue sorting through my old life, separating out everything having to do with my dead wife.

Chapter Forty-Seven
Kristen

Marcy is late once again. My assistant will offer a pretext concerning her childcare situation, and I'll tell her everything is fine—even when it isn't. I have little choice. I know there is nothing worse than a female boss with a disconnect between the challenges of maintaining a career and raising a family. It isn't easy. I know that. I wonder how I'll manage the balance between work and home when I have a child of my own. I used to only hope or feel it would happen for me. Now I'm certain. My certainty lets me exhale for the first time in I don't know how long.

Marcy is a whirlwind of justifications and phony good intentions when she arrives in a striking blue ensemble that she's never worn to the office. I'm sure she expects me to remark on how pretty the outfit is, but I won't.

"Sorry," she offers a final time after laying out her apology, but I really haven't paid any attention to the nuances of whatever it was that made her miss the first twenty minutes of the day. My mind is elsewhere.

"We need to get up to speed on the Barringer case," I say.

"Right," Marcy says, pulling out some files as she catches her breath and finds her way to a chair across from my monolithic desk. "Saw that thing on the news about the creep they think killed Sophie Warner out at Hood Canal."

"Yes," I say. Nothing more.

The curtness of my remark appears to trouble her. I can feel her eyes on me as I flip through the papers on my desk. The silence screams at her.

I knew it would.

"You think he did it?" she asks.

I look away for a second before returning Marcy's gaze.

I let out a sigh. "I hope so."

The word *hope* hangs in the air.

Marcy is wholly bewildered. "Is everything all right?" she asks after a beat, scooting herself closer to the edge of my desk.

I measure my thoughts carefully. Part of me wants to speak to someone about Connor and what might have happened the night we arrived at the Hood Canal cabin. It feels very much like a checklist for murder: the blood, his shoes, and the missed time.

Marcy can see that I'm worried. She can read me only to the extent that I let her.

"You don't think he did it," she says.

"Let's focus on Barringer," I say.

"Why don't you think he did it?" she asks.

"Marcy," I say, "just leave it. Please. Let's focus on work."

When we take a break just before lunch, I think of reaching out to the detectives on the Sophie Warner case. What would I tell them? My suspicions that Connor might have done something so vile, so out of character? His police record in California was a DUI, not a violent offense.

I drink coffee and look at the *Seattle Times* story about the manhunt for Jim Coyle in connection to Sophie Warner.

If they have evidence to charge him, I wonder what it could be. As I scroll down, there's a story about a man from Tacoma who had a wife there and two more in Spokane and Yakima.

The audacity of his deception doesn't shock me as much as it apparently shocked those quoted in the article.

I know something about being completely hoodwinked.

CHAPTER FORTY-EIGHT
KRISTEN

I sit there reading the bigamy article, and liars fly at me as though launched by a hurricane. Pinocchio. Any politician. Martha Stewart. Lance Armstrong. Bernie Madoff. Kenneth Lay. My mother, when she said I wasn't up to the task of being a lawyer like my father.

And at the top of the list, my husband.

My body tenses, and my knuckles go white.

Him.

A long needle stuck in your abdomen isn't the worst thing that can happen to you, though it's pretty bad. I've watched YouTube after YouTube on fertility. I've seen women get more needle pokes than a pincushion. And for what? Nothing sometimes. But as I have told myself time and again, that isn't the worst thing that can happen.

Learning that your husband is a cheat is worse. Finding out that it's more than sex, something—and really I want to laugh out loud about this—*deeper*, is an almost cosmic wound.

Yes, that's the worst.

My discovery turned the love of my life into nothing more than a stud service. Like he is a stallion that I procured from some local horse breeder, and I am the willing mare. I couldn't care less about him, but I knew at the time that he was still my best option to get a child. It's true, I could have gone to a sperm bank, looked through the online catalog, and selected a prospect with a strong chin and a PhD. I wouldn't have known him, though. I knew Connor. We had a history. I loved Connor. At least until that Sunday morning I did.

I was making buckwheat pancakes, and Connor was in the shower. He'd worked late on Saturday at the Blue Door, and I knew he'd be starving. I put some fresh blueberries, honey, and water in a saucepan and turned the heat on low. A nice compote would be perfect. Bacon too. I went to the refrigerator to get some, and his phone buzzed.

A text.

I didn't give it a second thought and turned on the oven. Connor likes his bacon crispy. *Very* crispy. In the restaurant trade they call it "shattered."

Funny, that word, *shattered*. I felt that way myself when another text came.

I bent down to look at it. It was from a number I didn't know.

First text: You up?

Second text: God, I'm tired. Last night was amazing. I can still feel you.

The room began to shrink. The buckwheat pancakes began to burn. I could feel myself being swallowed by the open oven door. I can't say for sure why I did it. Maybe just to see what would happen. Maybe just to help me understand that what I was seeing on my husband's phone was a misunderstanding.

"Tired" and "amazing" could be about last night's dinner service.

That last part, the part that said the contact could still "feel" him, was more problematic. It, to my way of thinking, could only be one thing.

So I texted back: Yeah. Great night.

I looked up and listened for the shower. Still running. Connor was standing there, letting the water run over him, while I was being run over by a truck in our kitchen. Nothing about our life together has felt equal. From the amount of money we made to the company we kept. Nothing. Not a single thing.

Next the texter wrote: I can't wait to see you.

I was a madwoman. I stood there in my kitchen glued to the tiny screen of my husband's outdated iPhone. I vowed right then I would not upgrade him. Not ever. The water in the shower was off. He was toweling off.

I texted back: Not going to happen. Not ever. This is over. I didn't press "Send." Instead, I turned on the garbage disposal and tossed his iPhone down the drain.

"Oh shit!" I screamed.

Connor came running. "What happened, babe?"

I hated when he called me that. *Babe.* Made me think of Paul Bunyan's blue ox, and I'm a size four.

"Connor, I don't know how it happened," I lied, "I think I just sent your phone into the garbage disposal."

"You couldn't have," he said, reaching past the rubber gasket and into the depths of the disposal. I thought of turning it on then, but I didn't. His face fell as he did indeed encounter what was once his phone. My face was a mask. I would never reveal to my goddamn husband what I knew. In court or in life, the element of surprise can only be used to great effect once.

"Sorry," I said, pretending to be merely upset at ruining a piece of electronics, when inside I was a Cuisinart of anger and regret about choosing a man who could kick me to the curb like I was nothing.

You goddamn idiot, Connor.

Why would you hurt me like this?

"It's okay," he said, looking at the mangled remains of his recovered phone while stacking his plate with pancakes and ladling on the blueberry compote. I would have added rat poison to it if I'd had time—or thought of it. But I didn't. He was oblivious. I wondered who the whore was that he was seeing. I suspected it was that Lynnette from the Blue Door. She had endless legs and was too pretty to be trusted.

"I was going to make bacon," I told him. "But the time got away from me."

Connor stabbed his pancake with a fork. "No problem," he said. "I could lose a couple of pounds."

He wanted me to say he looked great. Or did he not think he looked good enough for *her*? I didn't say anything.

"I needed a new phone anyway," he said, stuffing some pancake into his big fat mouth.

I loved him, but I wouldn't have minded if he choked just then.

I looked at the phone retrieved from the disposal. It looked like some junior NRA types used it for target practice.

"SIM card is probably shot," I said.

"That's okay," he said, always upbeat. "I don't have many contacts that matter. I guess I'm going to the phone store after breakfast, then off to run a few errands. Do you need anything?"

"No," I told him. "I'm good."

I wanted to say, "No, you've just crushed me to the core."

"I was going to make that bacon," I said.

"That's all right, babe. I'm good. Had a full meal last night."

"At the Blue Door?" I asked.

He looked at me quizzically. "Yeah. Of course. Where else?"

"I don't know," I said. "Thought maybe you went out after work. You've been doing that lately some."

"Once," he said, slightly defensively.

His tone made me feel good, as if I'd poked an open wound with a rusty nail.

"Oh," I said. "I have to prepare for a case this afternoon anyway."

With that, I left my stud husband in the kitchen with his plate of pancakes and the big lie he had told me. If I were an evil person, I would have killed him right then and there. But I'm not. I'm smarter than that.

Two days later, I went through the pockets of his shirt and slacks. Nothing. I was on a scavenger hunt. All alone. I needed to know who and what. I went by the Blue Door and saw Connor through the window as he worked a table. His handsome face caught the hanging light. He was beautiful. I wished he weren't. I went there at least three times. I thought that my timing was off, so I had Marcy go to the restaurant for takeout. I texted Connor at different times of the day to see how long it took him to reply. Though the tools were not the same, I was acting like the woman my mother had become when my father cheated on her with his law partner's wife. I looked at her with utter disgust back then. I told Mom that she was better than Dad. That she should just tell him to get lost and change the locks. God, how silly the advice of a fourteen-year-old must have seemed to a grown woman! Mom didn't answer me. She just cried. It's hard to unbraid a life with a man that you believe in. Like my mom did my father. Like I did with Connor Moss.

When I worked in the prosecutor's office, I'd ask a defendant anything.

Why did you kill your baby?

Did you get pleasure from stabbing the victim?

Did the cigarette burns you gave your girlfriend arouse you?

Are you turned on by hurting someone?

Why did you molest your granddaughter?

The list goes on and on. I ask. They answer.

Yet, when it came to my own husband, I was Helen Keller. I was blind and mute. I couldn't ask because I didn't want the answer. I didn't want to know for sure that he'd found a woman that he wanted more than me. I didn't want to mess up the dreams that I had since before law school. Graduate. Get a good internship. A good firm. Meet a great guy. Get married. Have a baby. Make partner at the firm.

I stupidly skipped the one thing that turns out to matter the most.

A few hours later, I was lying in bed with my legs in the air, waiting for my great guy's semen to be released inside of me to do some kind of biological magic. The sperm was from a man who I didn't trust; a man who was using what belonged to me—his seed—on some slut at the Blue Door.

Connor nuzzled me just then, and I breathed him in, trying to detect the scent of my rival. A perfume. Her bodily fluids. Her hair conditioner. Anything at all. When he was on top of me, I looked into his eyes and wondered if he was thinking of her or me. Did I need more Botox? Were my breasts starting to sag? The thoughts that raced through my mind had nothing to do with what we were doing at the moment.

Our lovemaking was mechanical. I did the bare minimum to encourage him to the finish line. Not that it took that long.

Connor has never had much staying power. A thrust later, he made that face he makes when he comes. It looks joyful and painful at the same time. I used to love seeing the ecstasy on his face when we made love. Now it made me sick.

So I just lay there without saying a word. The stud was done. He rolled off me. The mare caught her breath. I wanted to cry. Really, I did. Was I anything to him, or was I just a job to get done? Go to work. Fuck Kristen. Rinse and repeat. I didn't want to play the victim. I'm not about victimhood. But, goddamn it, I felt so wounded. So cast aside.

His face ruddy from exertion, Connor got up to get something to drink in the kitchen. I watched his naked butt as it disappeared out the bedroom door. At least, that's what he used to do when he left the bedroom like that. Now I wondered if he was texting on his new phone, telling her how much he missed her. How much he wished he were free of his wife.

Free of *me*.

I wouldn't put up with that. No, I wouldn't. I was better than that. Better than him. Better than *her*.

CHAPTER FORTY-NINE
ADAM

Aubrey sits on my lap as we look through a photo album Sophie had made for her parents the week before she died. Aubrey's warm and a little sleepy, but I'd promised. The pictures come at us one by one. Each makes her smile, laugh, or point.

"My birthday," she says, indicating the image of Sophie lighting a trio of pink candles on a chocolate cake.

"That's right," I tell her.

I'm unsure if Aubrey really understands the finality of what happened to her mother. She talks of her as if she's in the other room.

"I want to show Mommy," she says of the nightgown Helen gave her.

"She sees it," I say.

"I want Mommy," she says.

"I know. She loved you very much, Aubrey. You were everything she ever wanted."

She leans against my chest, and we look at more photos.

And as I sit there holding her, I think about the time I sat in that very chair and how my life vanished right before my eyes.

Nothing invites my prying eyes more than a folder on a computer marked "Personal." That's a goddamn fact. I'll bet that every time that a person with computing problems brings a device in to the Geek Squad or Office Depot, the first thing techs do is look for the "good stuff."

I know I would.

The discovery of such a folder is what led me to the emails between Sophie and her lover. She used the computer for work stuff when she needed to get some designs done and didn't want to spend the night at the office. During her pregnancy and even more so in the months after Aubrey was born, there was less of that, of course. Sophie, who'd been scattered and unreliable, was suddenly a new person. She had a focus on our family. At the time, I figured it was the natural course of things. A baby. A family. New priorities. No more late nights out. No overnight convention trips.

Just the three of us.

What an idiot I was. An imperfect idiot, I admit. When Sophie drifted, I found myself in the sack with Carrie LaCroix. It wasn't for any reason other than that I felt like I was being ignored. Big baby me. Bigger idiot. Carrie was ultimately far more trouble than she was worth. She literally screwed me over in every sense of the word.

I found Sophie's secret stash of emails when I was looking for my AmEx year-end report for our taxes. I wonder how many people wish they could unring a bell. I do. I feel that way right now when I think of that Saturday afternoon when I noticed that she had left her Gmail open and I clicked on a folder marked "Personal."

I sat there almost unable to breathe. Seriously. Sure, I

didn't have clean hands myself, but Carrie was nothing to me. This guy. This guy, whose name was only an email address, was more than some dude my wife fucked. The words they used were like shrapnel in my eyes.

Soul mate.

Love of my life.

Never felt such a connection.

I love your body, but I love your being even more.

I'm lonely when I'm without you.

The allness of you consumes me.

Your touch heals me.

I feel you inside me even when I'm away from you.

God, I can't live without you.

Is it wrong that we feel this way?

A noose was around my neck, and I couldn't breathe. That's the best way to describe that first reaction. Just no air. After I was able to suck in some oxygen, I bawled. Really, I did. I seriously doubt that I've ever cried as hard as I did reading those emails. It was an ice pick in my heart. I'm not sure why I sobbed like I did. I think I was just realizing that the world as I viewed it was not as it seemed. That everything I thought was true was a façade. In a way, I could kind of accept that. I worked hard to provide for Sophie and Aubrey, and maybe I'd taken my eye off the ball.

Maybe I had some blame here too?

I copied the folder onto a thumb drive and jammed it inside the pocket of my SkyAero laptop bag. I had a millennial at work who I knew could track the IP address and probably the sender if I ever wanted a confrontation scene. I chose not to take this step, though. Or didn't have the balls to take it. But I did hang on to the thumb drive.

I never told Sophie what I'd found. I never let on that I didn't trust her anymore. That she'd hurt me so bad, I wasn't sure I'd ever get over it. For a few days I couldn't stand the sight of her. The idea that she'd let another man fuck her.

Jesus! I wonder if they did it here in our house. I wonder how many times they fucked and what she said about me. Had she laughed at me when she lay in the bed next to him? Had she writhed when they had sex and proclaimed to him that his cock was thicker, bigger than mine?

I observed Sophie with newfound interest after my discovery. I studied her like a naturalist watching some strange animal in the wild, trying to understand why this creature does the things it does. How was she able to live that lie? Would it happen again? But in time I came to believe that whatever had gone on with her lover had passed. Suddenly she was attentive to me. We grew closer.

Deep down, I didn't trust her anymore. Even so, I really tried to let myself love Sophie the best way that I could.

CHAPTER FIFTY
ADAM

It had been raining for more than a week when the other shoe dropped. Typical Seattle weather. Sophie was preparing a presentation for the Starbucks annual shareholders' meeting, and even though I made twice her salary and had ten times the responsibility at my job, I was pressed into daddy duty. Don't get me wrong: I loved Aubrey. Being her dad was only one level below having a corner office with a view of the Duwamish River just south of Seattle, the building I was working in at the time she was born. I took the birthing classes with Sophie. I told everyone what kind of fruit or vegetable my baby grew to the size of each week as the iPhone app told me.

"Eggplant!" I'd say as though it were something that I'd done.

"Durian!"

"Head of lettuce!"

Being her father made me happy in all kinds of ways. Some professional—yes, my boss actually said at the time that I needed a bigger raise than a female peer because she was single and had no kids—and some personal. Saying I was a father made me feel like I was a grown-up. *Finally.* I know it's stupid, but before Aubrey, Sophie and I were living the single life even though we were together. We traveled like we had flight benefits from every airline. In our first year or two of marriage we went to Fiji, Australia, Cancún, Maui, and Bethlehem. Pennsylvania, that is: Sophie's aunt lived there. In any case, we went out to eat whenever we wanted to, and we fucked in every place we visited. Yeah, including some of the places we ate.

It was fun. Sophie was everything I'd ever wanted. And yet, all of that went *poof* when Aubrey was born. Just *poof.* Gone. And the weird thing? I didn't miss the restaurants or the travel. The fucking, yes. But nothing else. My daughter was everything to me.

That all changed that one rainy, daddy-duty Monday morning.

Aubrey was due for her two-year checkup. Nothing wrong with her, of course, but when you have something as precious as a daughter, you don't skip medical appointments. No matter how cursory they might be. What percentile? How smart is she? How tall will she be? No one has the fat gene in our family, does she? How can we tell?

God, she's beautiful, isn't she?

Dr. Mary was one of those no-nonsense types with her hair in a spray-on-tight bun and shoes that looked like they were fashioned of rubber and cardboard.

I bet she was wild out of the office.

She did her thing while I sat on a little stool and Aubrey stretched out on the paper-covered table in the examination room.

"Everything looking A-OK?" I asked.

"Yeppers," she said.

Who says *yeppers*? Only Dr. Mary. I knew for sure she was a wild animal when she was off with her boyfriend. Had to be a flipside there.

The doctor told me everything I wanted to hear. Aubrey was above average in every measurement. I was thrilled, of course. I'm *not* average. Neither is Sophie. There would have to be a big mistake to find anything average about our daughter.

"She's perfect, Adam," Dr. Mary said.

I beamed as I watched Aubrey, who was distracted by a puppy poster overhead.

Just then Dr. Mary's buzzer went off and she excused herself, leaving the iPad with Sophie's chart on the little table next to where I was sitting on the stool.

"Training a new nurse today," she said as the door swooshed closed behind her.

Since she was gone, I did what everyone else in my position would probably do.

I looked at the chart.

The notes were just as she said. I smiled at the mention of "Dad is concerned about her growth, and I indicated she's ten percent above average."

Only ten? I wasn't sure she actually said that. But that was fine.

I didn't touch the screen. I only read what I could see. At the top were the basics. My name. Sophie's name. Aubrey's birth date. Her blood type.

That was what stopped me.

It said she was AB.

I knew there had to be a mistake. I give blood at work at least once a quarter. More when there is some kind of disaster. One time after a Caribbean tropical storm, I gave until I was sure I was as white as chalk. My type is O negative. I'm a universal donor. I give because it makes me look good at SkyAero: a member of the ten-gallon club. I know it helps people too, but I'd be a liar—and that's one thing I'm not—if I said anything otherwise. Sophie was type A. I knew that. She gave blood too, though not as much as I do. She didn't have to prove herself as someone who cares at Starbucks.

In that moment, unless there was some gargantuan mistake, I knew something else. The room closed in on me. Like a total eclipse. A big fucking plastic bag over my head. A black one: one of those triple-thick, black plastic Hefty bags that can hold the weight of a MINI Cooper without tearing. Tight too. I couldn't breathe.

"Aubrey," I said to get her attention. She looked at me with a smile.

I saw parts of her then that didn't belong to me: her nose, the shape of her brow . . . I wondered if they could belong to the DNA of someone else.

I looked at the chart a second time.

It just couldn't be. I told myself to give my head a shake. The thoughts were pellets in a shotgun blast. None lethal on its own, but all together, effective enough to kill. One of them was the folder I found on her computer. The notes to a lover. He was more than a lover. They were notes to the man who got her pregnant. *Aubrey's dad.* I actually wanted to cry right then. The cut was so deep and so cruel.

Dr. Mary came in, then immediately saw the look on my face. Her eyes were full of what I was pretty sure was genuine concern.

"Is something wrong?" she asked.

"Sorry," I said, pretending to look at my phone before putting it in my pocket. "Took a call from the office. Fiasco with a project, and I'm not there to fix it, of course. Big mistake to take that call."

She gave me a knowing smile. "Big mistake to hire a new nurse when there's no one to train her but me. Goodness, how I hate Mondays."

"I hate them too," I said.

That Monday in particular was brutal. I'd brought my daughter to a medical appointment and left with someone else's kid. I did nothing to deserve this. Goddamn Sophie! She not only fucking cheated on me, but she had a baby with the guy. I can forgive myself for things I've done, but I can't forgive her.

After all, she was supposed to be better than me.

I took Aubrey for the drive home, barely looking at her in the car seat behind me. When I did, I saw only betrayal. I saw her mother in a hotel room taking it from another man. The affair might have been long over, but the consequences of it had ruined my life. After I handed her off to our nanny, Katrina, I returned to work. And since I'd made a big deal on Friday about being late because I was taking my daughter to her checkup, everyone asked me about it.

"She's great," I said.

A stranger to me, but great.

"Healthy as can be," I said.

Some other dad would be glad to know that.

CHAPTER FIFTY-ONE
ADAM

Bradlee Mitchell is my organization's millennial du jour. He's got the misspelled first name that signals überindividuality and a résumé with more stops than a suburban airport shuttle, all indicating he won't be around our office for long. That's fine. He's bright and eminently usable. I finally succumbed to my curiosity and deepening rage over Sophie's affair with her soul mate and handed him the thumb drive.

"They're emails. All from one sender. It's not work related," I cautioned him. "I'll pay you."

Bradlee, who has a degree from UW in accounting but hates his job, said he didn't care about money. He was more into experiences.

"No need, Adam," he answered. "I'll do it tonight. On the house. My folks are gone to Spokane for a few days, and I got the place to myself."

In my day that meant hosting a party that you could count on getting out of hand.

For Bradlee, it's a chance to sit around and play video

games without worrying that his mom is going to yell at him.

"What exactly are you looking for?" he asked.

"Basic stuff," I told him. "It's for my brother. He wants to know if you can track the IP. Figure out the sender's name if you can."

"Gotcha," he said.

I had scrubbed out Sophie's name and her replies to lover boy. Bradlee could probably find that info if he tried. I guessed I didn't care if he did. I just wanted to know. Who was my wife seeing?

"Want me to text you the info?" he asked.

"No," I said. "Just bring it in. I'll want the drive back too."

The next day Bradlee showed up with the thumb drive, a smile on his face. He looked excited. Excited for Bradlee, that is. His expression was decidedly less sleepy than normal.

"Dude," he said. "Your brother's wife is a total bitch."

I nodded. "Yeah, she is."

"Anyway, it was easy peasy to figure this out. The emails were sent from the Blue Door's IP. The guy logged on to his Gmail there using the restaurant's computer."

"Can you tell exactly who sent it?"

The kid shook his head. "But I bet if you go down there, you can scope it out. Been there once. Food's good. Small place. Can't be that many guys there shagging your brother's wife."

He returned the drive to my open hand. I squeezed it like a stress ball, and it dug into my palm.

I knew where I was going for lunch.

CHAPTER FIFTY-TWO
KRISTEN

Randall Howser is our law firm's senior partner. He's in his seventies and sports a shock of black hair that we assume to be a toupee. It seriously has to be. But of course, no one would mention it. He writes the checks, after all. And if he thinks he looks good, that's fine with me. In fact, make that fabulous.

It's my anniversary at the firm, and while I'm up to my neck in the quicksand of a case and the worry over what's happening with Connor, I have zero choice but to go to the obligatory lunch.

"Just you and me," Randall says.

I don't feel uncomfortable about this. He's harmless.

What isn't harmless is his insistence that we dine at the Blue Door.

"I love that place," he says.

I suggest a new Pan Asian place downtown, but he shakes his head.

"I really like the Blue Door," he persists. "I don't have a reservation, but I have a hunch you can get us a great table."

I want to push back. It's not that I'm ashamed of Connor working there. He's great at his job. And it's consistently rated as one of the best restaurants in Seattle. Really. It just feels awkward. And I admit to myself, the idea of sitting there with my boss while my husband serves us a meal is a little embarrassing.

Randall squires me in like I'm his date. He insists that Connor serve us.

"We're family," he says.

Connor does his unfailing best to charm. He's juggling three other tables, and his smile is omnipresent. But he can't hide it from me. Our eyes lock when he hands us the menus. I can tell that this is humiliating for him too.

"I'm a big fan of Chef Micah," Randall says, putting on his readers to review the fresh sheet. "And of you, Connor."

"You're too kind," Connor says.

As we sit there, and I process the moment, I can't help but think of the time my husband's connection to the Blue Door sent a monster to my office.

"New client's here," Marcy announced.

I checked the printout for the day.

Adam Warner, 2 p.m.

A minute later Mr. Warner was sitting across from me. He was a good-looking man, early forties, I thought, in a nice suit. A very nice suit for Seattle. Italian cut, I'd say. Marcy made the appointment, and I couldn't recall at the moment why he was seeing me. Our firm is big enough to manage cases both civil and criminal.

"You don't know who I am," he said.

I looked at his face. Did we meet somewhere? At a conference? Was he with another firm in town?

And then he looked at me like I was a tin rabbit at a shooting gallery.

Without preamble, he fired.

"Your husband fucked my wife."

Even before I could process what was happening, I wanted to defend Connor. It's what I do. "I don't know what you're talking about," I said, taking my eyes off him for a fleeting second that I knew would clue any juror in to the fact that I was lying.

"Yes," he said. "You do."

"I think you should leave, Mr. Warner."

"You might think that, but I think you need to hear me out. Things are about to get real ugly. The truth, as I'm sure you know, being in the legal arena, is sometimes not very pretty."

"I will call Security," I said.

"No you won't. Not until after I say what I'm going to say."

I watched Marcy walk by the window at the side of my door. A slow walk. I got up and lowered the blinds. In doing so, I noticed that my hands were trembling. I looked at the man who'd planted himself in the chair in my office like he was a suicide bomber and he was about to detonate both of us.

"How did you find me?" I asked.

"Once I found Connor Moss at the Blue Door, it was two clicks of a mouse to unearth that he's married to you. You're all over the Internet, Mrs. Moss. Seriously, though, a bus-boy?"

My hands were still shaking, so I hid them under my desk.

"He's the headwaiter," I said, again defending Connor.

Adam rolled his eyes.

"I know my husband had an affair," I told him. "It was a while ago. It's over. I'm sorry that you came to see me about something that is already handled. I'm sorry for any part Connor played in your marriage, but it's done."

He let a beat of silence fill the air as he walked over to the window to look out at the view.

"Her name is Aubrey," he said, without looking at me.

"That's nice, but I don't have any quarrel with Mrs. Warner. I hope you can work things out and get on with your life."

He turned to face me. "Aubrey is your husband's daughter's name."

And there it was. The end of everything I thought the world and life with Connor could be.

Aubrey was Connor's daughter's name.

CHAPTER FIFTY-THREE
LEE

It's almost one a.m. on the last day of June when my phone pulses on the nightstand next to me. I reach over Millicent, who somehow always manages to sleep next to my face. The name on the screen hits me like a jolt of caffeine from the bottom of a church-basement percolator. I think only a beat about whether I should pick up or not.

"Adam?" I ask in a whisper voice.

Silence.

I repeat his name.

Finally a response.

"Kind of late to call," he says.

"You shouldn't call me," I tell him as my feet find the floor.

"I guess not," he says.

I wait for more, but there's silence once more on the line. *Is he drunk?* I wonder.

"The investigation is open," I say, filling the empty space. "That means everything you say could become part of the case."

"Yeah," he finally says, "I guess so."

"Have you been drinking, Adam?"

"Little bit."

His words are slurred and "guess so" comes at me like a single word. I suspect his drinking was more than a "little bit."

"I think you should hang up," I tell him.

"I'm not calling about Sophie," he says.

I don't know where this is going, but his words come at me like a warning.

"What are you calling about, then?" I ask. "Are you all right? Is Aubrey okay?"

I hear ice in a glass. "Yeah," he says. "We're fine. Everyone's fine."

I should end the call, but I don't.

"Then what is it?" I ask.

"I've been thinking about Hodge and what he did."

I hate hearing my molester's name. It always feels like the jolt of a cattle prod. In print, on a report, or from the lips of another party.

Like Adam Warner. Just now.

"We're not talking about that, Adam," I say. "I don't want to."

"You don't get to own all of that," he says. More ice clinking. "You don't get to be the decider of what is yours and what can't be someone else's experience."

"I don't follow you, Adam. This call is over."

"Don't!" he says, his voice louder and more urgent. "What happened to you that day was only one side of it. Do you know what it did to me?"

You became a hero. That's what, I think. But there is a churlish quality to those words when I think them in my head.

"What?" I ask. "What did what to you?"

"Finding you," he says, his voice now fading.

Next, I hear ice cubes being released from a metal tray, and the sound of liquid pouring. He's getting more booze into his system.

"I'm very grateful for that," I say.

"Not about you," he says. "This is about me right now. I want you to know that as long as I live, I'll look back at the day I found you as the greatest moment of my life. There was no pretense. No trying to get something for nothing. No game playing. You need to know that finding you was the best I'll ever do."

His words touch me. He's right. I'd never really thought what the experience might have been for him beyond the award he got and his picture in the paper. I may have cheated death because of him. Nothing Adam would do would ever surpass the moment he found me that day. There was no ulterior motive behind my rescue. No jockeying for a better job. No manipulation. His finding me was untainted by anything. It was pure and selfless.

"There's something else," he says.

There's something in his tone that makes me want to run. But I don't. I do what I'm best at—what makes me effective as an investigator. I listen.

"I have always had feelings for you, Lee. Okay? I just wanted to say that to you because things are spinning out of control, and you deserve to know."

This isn't expected. Or wanted. My head spins.

"This call needs to be over," I tell him.

And it is.

The phone in my hand feels like poison. I don't need to hear any of that. I don't *want* to hear it. What Adam Warner feels about me or how he felt about the day he found me is best left unsaid. I set down the phone. Millicent is on my lap, purring and kneading her claws into my thigh. I don't wince. I'm just too caught up in the phone call. Tears fall. I always wanted to tell Adam Warner that I thought of him as a hero, like something out of a storybook. That I had feelings for him too—feelings that went beyond the fact that he'd saved me.

CHAPTER FIFTY-FOUR
LEE

As the days turn into weeks we have less and less to go on with the Warner case. It isn't for lack of trying. Montrose and I have knocked on every door. Interviewed a dozen people. Followed up on tips upon tips.

Abductions and murder are rare.

A cold trail is common.

Coyle and his red truck remain MIA. A conversation with his sister indicates that he'd been seeing a doctor for treatment of a serious illness—something he hadn't wanted the trucking firm to know. The reeds on his truck? They grow everywhere. I'd jumped to a conclusion.

The truth is, we need the DNA results back. Calls to the lab in Tacoma don't make things move faster. In fact, part of me thinks that a tech will put your request at the bottom of the pile if you ask too many times. Everything is a number-one priority. No such thing as a number-two.

* * *

It looks like a game, but it isn't. It's survival. Gulls circle over Oakland Bay in Shelton and drop oysters and clams on the rocks. They glide overhead, just at the water's edge, and then they aim and release. A shell falls and smacks a rock, and in an instant—before a crow or another lazy bird cuts in—the gulls drop in the air like yo-yos and land with the softest touch. Over and over they do this. All day. I wonder how *birdbrain* is even a term. The gulls of the Pacific Northwest are amazingly smart. They know a good way to get those shells open.

Montrose hands me a coffee.

"Thanks," I say as he takes the spot next to me and we face the water.

"You want to talk about it?" he asks.

It could be many things. None of which I want to discuss.

"Not really," I say.

"You need to," he says. "It's there, bubbling beneath the surface. It's doing both good and bad things to you, Lee."

"What's the good?"

"You're the cop you are because of what happened to you back then. You feel the pain that a victim feels, and you use all of that to fuel everything you do on the job."

I take that in. He's reaching, but it's a kind gesture.

"And the bad?"

"I'm not a shrink," he says. "I don't even believe in them. But I can give you what I think."

"And what's that?" I ask, letting the coffee go down my narrowing throat. "What is it that you think?"

"That there's a part of you that is still stuck back there at the end of Tamarack Lane," he says. "That you survived all of that, but you never let go of it. It clings to you, and it messes with your head."

My eyes stay on the water. "I thought you weren't a shrink, Montrose."

"You know," he goes on, "I'm not. Been to one or two.

Never really worked out for me. This is just two people talking here, okay?"

"Two people," I repeat. "Fine."

I don't say anything more as another gull drops another shell on the rocks right in front of us. The white fragments scatter, and the gull drops down to eat the oyster.

Finally, after what must have been the most annoyingly long pause, I speak up.

"You might have something there," I say, albeit reluctantly. "I think there is a part of me that was left under those branches when I was twelve. I think of me—that girl—and I wonder how it was that I was so stupid not to see what Hodge was up to when he first struck up a conversation that morning."

"You were only a kid," he says.

"I know," I say, now looking right at him. "But Cathy Rinehart was a young woman, and she made a mistake. Sophie Warner, she did too. They all experienced that split second when they knew there was no way out. Like me, getting in that car to see kittens."

CHAPTER FIFTY-FIVE
KRISTEN

A toilet has more uses than one might imagine. There are the obvious ones, of course. But as I sit here with the pregnancy test wand in my hand, I think of the toilet as a kind of gulag where I wait for an answer that eludes me month after month. I hold no doubts: I'm being tortured on that gulag toilet. No one can help me. No one can save me. I've put myself here, and I'm full of regret about it.

That wand is far from magical. It has failed me time and time again. I don't even want to glance at the little window that gives the response. It's like the sun burning into your retinas, making you blind. I don't dare look. It's like a scene in a cheesy 3-D movie in which a spike or sword is aimed for your eye. You wince. You turn away. You don't ever want to look at that again.

I've approached this quest from every angle. I've seen a psychic. I've pumped myself full of hormones. I've guzzled my way through more herbal tea than a taster at Stash. I've prayed to God so often that I don't even believe in him anymore. I'm bereft. I'm miserable.

I am not a mother.
Maybe I never will be.

I think of the women on TV who have gone off the deep end, feigned their own pregnancies with pillows and padding, and befriended an expectant mother. I almost understand the craziness that takes them to the point where they will cut a baby from a stranger's womb.

I don't think I could go that far.

I have never seen a case in which the baby snatcher had a happy ending.

I've also watched the news reports of the occasional woman who goes after a child in the park, in the schoolyard, in the hospital nursery.

There's a singular kind of desperation that links all of us who cannot conceive but think of nothing else. I wonder about us. What has made that message play over and over inside our heads? Is it biology? I want it to be that. I want the reason I sit on the toilet, hoping against hope, to be *biological* and not some kind of mental disorder.

I look down, finally. Tears come with the rage and disappointment that fill my bloodstream. I have never gotten the duo of parallel lines before, and I don't get it today. Still, I've done everything that I'm supposed to do. I should give up. I really should. That's the logical thing to do. I'm all about logic. In the courtroom. In every aspect of my being.

Except when it comes to this.

When it comes to this, I find that I cannot do anything but keep trying—trying until there is no hope.

A woman in China had a healthy baby boy at sixty-five.

I have decades to go.

A life sentence on my gulag toilet.

CHAPTER FIFTY-SIX
CONNOR

She's in the bathroom a very long time. I know why. It kills me every time Kristen goes through the ritual after we have sex. Baby-making sex. It's taken over everything in our lives, and I don't know how to stop it. I drink more than I should to cope, but it doesn't help. It's as if Kristen is on a tiny raft in the middle of the Pacific, and I can't reach her to get her back into the boat. She wouldn't take my hand anyway. She wants to put some of the blame, maybe most of it, on me. That I'm the reason why we don't have a son or a daughter.

I know full well that I'm not the problem. There's nothing wrong with me. I can't say that to her, though. It would crush her.

So I let her sling the poisoned darts and steel-tipped arrows when she feels the need. She told me one time that my underwear needed to be looser. That I sleep too hot. That my balls didn't descend as far as they should. There's not a damn thing wrong with my nut sack, but I let that go. I let all of it go because Kristen, as it turns out, is the love of my life.

So I do what she says. I do it when she says. If she wants me to come into a tube normally used for men about to go on chemo and wanting to bank their seed, then fine. I'll watch some porn and take care of business.

She comes out of the bathroom, and I can see she's been crying.

"Oh, baby," I say, though the word's a bad choice. "I was feeling it today too. I thought we had this."

Kristen melts in my arms. She doesn't let go very often. This time is different. She's sobbing, a messy kind of crying, and I hold her as tightly as I can. I tell her that she and I will be fine. I bring up for the umpteenth time that if we can't have a family biologically, we can adopt.

"I want our child to be part of us," she says. "I know it sounds terrible, but that's how I really feel, Connor. I don't want to raise someone else's kid and always know that he or she wasn't really a part of either one of us. It's like babysitting for eighteen years and then getting kicked to the curb when the real parents come home."

"It isn't like that," I say.

Her blue eyes are framed in red. "I've seen it. At the law office. On TV. Everywhere. The grass is always greener to these adopted kids."

"Not all of them," I tell her.

She pulls back. "Most of them. The saying 'blood is thicker than water' rings true because it *is* true."

"Not all," I say.

She stops crying, and it passes through my mind that my wife is beautiful even after a cry.

"Maybe not all," she finally allows.

It's no surrender, but it's the first time Kristen has opened the door on adoption. It's only a crack. A sliver. It's a beginning, though.

* * *

That night, while Kristen sleeps and dreams that I've finally gotten her pregnant, I take the tequila bottle and head for her office at the front of the house. My fingertips hover over the keyboard of the computer before I touch the space bar, and the blue light of the screen comes at me. I shouldn't do what I'm about to do. Nothing good will come of it. I know that. And yet, I find myself unable to resist the impulse. I look up the Warner murder case. It's been six weeks since everything happened. I remember nothing of it. Yet I can't get it out of my mind. I study pictures of Sophie, her husband, Adam, and their little girl, Aubrey. That same wave of nausea that hit me at the Blue Door finds me again. Did I do this? Was I the one who took her? Killed her? Dumped her in the water of Hood Canal?

I don't ask myself why I would do it. There is no need for that. I would never hurt anyone. Not Sophie Warner. Not anyone. Sitting there at my computer, looking at each of them, raises tears to my eyes.

I lost time.

I had blood.

My shoes were sandy.

I sit there reading and wondering what I should do. Should I go to the police? Should I post a tip online? The reality is I don't even know what I'd say.

"Hey, about that case in Lilliwaup. I don't think I did it, but I might have."

I don't think I could manage a list of reasons that would point to me. I don't remember. I could see the look of doubt in Kristen's eyes. I could imagine the hurt that this would bring to her. And the shame that would make her the subject of gossip all over our neighborhood.

Indeed, all over Seattle.

She wants to believe in me. I can see that too. I'm not imagining it. I know her better than anyone in the world. Kristen would do whatever she could to help me. I know that in the marrow of my bones.

I know all of that, and yet I wonder.

Would she still stand by me if she knew that I'd known Sophie Warner?

Would anyone?

"What are you doing up?"

I turn to see Kristen right behind me, and my heart rate ratchets up.

"Just thinking about what happened," I finally say.

My wife sees the tequila but doesn't remark on it. Or say a word about my increasing need to drink. A finger wag. A headshake. Nothing more.

"Let's go to bed," she says. "You are fine, Connor. You are a good man. I need you to stop this train of thought right now. Okay?"

She reaches over and shuts off the computer.

I look up and soak in the light that Kristen has always been. "Right," I say. "Okay. Right."

She's got my back, and I don't deserve it. I know that too.

CHAPTER FIFTY-SEVEN
LEE

I don't recognize the number when the call comes through to my desk phone.

"I know you don't give a shit," the voice says right after I pick up. "But I didn't do anything to Sophie Warner."

The connection isn't great. At once it crackles and fades. That doesn't matter. I recognize the voice.

"Mr. Coyle? Is that you?"

He doesn't answer immediately.

"It's me, and I'm done," he says. "I'm done being the whipping boy for investigators who have something to prove. I didn't do anything wrong in that other incident, and I didn't do anything to Sophie Warner."

The word *incident* sticks in my brain.

"You need to come in," I say, straining to hear any background noise, any clues as to where Jim Coyle might be. His truck is moving. That much I can tell.

"No point in it," he says. "I'm about done anyway. You're just making things move along faster."

"Please," I say. "You need to come in. You need to clear yourself."

"Look, Detective. I don't need to do anything. My life has been fucked up since I went to prison. I'm dying, lady. I'm about done."

"What do you mean? Dying?"

A long pause. "Cancer," he says, spitting out one of the hardest words anyone can utter when it's taken over their life. "If you really need to know. Probably caused by the likes of you and all the bullshit that I went through."

As the phone crackles and his voice fades in and out, he tells me his doctor's name and how he's been seeking an alternative treatment because he had no medical coverage through the trucking firm. I don't know how that could be, but I write down every word. He tells me how he kept it to himself because he didn't want to lose his job.

"They'd bounce me out the second they could."

"That's against the law," I say.

He lets out a morose laugh. "Seriously. The law? I just want you to know that you and your partner are wrong about me. I should have told you. But I didn't. I was in treatment the day before that woman went missing. I didn't get home until the morning you came to shit on me."

"You really should have told us."

"Right. Well, I'm telling you now. Not that it matters. I don't have a job. I don't have a reputation, and pretty soon I'm going to be done."

"You need to come in," I say.

Silence fills my ear.

"You need to make sure my dog is okay."

And with that, Jim Coyle hangs up. The word *incident* continues to reverberate. It's a familiar euphemism, well known by me and my family.

CHAPTER FIFTY-EIGHT
LEE

People used to ask me about what happened when I was a girl, and I always said that I didn't remember much of the "incident"—again, my mother's word. I explain it in a way that suggests memory loss due to trauma. For most, that's acceptable. I wish it were that simple.

The truth is that I remember nearly every minute of my ordeal with Albert Hodge.

That morning stays in my head like a graphic novel, images telling the story in bold swaths of black and white with smudges of jolting color roaring out of the lines. My point of view shifts from what I saw as my attacker undid his pants and forced his way inside me to how I know I must have looked to him. I see my face frozen in fear. I rise above the scene and watch everything like a detached observer.

It isn't happening to me.

Yet it did.

Thinking and dreaming of what happened is a far different experience than giving voice to events that haunt you. You cry when you tell someone something. You shake. You get sick. You seek comfort. When you don't speak about it and just think it, you don't fall apart.

I don't admit it to anyone. Even if they've asked. I'm private like that. The truth is I've had counseling. Gobs of talk therapy. I'm sure it helps others, but I think that any path to healing is the right one. Not talking about it and pretending that I can't remember is my chosen path. It's my right to hold that inside. Everyone makes a choice on what they want to do with what was done to them. I've chosen to bottle it up. Sequester the evil. Move on. I do it because I'm so ashamed of the stupid mistake that I made. My therapist would chime in right now and interrupt my thoughts to remind me that I was a child and that I had been victimized. That I had no hand in what happened to me. That what Albert Hodge did was his doing—and none of my own.

That's fine for some to say. That makes them feel better. I'm not mad at anyone.

Just me.

My mother and I had a fight that morning before school. I'd put on some mascara and what I thought was a subtle smear of eye shadow. I was just messing around. It wasn't that I wanted to be older, more attractive, garner attention. Honestly. I was just being a girl experimenting with makeup.

"You march yourself into the bathroom before your dad sees you," she said.

My face went hot. "Sorry, Mom."

"You'll be sorry if Dad sees you looking like that. No makeup until you are sixteen."

"And no ears pierced until I'm eighteen," I told her, with what I'm sure now was a sassy intonation.

My mom gave me a look, and I knew better than to stand there and provoke her into an argument. In truth, it wasn't that big of a deal. I did what she asked, and I was glad that my dad didn't get involved. Yes, I was embarrassed.

On the walk to school, I fumed a little. Only a little. This is not an "I'm mad at my mom and running away from home" story. Not at all. It was, in my mind at the time, a little manufactured drama that I could tell everyone. I wanted to start with Charlene, but she had that dental appointment.

So, yes, I had a fight with my mother over makeup. Maybe that did a number on me. Maybe it left me feeling sorry for myself. As much as I've thought about it in the years since, I'm still not sure. Sometimes being certain of something is impossible.

I love my mom so much that I never told her everything that happened. I know that if she thought our little conflict had played a part in what I did, it would kill her.

The truth is that Albert Hodge didn't lure me with kittens, then overpower me. I got inside his vehicle on my own. Stupid. Stupid. I was so unbelievably stupid.

"I'm lost," Albert said, pointing to his newspaper.

"Yeah," I said, "you're on the wrong side of town."

"Crap!" he said. "Excuse my French."

"No problem."

"I'm Al."

"I'm Lee."

Back to the paper, perplexed. "Clear across town? Now I'm really turned around."

Just a little older than my brother. Young to have a big blue boat of a car.

And then I said it. I don't know why for sure.

"I can show you where to turn. It's on my way to school." And I got in.

And really, that was that. The locks went down. Hodge reached over to the passenger seat with a fist wrapped in a cloth dipped in what the police later said was chloroform, though at the time it reminded me of my aunt Martina's vodka-perfumed breath.

In the graphic novel in my mind, Aunt Martina is in a panel, holding her martini glass and wagging her finger at me.

I missed some of what happened. Lost a little time. Not so much that I don't remember how he tore off my clothes in the vacant lot. Or how he pinned me down and shoved himself inside of me. I was in shock. I remember a red admiral butterfly floating over us, and I thought to myself how I wish I could fly. He raped me. Choked me. He whispered things in my ear that reverberate today.

"You're such a good girl," he repeated over and over. "You like this, don't you?"

I didn't, of course. His face grew redder and redder. I was thinking that he might have a heart attack. Hoping he would. Praying that God would hear me and strike him dead. I never blamed God for not following through in that vacant lot. I know that I would not have been there if I hadn't stepped into his car.

Trust and stupidity are close friends. Of course, no one really knows that until it's too late.

Two hours after Coyle calls me, Montrose confirms that our person of interest has been seeing a practitioner of sorts in Centralia, a small town on the interstate best known for its outlet malls.

And, I guess, its alternative healers.

"A quack," he says. "A nice quack. He says Coyle checked in there for some kind of overnight herbal infusion the Friday before Sophie Warner was abducted. Get this, Lee. The treatments are usually at the Super 8, but they don't allow pets, so Coyle and that insufferable dog of his stayed at the Bellflower Motel. The quack videotapes all treatments, he says, and would be glad to show us Coyle's. Not real big on HIPAA and all that, evidently. I said sure, send me some footage. He says Coyle wasn't out the door until noon on Saturday. Assuming the video checks out, I'd say that he's not our guy."

I want to ask about Montrose's own medical problems. It seems the door is a little open. But I don't do it. Montrose isn't the kind of man who likes to talk about himself. I don't like to talk about myself, either. We're good that way.

"We need to find him," I say. "He's suicidal."

"We can't save everyone, Lee."

Don't I know that.

CHAPTER FIFTY-NINE
ADAM

The reception area at the law offices of Belding and Son is empty except for a bunch of children's and parenting magazines and a play area strewn with toys. And me, of course. I sit quietly, playing Candy Crush on my phone while I wait for Dan Belding Jr. to see me. I'm early. I'm unemployed. I'm a widower. None of those things define me. At least I hope not.

Dan and I went to school together. His father, Dan Belding Sr., coached the Shelton High School basketball team. He was a pleasant guy with coffee breath and an overbite. He was also the first professional person I really knew. He was a lawyer. In Shelton, that was pretty much the top of the food chain. Dan Jr. was too short to play hoops, but as it turned out, he was able to follow in his dad's footsteps by getting a law degree.

"Sorry about your dad," I say when Dan comes to greet me with a hello and a handshake. He's a younger version of his father. Coffee breath must run in the family.

"He went quick," he says. "That's a blessing."

Dan Sr. had cancer. Testicular. Any man's worst night-mare.

"Good," I say.

I follow him to his office, which is surprisingly modern considering that he's from Shelton.

I don't know why that always surprises me on the rare occasion I run into someone I knew or someone from a family I knew. I have it in my mind somehow that my Shelton past was set in a blend of Appalachia and Hooterville. It wasn't. Not really. The town was working class, and the bosses who managed the mill were working class—at least in spirit and lifestyle. Sure, we had some poor outliers, but not many. And besides, every time I stand in front of the mirror, I no longer see any evidence that I personally came from a Pacific Northwest backwater.

"You made your dad proud," I say, indicating the firm's name in gold letters on the glass door to his office.

Dan gives me a sheepish grin. "Yeah. Dad thought it was some big bait to get me to come back here, but this place has always been home."

I hold my tongue about Shelton. I'm not ashamed I'm from here. Not really. I just like to keep it in the past. Way past.

"So you and your wife are looking to adopt," he tells me as we get down to business.

He hasn't read the news stories, at least not closely enough to get to my name.

"No," I say. "I'm here on another matter."

He takes off his glasses and studies my face. "What kind of a matter?"

"My wife died," I say, "and, well, I don't think I'm equipped to raise our daughter."

The words I have aimed at him are a double-barrel load, and I know it. I let him process them for a minute.

"I'm sorry," he says. "I didn't know about your wife."

I take a breath. I actually need one. A really big gulp of

air. This is harder than I thought. My emotions are a whirlpool, and I'm hanging on the edge of something that I know is impossible to completely explain. Not to anyone who hasn't been where I am right at the moment. I try anyway.

"Sophie was murdered over Memorial Day weekend. Up at the canal." I watch him as the synapses of recognition finally fire. He drops his eyes from mine. He knows the case. Everyone in the region does. Linda London has received quite the uptick in her teetering career from her exploitation of my private family business.

"Wow," he finally says. "That's terrible. Saw something about that. I guess I really didn't place that it was you, Adam. Really sorry for your loss."

"Thanks," I tell him. "I appreciate it. Been rough. Rougher than anything I could have imagined. That's why I'm here."

He sets his glasses on the desk. "And why is that? How can I help you?"

"I don't think I can raise my daughter by myself," I repeat.

"Hey," he goes on, "you're going through a rough patch. You'll get through this. Tell me about your little girl."

"I doubt I'll get through it," I tell him. "She's three. She's great. Smart as can be. Cute like her mother. Her name is Aubrey. She's wonderful, but I can't raise her."

"You don't want to do this," Dan says, pushing back. "You're just in a bad place at the moment. Maybe you could get some help. A relative? A nanny?"

He's trying to be helpful. That's Dan Jr. to a T. I remember how he served as equipment manager when he didn't make the basketball team. Always there with a clipboard and an earnest expression.

"I have a nanny. It isn't that I can't take care of her. Like I said, she's great. The fact is that—and don't think less of me because I'm honest—I don't want to be bogged down. I don't want the life of a single dad. Dan, we both grew up in Shelton, where most families stuck together; and honestly, they were better for it. A mom and a dad. Traditional, right? But still the best way."

"Is there a relative?" Dan asks. "Grandparents?"

I shake my head. "God, no. I can't have Sophie's folks take Aubrey. Not after how her dad molested my wife when she was a girl."

Another blast and this guy will start ducking whenever I say something.

"Jesus," he says, now a little flustered. "Of course not. You can't have your daughter around a pedophile."

"Sophie hated her parents," I say. "Her dad for molesting her. Her mom for putting up with it."

"I hear you," he says. "Were there any charges brought against her father?"

"No," I say. "It was more than thirty years ago, when no one really talked about what sick fucks like Frank Flynn were doing to their daughters."

"Has he heard these charges before?" he asks. "From you? Your wife?"

I nod. "Yeah. Sophie confronted him years ago. She acted like she forgave him, because she let him come around and we had to go to their place for Christmas. Not sure why she did that. But that's what she did."

He puts his glasses back on, gets out a notepad, and starts writing. "And what about Mrs. Flynn?"

"She's like a scoop of Crisco," I say. "She's weak. No backbone. Won't stand up to her husband."

He sets down his pen. "They'll fight for custody," he says. "Those freaks often do. See it as a pathway to vindication."

"Wouldn't surprise me," I say. "He's threatened it. But I doubt he'd go balls to the wall if he was going to be exposed for being a pervert."

I give him Frank's information. Everything I know about him. Helen too. I give him Aubrey's birth date. He asks for little details as I lay out my hopes for Aubrey. Parents with education and some means. I'm giving her up. I'm not throwing her to the wolves. None of this is her fault. He takes down every word.

"Giving up your child for adoption is huge," he finally says, now treating me like some teenager who got knocked up by her older boyfriend. He's using his preacher's voice now, all calm and composed as if I could be persuaded somehow.

"I want you to think about it over the next few days, and then we'll get together and finalize how this will work," he tells me. "After that, we'll meet with the prospective parents. You want this an open adoption, right?"

"No," I say. "I want the new parents to be the sole parental figures in Aubrey's life. If she wants to poke around the Internet in twenty years or so to find me, that's fine. That will be up to her. I'm not going to confuse Aubrey by hanging on and playing part-time, half-assed father figure."

"But Aubrey is not an infant," he says. "She's three. She knows you are her father."

"I know what's best for her."

Dan Jr. gives me a nod that indicates understanding, but I seriously doubt it. I gave the same headshake in a meeting at SkyAero when I wanted the damn thing to end so I could get on with more important things. Like anything other than what that slutty boss of mine was talking about.

"I just want you to think about it," he says.

"I have," I say. "Long and hard."

"Fine." He puts his notebook away. "Why don't you come back in a week? I'll sleep better and be a stronger advocate for you against the Flynns if you agree to some time to process what we've discussed. It's a lot. You've been through the wringer. Let's not make a mistake."

* * *

Look, I know the world will hate me for what I'm thinking as I return to my car for the drive back to the house. But it is true. I don't want to raise Aubrey without Sophie. Sophie was a good mom. She was the better half of our parenting. No doubt. I'll give her that.

I dig a little deeper for the truth. It's below the surface, but I can access it all right. It's always on my mind, but it is something I could never verbalize to anyone. Not a trusted friend. Not even my lawyer.

Seeing Aubrey is a reminder of the worst betrayal my wife ever perpetrated on me.

And the worst thing I've ever done.

Besides, it's not like I'm foisting off some kid who plays with matches or who has some kind of weird and unpronounceable disorder. Aubrey's a sweetheart. I'll miss her. I know in my bones that this is best. That I can't be the one to raise her. It's ugly, sad, but true. She's better off with someone else.

When I get inside, Katrina goes for her coat, and Aubrey runs to me as she always does. I scoop her up and lift her almost to the ceiling. I wonder how many more times I'll do that.

I also wonder if she'll remember me when she's gone.

CHAPTER SIXTY
ADAM

Sophie rides in the passenger seat on our way to the cabin. I don't strap her in with the seat belt. No need to. The cabin's owner alerted me of a cancellation, and I decided the time was right and taking Sophie there, where it all started, was the best thing to do. Sure, she is in an urn now, but she was there when she last wasn't. I am bringing her back to scatter her ashes off the beach that she vanished from. It's a good-bye party of one. Aubrey's too young to understand, so I left her with Katrina. The Flynns are too obnoxious to invite to anything, let alone a celebration of their daughter's life. So I didn't even text them about what I am doing.

Sophie always liked surprises.

"It's just you and me, babe," I say to the cheapest urn the wet-handed funeral home director offered as I go past the shingled exterior of the Alderbrook Resort and the hidden compound belonging to Bill and Melinda Gates. Lots of money here, I think. Money. My mind goes to that sore subject. My savings will only last until the end of the year. Sophie's life insurance will pay off the mortgage. I will need more money. A new job. A push of the reset button of my life.

I park under an ancient rhododendron, more tree than bush, next to the Wisteria's detached garage. Another car for one of the other cabins is already there, so I know that I won't be completely alone. That's fine. I'm not going to make a show out of this. That's not Sophie's style.

The urn, a pewter-colored aluminum, is cold from the AC. Sophie hated the cold weather. I smile. I carry the urn up the fern-lined path to the cabin door. I put it on a bench as I rotate the numbers on the lock box and open the door.

I haven't been here since the weekend Sophie died. I put her on the counter in the kitchen and survey the place. It is just as it was when we were here last. Like a moment had been frozen in time. I think of that day and the night before as I wander from room to room. I have no idea how many people have stayed in the cabin during the month and a half since then. Dozens, maybe? Yet I can still feel Sophie as if she's just left the room. I can smell her. It unnerves me a little, and I return to my car to get my bag and essentials.

Maker's, of course. It's five o'clock somewhere, as they say.

I'm not a fancy drinker, but I am a drinker who likes a half-good whiskey and isn't willing to pay for something better. I pull at the red wax that surrounds the neck of the bottle. I taste that first splash over ice.

Sophie, I think, *I brought you back here because I can't think of a better place to say good-bye forever.*

The whiskey burns a little. I like the burn. I drink more.

I'll use the same little rowboat that Aubrey and I took out the day Sophie was taken. I don't have anything to say as I deposit her ashes in the canal, but in case anyone is watching, I'll probably linger over the dust as it settles downward into the deep blue of the water. Maybe I'll mouth something. Or if someone is close by, I'll cry.

The surface of the water is an amplifier.

I sit on the couch and peer through the slats of the blinds at Hood Canal. The old wavy glass sends a thousand stabbing shards of light at me. I don't care. I look anyway. Facing up to what happened is necessary in order to truly let go of the past.

As I face my phone, I carefully consider whether I should text Lee again or not. She treated me badly in that fucked-up interview, that's for sure. But she's my only conduit for information on Sophie's case. Can't believe that after Jim Coyle there's been zero activity. That I know of anyway. As I sit here and look at the water, I can only half blame Lee's chilliness on her partner, but, Jesus, she shouldn't suppose that, just because of my mistake with Carrie, I'm capable of killing Sophie. Has she forgotten everything else about me?

I drink some more and then send the message.

I know you were just doing your job.

A second later she answers.

Right.

I sip more whiskey.

You know me at my core, Lee.

I do, Adam.

Anything new on the case?

Working it, Adam. Will never stop.

I know that about Lee. I know that the case that almost undid her haunts her. She won't fail twice. I want her to catch Sophie's killer so everyone can move on. It hangs over me. It hangs over everyone. I consider my next text very, very carefully. I don't want to send the wrong message. I don't want to scare her off. I want her to know that I am the grown-up version of the boy who found her that day under the branches of the plum tree. That I haven't morphed into something vile and hideous in the years since Albert Hodge took her. That maybe there was a purpose for our being reunited after all these years.

I start typing.

I'm up at the cabin. Brought Sophie's ashes to spread. Not sure I really want to do it alone.

She's typing. I watch the dots bounce on my phone.

She pushes "Send" and I read: I don't know.

I write back without hesitation: That's okay. I can do it alone.

I know Lee. I know why she went into police work. She wants to be a help to people. She's not motivated by revenge. She will never forget what I mean to her, and I can count on that no matter what anyone—including Frank Flynn, Carrie LaCroix, and Zach Montrose—has to say.

A second later, the response I hoped for: I'm coming. I can be there tomorrow. Late in the day.

I write: Perfect.

CHAPTER SIXTY-ONE
LEE

I'm still holding the phone in my palm after texting with Adam when Sarah Leonard from the Washington State Patrol Crime Lab texts me to call her.

Finally! Got a hit on the Warner case.

Sarah and I were working the Rinehart case when it unspooled into a disaster. We were both new in our jobs at the time and took the brunt of the blame for the botched case. None of it was really Sarah's fault. The officers responding had contaminated the scene, which was a gift to the killer. With the DNA compromised before it got to the lab, there was nothing she could do. I made mistakes too. I can't say that I didn't.

Social media had a field day, of course. That we were two young women in a mostly male-dominated field was red meat for those who'd rather have us serving coffee than warrants.

"I hope you're sitting down," Sarah says when she answers my call.

"With the shoes I stupidly wore today, you bet I am. What do you have?"

"Got a hit, and it's not James Coyle."

"Are you serious?"

"As a heart attack."

That's her favorite phrase. Everything Sarah does is as serious as a heart attack.

She goes one more. "The DNA Dr. Collier collected from the victim belonged to Connor Justin Moss."

I'm stunned.

"Connor Moss?"

"Yeah. Huntington Beach PD collected DNA in conjunction with a DUI when he was barely in his twenties."

"DNA for a DUI? Who does that?"

"California does," she says. "Or did. Not sure if they do now."

As Sarah goes lab-rat technical on the markers and the incontrovertible scientific analysis that connected Connor to Sophie's body, I think about the Mosses. They were in the Lily cabin that weekend. Connor was too sick to give a statement until the next day when he and Kristen, his lawyer wife, came to our offices. I remember thinking that he was a pleasant guy, a waiter.

"We ran all of the witnesses through the system and didn't come up with anything on Moss," I tell her.

"You couldn't have," Sarah says. "His arrest record was part of the disaster ten years ago when California upgraded systems and 'lost' records. Thankfully, the DNA-collected data was on a different system."

"So much for technology."

"Not the technology, Lee. It's always the people running it."

She's right about that.

I text Montrose right away.

I need to see you ASAP.

I keep my message vague, because I know that the contents of my phone are a public record and anything I share on it could become part of the case.

I want to text: Holy shit! It's Connor Moss!

A beat later, Montrose texts back that he's five minutes away.

While I wait for Montrose, I go on Facebook. This is well-trod ground, no doubt. Montrose worked the social media aspect of the case the first day of the investigation and turned up nothing.

I scroll down the page. I friended Adam a few years ago. I admit that I waited like a schoolgirl for three days—imagining that he didn't remember me or care about me—before he accepted my request. I posted some innocuous message, and he gave me a like. That was the sum of our social networking. He had almost a thousand friends—which, where I come from, is a very big number. I have less than a hundred. Popularity has never been my thing.

I look at Adam's page. He's updated it since I last viewed it to include a beautiful picture of Aubrey taken, I think, the day her mother went missing. She's standing in front of the Wisteria with her little pink suitcase and the biggest smile I've ever seen. I know that the photo will haunt her when she's older and puts into context what happened later at the cabin.

I read the words of encouragement and the—for once—proper use of the love emoji.

Next I click over to Sophie's profile. Her page is public, and it's frozen in time, of course. She posted a message the day before the trip to Hood Canal that she was heading out to what she hoped was her new "happy" place.

We all need a happy place, right? she wrote.

We all do, though clearly Sophie certainly didn't find hers.

I scroll through a mix of posts in which she was tagged. Some were from friends at Starbucks. She shared images of

Aubrey and Adam too. Those were heartbreaking. A life lived in the real world but now only existing online.

I note the VRBO travel website listing for "Historic Hood Canal Cabins—rent one, rent all three." The picture shows the Wisteria, Chrysanthemum, and Lily from the beach at low tide. The crescent-shaped bulkhead is studded with oysters and barnacles. Sophie had 640 friends. I scroll down and quickly recognize Janna Fong and Helen Flynn's pictures.

And one more.

Connor Moss
Works at: The Blue Door
Studies at:
Lives in: Seattle, Washington

"What's the ASAP all about? You finally crack ten likes on a video of your cat?"

Montrose has arrived and seen me scrolling through Facebook. He's wearing tan Dockers and a light blue long-sleeved shirt that makes him look like he should be parking cars somewhere. He smells like cigarette smoke, and I hope he's brought his Tic Tacs.

I pass my phone to him.

"Lab called," I say. "DNA on the Warner case matched Connor Moss."

My partner widens his gaze. "I didn't see *that* coming."

He doesn't surprise easily. It's clear he's as astonished as I am.

"Yeah, I just got off the phone with Sarah," I tell him. "What's more, Montrose, while I was waiting for you to get here, I went to Facebook—and get this—Connor and Sophie *are* friends. And Sophie posted on her wall where she was going for Memorial weekend."

He tilts his head as he looks at the small cracked screen of my phone. "They knew each other? How'd we miss that?"

He'd missed it, but I can't blame him. He hated social media because it was a weak area for him.

"Yeah, seems like it slipped by us," I say. "And he would have known where she was going the weekend she was killed. I don't know what was going on between them, but there's something there."

Montrose sets down my phone and slides it over to me.

"Good work, Lee."

I smile at him as I get up.

"Honestly," Montrose says as we walk down the hall to let our sheriff know what's happening, "I would have bet my house on Jim Coyle being the perp."

"Me too. Let's get over to the prosecutor's so we can get a judge to sign an arrest warrant."

CHAPTER SIXTY-TWO
CONNOR

I've just stepped outside for a run when I hear my name. It's the detectives from Mason County, Lee Husemann and Zach Montrose. I turn in their direction, and in a nanosecond I know that whatever is about to happen to me is not going to be good. Their faces are grim. Their eyes are piercing. Their mouths are straight lines.

I feel a ripple of nausea.

"Connor Moss," Detective Montrose says, "put your hands where we can see them."

I lift them in the air. "What's happening?" I ask, though it is obvious.

Kristen, who is about to leave for work, swings open the front door.

"What's going on here?" she calls out.

Detective Montrose tells me to put my hands behind my back, and I comply with jittery hesitation.

"I'm a lawyer," Kristen says.

"We know," Detective Husemann says, giving a little glance in the direction of her partner.

Kristen persists. "What are you doing here?"

They ignore her.

"Connor Moss," Detective Husemann says, "we're placing you under arrest on suspicion of homicide."

I hear my Miranda rights being read. I think back to the first time that I'd heard those words: after the accident in Southern California. Since then I have never so much as driven five miles over the speed limit. I never cheat on reporting my tips. I actually overpay my taxes. I have spent every second of my life trying to be on the right side of the law. I do all of that because I am sorry for what I've done. I'm not bitter that the drunk-driving conviction has hung over me for my entire adult life. It was my fault. I have never—not even one time—not owned up to what I did.

As the cold metal of the handcuffs encircles my wrists, I feel the blood drain from my face. I am physically fit. I run nearly every day. I do a weights circuit twice a week at the gym. I work in a restaurant and know what food is good for you and what isn't. And yet, as I stand there in a T-shirt and jogging shorts, my wrists locked together, I wonder if I'm going to collapse in front of the detectives and my wife.

"I didn't do anything," I say.

"Don't say another word. I'll get my purse, and I'll follow you."

It's Kristen. She's hovering just beyond the detectives. Her words are measured and calm, and her demeanor soothes and steadies me. She knows me. She knows I would never hurt anyone.

They say her name.

Sophie Warner.

My eyes go wet as I go deeper into the vortex of a murder arrest. Oddly, though, I'm not ashamed of my emotions. The tears come, and I let them. I am being sucked downward. I am helpless. I have no control over what's happening. My vision is blurred, but I can see Kristen clearly enough to see she's moving her mouth and saying that everything will be all right. Somehow her emotions don't track with her words. It's like an old Japanese movie dubbed in English. Just not quite right. I wonder then if she's thinking back to Hood Canal. I wonder then if she's looking at me in a way that she never has.

When she first met me, she saw me as broken but deep down, like the fixer upper on our street, good bones.

"You got this wrong," Kristen calls out to the detectives. "Not my Connor. He'd never hurt a fly."

As they slide me into the backseat of their car, I catch another fleeting glimpse of her beautiful face.

I wonder if she sees me as guilty.

I wonder if that's what I am.

Hours pass before I see Kristen. I've been strip-searched, fingerprinted, and photographed in the Mason County jail by a couple of deputies who glower at me like I'm subhuman. In the holding cell, another man asked me if he could suck my cock when the guard is out of view. I declined. I sit motionless on a bench as a fruit fly circles overhead. I don't swat at it because it is superior to me. As good as I've tried to be in my life, I know that I have been a fraud. I cheated on my wife. I cheated with Sophie Warner. It was a deliberate act. I can't make it into anything less. I could rationalize all I want, but God knows what I've done. God knows that I have been a fraud to a woman who adores me—a woman who wants nothing more than to make a family with me.

I slept with Sophie. Yet it was far more than that. I fell in love too. We both did.

Kristen is in the jail's small visiting room when they bring me to her. I know she must have taken her time to follow me here, because she is no longer dressed for work. She wears no makeup, and her hair is clipped back—her look for days when she doesn't have the time or the desire to wash and style it. Mostly Saturdays. But this isn't a Saturday. I don't know why I thought that she was just outside the jail the whole time, telling the police that I was innocent.

I take the chair across the table from her. The guard shuts the door.

"I'm sorry about all of this," I say.

Her attention stays on the table between us.

"I'm not here as your wife," she says.

I'm not sure I heard her correctly. "I don't understand."

"I can't be your lawyer after today, either."

"Kristen, what's going on?"

She looks up at me. No, right *through* me. I can see her eyes are bloodshot. She's kneading her hands together, and I detect a palpable heaviness in her breathing. I'm worried about her.

My pulse begins to accelerate. "Are you all right?"

She shakes her head. "Are you really going to ask that?"

Now her eyes are darts, and they are aimed at me with Kristen precision.

"I don't get it," I tell her, glancing around as if there were someone else here to help me explain.

Kristen keeps up her stone face. "You raped and murdered that woman," she says, her words carved out of ice. "The police have DNA. *Yours.*"

"They are wrong," I say, scrambling for words of certain denial. "They can't have my DNA."

"Connor," she says. "Stop. Just stop. The lies have to end now. They can't make me testify against you. We're married. That's in your favor. I won't tell them about the bloody sheets. But you can't keep lying to me. You raped her."

"I never did that," I say. "I could never do that. You know me, Kristen."

"I thought I did, Connor. I really thought I did." She stops to take a breath. "I don't know you at all."

I stand and lean across the table. I want to believe that this isn't really happening, but it is. I feel my heart beat as it pulses against my rib cage.

I am alive. This is not a dream.

"Why are you saying that?" I ask.

"Sit down, Connor, or the guard will come in."

I sit and start to beg. "You have to believe me."

Kristen puts her hand up as if to stop me from any further nattering.

"I believe the evidence, Connor," she says. No emotion. "Your semen was inside of the victim. That's a fact. That's something that will carry you through to a conviction. Maybe you don't remember doing it. I don't know if there's a plausible excuse for that kind of a lapse—and, really, I just can't believe it."

"You know me, Kristen."

"You lied to me. You lied to everyone. Didn't you?"

"No. I didn't," I say, suddenly feeling like I'm involved in a tit-for-tat kid's game.

"You knew Sophie Warner, didn't you? Isn't that true?"

Having her stating the truth like that, so starkly, is like a sledgehammer to the chest.

"I didn't kill her."

"The evidence the police have says otherwise."

"I loved her," I say. "I would never kill her."

Wrong words. I know that immediately. I'm not thinking clearly.

Kristen starts to break. I can see it in her face. In the way her hands are now clenched. She's hurt and angry.

"You shut up, Connor," she says. "You don't say that to me. Ever. I don't know how long I knew about an affair, but it has been in my mind for a long time. It haunts me even now. I think about how we ended up at those cabins in the first place. How you must have stalked her."

"I didn't," I tell her. "It was your idea to go there."

She brushes my words aside. "I don't remember it that way. All I remember is all the goddamn blood. All the lame excuses you had for whatever it was that you were doing. Or who you were doing it with. Something went wrong, Connor. She dumped you. You got mad. You paid her back, and you will not drag me down with you."

My voice cracks. "I never would do that."

"Look," Kristen finally says, "I'll stand by you. I'll be the wife at your side. I'll get you the best lawyer in Seattle. I'll do all of that to keep you alive. But you'll need to do the right thing. You'll need to stop being a selfish little boy and grow a pair."

Keep me alive? I have no idea what she's talking about.

"I don't know you right now," I say. I *don't*. She's hard. She's a block of limestone, and she's holding me with a cold stare that eviscerates me.

"The Mason County prosecutor told me she'll ask for the death penalty, Connor. Neither one of us wants that, right?"

I don't answer, because I can't even breathe.

"You'll plead guilty. That's what you'll do."

"I didn't do it."

"Your DNA and your lack of an alibi, Connor, will get you a needle in your arm."

"But you're my alibi."

My wife's head drops, because either I'm not listening to her or I don't understand.

"Am I? I can't say for sure where you were, Connor. And, unlike you, I can't lie to the court."

CHAPTER SIXTY-THREE
LEE

I sit at my desk and leave a voice mail for Adam after several failed attempts. I could've waited to talk to him when I see him later at the cabin, but it felt wrong to withhold the news. And I want him to know that I never thought he was involved, that I knew he was innocent from the moment I saw him by the concrete bulkhead at the cabin on Hood Canal.

I fill him in on Connor Moss's DNA match and arrest in Seattle. I watch my tone. I'm elated, of course. But the man I'm calling has suffered in so many ways since everything happened. Joy and relief are not the same thing.

"I'm sorry about everything you've gone through since Sophie was taken, Adam. I'm sorry about all of it. I hope you and Aubrey are doing all right. I'm looking forward to seeing you later."

I look out my window. The plum tree is fully leafed out. Its green leaves are touched with a little bronze from the heat of the summer. *The tree*. The branches. Adam and I will always have a bond because of the day he found me. I know now that if I transferred some feelings of affection to him, they were misplaced. I'm a Shelton girl. The Shelton boy is now in Seattle making a new life for himself.

I reach for my coffee cup.

"You hungry?"

It's Montrose.

"Yeah," I say, setting down the cup. "You drive."

He nods, and we make our way to his car and drive down Fourth to a Mexican restaurant that I've wanted to try since it opened over Memorial weekend.

I notice his grip on the steering wheel.

"Tremor's better," I say.

He gives me a smile.

"Yeah," he says. "New meds. Can't stop the progression completely, but we're doing our best to slow it down. How long have you known?"

"Awhile," I say.

He doesn't ask me not to tell anyone.

He knows he can trust me.

At the end of the day, trust is everything.

CHAPTER SIXTY-FOUR
LEE

I don't know why for sure, but I put on a new dress I bought from Anthropologie's online store just before the Warner case. I'm no trendsetter. In Shelton, I don't have to be. The dress is a cotton blend with a pretty, modern floral print. Not a grandma dress at all. I saw Chrissy Teigen wear something similar on Instagram. I don't even allow myself to think that it's a sexy choice, because that's not the message I ever send to anyone. The truth is I seldom feel sexy. I'm not terrible to look at, but not gorgeous, either. I do the best that I can. I exercise. Eat right. My makeup is light and professional during the week. On the weekends I don't usually wear any at all.

Today, however, I do. It's not a celebration. Connor Moss hasn't gone through the legal system yet. But still, I can't help but feel that his arrest will start Adam toward healing.

He'll get what I didn't with Albert Hodge: justice.

I stare at myself in the rearview mirror as I back out of my driveway for the drive up to the cabins near Octopus Hole. I look pretty good. I just wonder why that's so. As I drive, I listen to country music and the sad-sack stories of love, loss, and pickup trucks on dirt roads. The sun shimmers on the waters of Hood Canal, and I put on my sunglasses. I know that Adam Warner is not a killer. The DNA found inside Sophie proves it. We were doing our job when Montrose and I interviewed him, but now I realize the price of due diligence was a friendship that mattered.

When I pull in to park, I see that Adam is out in the rowboat. He's about fifty yards out, adjacent to a clutch of white mooring buoys. I make my way over to the bulkhead where Sophie was last seen alive, and I think how similar her final view of her husband had been. He doesn't seem to have seen me, so I sit and watch.

It dawns on me that he's decided not to wait: he's pouring her ashes into the canal. That's fine with me. A light breeze moves some dust over the glassy surface, while the majority of what is coming from the urn cascades into the water. The scene brings tears. I cannot imagine a lonelier, more personal moment than the good-bye he's experiencing now. I feel like I've intruded in that way when you see something that you know you shouldn't have. He looks up in my direction, and I give a slight wave.

Adam's done with a final, sacred moment with his murdered wife and starts rowing in my direction.

"Hey," he says, stepping out of the boat into the shallow water along the shore.

"I'm sorry," I say. "I feel like I'm intruding."

He gives me a sad smile. It's to relax me, but I know that there's no truth behind it. He's heartbroken over his loss. His eyes can't lie.

"It's all right," he says, setting the empty aluminum urn on the beach. "I wanted you here. I pretty much have no one else now. No friends who could possibly understand."

"You have a daughter," I remind him.

He drags the boat to its storage spot on a bunch of driftwood and picks up the now-empty urn.

"Yes," he says. "I do."

"We caught him, Adam. He's going down."

"Her killer was here that weekend," he says. "Not some freak driving by or stalking her at the IGA. Right here, two cabins over."

"I know. The DNA is conclusive."

"I want to see that creep. I'd like to fucking kill him."

"He's going to prison. That's how it works."

Adam shrugs a little, and I follow him up to the cabin. He offers me ice tea or a beer.

"Maybe later," I say.

We watch the water for a long time. At first we don't talk about anything important. We don't talk more about Connor. It's just too ugly. Instead, we just watch the birds fly. Kayakers paddle around the cove. Laughter from kids staying in the cabin next door, giving the rope swing a good workout, breaches the serenity of the moment. But in a good, life-affirming way. It's a beautiful, sunny day. If I could be anywhere in the world, it would be right there. If I could change all the circumstances that brought me there, I would do that too.

"You hungry?" he asks.

I didn't eat breakfast or lunch, so I'm basically starving.

"I could eat something," I say.

He stands. "Let's head up to Hama Hama."

"Sounds good," I tell him. "I haven't been there in ages."

We walk to his car, and the empty car seat makes me think of his little girl. "Is Aubrey with Sophie's folks?"

Adam glances over and shakes his head. "Not a chance. The nanny has her. Just didn't want the drama of Frank and Helen on this day."

The Hama Hama Company's "oyster saloon" has been a fixture north of Lilliwaup for decades. It's not fancy, but it's authentic. Locals needing an oyster fix blend in with out-of-towners who have made the place a must-visit for any Hood Canal itinerary. Adam and I order oysters two ways, pan-fried and on the half shell. I'm not a huge oyster fan, but under the right circumstances nothing is better than a cold beer and some very fresh oysters.

We sit there facing each other across a picnic table. We don't talk about the case. In fact, it's as if there is no case. We talk about his family. *My* family. We laugh about some of the things we used to do to pass the time in Shelton when we were kids.

"Can you believe we actually played kick the can?" he says.

"Yeah," I say. "It was the nineties, but Shelton was stuck in the forties."

He asks me if I've been seeing anyone. It's not a creepy question. Just a summation of the fact that we don't know much of each other's lives after he left town.

"Not now," I tell him. "Dated a guy I met at the academy in Burien, but things didn't work out. He took a job in Mesa, and I just don't do well with heat."

"A true Pacific Northwest girl."

I drink more beer. "That's me."

He talks about making a career change and that he's got his résumé out but hasn't found anything yet. "I'm going to run out of cash soon," he says. "Hate to dip into my 401(k), but that's probably in the cards."

I know there was life insurance through Starbucks, but I can imagine that money goes fast when you live in the city and have childcare and other expenses that I don't have.

"Hard to find an executive position, I guess," I say.

He nods. "Hard to find the right one."

The sun is dipping low as we head back to the car. I'm feeling the effects of the beer. It'll be a while before I can drive back to Shelton.

"I'm glad I came up to see you," I say as we cross the Lil-liwaup bridge.

"Me too, Lee. Maybe the only good thing about every-thing that happened is reconnecting with you."

"I'm sorry for all you and Aubrey have gone through."

"Thanks," he says.

"No, really I am."

"I know, Lee."

When we arrive at the Wisteria, we sit in the same Adiron-dacks on the deck. The mood feels different. The breeze has stopped. The kids next door are no longer on the swing. Si-lence fills the air. Adam and I are alone.

"I don't think I should drive," I say.

"That's fine. Let's just sit."

CHAPTER SIXTY-FIVE
ADAM

Lee drank too much, and I can't let her drive back to Shelton. In a way, I feel protective of her, even after all these years. It's that bond again.

I retrieve a couple more beers from the kitchen.

"Oh, God," she says. "I'm half drunk now."

"Not even a quarter drunk."

She laughs but pushes back on my offer.

"Lee, you might as well stay," I say, sitting back down. "Your cat will be fine without you."

"Do I talk about my cat that much?"

I grin at her. "Constantly."

She makes a face and accepts the beer.

"Sorry," she says. "I never thought I'd end up being a cat lady."

"You're not," I say. "I think you are great."

She drinks some more, and we sit there on the deck as two kayakers paddle by. A seal plunges into the water from a float. I'm thinking of the ashes that I sifted out of the urn and wonder if the current has carried them all far away or if maybe bits of Sophie are on the crescent shoreline fronting the cabins.

I have no idea what Lee is thinking. I can only hope it's that she sees me for who I am.

When it starts to get dark, I put a frozen pizza in the oven, and we eat it outside in the still but cooling air. My phone buzzes, and I read the text.

"Katrina says Aubrey went to sleep without a hitch," I say.

"That's good," Lee says. "I thought you didn't get great cell service here."

"I texted *you*, didn't I? But yeah, it's far from great. So spotty that I don't think anyone out here can truly be connected without Wi-Fi."

When she's finished with her beer, I ask if she wants to check out the sauna.

She hesitates a little. "I don't have a suit."

"I don't, either," I say, "but the owner has some really big towels. Come on. It'll be good for you. Get out those nasty toxins."

"Do I look like I'm full of nasty toxins?" she asks with a smile.

I shake my head. "No. You look great."

Inside, I turn on the sauna to let it heat up. I give Lee a towel and show her a little room off the kitchen where she can change. I go to the bedroom and do the same. A few minutes later we're sitting on the cedar benches, feeling the heat pouring from the firebox.

I tell her about rumrunners on Hood Canal during Prohibition. How the cabin had even been a speakeasy.

She notices the small panel on the wall near the firebox.

"What's that for?" she asks.

"Nothing," I tell her. "Lots of passageways in old places like this."

She gives the panel a little kick and smiles. For only a second, the moment does seem a little strange. It isn't like I thought things would go this way, but I can see the way that she's regarding me.

CHAPTER SIXTY-SIX
LEE

It's the darkest of nights. An unfamiliar clock ticks from another room. For a second I forget where I am, and I reach for the warmth of Millicent. She's not there.

Adam Warner is in the next room.

I'm naked, covered by a white eiderdown.

He's sleeping.

I'm awake.

My muscles tighten, and my heart begins to race. I'm in the cabin at Hood Canal. I came to offer support to Adam. At least, I think that was the reason. I play back the day. The ashes. The oysters. The beer. I don't remember anything after the sauna.

I don't remember how I ended up naked on the sofa. Adam is snoring softly in the other room. I drank too much, but not so much that I would have blacked out. I felt woozy at Hama Hama and then a little more so after dinner. Maybe it was the heat? Maybe I passed out there, and he carried me here?

As quietly as I can, I find my clothes, get dressed, and slip out the back door. This isn't happening right now. I start my car, and as silently as possible I pull away from the inky waters of the canal.

I'll be okay. This is not the worst thing that could ever happen, I think. Mostly because I don't know what happened at all.

My phone pings.

Adrenaline is a river through my body. It's a text from Adam.

Hey. You left. Hope everything is good. Nothing happened, by the way. I was a perfect gentleman.

I let out a sigh of relief.

I know that's true.

CHAPTER SIXTY-SEVEN
LEE

It's a sunny Saturday morning a month after Connor's arrest, and I go where I always go on Saturday, Sister's Restaurant on Railroad Avenue. I don't have a sister, of course. I have a cat that thinks she's a person, so on some level I think I qualify. In any case, I order my usual, a Swiss-and-mushroom omelet and whole-wheat toast with raspberry freezer jam. As I drink coffee and wait for my waitress, Diane, to bring my order, I ruminate on the past. I replay the same scenarios over and over in my head. It's a wonder that I can move forward when so many things keep me glued to the past. I'm a fly on flypaper. I think about how I was the one to survive when Cathy Rinehart and Sophie Warner were not. How it was me who went on to live a full life—or as full as I can manage—and they were left to dust or memories. I almost never think of the perpetrators of crimes like these, but rather the what-ifs of the lives they've stolen.

Cathy would be out on her own now. Maybe have a family. Sophie would be reading to Aubrey and telling her silly stories about her father. My mom did that. She teased my father, and he went along with it. If she said he'd hunted bear in Alaska, then he'd join in and have me help dig for a bear's tooth in the backyard. One time she told me that Daddy had been to the moon, and he took me out to the backyard and pointed out where he'd left his footprints. I think I knew it was a game very early on, but I loved it anyway.

When Diane leaves, I see Dan Belding Jr. a couple of tables over from me. Dan was two years ahead of me in school. I remember how Kip and Adam used to tease him by calling him Water Boy. Now we call that bullying, of course. Back then everyone just laughed it off.

At least, my brother and Adam did.

I wonder if Dan ever thought it was funny.

"Hey," he says, getting up. "You alone?"

I give him a smile. "Yeah. Same as every day."

"Join you?"

I don't get the uncomfortable "I'm interested in you" vibe, so I gesture for him to sit. Dan's a good guy. He's one of the locals who made good and did something with his life.

"I'm sorry I haven't stopped by since you moved back to Shelton," I say.

Dan rolls his shoulders a little. "My return was inevitable. Sawdust runs in my veins, you know."

"Same here," I say. "Anyway, welcome back home."

Diane sees that Dan has moved and brings his food. She gives me a little wink. She's completely wrong about Water Boy and me, but I don't say anything. My omelet arrives too.

"You must be relieved about the Sophie Warner case," he says.

I can't tell if he's making a dig about the Rinehart case not being solved or if he's being kind. I choose to think he's being kind, because that's the kid I remember.

I swallow a bite of my omelet and consider the raspberry jam.

"I am always glad when things end with a solid conviction," I say.

He looks at me, then around the restaurant.

"What is it, Dan?"

I notice sweat on his brow, and while it could be the hot sauce he's doused his eggs with, it seems as if anyone who had a penchant for doing that would be used to it.

"Attorney-client stuff," he says. "I hate that rule."

I smear jam on my toast and give him a moment to think about what he really wants to say. I'm on the edge of my seat, but I don't show it. Dan's holding something, and it's like a ball made of razor blades that he wants to hand off.

Quickly.

"Yeah," I say. "That's not my favorite legal privilege. I understand it, though. I see the need for it, but I see the abuse too."

"Right," he says, staring down at the big yellow eyes of the eggs on his plate.

I push a little. "Dan, come on, I've known you since we were kids."

It's true, though a stretch. I took my position on Dan Belding Jr. from my brother. I didn't mock him. I would never do that to anyone. But, admittedly, I laughed at the water-boy jokes.

Dan has egg yolk in the corners of his mouth, but I don't say anything. I try not to look at it.

"All right," he says, setting down his fork. "I don't think I'm really violating much."

"That's good," I say.

He doesn't break his gaze from mine. It's a penetrating, unflinching stare.

"One of our classmates came to me after his wife died," he says.

I don't need to ask who he's talking about. And I can see that we're playing a game, so I go along with it.

"That's interesting," I finally tell him.

"I'm not saying who it is," he says.

"Right. I got that. Because that would be a violation."

"Possibly," he says. "Yes. But the truth is, he didn't hire me."

"So he wasn't a client."

"Like I said, it's a sticky wicket," he says. "He did come for legal advice."

Diane brings more coffee. She's worked here for twenty-five years and still has the worst timing in the food-service industry. We wait for her to finish pouring.

My heart is sinking, and I'm not sure why. When Dan doesn't say anything for what seems like the longest time, I ask, "Is this going to be twenty questions, Dan?" I'm not irritated. I just need to know what the ground rules are here. I can see that he wants to tell me something important. It's not idle gossip about someone we know.

He sets down his fork. "Adam came in about an adoption."

I almost say, "*My* Adam?"

But I don't.

"Adam Warner?"

"Yeah."

"I didn't know he and Sophie had wanted to adopt," I say, whispering now because I know how keen the hearing is of the old man in the booth next to ours. I know that gossip travels faster than Wi-Fi in Shelton.

Dan's expression is, well, expressionless. I can't tell what he's thinking as he sits across from me processing my question.

"Like I said, it wasn't Mr. and Mrs.," he says. "It was just Adam. It was after his wife was murdered."

He's losing me. I'm not sure what to make of what he's saying.

"Did he say why, Dan?"

"Yeah. He said that he didn't think he could manage the responsibility on his own."

None of this makes sense.

"Then why would he come in to adopt another child?" I ask.

Dan looks down at the table and rubs his forehead. "You're making me say everything."

I wait for him to return my gaze. "Because you aren't telling me anything. At least nothing I can grasp, Dan. Come on, now, tell me."

"He was going to adopt out his little girl."

I'm stunned. "Aubrey?"

"Yes."

"To the Flynns?" I ask.

He shakes his head. "He wouldn't say. It was going to be a private adoption, and he specifically didn't want the Flynns involved. I told him they'd fight him and certainly win visitation. Maybe even full custody."

I don't say it, but I think it: *This is the Adam Warner I know?*

"What happened?"

Dan pushes his plate across the table and thankfully wipes the egg from the corners of his mouth. "Never came back. I figured once things calmed down he'd had a change of heart. Maybe didn't want to go through with it. Grief and shock make a lot of people do the craziest things."

Diane drops off our checks. We sit there in silence while I get my wallet from my purse and Dan fishes for his credit card.

"Just thought it was weird," Dan says as we get up to pay.

"I can't make sense of it," I say.

"See you around," he tells me as we head out the door.

"Welcome back home, Dan. And thank you. I think."

He reaches over and gives me a quick hug.

"I always liked you, Lee," Dan says. "Maybe we'll run into each other soon."

"Small town," I say, stepping back, surprised. "I'm sure we will."

appreciate it."

hands are folded, and when he breathes, the belly
linked to his handcuffs rattle against the stainless
ble.

not sure why I came," I say.

gives me a nod. "Your being here," he says, "gives me
hope. I didn't do this. I didn't. I know that I have no
ut I just couldn't have killed her."

've said that," I say. "Tell me more. I'm listening."

ts out a breath and starts talking.

n't you think I would have a list of things to tell you
was anything I could add? I passed out in the cabin.
o memory of attacking Sophie, let alone raping her
getting rid of her body."

that's what you did," I say.

akes his head. "I *didn't*. I couldn't do that."

. Fine. Let's go back to what happened. What, if
, do you remember about that weekend, before So-
killed?"

't do it, so how would I know anything other than
on the news?"

' I say. "Tell me about what you, specifically, can

r leans as close as his chains allow. "First of all,"
didn't even want to go there that weekend. I wish
d, obviously. It was Kristen's place. She and her
rented the Lily for years. She loved the history of
I would prefer a place like Walla Walla for a
etaway. You know, someplace with decent food
ine."

Walla is fun," I say. "But you went to Octopus

he says. "Kristen insisted. She makes the money,
o decide."

at bother you?"

says. "It's the way it is. I love my wife. She

The rest of the morning, I attempt to work through my
completely manageable to-do list. The bedding plants that I
put out in the spring have bolted with the recent hot weather,
and I decide to swap them out with late-summer bachelor
buttons and daisies. The white-and-blue combination was
always my mother's favorite, so it became mine. I pick up a
flat of each at the Fred Meyer garden store and return home.
I start ripping out the old stock and planting the new. I wave
at the new neighbors across the street while their kids play in
the sprinkler. I'm so preoccupied that I forget to smile. The
air is heavy. The kids' laughter only registers as an annoy-
ance.

All the while, I think about what Dan told me at Sister's.
I can't make sense of why Adam would want to put Aubrey
up for adoption. He seemed to be a doting father. He was
adamant about wanting to protect Aubrey from the Flynns.

When I go back inside, the letter sent to my home from
Connor Moss draws me like a magnet. I opened it and set it
aside, meaning to bring it into work for the case file, now
closed. I fill a glass with tap water and sit down. Millicent is
immediately on my lap and looking for some attention. The
letter is dated a few weeks after Connor was processed and
sent to the prison, all of which took a fraction of the time it
usually does, like the system just couldn't wait to welcome
him in. His handwriting is a little shaky. I wonder about that.
Was he nervous? Scared? Desperate? No doubt all three.

Dear Det. Husemann,

*I want you to know that even though I confessed to
this terrible crime, I honestly don't think I did it. I
don't think I am that kind of person. I know that soon
enough everyone will have gone on with their lives
and forgotten about me. I'll be just another killer put
away for rape and murder. I can't explain the evidence
against me, but I know in my heart I would never have*

killed Sophie. I loved her! She was the mother of my little girl. I just want you to know that. I should have said this in court before sentencing, but I was still in shock. Good-bye.

 Sincerely,
 Connor Moss

I scratch Millicent under her chin and put the letter back into its envelope. She purrs like a chain saw.

"I hate to do this to you, Milli," I say, setting her gently on the floor, "but you'll have to get along without me. I'm going to prison."

CHAPTER SIXTY
LEE

You hear it all the time.
 My high school is like a prison.
 My boss keeps me chained to m
 I feel like I'm trapped here in t
 I am a prisoner.
 The truth is, nothing is like
sound a heavy gate makes whe
room pushes a button. Even thou
tution that provides so much en
the impact of being held in a
escape.

Connor Moss sits in a room
forcement to meet with pris
Maybe fifteen. His cheeks ar
thing in his eyes as the guard
the table where he's sitting.
lieved too.

"I didn't think anyone w
"Your letter," I say. "I gu

"I
Hi
chain
steel t
"I'
He
a little
proof,
"Yo
He
"Do
if there
I have
and the
"But
He s
"Oka
anything
phie was
"I did
what was
"Fine,
recall."
Conno
he says, "
I never h
family had
the cabins
weekend
and good
"Walla
Hole."
"Right,"
so she gets
"Does th
"No," h

works hard. We both did. She just made ten times more money than I did."

"Back to the trip, Connor," I say. "You left Seattle late Friday."

"Right."

"Make any stops?"

"Yes," he says. "We stopped at a bar for some drinks and food. A Mexican place. I drank too much. Seriously, I did. I have a drinking problem. That's no big secret. I know that better than anything now that I'm here."

"That's good," I tell him. "Then what?"

"We stopped at a liquor store and got some more tequila. I stayed in the car. Kristen said we were going to party that night and do shots or something. I'm telling you, I had no business drinking any more. I felt sick and out of it."

"So you stopped drinking, did you?"

"I had a flask and Kristen filled it. I drank all the way up to the cabin."

"And after that?"

Connor looks upward. A tear starts to fall, and he awkwardly tries to wipe it with his cuffed hands.

"Nothing, Detective. Nothing at all. I was drunk. I passed out."

I've heard of sleepwalking murderers, and I've felt sorry for them. Being a drunken murderer is different, however. I'm less forgiving. Sure, it's possible that such a killer had no idea what they were doing, or it was a case in which they did what they had always wanted to do—with the help of a 110-proof shot of courage.

I'm unclear about the dynamic between Connor and Adam and Sophie. I ask him if he knew Adam.

He says he didn't.

"Never seen him in person," he says. "One time after Aubrey was born, Sophie met me at Café Cirrus to show me the baby. When we were there, I asked her if she thought Aubrey favored me. She thought a little bit, but surprisingly, insisted Aubrey looked like Adam too. I didn't see how that was possible, so she showed me Adam's photo on her phone. I didn't see the resemblance at all. I think Sophie was trying to make things work and wanted to believe what she needed to in order to save her marriage."

"Did you continue to meet like that?" I ask.

"No. That was the last time," he says. "That was the only time I ever saw my daughter. Sophie made it clear that she was going to fix things with her husband and that I should do the same with Kristen."

A guard pokes his head in, and I indicate that we're fine.

"What about the DNA?" I ask. "Your DNA was in her body."

"Was it really?" he asks. "I hadn't been with her in a very long time. I wouldn't forget that, Detective."

"Yes," I say. "You know it was."

"How do we know it wasn't put there later? Maybe in the lab?"

"Because our lab isn't crooked, Connor."

"Others are."

I ignore this and remind him of something very important: a bell that's nearly impossible to unring. "You confessed," I say.

"I did that to avoid the death penalty."

"Right," I say. "It was a good move. Your relationship with Sophie and your DNA inside her would have convicted you by any jury."

"Good move?" he says. "I'm in here for a life sentence. Life without. I'm not some tough guy. I wanted to do social work and fix problems. Help people. Now look at me."

"Maybe you can help people in here," I tell him. I don't mean for it to be a cheap shot, but I know that's how it came out.

"You don't even want to go there," he says. "The guys in here can't be helped. At least, I haven't met any. I was a waiter before I came here. I was married. I wasn't dealing drugs or doing anything to anyone."

"But you're here because you killed Sophie Warner."

"Honestly?" he asks. "Why would I kill her?"

"I don't know why, Connor," I say. "Maybe Sophie dumped you? You wanted revenge or something along those lines?"

He stays fixed on me.

"She didn't dump me," he says, his tone now insistent. "It was mutual. It was the best thing for everyone. When she told me she was pregnant and she wanted to try to make things work with her husband, I agreed."

I push a little. "It made you angry."

Connor's chains rattle against the edge of the table. "Hurt," he says. "Not angry. Disappointed. I wanted to be a father. Kristen and I had been trying for a long time."

"But you cheated on her."

"You know that I did," he says. "I've never said differently. I fell in love. I fought it."

"You deceived your wife, Connor. Kristen's smart. She fell for whatever it was you told her to cover your affair with Sophie."

"Yes, I lied to her. Everybody lies for one reason or another."

His voice is shaky now. I watch him struggle to stay composed.

"Everybody lies," I repeat to fill the gap in the air while Connor Moss pulls himself together.

"I lied to Kristen. Sophie lied to Adam. Adam lied to Sophie. You've probably lied about something too."

CHAPTER SIXTY-NINE
CONNOR

I almost never work the lunch rush, but that's what I was doing that fall day when Sophie Warner and some others from her office came to the Blue Door. It was raining, and the entire party of four was soaked to the skin. Sophie just laughed it off and said it was the cost of living in Seattle.

"The rainy season," she said.

I took her coat.

"Which is every season," I said.

She gave me a warm smile, and some serious electricity passed between us. I felt it. I didn't know if she did or didn't. Hasn't everyone experienced that moment when there's a charge in the air between you and another person?

I hope so.

And really that was it. I thought Sophie was beautiful, of course. When I served her group, she was friendly and funny in the way that makes everyone feel more comfortable—servers included. That's a rarity in Seattle. When she paid, she used a Starbucks corporate card. She thanked me for taking care of her coat and left.

The busboy found me in the kitchen a short time later.

"That four top by the window left this," he said, holding out a packet of what appeared to be work material. The familiar Starbucks mermaid logo greeted me when I opened the dark green folder.

"Looks important," I said. "I'll make a call."

Her direct line was on her business card in the folder. Sophie was relieved beyond words when I told her what I'd found.

"I must have put it under the seat next to mine," she told me. "It's a month's worth of work. Crap! Completely forgot about it."

I told her not to worry. It was safe in my hands. "Want me to bring it to you? I'm off in an hour."

She thanked me, but insisted that she'd send a messenger to retrieve it.

"Seriously," I said. "It's on my way home."

I could feel her relax over the phone.

"Are you sure?"

"Completely," I said. "Hang tight. It's not a problem. I'll be there."

An hour later I asked for her at the Starbucks front desk, but she was busy. I left the packet, my work number, and a note. *I like option B,* I wrote of the designs for an in-store promotion I'd seen inside. I added a smiley face.

I didn't leave my information for any other reason than to let her know that I'd brought it and had ensured its safety.

I thought that was it. And really, that was fine. But the next day she called me.

"You saved me," Sophie said. "Not even kidding. Everything was backed up in that folder but the notes my design director made. I didn't want to go back and tell her I lost it."

"No," I said. "Don't want your boss in your face."

"That makes me wonder if you know her," she said, with a short laugh.

"I know the type," I said.

I told her that I was glad to bring it, and she insisted that she repay me with a drink at a little place in Pioneer Square. I'd been trying to quit alcohol, but I said yes anyway. She was so appreciative, and I honestly could feel that energy passing between us.

Micah was installing a new freezer at the restaurant, so I had the night off. I met Sophie at six forty-five, and we talked for two hours. She told me about her job. I told her about the restaurant business and the things people forget to take with them when they dine: birthday presents, phones, and condoms.

"Condoms?" she asked. "What kind of place is the Blue Door?"

"Special occasion," I said with a grin.

And it went like that. Neither one of us mentioned our spouses, though we both wore rings, and it was obvious we were married. It didn't feel like a first date or anything. Instead, our two hours felt like five minutes with a best friend you haven't seen in years, when you are somehow able to cram in a range of dozens of topics like an episode of *Jeopardy!*

Here's the thing: I didn't stop loving Kristen when I met Sophie. I loved Kristen with all my heart. She and I were going to start a family. And while all of the drama—sadness— associated with that weighed on us, I never doubted that we'd work our way through it. Kristen had an innate need to be a mother. I understood. I cried with her whenever we failed. I held her at night, because that's what you do when someone is in emotional agony. I didn't ever say to her that it was killing me too. I couldn't do that to my wife. I didn't think it was right to say anything about *me* when she was in the morass of motherhood denied.

Then Sophie Warner came along. She was beautiful and fun. She wasn't weighed down by constant disappointment. She was buoyant. There was just another part of me that Sophie seemed to easily tap into. She didn't care that I was a waiter. She looked at me with eyes that seemed to really see me. Not my job. Not my past. Just me.

When we started sleeping together, I'd go home feeling less of a man than I ever had in my life. Kristen would be there waiting, and I knew on some vague level that she suspected something. My betrayal was a poison. I tried to rationalize what was best for Sophie, her SkyAero manager husband, Adam, and me. If Sophie and I were soul mates, then we should be together, right? I even asked God to help me sort out what I should do.

God didn't give me the answer, though Sophie did.

I met her at our place in Pioneer Square.

She started crying before we even sat in our usual booth, one in the back that we were sure had been the territory of adulterers before us.

"What is it? Is everything okay?"

I wondered if she'd lost her job. If her husband had found out about our affair. Or maybe she had cancer.

"No," she said. "Not by a mile."

She didn't say anything for the longest time. When the waitress came and she ordered a club soda with lime, I knew.

"You're pregnant," I said.

She shifted her stare to the tabletop. "I found out this morning."

I was in shock. Really, I was.

Nothing but silence.

"Is it mine?" I finally asked.

She pushed a lock of her hair behind her ear and drank her club soda. She fiddled with the lime.

"I don't know," she said.

Sophie's answer astonished me, though it probably shouldn't have. She had insisted that she and Adam barely slept in the same bed. That he was probably having an affair at work, and she didn't even care. She told me that I was the only man she wanted to touch her. I was her soul mate! And yes, I was sleeping with Kristen. But that's because I had a job to do. Kristen wanted a baby. I felt I owed it to her.

And now this.

I ordered another tequila.

"What are we going to do?" I asked.

I knew the answer before she reached for my hand. "We're going to say good-bye, Connor," she said. "We're going to stop."

My throat tightened. I could hardly talk.

"But I love you," I said.

She nodded. "I know. I love you too."

It didn't seem right to me. It seemed all kinds of wrong. "This is my baby," I told her.

As much as I loved Sophie, I could see in that moment that I was alone in this relationship.

"I don't know that," she said. "But I do know that I don't want the complications of our relationship, my marriage, and a baby. I can't handle it, Connor. I've made up my mind. We have to end this."

By then I could feel my own tears coming.

"I don't want to say good-bye."

Sophie, however, was full of resolve. I knew in that moment that it didn't matter what I wanted or what I thought. She was going to do what she believed was best for herself and for the baby.

She leaned in and gave me a kiss.

And then she got up and left.

CHAPTER SEVENTY
LEE

As Connor spins his story of how he and Sophie met and became lovers, I see no guile whatsoever. He loved her. That's undeniable. I believe his story that he doesn't really know what happened to Sophie, that he has no memory of what, if anything, he did after arriving at the cabin. I've been lied to by the best—and worst—of them. My BS meter almost never fails me.

Even so, undercurrents of jealousy can be a hidden Niagara. Add some liquor to the mix, and it's possible there was an explosion he can't recall.

"You only saw Aubrey one time?" I ask.

"When she was a baby," he says. "Yes, that one time."

"Did you and Sophie communicate after that?"

"Not once. No calls. No emails. No texts."

"Were you stalking her?" I ask.

He pushes back from the table. "Seriously? No. I wasn't. When she said it was over, I accepted it. When she said she wanted me to see the baby, I said all right. I never initiated any contact."

"Connor," I say, "I don't know how I can help you or even if I should. I do believe you don't have any recollection of what happened."

"Small consolation, but thanks, Detective. I appreciate someone believing me."

"You aren't alone," I remind him. "You have Kristen."

"I *had* Kristen," he says. "We're getting divorced. It's for the best. She can't wait, and there really are no appeals if you plead guilty, which I did."

"I'm sorry," I say. And I am. I really am.

He keeps his gaze cast downward. "Me too. I really fucked up my life. I dragged her down, and now maybe she's got a shot at happiness. I hope she finds it. She's a really good person."

I think of how shell-shocked Kristen looked after her husband's arrest, standing there in front of their house all dressed for work. She was both beautiful and strong. I felt sorry for her. I knew she was a lawyer—she reminded everyone of that fact—and the profession relies on keeping one's emotions out of the worst of circumstances.

"This can't be happening," Kristen said as we picked up Connor on an arrest warrant for Sophie's murder. "Not my husband. Not my Connor. He'd never hurt a fly."

She stuck with him through a process that must have been excruciatingly humiliating for an officer of the court married to an accused killer. TV, newspaper, and online coverage rained like the worst Seattle storm in history. Later, Kristen added to the case against her husband by revealing her suspicions of an affair.

"I had no idea that he was seeing Sophie Warner," she told TV reporter Linda London in an interview that aired before his plea deal, "but now it makes sense. It's the reason we went to the cabin. I wanted to go somewhere else, but he was so insistent. I wonder if he was planning to meet up with her."

As I sit across from him in that chilly prison interview room, I tell him I don't know what to say to him. "Axel Bakker saw what he saw, Connor. You can't dismiss his eyewitness account. A woman being abducted in broad daylight while her husband and daughter were offshore crabbing."

"I know," he says, "but he didn't see *me*. I was wiped out in our cabin. That was supposed to be us out there crabbing. We had the pots in the trunk. But I got all messed up and ruined it." He shook his head miserably. "Not that we would've been able to go anyway."

"Why's that?"

"Found out Sunday when we tried. Turns out the crab fishery was closed until June sometime. Big notice in all the little boats that go with the cabins."

"But Adam Warner and his little girl went crabbing," I say.

He just shrugs. "Outlaw crabbers," he says. "Great way to get a massive fine. They take it seriously on the Sound."

I nod, knowing that to be true. I picture Adam ignoring the sign in the boat, loading Aubrey and the crab pots in anyway—

"I need to leave," I tell Connor.

"Are you going to help me after all?" he asks.

"I don't know if I can," I say, getting up and tapping the glass for the guard.

"Thanks," he says. "Thanks for seeing me. I want you to know that if I ever get out of here, I'm going to fight Adam Warner for custody or visitation. Aubrey's my daughter."

"You don't know that for sure," I say.

"I do," he says. "I knew Sophie better than anyone. She lied to me when she said she thought it could be Adam's baby. I know that beyond a shadow of a doubt. When I looked into Aubrey's eyes, it was my own that I saw."

CHAPTER SEVENTY-ONE
LEE

I stand on the bulkhead and look down at the three little boats associated with the three cabins just south of Octopus Hole—and wonder why I've rushed here. Something to do with crabbing, and these little boats, each of which is now chained to the dock, and each of which once again displays a sign announcing the closure of the crab fishery.

Yet Adam and Aubrey, outlaw crabbers, went out anyway. And Adam, seeing his wife being attacked, had then rowed like a madman to shore to save her. Thrown his little boat up onto the sand, yanked his daughter free of it, and started searching for his wife, yelling for help, leaving Aubrey with the nice older woman there and charging up into the brush.

That little boat had still been there, beached cockeyed on the sand where Adam had left it, when Montrose and I arrived.

That little, utterly empty boat. Containing not a single crab pot.

Was *that* it? Was that what had sent me scrambling back to this place? Crabbing was banned on that weekend, and Adam's boat had contained no pots anyway. Maybe he just left his outlaw pots out in the canal when he saw Sophie being attacked.

Like an idiot, I scan the water for crab-pot markers, as though they'd still be out there nearly three months later.

I heave a sigh and turn around. My eyes settle on the big gray cabin where Sophie Warner spent her last night on this earth. It's a straight line from the steps through the seawall to the trail to the Wisteria's front door, hidden by a big old cedar. I scan over the middle cabin where Teresa Dibley and her grandchildren slept—and think of how the kids got up in the middle of the night and the little boy heard something. Finally, I cast my attention in the direction of the Lily. The Mosses arrived late the night before the crime.

The tide is out, so I walk farther back over oyster shells and rocks to take in everything at once.

I have no idea what I'm searching for until I see it.

A faint indentation runs across the lawn from the Wisteria to the Chrysanthemum, and from the Chrysanthemum to the Lily. A buried water line? No, each cabin has its own well house. Power, I know, comes across from the road above. It would make no sense for a sewer line to run from cabin to cabin. Patches of bright green grass indicate separate drain fields for septic systems.

I remember the code for the Wisteria's lock box, the wholly unsafe and unwise "1234" I saw Adam key in when we came back from the Hama Hama Oyster Saloon.

Down the beach I see a dad and two boys turning over rocks hunting for crabs. I feel like I'm doing the same thing.

Though there are no cars in the parking area, I knock anyway before turning the key in the lock. No answer. Inside, it appears that the housekeeping service has just left. The kitchen floor is still damp. A big, loose bouquet of cosmos commands the space atop the dining table. It, like delphiniums and daisies, reminds me of my mother. She loved blue and white.

I think more about how it was that the Warners and Mosses ended up at Octopus Hole over that long and deadly Memorial Day weekend. It was on purpose, of course. The assumption all along was that Connor stalked Sophie on Facebook, where she had posted their weekend plans: "Adam and I are headed to Octopus Hole #MemorialWeekend." Kristen said that her husband was resolute in his desire to spend that particular weekend there.

But in reality it was *her* place.

She'd been going there for years with her family.

She knew the history of the cabins.

But so did Adam.

I think of that night that I spent here. Stupid me. Drunk and infatuated with the memory of a boy who found me. He told me about rumrunners on Hood Canal during Prohibition; how the big gray cabin had even been a speakeasy.

"Whenever the government agents came calling," he told me, "they moved a bookcase, and it hid the hard stuff, revealing the kind of drinks only a kid would want. Lots of people out here back then with things to hide."

"Hood Canal was a good place to get lost back then," I said. "They never teach that in school."

I remember how Adam and I sat in the sauna after eating oysters and drinking too much beer. Something struck me as odd back then. It comes to me as I return to the little sauna—the strange little panel by the firebox. He was dismissive about it. It didn't seem peculiar at the time, but now I wonder as I examine it. The door is small, but not *that* small. It's paneled in clear cedar like the rest of the space. When I give it a firm push, it springs open. The cedar is a cover over tight-grained fir, the original wood used to build the cabin. The hinges are timeworn, but the screws fastening them in place are new.

When I open it, I poke my head inside. It's dark, so I reach for my phone and turn on the flashlight. Its beam points downward to some old, worn steps.

I start down the steps.

The space isn't very large—maybe the size of a small bedroom. The floor is dirt, but the walls are concrete. As I swipe the beam of light over into the dark, something catches my attention.

A straw hat.

A jolt goes through me, and I think of Axel Bakker. He said Sophie was wearing a straw hat before she vanished after the struggle above the seawall. Adjacent to the hat, I see something darkening the soil. When I bend down, I'm met by what I'm nearly certain is a pool of dried blood. It's mahogany in color. It has been there awhile, but it isn't black. It's still the color of blood. I know the lab can tell me how long it has been there. I know, however, how long it's been there isn't as important as whose blood it is.

I'm focused on what happened down here. How is Sophie's murder connected to the space?

Connected.

The cabins are connected.

I make my way to an opening that leads down a short passageway. It's musty, but cobweb-free. Water drips. Through some gaps between the slats in the passage ceiling, I notice I'm under the little cabin. It passes through my mind that young Clark Dibley probably had heard something that night after all. And it wasn't a door closing. It was a body being moved. Only twenty yards separate the cabins. In another minute I'm under the Lily, the last cabin—the one Kristen and Connor had rented. The tunnel goes farther, and I keep going. I find that I no longer need my phone for illumination. I feel the breeze of the outside come at me.

In front of me, partially obstructed by reeds and a snarl of driftwood, is an opening to the waters of Hood Canal.

Connected.

Connor and Kristen came to Hood Canal for the weekend because *she* had wanted to—and it wasn't because she wanted a long holiday with her waiter husband. She knew what was beneath the cabins. She wanted her rival gone.

Ragged as they are, the pieces are falling into place. I find myself back in my car driving to Seattle.

I need to talk to Adam.

CHAPTER SEVENTY-TWO
LEE

Adam greets me with a surprised look when I arrive. I know I'm a mess, but I really don't care how I look. I'd spent the morning gardening and the afternoon crawling around the passageway between the Octopus Hole cabins. He's dressed to go out.

"Hey," he tells me, pretending to ignore my appearance. "Wish I knew you were coming. Made other plans and would have ditched them for you."

"That's fine," I say. "I'm not up for going out."

"What's up?" he asks, letting me inside and leading me to the living room. Everything I take in is out of a magazine. And not one I subscribe to. Fashionable. Perfect. Lavish.

Adam's wearing a blue linen shirt, and his shoes gleam like a pair of mirrors. I also notice new eyeglasses with Prada frames. I wonder how it is that he's able to spend so freely on himself.

"You must have gotten a job," I say.

He motions me to sit and offers me a drink. I decline.

"Nope," he says. "A few prospects, though."

"I see," I say.

He pours himself a whiskey over ice. "You didn't come all this way to tell me how good I look."

He's right, of course.

"I didn't," I say. I'm searching for the words to tell him that I think Kristen Moss was involved in Sophie's murder. I'm thinking that Connor lied to me. The Mosses did it together. It *had* to be the two of them. She was a small woman; there was no way she could wrestle away Sophie and drag her off to the bunker below the house. There was also the matter of his DNA. I wonder if Connor raped Sophie the night before he and Kristen killed her. I feel like he wanted to tell me something more, but he didn't want to admit to his own culpability. When Kristen served him divorce papers after his incarceration, he wanted to hurt her back.

This was clearly one way.

"I think I know what happened to Sophie," I say.

Adam takes a drink. "We know what happened to her."

I weigh his expression. I study him behind those fancy new frames. I want to see his reaction to what I'm about to tell him.

"Yes," I say. "And no."

"That's a strange response," he says, playing with the ice cubes in his glass. "Are you sure you don't want a drink?"

"I do," I say. "But I better not. Long drive back."

"Yeah," he says, shifting his gaze back to his glass. "Right. So what's the *no* part?"

"I think Kristen was part of it," I say.

His eyes widen. "Shit! That's a hell of a thing to say. Kristen would never do anything like that."

Everything stops right then. He's defensive. It's a strange and unexpected jolt.

"Sounds like you know her," I say.

He shrugs a little. "Not really," he says. "But it goes without saying that we've become bound together by the legal stuff. My wife. Her husband. It's a mess that only we can really share."

I ponder that a moment. It happens. I've heard stories of the family of a murder victim befriending the killer's family.

"So you're friendly now?"

"I guess," he says, looking at his watch, a gargantuan and gleaming chronograph. "In fact, we were going to hang out tonight. She's going through stuff at work. Related to a case."

He's trying to sound casual. I don't push. Deep down, the alarm bells sound louder. I try to mute them. I really do.

Adam saved me.

"What would you do if she had been involved?" I ask him. "What would you say about that?"

Adam blinks. "I guess I would say, 'Lock her up and make sure she never gets out.' But she didn't. She's not that kind of a woman. She's brilliant. Kind. Very giving."

"Sounds like you've gotten to like her."

"Well, honestly, Lee," he says, "I barely know her."

His words suddenly feel like a lie, but this is Adam Warner. He's not a liar. He wouldn't know how to lie if someone taught him.

I am sure of that.

Chapter Seventy-Three
Adam

The first time I saw Kristen Moss was when she knocked on our door one Sunday afternoon. I'd been watching football on TV, and the Seahawks were losing. Big-time. Sophie, as she had been far too much at that time, was gone. I was ready for a distraction. I hated seeing my team go down in flames. *Again.* I was a winner. So of course I expected the Hawks to be winners too.

I wouldn't have opened the door, but seeing Kristen through the peephole, I gave the knob a turn. She was pretty. Easy on the eyes. No doubt about that. If she had been selling something, I might even have been a buyer.

Looking back now, I would have been a lot better off if it actually *had* been a kid selling chocolate bars for the school band, or even a pair of Jehovah's Witnesses.

"Adam Warner?" she asked in that way people do when they know exactly who you are and think that you should know them as well. I looked her over, but nothing registered. Maybe we'd talked at a conference? She was too beautiful for the accounting pool at SkyAero, that's for sure. I'd have kept my eye on her.

"Sorry. Have we met?"

"No," she said. "I know your wife. Is she home?"

I opened the door a little wider. "No. Sophie's out running errands with our daughter. Might be home in an hour. You want to wait . . . ?" I let the last word hang out in the breeze, an invitation for her to tell me her name.

"Kristen," she says. "Kristen Moss. You might know my husband, Connor."

I knew that name. Indeed, I knew a lot about Connor Moss. I'd Facebook-stalked him after my office millennial helped me figure out who the hell he was. I'd gone by the restaurant where he worked, hoping to get a glimpse of the piece of shit. I even went to lunch there, but I missed him. I never even saw him. After a few days of being pissed off, I let it go. I'd been messing around with Carrie. I had no right to call Sophie out on it. And then things got better.

"What do you want?" I asked.

"I want your wife to stop fucking my husband."

I didn't even flinch at this. I'd seen the emails between Sophie and her lover by then. I knew that things were bad between Sophie and me. I deliberately chose to ride it out. This woman in front of me was taking a different, more direct, approach.

"It works both ways, Kristen."

She clasped her hands as if to steady herself. She'd been undone by the affair, less able to put up with it than I was. That was probably because Kristen Moss was a far better person than I ever could be.

"My situation is complicated," she told me. "I have things to do that require Connor in my life at the moment."

"Sounds ominous."

"Just personal," she said.

Affairs are very personal, I thought.

"But what these two are doing has to stop," she went on, the anger in her eyes flashing. "Have you told her?"

I didn't want a scene on my front steps, but I didn't want to invite trouble into my house.

Like Sophie did when she had sex with this intruder's husband.

I shook my head. "I don't exactly have clean hands myself."

She let out a huge sigh. I was only glad that it wasn't a scream. She looked that frustrated and angry.

"Great," she finally said. "What's wrong with everybody these days? God help me. I can't deal with this now. Not with all that I have going on."

I didn't ask her to elaborate, because I really didn't care. I knew that if I went to Sophie, she'd toss the possibility of an affair with Carrie LaCroix in my face, and I'd have to deny and lie. We just didn't talk about it because we didn't like lying to each other. Who does?

"I wish they'd get in a car crash or something. The both of them," she said, testing me. "I bet you'd get over her in a New York minute."

I started to ease the door closed. "I don't want to hear this kind of bullshit," I told her. "You need to leave now, Kristen. Do whatever you want to do with your husband, but keep my wife out of it."

And then I shut the door. I didn't see Kristen again. Not for quite a while. Not until the day I found out that Aubrey was not my biological daughter.

CHAPTER SEVENTY-FOUR
LEE

I don't tell Adam about the straw hat. How I found it under the Wisteria when I searched the old rumrunners' passageway between the cabins. I don't tell him as he stands there in his fancy clothes that I know I've been lied to. I don't tell him any of that because when he sets down his phone to refresh his drink, I notice the pendant that caught my eye in the interview with Kristen and Connor.

Art deco. Platinum. Sapphires.

It's coiled like a snake on the table next to Adam's drink. It is almost like I've been swallowed by a black hole in the middle of that expensive sofa. Down some huge drain and into the sewer.

Everybody lies.

It wasn't Connor at all.

It was Adam and Kristen.

I try to slow my heart rate and appear calm.

"I'll take that drink," I tell Adam. "If you're still offering."

He's oblivious to my shift in demeanor. Or maybe I'm more adept at hiding how I feel than I think I am.

He flashes that perfect smile. Before I saw a Cruise smile, a Clooney grin. Now I see *Jaws*.

"I can do that," he says. "One quick drink, and then I need to get out of here." He turns his back to me and makes it, then hands me a glass. I take the smallest of sips. I wonder now if he spiked my beer that night at the cabin. It passes through my mind now that the boy who saved me when I was a girl has become a worse monster than my rapist and captor, Albert Hodge.

How is it that I could be so intuitive with so many, but fail with the one who had saved me? The one I thought I knew better than anyone?

"How's Aubrey?" I ask, trying to keep the conversation going. "Must be hard caring for her."

He wipes the lenses of his glasses with a tissue.

"I have Katrina," he says.

"That's right. She must be a big help."

He sees me a little differently now. I can feel it.

"Where is she now?"

"They stay at Katrina's on Saturdays so I can get things done around here. It's tough doing it on your own."

You don't have a job, I think.

"I'm sure."

I avert my stare.

"Something's up," he says. "What's going on with you? Are you all right?"

I think about what card to play. Adam knows me well. He knows every tell that I have.

I start with Aubrey.

"I ran into Dan Belding today at Sister's."

He shakes his head. "That place still open?"

My heart pounds.

"Yeah, and Diane still works there. But that's not the interesting part."

"What might that be?"

The energy in the room has altered. The blood vessel in his temple pulses like the beating heart of a frog. It's rapid. He's got to feel it.

Yes, in fact, he does. He wipes the back of his hand over that very spot.

"Says you sought some legal advice, Adam."

I watch him very closely.

Adam doesn't play dumb. He's smarter than that. No. Maybe *devious* is the word. My brother used to tell me that Adam should join the drama club and give up the basketball court.

"I was at my wit's end, Lee," he says. "Didn't know what to do. Didn't know how I'd make it."

"But as you said, you have Katrina," I say. "I thought she was a great support."

He pretends to brighten a little. It's phony, but I give an empathetic smile in return.

"Yeah," he says. "I'd be lost without her."

You're lost now, I think.

I weigh my options. I'm not afraid of this man. I could be direct and confront him, or I could try to extract from him what I want to know. But I'm not stupid. I know the risks of such a confrontation.

"I need to use the bathroom," I say.

He points down the hall. "First door on the left."

I find my way down the hall. I lower the toilet seat as though I'm about to use it. I turn on the water. While I stand there, I look at my reflection in the mirror. Without makeup I am a blank canvas. Freckles bridge my nose. My eyes are full of sadness, and I almost make myself cry. I see someone who was blinded by a traumatic event, so blinded that when the truth was right next to her, she couldn't see it. I can see it all now. I can see the woman that I was meant to be, and I'm not letting this SOB get away.

I can't have Adam hear me make a call, so I text Montrose.

I'm at Adam's. He's Sophie's killer. Call SPD and get them over here ASAP.

I press "Send" and flush. I stay riveted to my phone until I see the dots moving up and down.

Montrose: Roger that. Be safe.

When I return to the living room, I notice that Adam has moved his phone. I bet he sent a message of his own. I decide to be direct.

"Aubrey isn't your daughter, is she?" I ask.

He holds my gaze for a very long time. It's clear that he's weighing his options too.

"I saw Connor today at prison," I go on. "He had a lot to say."

Everything I say now is a log on the fire. I'm going for a bonfire. I'm going for the biggest blaze I've ever seen.

"Connor is a murderer," he says. "And a liar."

"I don't think so." Before that moment I might have added, *And I'm a pretty good judge of who is truthful and who isn't.* "I know you killed Sophie," I say.

He looks at me like I'm crazy. But I know I'm not.

"I was in the boat," he says. "Axel Bakker saw me. You know that, Lee."

The eyewitness is trotted out once more. I feel so stupid about that now. Mr. Bakker saw something, all right. But not what Adam had said.

"You counted on him," I tell him. "But, Adam, I know better. I found the hat and the blood under the cabin. I know that you knew about the passageway because the night I stayed at the cabin you told me about the history."

"Oh, Lee," he says, moving closer. "You were drunk that night at the cabin."

He's a stranger. I know that now.

"I *was* probably drugged," I say, holding my arm out to keep him from moving any closer. I feel my gun against my rib cage. I have seldom had the need to draw it, but now it dawns on me that it might come to that. "Did you drug me?"

He shakes his head. "I'd never do anything like that, Lee. Come on. You know me."

I wish I did.

"I don't, Adam," I finally say. "I never did. Whatever you did for me when I was a kid was appreciated, but who you are today has nothing to do with who I thought you were."

If this affects him in the least, he's not showing it. He's just flatly staring at me.

"Kristen's getting a divorce," I say.

"What's the big deal about that?"

"You know, Adam. I know."

"I really don't," he says. "Not for sure."

I give it a go. I bluff.

"I know you're seeing her," I say.

"So we got a little close."

I suck in some air. I hate confronting a liar. Like Adam. My Adam.

"You've been having an affair with her all along," I say. "Haven't you?"

He suppresses a laugh with a tight smirk.

But I see it. I see it all.

"You couldn't be more wrong," Adam says.

CHAPTER SEVENTY-FIVE
KRISTEN

Jesus, I'm terrible at picking men. I'm reminded painfully of that when Adam texts me that Lee is at his house. He's weak. He'll crumble like a dried autumn leaf. I wonder if he's told her that we are going to get married. That I am going to adopt Aubrey. He's so pathetic that I'm sure he has. I get in my Lexus and pull into traffic. I can take care of Lee.

Just like I took care of Sophie and Connor.

Even now, as I make my way to Adam's, tears come when I think about the betrayal that set all this in motion. I'm a good person. I was doing everything that I could to be productive. I gave money to the Humane Society. I sponsored three kids in World Vision. I worked hard at my job. I only wanted one thing: a baby. God, why was I denied when I see so many kids come through the system who've been abused or abandoned? Jesus, help me. I honestly don't get it. I did every single thing that the doctors told me. I might as well have been forced to walk down Westlake Avenue completely naked with a sign on my back that read "Barren." That's how humiliated I was by my inability to conceive.

And then Adam Warner comes to my office and drops a dirty bomb.

Connor has had a child with that whore Sophie.

When Adam left, I told Marcy that I wasn't feeling well, and I drove to Green Lake and just sat there on a bench looking at the mallards and Muscovies, thinking. My mind was spinning so fast I know I wasn't thinking straight. It was emotion driving a decision. I never, ever do that.

And yet that day I did. I knew that I wanted that backstabbing husband of mine gone. I wanted that bitch girlfriend of his gone too. When they were fucking each other, they were really fucking me. My legs were wide open, just letting them do whatever.

This was my fault. I knew it. I also knew that I could fix it. I sat there with those smelly ducks, imagining what it would feel like to grab one by the neck and choke the life out of it. I closed my eyes.

I thought it would feel good.

When I got home, I went to the kitchen calendar hanging next to the coffeemaker. I flipped its pages to see the best time. To see how long I'd need to pretend that all was well between us.

Memorial Day weekend looked good. It wasn't far off. I could survive the routine of our lives with an end in sight. The date held some irony too. I liked that. It would forever be a time to remember what I'd done and the reasons why I had done it. Years later, while others had fresh strawberry shortcake, I'd savor the memory of making things right. It would be far sweeter than any dessert.

Just desserts. I smiled at my little joke.

I could do this.

Still, I needed help.

I put a big circle around the weekend with a Sharpie.

The next day, Connor stood in his underwear pouring some coffee. When I looked at him, I imagined castration as a solution. I could grab that two-timing cock of his and slice it with a Henckels on the butcher block. While he is writhing around, I'd toss the severed member in the garbage disposal and turn it on.

"Hey, babe," I said. "Change in plans for the three-day weekend."

"Crap," he said, looking at me while I sat across the kitchen in the banquette we'd built together. "You have to work? I already got the time off."

"No," I told him. "I'm thinking of somewhere close to home."

He made a disappointed face.

I wonder how he'd feel if I cut off his nut sack and flung it against the cupboard door.

Splat!

"I was looking forward to Walla Walla."

"Me too," I said. "But I'll find something closer. I don't want to spend the weekend on the road. The Seattle traffic has really gotten to me. I'm beginning to hate my car."

He sipped his coffee.

"I hear you on that, babe."

I hated when he called me that.

"Love you," I told him as he returned to the bedroom.

Hate you, I thought.

There are a million ways to kill someone. I know that from practicing law. Most people only know about it from TV. Those of us in the profession—on either side of the law-and-order equation—know how to get away with something as egregious as homicide. Be very careful. Trust no one. Tie up loose ends. And never get caught.

No. Never.

A few days later, I make it a point to run into Adam Warner. I learned his routine and his wife's in about two minutes on Facebook and by sitting out in my car two doors down from their house. Sophie left first. It made my stomach roil to see her. She was very pretty. I could see how Connor would like her. She was younger too. Probably more fun than me. I didn't even want to go there, but I couldn't help myself. I wondered what the two of them said about me. How they must have laughed at my inability to become pregnant. How it came so easily and accidentally to them when I put so much effort into it.

That wasn't what made me sick when I watched Sophie. It was seeing her and that little girl—a girl that I felt was half mine. Or *should* be half mine. It was my husband that made that baby! Aubrey was perfect. She was the little girl that I dreamed about when I went to sleep in tears after having Dr. Y or some stupid girl at the herbal store tell me that I was not going to get pregnant.

That I should just give up and adopt!

Idiot.

Twenty minutes later, Adam backed his car out of the driveway. I followed him half a block, and then I started honking and waving frantically. He pulled over and got out, thinking that there'd been an accident.

"What do you want?" he asked, recognizing me right away.

"The same thing you do," I said.

He pretended to push back, but I'm persuasive. That's what I do.

"I don't know what you're talking about."

"Yes, I know you do," I said. "I want you to meet me in the bar at the Four Seasons at seven."

"I won't meet you anywhere," he said.

"We have the same interests here, Adam. Our spouses betrayed us, and your marriage is going to end. You know it. And you'll be stuck paying child support for a kid that's not yours. You'll hate every minute of your life for the next fifteen years. Aubrey will be a reminder of how Sophie betrayed you. A knife in your back. You know it. I know it. I have a solution. Meet me there."

He looked at me like he'd been hit with an air gun. Just flat-out stunned. I had no idea if he'd come or not.

He did, of course.

God, men are so easy.

I see the detective's crappy car in front of Adam's house and park behind it. I remove the gun from my glove box and go to the door. Connor bought it for me after our neighbor was assaulted.

Connor had his good points.

All right. One good point.

CHAPTER SEVENTY-SIX
LEE

I hear a knock at the door. That will be the Seattle police. I silently thank Montrose and God. In that order.

"Better answer that," I tell Adam.

He gives me a nervous look and then heads to the foyer.

It isn't the police, though. It's Kristen Moss. She's dressed to the nines for a night out, but her manner is anything but celebratory. There's a hardness to her that unsettles me. Her face is stiff, her features unyielding.

"What are you doing here?" she asks me.

"You know why I'm here, Kristen," I say.

She looks at Adam. Her eyes spark. "Can't you keep your mouth closed?"

"I didn't say anything," Adam says. Then he looks at me. "Drink your drink. Kristen and I have dinner plans."

I most definitely will not drink anything.

My eyes go to the necklace, and Kristen snatches it without a word.

"I don't know how you did it," I say to her as her heels

dig into the thick black-and-white area rug, "but you killed Sophie, didn't you?"

Kristen stands still as a statue. It's as if the words are running loose between the synapses in her brain. Her affect is so strange. Something's seriously wrong with her.

"I didn't kill anyone," she says.

I poke the hornet's nest.

"You were so enraged about Connor having that baby with Sophie."

She glares at me. "I won't lie," she finally says. "I was. If you ever have a husband, and he does that to you too, you'll feel the same anger. It's universal, Lee. It's not a motive for murder."

She's baiting me. I can see that now. She wants to talk. *Where are those Seattle police officers?*

"So you killed her," I say.

"I said I didn't." She frowns at Adam. "*He* did."

The air escapes my lungs.

"He couldn't have," I say. "He was on the boat."

Adam's face is blank. The moment is surreal. Maybe it *isn't* real. Maybe it is another bad dream. In some ways, I hope so. Adam might be a liar, but I don't want to see him behind bars for the rest of his life.

"Adam," I say, "Mr. Bakker saw you."

Silence fills the room. I swear I can feel heat rolling off Kristen's body. She's about ready to blow. But Adam just sits there in a strange stupor.

"I had a bad feeling about this," he finally says, "from the very beginning."

CHAPTER SEVENTY-SEVEN
ADAM

We sat at the back table of the Goldfinch Tavern in the Four Seasons. Kristen had just come from work. I didn't have to make an excuse. Sophie was on a project—at least that's what I thought—and I did some shopping before we met.

She noticed my Saks bag. "You have good taste," she said.

"Yeah, but a craft-beer budget," I said. "But that's not why we're here. What do you want?"

"Like I said," she went on, "I think we want the same things. I want Connor gone. You want Sophie gone."

"You can't be serious," I said.

"Do I look like I'm joking?" Kristen asked.

The waiter brought our drinks. Maker's for me, obviously. An expensive merlot for her. It was clear: she had good taste, and more money than I did. I acted like I wasn't interested in what she had to say, except that I was. I asked her to elaborate while I drank my whiskey.

"What if both Sophie and Connor were gone?" she asked.

"Like dead?" I asked. I felt strangely giddy at the prospect. Like we were playing some stupid and dangerous game.

"Yes," she said. "Like dead. Look what they did to us, Adam. They fucked up our lives for all time. The chances that I'll have a baby one day are slim. I can thank Connor for wasting my chance to have a family now. And you, you're going to end up paying for a child that isn't even yours for the rest of your life."

The truth was I no longer felt for Aubrey the way I did before I found out she wasn't mine. I would never utter the words out loud: it would have made me sound so callous and pathetic. I saw Sophie and Connor whenever I looked at her. That's the only thing I could see. It made me angry and sick to my stomach. I thought of how the cuckoo pushes the offspring from a host's nest. I understood.

Inexplicably, however, I defended Aubrey.

"It's not as if she's a brat, Kristen. She's a good little kid."

Kristen raised her perfect brow and swirled her wine. "In any case, she's not *your* brat. She's Connor's. I know you hate that. *I* would. My dad once told me that no man wants to raise a child that's not his own."

I ignored her remark. Instead, for some reason, I egged her on a little. I lowered my voice.

"I could never kill Sophie."

"You don't have to, because I could."

Her eyes were ice. She actually meant it. It stunned me.

"And then I suppose you want me to kill Connor," I said. "Is that it?"

When she shook her head, big fat diamond earrings caught the light and sent sparks off into the room. I looked around to see if anyone was watching. It was a reaction to the circumstances. She was plotting. I was listening.

The conversation was going way too far.

"No," she said. "You don't have to kill anyone. I'll do it all. You just have to help in other ways."

The more she went on, the crazier I assumed she was. She had it all figured out. Even had the time and place picked out—some cabins on Hood Canal over Memorial Day weekend. She planned to frame Connor and give him the boot to prison for the rest of his life. I'd have an alibi. She knew that an old man walked the beach every single morning at ten forty-five. He'd done it for years like clockwork. She even made a reconnaissance trip up there to confirm it.

Axel Bakker was the key.

"Your cheating wife's abduction will be done in broad daylight," she said.

"By who, if I'm in a boat?"

Kristen locked her eyes on mine. It was as if she didn't need to blink. "I'll kill her the night before," she said. "You'll be traumatized. You'll clean up the mess. That's easy. I'll plant Connor's DNA on her body. He'll go down for it. We'll be free. You want to be free, Adam. Right?"

I admitted that I did.

"Think about it. Divorce will never make you free," she said, still cool and resolute. "You'll have to pay for Aubrey. I know women like Sophie. She'll bleed you dry, Adam. She'll be a bloodsucker. A leech. You and I both know it. The cheaters are always the most vindictive."

I took a breath as I tried to process what she had planned. I really didn't understand.

"If Sophie's dead, how is that going to free me of raising Aubrey?" The words felt like bile coming up my throat, but I said them anyway.

"You'll give her to me," she said.

I had sat there for more than an hour, and while Kristen

spun a plot for murder, my misgivings were small enough to push aside. Offering up my daughter for sale was too much.

"You are sick," I told her. "I'm not going to sell Aubrey."

Just then Kristen reached her hand over to mine. It was a move to quiet and control me.

"Not sell," she said with complete conviction. "Let me *adopt* her."

CHAPTER SEVENTY-EIGHT
LEE

I see the barrel of Kristen's handgun. It's pointed in my direction, but she keeps her attention on Adam. I detect a slight tremor in her hand, I expect she's not used to shooting anyone. Then again, I really don't know her at all. I suspect that Adam doesn't really, either. People like Kristen wear a mask every day. It isn't makeup. It isn't latex or anything overt like that. It's their ability to keep their emotions hidden by pretending to be normal.

Or happy.

When they never really are.

"Did you give her the GHB?" she asks.

Adam nods nervously and indicates my glass. "Yeah, but she's not drinking it."

Kristen stabs her gun in my direction. "Drink it."

"No," I say. "I won't."

Adam looks at me with sympathetic eyes. "It will make things easier," he says.

The words swing me back to Albert Hodge. When he put

his hand over my mouth and said to breathe in. "Everything will be easier."

I didn't fight him. I did what he said because I was so scared. But not now.

"You'll have to kill me," I say. "I've called the police. They'll be here soon. You'll go down for this, Kristen. You too, Adam."

"She's bluffing," Kristen says, measuring my words. "When did you call?"

"When I was in the bathroom."

Kristen gives Adam a hard glare. "Well, that's pretty stupid, Adam. Letting her do that."

"I didn't kill anyone," Adam says. "It was *all* Kristen. I didn't even know she was coming to the cabins. She stalked Sophie. She and Connor. Both had their reasons."

"You're such a liar, Adam," Kristen says.

Adam shifts his attention to me. "You know me, Lee."

I *thought* I did. Now I know that I only had a fantasy of who my rescuer and my beloved big brother's best friend really was.

The gun moves closer.

I need one of them on my side. I also need the police to get here.

Where are they?

"I know you couldn't have done it, Adam," I say.

Kristen won't back down. "We did it there because Adam told me an old friend, someone who looked up to him, who owed him, would be the responding detective. Didn't it ever strike you as strange, as a coincidence, maybe even fortuitous, that your old friend's wife was abducted in your Podunk jurisdiction?"

I don't respond. I had thought it was fortuitous, actually. At the time, I thought that it gave me a chance to do something for Adam Warner as he'd once done for me long ago—that I could help him at the worst possible time of his life.

Kristen Moss is a talker. She talks in front of a jury for a living. She might also be the biggest liar on the planet.

"I know you are going to kill me," I say. "I want to know what happened. I deserve to know."

Adam looks away.

"This is really messed up," he says.

He's not who I thought he was. Or who I wanted him to be.

"*You* messed it up, Adam," I tell him. "*You* did."

Adam seems scared. Like he's about to crumble.

"I didn't do anything, Lee. Really, I didn't."

Kristen remains stone. But she can't stop talking. She wants to control the narrative.

"The night before her supposed abduction, Adam drugged Sophie with GHB," she says. "I got it from a client who was stupid enough to bring it to court. Of course, I don't use the stuff. I gave some to Adam for Sophie and kept a good dose for Connor."

"Connor was drugged too," I say. "That's why he can't remember."

Kristen lets out a little tense laugh. "You should be a detective."

She'd be proud of that little retort in front of a jury.

"What happened?" I ask, trying to buy some time. "I need to know."

Kristen, thankfully, is on a roll.

"Adam brought her down to the basement. I did what I had to do. I snuffed the life out of her because Mr. I'm-Not-That-Kind-of-Man didn't have the balls for it. Typical male. All talk. Little action. I put some of Connor's semen from a fertility-collection kit inside her. Done. We carried her body down the tunnel and stowed it there, then shoved her into the canal when the time was right."

She stops and looks at Adam. "And you, Adam, had one little job to do. You must have screwed that up. The detective is here. That can only mean you either told someone or you didn't get rid of all of the evidence, did you?"

He doesn't answer.

"I found the hat," I say.

Kristen gives a knowing nod. "Of course you did," she says. "I knew I should have gone back there myself. Stupid me. Stupid me."

A disconnect infiltrates everything that comes out of her mouth. Her words are delivered with an odd flatness. I've never heard such a vile string of words expressed without one iota of emotion. She might as well have been ordering a pizza.

"I had nothing to do with it," Adam says, urging me to believe him. "You need to believe me. She's batshit crazy."

Where are the police?

"You came up with the best part of the plan," Kristen says, looking at Adam, who's now silent.

"What was that?" I ask her.

Kristen smiles.

"The blow-up doll."

CHAPTER SEVENTY-NINE
KRISTEN

I'd racked my brain over the alibi situation. I've practiced law for more than a decade; I know the keys to avoiding a conviction. Have an unbreakable alibi and never talk about what you've done once everything goes down. I'd have Connor, of course, to alibi me, but there was the issue of Adam. In order for us to get away with it, I needed to make sure that even a narcissistic fool like him wouldn't get caught.

Narcissists are very unreliable.

Adam had to be positioned in that rowboat, and the old man needed to see a struggle. It was as simple as that. Simple is always a good starting point. Complicated only trips up the best—or worst—of intentions.

I met Adam at the Goldfinch in the Four Seasons a second time. The place was crawling with out-of-towners, and that's why it was such a great place for what we had in mind. Everyone was too busy one-upping the person across from them to pay us any mind. That was good. We had a lot to get done. Memorial Day weekend was ten days away, and we needed to be in sync. Completely so.

I slid a packet of GHB across the table. "The kids call it cherry meth."

He put it in his coat pocket. "Sounds yummy."

We ordered drinks—whiskey and wine—and after they arrived, we got down to business. I studied Adam as we talked. He was all in. That was not only good, it was necessary. He had more to risk here. She was *his* wife.

"The old man has to see a struggle on the lawn above the beach," I told him.

"Right," he said. "So you'll dress in Sophie's clothes, and you'll make a scene. The old dog walker will see you fighting off someone, and then you'll vanish from view."

Adam isn't a detail person. That was obvious from the start.

"That won't work," I said after swallowing some wine. "I can't just pretend to fight someone. The old man's not blind. Just near-sighted."

"Can't you zombie up Connor and make him struggle with you?"

It was intended as a joke, but there was a nugget of a genuine idea wrapped in his stupid idea.

"He's going to be completely zonked out so that he won't know what he's done," I told him. "I'll set him up, and you don't have to worry about that. He'll go down for it. I'm going to let nature take its course. No need to call the police on him. I know Connor Moss. He's always been about doing the right thing."

"I almost feel sorry for the guy," Adam said.

"Don't," I said, meaning it. "He fucked your wife. He made a baby! He ruined our lives."

Adam gulped his drink. He was nervous. I wondered if he was cut out for this.

"I won't ever forget that," he said.

Good, I thought.

"Now, about that zombie idea," I went on. "What about a mannequin?"

"I don't follow," he said.

Adam may have been good-looking, but he most definitely was not a quick study. He'd always be the weak link in what we were going to do. I made a mental note of that.

"What if we dress a mannequin up as Sophie, and I dress up as Connor?" I asked. "Wear his jacket. Hat, maybe. I struggle with the mannequin."

He put down his empty glass and indicated to the waiter he wanted a second drink.

"I like it," he said. "But we don't have a mannequin. Do we?"

I shook my head at the waiter that I was fine with a single glass of wine.

"No," I said. "And we don't need to be seen running around Goodwill, trying to find one, either."

Adam sat there quietly for a minute.

"I have one of those sex blow-up dolls in my trunk," he said.

"You're disgusting," I said.

He gave me a shrug. "It was from a bachelor's party at work. I keep meaning to get rid of it. My worst fear is that I'm going to get in an accident on I-5, and the trooper is going to find it in the back of my car."

I had a lot bigger reservations than that. Spending the rest of my life in prison was at the top of the list.

"That'll work," I told him. "Better than a mannequin. It'll be more flexible probably."

As we sat there, I ran everything over in my head. Backward and forward. This could work. It was risky being at the same group of cabins, but that could be explained too.

"Remember," I reminded Adam. "We have never met. We wouldn't know each other by sight. My husband tracked your wife to Octopus Hole. It was a surprise. Sophie had heard about the cabins too—from Connor. She booked the Wisteria cabin, posted it on Facebook, and Connor booked the Lily for us. Neither one of us had any idea what was about to take place."

"Yeah," he said. "We're both victims here."

"You know that's true," I said, thinking of our betraying spouses.

"What about the third cabin?"

"I already know who booked it."

"Who?"

"Some grandmother with some little kids. She'll be distracted."

"How can you be so sure?"

"Because I know. Things happen fast. This will all be done in a blur."

When we get up to leave, Adam gave me that obvious and unmistakable look that men give to women when they think they have a shot.

I made a note of that too. Never know when you'll need to use something like that.

CHAPTER EIGHTY
LEE

"She's a liar," Adam says flatly. "I could never hurt Sophie. Sure, I was pissed off at her. Yes, I hated that Aubrey wasn't mine but in fact was some other guy's kid. I would never be a party to killing my wife. You have to believe me, Lee."

"I don't know what to believe," I say as the three of us face each other in the living room of Adam's pricey Seattle home.

Kristen is calm. Adam is unraveling. *I* know *you are a killer, Adam,* I think. *Janna Fong told me about the blow-up doll in your trunk.*

He jabs a finger in Kristen's direction. "She's crazy."

Again, Kristen doesn't react. She's oddly flat. Calm.

"Not crazy," she says, her gun now a divining rod, pointed at her greatest threat—Adam. "Just tired. Tired of working so hard and giving so much while everyone else just takes. If you had anything to give, you'd understand. But you don't.

You're too wrapped up in your 'poor me, my wife slept with another man' pity party."

The way Kristen is talking removes any doubt that this is going to end badly for me and for Adam. But only if I let it.

"I actually do understand," I say.

She swivels her attention to me.

"How is that, Detective?"

No one can really understand deranged. However, I know that a crazy person can be manipulated just as easily as anyone.

"You've been through a lot," I tell her. "Connor told me. I know that you had struggles with infertility."

She gives me a hard stare but says nothing.

"I know you did all of this because you wanted a child. Didn't you, Kristen?"

Her eyes flutter. "I know you saw Connor," she says. "He's a liar too."

"Kristen," Adam says, "put down the gun. This isn't going to work."

His voice is a rasp, choked with what I think is genuine emotion.

Kristen looks at me, then over to Adam.

"Don't you think I know that?" she asks. "Don't you think that I knew almost from that first night at the cabin that this would fall apart? I should never have gotten involved with you, Adam. You made me do all of this. You talked me into this, you bastard."

And just like that, she fires the gun into Adam's chest. He gasps and puts his hand over the growing red pool on the shirt I admired when I first arrived. He seems stunned. Even though Kristen has been aiming a loaded gun at him, it dawns on me just then that Adam thought he was invincible. In his perfect marriage. His job. His plot with Kristen. Now that's all gone. He slumps silently downward onto that thick black-and-white rug, which is now splattered with blood. He doesn't say a word.

Kristen's still watching him when I pull out my own gun and fire.

She goes down, her fingers still gripping her weapon. Her eyes are open and staring into the room, but I know that my shot has killed her. I went hunting with my father when I was young. I know the confused, frightened look of a buck when the life force ebbs from him. Kristen Moss is that animal now.

The smell of gunfire fills my lungs. I've never fired my weapon at another human being. Tears come. I glance around the room like a caged animal. I've been trained for this all of my career. I know what to do. I kick the gun from Kristen's hand and go to Adam, who is making horrific guttural sounds.

"I'm really sorry, Lee."

I don't know why, but I get on my knees to comfort him.

"I know, Adam," I say. "It will be all right."

I'm back on Tamarack Lane in Shelton. But now Adam Warner is under the branches of the plum tree. He's asking for help. I'm reaching down for him and promising to take him home.

And as he did to me, I lie.

"It will be okay."

"Kristen did all of this," he says.

"I know," I tell him.

I look at his handsome face, his stylish glasses now splattered with tiny specks of blood. I wonder what turned the boy who rescued me into a monster. I find it hard to breathe, but I know I'm breathing. I wonder if anyone can ever know the reasons why we do the things we do. Even the most terrible things. His eyes are starting to dim.

I hear sirens.

"Hang on, Adam," I say. "Help is on the way."

EPILOGUE
LEE

Adam Warner survived only to face murder charges after the labs went back for a second review of blood samples taken at Sophie Warner's autopsy and discovered trace amounts of GHB. It's one of those drugs that isn't part of the standard tox screen. No one looks for it unless you think it might be there.

Oyster gatherers had found Connor's red jacket but didn't know it was part of the criminal case until Linda London made a news report about what had really happened in the cabins not far from Octopus Hole. Kristen and Adam had left it out on the water after Sophie was supposedly abducted. It was the kind of mistake that could easily have been their undoing—the jacket was purchased at Nordstrom in Seattle. A receipt carelessly left inside a pocket indicated Kristen's account. It had been part of her disguise. Synthetic wig hairs were recovered from the straw hat.

The blow-up doll.

It was true. Kristen's last words had not been a lie.

One thing, however, had been.

Dr. Collier called me about Kristen's autopsy.

"I read your report," she said. "Saw all the notes on her quest for a baby. Holy mackerel. I hope you're sitting down."

I wasn't. But I said I was.

"Kristen couldn't have a baby. She didn't have any ovaries. Born without them. She had what we call ovarian agenesis."

"But she was seeing a fertility doctor," I said.

"I checked on that too. Dr. Yamada is a psychiatrist. Once you get back to work you'll want to see if you can get him to talk to you. Interesting case, I bet. She was trying everything she could to get pregnant, but she didn't have the goods to get there. I wonder if her husband knew?"

"I doubt it. He was all in on her quest to have a baby. What a mess."

Dr. Collier said her report was in Montrose's email.

"Just wanted you to know," she said.

I thanked her and found a place to sit down. I hadn't expected it, but I felt sorry for Kristen. She was sick. She wanted something that she could never attain, and she clearly snapped.

Adam was another story.

I had a long week off pending a review of the shooting. Millicent and I got caught up on Netflix, and, in the surprise of my life, Dan Belding Jr. asked me out for a date. Bigger surprise, I said yes. He's decent, and decent has been in short supply in my life as of late.

When I was growing up in that little house in Shelton, I didn't dream of being a cat lady.

Like Kristen Moss, I wanted to get married and have a family.

Probably not as much as she did, though.

Two weeks after Adam's arrest, a young woman followed her dog into a ravine off a remote logging road near Hurricane Ridge on the Olympic Peninsula. The red of Jim Coyle's much-sought-after pickup truck caught her attention, and she dialed 911. It was true. Coyle hadn't killed anyone but himself. I thought of his request about his dog during his call to me. Sad relief washed over me when I checked with Animal Control. A young couple from Union had adopted AJ, his beloved Pomeranian.

The dog that unremittingly yapped had the only happy ending.

At least as far as I could tell.

CONNOR

You'd think that a confession and supporting evidence would get a guy out of prison in short order, but the wheels of justice move slowly even when the right thing to do is so obvious. My lawyer tells me that I should be out of here in a couple of months. Undoing a guilty plea isn't easy.

A paternity test confirmed what I already knew deep down when I first saw her: Aubrey is my daughter. Aubrey's grandparents have her now. Frank and Helen seem nice enough and have been here to see me twice. My lawyer has already put in the paperwork to fix the custody issues that will undoubtedly come up when I'm released. So far, I get the vibe that the Flynns won't fight me. They don't seem like the controlling type. In fact, as I sit in the visitation room, my heart flutters a little. This is all so new. Helen, dressed like she's headed to a garden party, looks nervous, and Frank's giving me a smile as the corrections officer gives them one last bit of instructions. And Aubrey? She comes at me now as a familiar face, with a smile that would melt anyone's heart.

One day she'll call me Daddy.

Turns out being a parent is all I ever really wanted.

Same with Kristen.

ADAM

As I await trial in jail, I weigh all the things that brought me here. I think about what I could have done differently to avoid this mess. Would my life have been better if I hadn't found Lee Husemann in that vacant lot? I was a hero in everyone's eyes on that day. Just below the surface, like a bug bite that had yet to emerge from my skin, I knew that I was nothing but a guy who was in the right place at the right time.

Or was it the wrong place?

Here's the funny part, though I know *funny* is the wrong word. I actually loved Sophie. I really did. She hurt me so bad with the affair that the wheels came off the bus. I can't explain it. I gave her a second chance. I looked the other way. If only I hadn't taken Aubrey to the doctor that day. I might never have known she wasn't mine. Seeing her face. Seeing Sophie's. I just couldn't get it out of my mind. It consumed me. I acted out with Carrie LaCroix. I admit it. But that's all. Kristen Moss was a liar. I had nothing to do with my wife's murder.

I need everyone to believe me.

Visit our website at
KensingtonBooks.com
to sign up for our newsletters, read
more from your favorite authors, see
books by series, view reading group
guides, and more!

Become a Part of Our
Between the Chapters Book Club
Community and Join the Conversation

Betweenthechapters.net